Praise for the novels of Deirdre Martin

JUST A TASTE

"A warmhearted romance with in-depth characters, this story will leave you satisfied, salivating, and ready to try one of the recipes included. Martin serves up a real treat."
—*Romantic Times* (4 stars)

"Be prepared to get a little hungry . . . Pick up *Just a Taste* for a tempting read you won't want to put down."
—*Romance Reviews Today*

"Will make you laugh and melt your heart at the same time."
—*Fresh Fiction*

"The revelation of deeper emotions makes this another victory for Martin."
—*Booklist*

"Delightful! Romantic, funny, and wildly fast paced . . . A great story that pulled me in right from the beginning."
—*Romance Reader at Heart*

"This engaging tale will keep readers entertained to the very end of the story. Ms. Martin has written a winner with this one."
—*Romance Junkies*

"Ms. Martin does a terrific job in writing dynamic characters you will come to know intimately and care for . . . I thoroughly enjoyed this book, enthusiastically recommend it, and anxiously await future books by Ms. Martin."
—*All About Romance*

continued . . .

Be sure to visit the Blades' website at
www.nyblades.com

CHASING STANLEY

"Martin has created an enjoyable sports community with quirky characters and lots of humorous dialogue. You'll cheer as Delilah and Jason slowly overcome their fears and the obstacles keeping them apart." —*Romantic Times*

"Martin has a way of bringing her dissimilar characters together that rings true, and fans and curious new readers won't want to miss her latest hockey-themed romance."

—*Booklist*

"Sometimes it's not the one-plus-one-equals-two that matters but everything that comes in between. On that score, *Chasing Stanley* is a real winner." —*The Romance Reader*

THE PENALTY BOX

"It will make you think even while you laugh and cry . . . A crowd-pleaser. You won't want to miss *The Penalty Box*."

—*Romance Reviews Today*

"Scores a goal with this reader . . . Deirdre Martin proves once again that she can touch the heart and the funny bone."

—*Romance Junkies*

"Martin scores another goal with another witty, emotionally true-to-life, and charming hockey romance." —*Booklist*

"Fun, fast rinkside contemporary romance . . . Martin scores with this witty blend of romance and family dynamics."

—*Publishers Weekly*

"Ms. Martin always delivers heat and romance, with a very strong conflict to keep the reader engaged. *The Penalty Box* should be added to your 'must-read list.' "

—*Contemporary Romance Writers*

TOTAL RUSH

"*Total Rush* is just that—a total rush, an absolute delight. Deirdre Martin is the reason I read romance novels. This contemporary romance is so well written [and] has a hero to die for and a romance that turns you into a puddle. It fills your heart to overflowing with love, acceptance, and the beauty of uniqueness. I laughed, I cried, I celebrated. It's more than a read, it is a reread. Brava, Ms. Martin, you're the greatest!"

—*The Best Reviews*

"Well written . . . Makes you want to keep turning the pages to see what happens next." —*The Columbia (SC) State*

"Martin's inventive take on opposites attracting is funny and poignant." —*Booklist*

"A heartwarming story of passion, acceptance, and most importantly, love, this book is definitely a *Total Rush*."

—*Romance Reviews Today*

"Fast paced, sexy, fun yet tender, the pages of *Total Rush* practically turn themselves. This is Deirdre Martin's third novel and is as sensational as the first two . . . A definite winner."

—*Romance Junkies*

FAIR PLAY

"Martin depicts the worlds of both professional hockey and ethnic Brooklyn with deftness and smart detail. She has an unerring eye for humorous family dynamics [and] sweet buoyancy." —*Publishers Weekly*

"Fast paced, wisecracking, and an enjoyable story . . . Makes you feel like you're flying." —*Rendezvous*

"A fun and witty story . . . The depth of characterizations and the unexpectedly moving passages make this an exceptional romance and a must-read for all fans of the genre."

—*Booklist*

"A fine sports romance that will score big-time . . . Martin has provided a winner." —*Midwest Book Review*

BODY CHECK

"Heartwarming." —*Booklist*

"Combines sports and romance in a way that reminded me of Susan Elizabeth Phillips's *It Had to Be You*, but Deirdre Martin has her own style and voice. *Body Check* is one of the best first novels I have read in a long time."
—*All About Romance* (Desert Isle Keeper)

"Deirdre Martin aims for the net and scores with *Body Check*." —*The Romance Reader* (Four Hearts)

"You don't have to be a hockey fan to cheer for *Body Check*. Deirdre Martin brings readers a story that scores."
—*The Word on Romance*

"A dazzling debut."
—*USA Today* bestselling author Millie Criswell

"Fun, delightful, emotional, and sexy."
—*Romance Reviews Today*

"An engaging romance that scores a hat trick [with] a fine supporting cast." —*The Best Reviews*

POWER PLAY

Deirdre Martin

BERKLEY SENSATION, NEW YORK

THE BERKLEY PUBLISHING GROUP
Published by the Penguin Group
Penguin Group (USA) Inc.
375 Hudson Street, New York, New York 10014, USA
Penguin Group (Canada), 90 Eglinton Avenue East, Suite 700, Toronto, Ontario M4P 2Y3, Canada
(a division of Pearson Penguin Canada Inc.)
Penguin Books Ltd., 80 Strand, London WC2R 0RL, England
Penguin Group Ireland, 25 St. Stephen's Green, Dublin 2, Ireland (a division of Penguin Books Ltd.)
Penguin Group (Australia), 250 Camberwell Road, Camberwell, Victoria 3124, Australia
(a division of Pearson Australia Group Pty. Ltd.)
Penguin Books India Pvt. Ltd., 11 Community Centre, Panchsheel Park, New Delhi—110 017, India
Penguin Group (NZ), 67 Apollo Drive, Rosedale, North Shore 0632, New Zealand
(a division of Pearson New Zealand Ltd.)
Penguin Books (South Africa) (Pty.) Ltd., 24 Sturdee Avenue, Rosebank, Johannesburg 2196, South Africa

Penguin Books Ltd., Registered Offices: 80 Strand, London WC2R 0RL, England

This is a work of fiction. Names, characters, places, and incidents either are the product of the author's imagination or are used fictitiously, and any resemblance to actual persons, living or dead, business establishments, events, or locales is entirely coincidental. The publisher does not have any control over and does not assume any responsibility for author or third-party websites or their content.

POWER PLAY

A Berkley Sensation Book / published by arrangement with the author

PRINTING HISTORY
Berkley Sensation mass-market edition / October 2008

Copyright © 2008 by Deirdre Martin.
Cover art by Aleta Rafton.
Cover design by George Long.
Interior text design by Laura K. Corless.

All rights reserved.
No part of this book may be reproduced, scanned, or distributed in any printed or electronic form without permission. Please do not participate in or encourage piracy of copyrighted materials in violation of the author's rights. Purchase only authorized editions.
For information, address: The Berkley Publishing Group,
a division of Penguin Group (USA) Inc.,
375 Hudson Street, New York, New York 10014.

ISBN: 978-0-425-22451-9

BERKLEY® SENSATION
Berkley Sensation Books are published by The Berkley Publishing Group,
a division of Penguin Group (USA) Inc.,
375 Hudson Street, New York, New York 10014.
BERKLEY SENSATION and the "B" design are trademarks of Penguin Group (USA) Inc.

PRINTED IN THE UNITED STATES OF AMERICA

10   9   8   7   6   5   4   3   2   1

If you purchased this book without a cover, you should be aware that this book is stolen property. It was reported as "unsold and destroyed" to the publisher, and neither the author nor the publisher has received any payment for this "stripped book."

For David Campbell
"In my friend, I find my second self."
—Isabel Norton

ACKNOWLEDGMENTS

Thanks to:

My husband, Mark.

Miriam Kriss and Kate Seaver.

Binnie Braunstein, Eileen Buckholtz,
and Jeff Schwartzenberg.

The Actors' Workshop of Ithaca Saturday
morning class—you guys help keep me sane.

Mom, Dad, Bill, Allison, Beth, Jane, Dave, and Tom.

Rocky.

ONE

ROXIE: *You'll walk again, Grayson. You have to believe that.*

GRAYSON: *Stop deluding yourself, Roxie. We've been to the top neurologist in Zurich. We've traveled to Lourdes. Even that Yaqui shaman did nothing. Nothing!*

ROXIE: *I can't give up! I won't!*

GRAYSON: *You must. (HE TRIES TO RISE FROM HIS WHEELCHAIR BUT FALLS BACK, FRUSTRATED.) We must accept it; just as an Eskimo can't feel the cold, so I will never again feel my legs.*

ROXIE: *Where there's love there's hope, my darling. And I love you. (KISSES HIM TENDERLY.)*

"And cut!"

Monica Geary glared at her costar, Royce Lindstrom, as he rose from the wheelchair and ostentatiously shook out his legs, admiring the definition of his calves. "How many times have I told you not to stick your tongue down my throat?"

For ten years, Royce had played Grayson Lamont, the on-again, off-again love interest of Monica's character, Roxie

Deveraux, on daytime's top-rated soap, *The Wild and the Free*. And for ten years, Royce had taken any opportunity he could to probe the depths of Monica's mouth, claiming he was simply keeping in character. This time, however, rather than claiming a De Niro–like dedication to his craft, Royce sported an unapologetic smirk.

"I thought you might start to like it, since you've been without a man in your life for so long."

"Quit perving me, or I'll tell *TV Guide* your hair comes out of an aerosol can. I mean it."

"Threats, threats . . ." Royce trilled, whistling to himself as he sauntered off the set.

Monica turned to the show's director, Jimmy, a slight, haunted-looking man with dark circles gouged beneath his eyes. "He's unbelievable."

Jimmy leaned in close to Monica, his eyes assessing the bustling TV studio to make sure that no one on the crew was paying them any attention. "Rumor has it the writers are lobbying to get rid of him," he murmured in a voice just loud enough for Monica to hear.

"Why? Because he constantly screws up what they've written? Or because his idea of acting is lifting his eyebrows?" Monica hated wishing unemployment on any of her costars, but Royce was an exception.

Jimmy chuckled. "That, and he's a huge pain in the ass. Keeps going up to their office and asking what's going to happen with his character."

Monica shook her head in disbelief. One of the cardinal rules in daytime was not to bug the writers. They *might* tell you the basic story arc for your character for the upcoming months, but that was it. Otherwise, you were pretty much kept in the dark. For all Monica knew, Roxie could wind up being the victim of a voodoo curse (zombies were quietly invading Garrett City), or she could be back on the streets hooking for a living, as she did before she and her estranged father reconciled when he was dying of a rare tropical fever, making her the head of his publishing empire.

"I'll keep you posted," Jimmy promised, trudging back toward the control booth.

Tired, Monica headed for her dressing room in the hopes of stealing a quick nap. It was going to be a long day. She still had three scenes to shoot that afternoon, which meant she'd be lucky to be home by nine. Her Friday night would be spent in front of the tube, snarfing down a Healthy Choice dinner and thumbing through the scripts she had to memorize for next week. She hoped the writers had something interesting planned for Roxie beyond wringing her hands and worrying whether Grayson's legs would work or not. She closed the door, dimmed the lights, and lay down on the couch, closing her eyes. One hour. Then it was back to work.

It wasn't to be. Ten minutes into pretending she was in a warm bath soaking her cares away, there was a firm knock at the door, and her costar, Gloria Hathaway, poked her head in the door. "Smoke?"

Monica sat up and turned up the lights. If anyone else had interrupted her, she'd be annoyed, but Gloria was a different story. Monica adored Gloria, who had taken Monica under her wing when she'd started on *W and F* ten years ago and had no damn idea what she was doing. Gloria taught Monica how to deal with fans and difficult costars, how to give an interview without making a fool of herself in the press, even how to be a gracious loser when she was nominated three times for a Daytime Drama Award and didn't win. Gloria had been Monica's daytime fairy godmother.

"No cigarettes for me. I'm trying to quit," Monica told her.

"Well, I'm not," said Gloria, shaking a cigarette out of the pocket of her hot-pink chenille robe, which always seemed on the verge of falling open, intentionally so. At seventy (not that anyone knew Gloria's real age apart from Monica), Gloria still had a decent body, but she was—well, seventy. Monica didn't have the heart to tell Gloria that her once-magnificent boobs (which Gloria claimed had "provided succor to Richard Burton when he and Liz had temporarily split") now looked like two deflated balloons, or that it horrified the wardrobe mistress when Gloria would wander in with her robe half undone, revealing her obviously dyed bush. To Monica's mind, Gloria deserved respect. She'd been a huge movie star, until juicy roles began drying up along with her body parts. Determined to keep working, Gloria had joined *W and F* fifteen years ago and had never looked back. She was called "the Grand Dame of Daytime," a title she deserved. She was also the only person Monica knew who could wear a turban and not look like an idiot.

Gloria lit her cigarette, sitting down next to Monica on the couch. "I'm looking forward to that catfight we're shooting this afternoon. Should be fun."

Gloria played Antonia Lamont, Grayson's controlling, alcoholic mother. Antonia hated Roxie and was determined to take her down. Monica loved when she had scenes with Gloria, because Gloria could act. In fact, a number of Monica's costars were fine actors. She counted herself lucky.

Gloria took a drag off her cigarette and tilted her head back, blowing a geyser of smoke up to the ceiling. "I heard Royce might be history."

"Where?"

Gloria looked back at her. "Jimmy."

"Jimmy told me, too! But I thought it was a secret."

Gloria snorted. "As if anything is a secret around here."

Everyone knew everyone else's business on a soap set, and rumors flew faster than bullets. Perhaps there was a grain of truth to it, then. Monica could only hope.

"Hear anything else?" Monica asked, casually relieving Gloria of her cigarette. One puff wouldn't kill her.

"Well, that new little tootsie starts next Friday."

Monica had forgotten. A fresh, young face (*Younger*, Monica corrected herself. At thirty-one, she was not old!) was being brought on to play Monica's younger sister, Paige, the half sister Roxie never knew she had. All Monica knew about the actress was that she was twenty-one, the same age Monica was when she started on daytime, and that her breasts were impressive. At least that was what Ricardo, the casting director, thought. But he panted after anything with long legs and basic brain function.

"What's her name again?" Monica asked.

"Chessy Matthews. What the hell kind of a name is Chessy?" Gloria scoffed.

"Either fake or it's her boarding school name."

Monica had never had a boarding school name, though she remembered plenty of girls who did. Sparky. Chessy. Binky. Mon just didn't cut it, though Monica remembered one of her classmates, Juliet "Jools" Spencer, always talking to her in a fake Jamaican accent, saying things like, "*Irie*, Mon, help me with this calculus," which Jools thought was hilarious. Monica wondered where Jools was now. Probably finishing up her summer in the Hamptons with investment banker husband number two and spoiled kids named Lincoln and Madison. A slight shiver of envy went through Monica.

"I'll be curious to see if she can actually act," said Gloria, "or if this is another case of Ricardo being blinded by a C-cup."

"We'll see." Monica was actually looking forward to someone new on the show with whom her character would interact frequently. It could be challenging.

Gloria snuffed out her cigarette and rose. "I'll let you get back to your shut-eye. See you on the set in forty?"

Monica nodded as Gloria departed, quietly closing the door behind her. A new costar. Something interesting was happening next week after all.

"Yo, the savior of the Blades has arrived."

Brimming with self-confidence, Eric Mitchell scanned the locker room, waiting for his new teammates to respond to his announcement. Instead, he was greeted by scowls, glares, and the unmistakable look of resentment. What the hell was wrong with these guys?

One of the most piercing glares came from Eric's twin brother, Jason, who now thought he was hot shit because he was an assistant captain. The team had a new assistant coach, too: Michael Dante. The head coach was still the legendary ballbuster, Ty Gallagher.

"What my brother means—" Jason began.

"Is what he said," defenseman Ulf Torkelson finished for him, planting himself so close to Eric their noses were practically touching. "Listen up, dickwad: until you prove yourself on the ice, no one in here believes you're the next Brian Leetch. Got it?"

Eric returned Ulf's attempt at an intimidating stare. He'd gone toe-to-toe with him on the ice for years. If his new teammate thought he was going to squeak out a meek, "Okay, whatever you say," he was wrong.

Ulf kept staring. Eric stared back, though out of the corner of his eye, he caught the look of mortification momentarily crossing his brother's face. Clearly Jason thought he was handling this all wrong. *Not to worry, Bro. I can hold my own.*

The staring contest ended with Ulf shoving Eric's shoulder. "You hear me?"

"Tell me again. I forgot."

By now, all the Blades had drawn closer to the two men, ringing them in a semicircle. Were he and the Ulfinator on the ice, gloves would have been dropped, and they'd already be at it. As it was, Eric could feel his adrenaline begin to rise. Ulf wanted a fight? He'd picked the right guy.

"Cut the shit, both of you."

New captain Tully Webster pushed the two men apart, his glare outshining everyone else's. "This is not the way *I* want to start the new season." He turned to Eric. "Glad to have you aboard, but it might serve you better to keep your mouth shut for now, okay?" His body swiveled to Ulf's. "As for you, save the threats for the ice."

Eric gave a curt nod that mirrored Ulf's. Ulf turned away, angrily pushing his way through his teammates to head for the showers. One by one, the other Blades drifted toward their lockers or the shower, but not before throwing Eric a dirty look. Eric met each and every look with an unapologetic expression.

Whether they liked it or not, they did need him, which is why he'd been traded from Jersey for two young prospects and one of the Blades' most beloved players, defenseman Guy Le Temp. Eric was one of the top scoring defensemen in the NHL. His trade to New York from New Jersey had been one of the top stories in local sports, along with the ego-stoking fact that he'd made *People* magazine's "Fifty Hottest

Bachelors" issue, coming in at number forty. Eric thought he should have been higher. It wasn't hard to figure out that his new teammates were envious of him, both on and off the ice.

In need of a shower himself, Eric grabbed a towel and his toiletries from his locker when someone gripped his forearm.

"We need to talk," Jason said tersely. Eric refrained from rolling his eyes. He knew what was coming: big lecture, blah blah blah. He'd indulge Jason—this time.

"Sure. Just let me shower, and I'll meet you in ten."

Eric had no sooner closed the cab door behind him than Jason fixed him with a death stare.

"What the *hell* was that all about?" Jason demanded, directing the cabdriver to West Eighty-fourth Street, where they both lived. Three years ago, when Jason was first traded to the Blades from the Minnesota Mosquitoes and Eric had already been playing for Jersey for a year, Eric had found him a primo apartment in a building four doors down from his own. Both of them loved their places, though Jason's had become a little cramped now that he and his wife, Delilah, who ran a dog-walking business, lived there together along with their four dogs. Luckily, building rules wouldn't let her maintain her dog-boarding service; otherwise their place would really be a zoo.

Eric was nonchalant. "What?"

"*What?* Your egomaniac display back there in the locker room."

"I was just stating fact."

"Big deal!" Jason retorted. "You know how this shit works: you bust your hump until your prove yourself." Jason shook his head in despair. "They're starting off hating you, man. You're already at a disadvantage because everyone loved Guy. The guys, the fans . . ."

"I was just trying to be, you know—"

"What? A macho, arrogant dick?"

"We're all macho, arrogant dicks," Eric pointed out in his defense. "We're professional hockey players."

"Yeah, but you're the *new* macho, arrogant dick. That means eating humble pie until further notice."

"They're just jealous. Especially with the *People* magazine thing."

"Christ." Jason opened his window a crack. "You've been even more insufferable than usual since that came out."

"I believe you mean self-confident, not insufferable," Eric replied smugly.

"No, insufferable."

Eric enjoyed the image of himself as Manhattan bachelor at play, which was why he only dated brainless bimbos: it saved him having to put himself out emotionally. That was certainly the case with his last squeeze, Brandi. Sweet, great in bed, but the brains of a mackerel. When she started pushing for a relationship, he ended things—like a gentleman, of course. Shallow he could do. Mature? That he wasn't so sure about.

"You should go in there tomorrow and tell everyone you're sorry about coming on like such an asswipe; say that you were just nervous or something," Jason advised.

"Maybe I'll just tell them what's happening next week," Eric said boastfully.

"Yeah, what's that?"

"I'm doing a cameo on the *The Wild and the Free*, Bro."

Jason's eyes doubled in size. "No. Fucking. Way."

"I kid you not, my man. The show got in touch with Lou in PR after *People* came out, and they asked if I wanted to do an 'under five'—that's TV talk for under five lines, by the way," Eric added.

"You have got to be shitting me."

Eric draped his arm around his brother's shoulder. "Would I shit you?"

"Yeah. Daily. But I can tell you're not ringing my bell on this one. I haven't seen you look this happy since eleventh grade, when Kylie Jacobs told you the rabbit *didn't* die." Jason punched his arm enviously. "You *bastard*. You're probably going to meet Monica Geary, aren't you?"

"I have a scene with her," said Eric, feeling quite pleased with this small coup. "I even get to play myself."

Everyone in the league watched *The Wild and the Free*. Soaps were a favorite way for them to pass the time in hotel rooms when they were on the road, and they all watched when they were home, too, since the teams' workout and weight rooms had TVs. Eric couldn't count the times he'd been sweating his ass off on a cross trainer with his eyes glued to Monica Geary.

Jason had a faraway look in his eyes. "Remember that time Roxie's fiancé plunged into a volcano, but it turned out he didn't really die, and he secretly came back to Garrett City, gaslighting Roxie for a while?"

"That was great," Eric agreed. Talking about the show was getting him pumped.

"Or the time Roxie was reunited with the baby she'd given birth to in high school but didn't know she had, because she'd been kicked in the head at the prom by a runaway horse and got amnesia?"

"Oh, man. The way Monica turned on the tears during that scene? You could hear guys sniffling all over the weight room that day. She's a great actress."

"When will you be torturing the cast and crew with your presence?"

"I shoot next Thursday afternoon, I think. I should be getting my script by FedEx today." It sounded so cool saying that.

"Do you know when it airs?"

"No. But I'm sure they'll tell me."

"Bastard." Jason paused thoughtfully. "You know what you should do? Get an autographed pic of her for the locker room. Or have someone take a picture of the two of you together. That'll help redeem your ass a little."

"I'm not doing that," Eric scoffed. "It's so fannish."

"You *are* a fan."

"Not on Thursday I'm not. On Thursday I'm a guest star."

"Oh, please."

"Seriously: I don't want to come across as a geek."

"You could never be a geek. But an asshole? That's another story."

Eric yawned. "Yada yada yada."

"Delilah wants to know if you want to come for dinner tomorrow night."

"I'd love to," said Eric, "but I can't. I have to start studying my part."

"Your cameo is a *week* away, Eric, and you have less than *five* lines."

"No," Eric said emphatically. "I need to be make sure that when next Thursday rolls around, everything goes perfectly. I want to impress Monica."

Jason frowned. "Fine, but if you change your mind, just come over. We're hanging out and watching some special on aardvarks on *Animal Planet.*"

"Now that's love."

"You're damn right. You might want to try it sometime."

TWO

ROXIE: *Wait until you see the surprise I have for you, Grayson. (SHE WHEELS HIM, BLINDFOLDED, INTO A LOCKER ROOM. HOCKEY SKATES AND HELMETS HANG FROM SEVERAL OF THE LOCKERS. A FEW BATTERED HOCKEY STICKS ARE PROPPED UP IN THE CORNER. ERIC MITCHELL ENTERS. ROXIE UNTIES GRAYSON'S BLINDFOLD.) You can look now!*

GRAYSON: *My God! It's Eric Mitchell of the New York Blades, my favorite team!*

ERIC: *It's an honor to meet you, Rox—I mean Grayson."*

"Cut!"

Monica heaved a sigh of frustration as Jimmy the director flew out of the control booth for the third time, making a beeline for Eric Mitchell. The first time Eric screwed up his lines, Jimmy was patient. The guy was a hockey player, after all, not an actor. The second time he screwed up, Royce, who usually ate guest stars alive, assured him that he just needed to relax and things would be fine. But the third time was too much. As always, they were on a very tight shooting schedule and had no time for multiple takes.

"For the third goddamn time, the line is, 'It's an honor to meet you, *Grayson,*'" said Jimmy through clenched teeth. "Grayson! Grayson! Grayson! It's not that hard!" He stormed back to the booth.

"Yowza," said Eric sardonically, looking at Monica. "Someone should give that guy a chill pill, huh?"

"This isn't a joke," said Monica, wheeling Royce back out of the locker room as he retied his blindfold. Eric took his place, too. Sauntered to it, actually, then had the balls to wink at Monica. This guy was unbelievable.

"Action!"

This time, the jock managed not to call Grayson Roxie, but when it came to his line, "I know you'll score a goal of your own, Grayson, and walk again," he said "talk again" rather than "walk again."

"Do *you* know how to talk?!" Jimmy shouted through the mike from the control booth. Monica winced as Jimmy turned to the executive producer, Michael Herrera. "Whose bright idea was this to have this guy do a cameo?! Yours?! We'd have better luck with a trained seal!" With that he grabbed the giant bottle of generic aspirin he always kept on the ledge of the control panel, shaking out what looked like a small mountain into his palm before cramming them into his mouth as if they were M&M's.

Herrera, *W and F*'s long-suffering producer, recently back from a second stint in rehab for addiction to Valium, got on the mike and said, "All right, everybody, let's take five."

"We don't have five!" Jimmy screamed.

Michael ignored him, focusing all his attention on Eric. "Listen, you have *got* to nail it the next time, or we're gonna have to cut the scene; we just don't have time to fool around with this." He paused, thinking. "I'll check with the writers to see if they can write up a few new lines for a different surprise for Grayson if we need to. Maybe Roxie can do a lap dance or something."

"You do that, and the only dance I'll be doing is on my way out of this studio!" Monica shouted up to him. She

couldn't even bear to glance at Royce, whom she knew had to
be praying for Eric Mitchell to hang himself the next time he
opened his mouth. God, she wished she had a cigarette. She
would just have to do with moving off set and doing a few
deep-breathing exercises instead.

"Hey."

Monica cracked open an eye in the middle of a deep inhale
to see Eric Mitchell standing in front of her. Out of polite-
ness, she opened the other eye. "Yes?"

"I'm sorry I keep screwing up. I thought it would be
easy."

Monica frowned. "Everyone does."

It amazed her, the way everyone thought they could act.
She could tell him that the sign of a good actor *was* making it
look effortless, but what would be the point?

Part of the problem was that for every good actor in daytime, there was one bad one. It was one of the reasons the
genre got no respect. That, and the fact that to hold the interest of viewers and not repeat themselves five days a week,
fifty weeks a year, year in and year out, the writers were
sometimes forced to write fantastical story lines ripe for
mockery. Evil twins. Characters returning from the dead.
Amnesia, demonic possession, characters marrying each
other multiple times—it was all there. But there was reality
there, too: characters grappling with serious issues of life and
love. That was what hooked the viewers. That was what allowed them to suspend disbelief and follow these characters
wherever the show's writers took them.

The hockey player was looking at her like she was a piece
of succulent filet mignon on his plate. She should have been
used to that by now, but it never failed to irk her just a little.
I'm more than boobs, legs, and a face, she wanted to tell him.
Not that it would make any difference.

"You and I have something in common," Eric murmured.

"What's that?" Monica asked, trying desperately to see
past him to the clock on the studio wall. Three more minutes.
She only had to endure three more minutes of small talk with

the jock who thought he could act. Anything was doable for three minutes.

"We're both sexy," he whispered through hooded eyes. "You were voted 'One of the Sexiest Women in Daytime,' and I was voted one of *People* magazine's 'Top Fifty Bachelors.'"

"I didn't know that," Monica replied with affected boredom she hoped would repel him. She could see why he made their list, though. Great bod, sandy blond hair, sparkling blue eyes. She hated to admit it, but physically speaking, he was the male version of her.

"You really don't think it's fascinating we're both sex symbols?" Eric prodded.

"No."

"Oh, c'mon. You and I both know it says, 'These two people were fated to meet.'"

"Actually, to me it says, 'Delusional athlete.'"

She knew she was taking a risk in being snarky to him. First rule of being in the public eye: be unfailingly polite, even if you are dealing with a crazed fan or an antagonistic journalist. But this guy was being such a horse's ass she couldn't hold back.

Undeterred, Eric leaned in to her. "Two famous people who are hot, the big city at night . . . how about you give me your number, and we set the world on fire?"

Monica recoiled. "You're kidding, right? Who do you think I am, some bimbo?"

Eric looked mystified. "Huh?"

"That has got to be the most atrocious pickup line I've heard in my life. Do you really think a woman would *fall* for that?"

Eric rocked confidently on his heels. "I thought it was pretty good, myself. What do you say?"

"Thanks, but no thanks." Just a minute and a half more. *Tick, tick, help.*

Eric chuckled. "Look, Rox—I mean, Monica—I occasionally glance at *Soap World* magazine when one of the other players brings it into the locker room, so I know you're foot-

loose and fancy-free these days. As am I, remarkably. You can't
deny there's some kind of chemistry between us here."

Monica cocked her head inquisitively. "Have you ever
spent time in a mental hospital? Just curious."

"Take a chance, babe. Go out with me."

"*No,*" Monica repeated firmly. "And don't call me *babe.*"

Eric winked at her, and it was even more annoying the second time than it was the first. "How about *gorgeous*? *Hot?
Goddess? Stone-cold foxy lady supreme?*"

"Let's make a deal, okay? You don't talk to me again unless we're in character, and I don't publicly accuse you of
harassing me."

Eric shrugged. "Your loss, babe."

"Aaarrrr!" Monica growled in frustration, storming back
to the set, fingers twitching for a cigarette. It was a pity that
someone so good looking was such a vapid, annoying *tick*.
The minute their scene together was over, she ran to her dressing room and locked the door until she got word Eric Mitchell had left the building and crawled back to the rink he came
from. Sometimes, acting was the easy part. It was getting
men to see past her status and body that was hard.

"So, Mr. Soap Star, how did it go?"

Eric turned from his locker to see Ulf Torkelson standing
behind him, arms crossed, a mocking expression on his face.
Word had spread like wildfire that Eric was doing a cameo on
The Wild and the Free, and just as he'd expected, some of his
new teammates were regarding him with envy.

Eric slung a towel around his sweaty neck. "It went great.
I had four lines. Could have done it in my sleep." Fearful of
his scene being cut, he *had* aced it on the last take. Thinking a
touch of humility might get Monica to reconsider her refusal
of a night on the town with him, he'd turned to her the second
the director yelled, "Cut!" to thank her for her patience, but
she shot off the set so fast she was a blur. He took it in stride,
knowing that eventually she'd regret turning him down and
seek him out.

Barry Fontaine, a teammate and a friend of his brother's, wasn't looking at him with any resentment at all as he asked in a worshipful voice, "Did you meet Monica Geary?"

"Yup. That's who my scene was with. We got along great. Truth be told, I think she was kind of into me."

Ulf snorted. "Yeah, right."

"Seriously. We hit it off right away. Couldn't stop talking between takes."

"She probably felt sorry for you," Thad Meyers said with scorn.

"Why would that be?" Eric asked, grabbing his shampoo and soap.

"Because you're no Guy Le Temp and never will be," Thad replied. Scattered nods of assent filled the locker room.

I'm better than Guy Le Temp, which is why I'm here, you asshole, thought Eric. He'd just done great at practice, and that wasn't just his ego speaking. Tully had told him so, and so had Assistant Coach Dante, who had a tendency to be extra hard on players since he moved behind the bench. The only one silent and watchful was Ty Gallagher. Always scribbling notes on his fucking clipboard. Eric imagined him checking off some kind of score sheet as the Blades progressed from drill to drill. Ty seemed particularly fond of making them sprint up and down the ice, which Eric hated. Luckily he didn't lag in any way, and in fact skated more quickly than his brother, which gave him pleasure. Jace might be assistant captain, but Eric was still the better player. He couldn't wait to prove it on the ice.

"When's the episode airing?" David Hewson asked. Hewsie was now the team's top goalie after the departure of Denny O'Malley, who'd retired after taking one too many pucks to his melon. Hewsie seemed not to have any issue with Eric replacing Guy, perhaps because he had only been a Blade for a year himself. Or maybe he just wasn't a schmuck.

"Two weeks."

"Two weeks?"

Eric shrugged. "That's the way it works. They shoot stuff two weeks in advance."

"Did you bring your camera and have anyone take a pic-

ture of you with her—you know, to preserve the memory?"
asked Thad sarcastically.

"No."

"Why not?" asked Ulf. "She refuse to pose with you?"

"I didn't *ask*," Eric retorted.

"That was fucking stupid," said Ulf.

It was. He should have listened to his brother. Gotten an
autograph that said, "To the New York Blades, My Favorite
Team, Love, Monica," or one that said, "To Eric, Great Working with You, Monica," with a bunch of *X*s and *O*s across the
bottom. He'd pop in and see Lou Capesi in Blades PR, find
out if he could call the show and have them send over a few
autographed pictures.

"I vote we have a Watch Mitchell on TV party," said Thad.
"I could use a good laugh."

Heads nodded. Of course they'd watch it together. Eric
would watch it with them. His five minutes of fame off the
ice. He couldn't wait to see it. He couldn't wait for them to
see it, either. That would shut them up.

"Everyone, meet the latest addition to the *W and F* family,
Chessy Matthews."

In seeming perfect synchronization with the rest of her
cast mates, Monica smiled and said "Hello" to the petite,
buxom blonde who had just been introduced to them on set
by the executive producer. From the little bit of info the writers had provided, Monica knew that Chessy's character,
Paige, was Roxie's half sister through their late father. Paige's
mother was their father's secret plural wife, taken after his
previously unknown conversion to a fundamentalist Mormon
sect. Now Paige had come to Garrett City to take over Roxie's
publishing empire, claiming their father had written a subse-
quent will to the one that left everything to Roxie. *More cat-
fights and lots of bitchy lines,* thought Monica. *Could be fun.*

Much to her horror, she had dreamed of Eric Mitchell last
night. In the dream, she had put masking tape over his mouth
and told him to just "Shut up and fuck me." Which he did—
quite skillfully. She woke up moaning with pleasure, her sheets

twisted around her. As consciousness dawned, sexual satisfaction turned to horror. How could she have dreamed of *him*, New York's most obnoxious man? Easy: he was the finest-looking specimen she'd set eyes on in a long time. The dream haunted her all day, shameful and somewhat embarrassing. Her libido had never ambushed her with a dolt before.

Gloria stood next to Monica, imperious as ever as she watched Chessy make her way toward them, introducing herself to the cast one by one. "Her name should be Chesty, not Chessy," Gloria whispered out of the side of her bright red mouth. "I hope her boobs can act."

"Don't be mean." Monica believed in giving everyone new a fair chance, always remembering back to when she was the newest cast member. She could still conjure the terror of it, the fears of not fitting in and screwing up. Thank God Gloria took Monica under her wing. Maybe Monica would do the same for newbie Chessy, though her perpetual smile did grate a bit. Monica hoped she hadn't been that—toothy—on her first day.

Chessy finally made her way to Monica, standing breathlessly before her. "Oh my God. I have soooo wanted to meet you for soooo long. I have been, like, your biggest fan since I was a little girl! It's been soooo great to watch Roxie mature over the years. I can't wait for us to work together. I just *know* I can learn a lot from a veteran like you."

Monica's mouth froze into a rictus. "Yes, I get the feeling there is a lot you need to learn." *Like how not to assault someone with backhanded compliments the first time you meet them.* Chessy smiled at her again before moving on to Royce.

"Little bitch," Gloria hissed as soon as Chesty was out of earshot.

"Now, now."

"Watch that one," Gloria warned.

Monica waved her hand dismissively. She'd been on the show ten years, and she'd seen a parade of ingénues come and go, many of them intent on unseating her. What they didn't know was that if their story line tanked and the writers couldn't come up with another, they'd be collecting unemployment faster than you could say evil twin. Monica patted Gloria's bony shoulder before heading for her dressing room. "I'm not worried."

A minute later, it was painfully clear she should be. Every Friday each member of the cast had a copy of the latest issue of *Soap World* delivered to their dressing room. This week's issue had a giant picture of Chessy on the cover, the headline blaring, "Is This the Next Monica Geary?"

Monica stared at the cover a few seconds before forcing herself to sit down on the couch. She knew she was letting herself in for a world of misery, but she opened the magazine anyway and flipped right to the article. It was a two-page color spread in the center. Her guts plummeted to her feet faster than a jet losing altitude.

Shit, the pictures. Chessy smiling, radiating girl-next-door appeal. Chessy looking sexy. Chessy pretending to pore over a script. The text was worse, the writer (whom Monica hated but was always nice to) talking about how with Chessy's talent and remarkable looks, she could skyrocket to soap superstardom faster than Monica did.

What talent?! No one had seen her act apart from the casting director. Monica skimmed the article for a quote from Ricardo. "The minute Chessy read for me, I was just blown away." Wanting to *get* blown was more like it. She continued skimming, uncovering the fact that though Chessy had never acted before, Ricardo sensed "a unique energy coming from her that couldn't be ignored" as she took his order at La Artista, where he found this "unknown jewel."

A waitress. The casting director had hired a goddamn waitress who had never acted. Monica knew she should throw the magazine down right now, but it was like witnessing a car wreck: she just couldn't stop looking. She read on, shocked at the quote from the executive producer who said he hoped Chessy's character would help turn the show in a "new and vibrant direction." What the hell did that mean? The article concluded with the writer speculating on how much fun it was going to be to see Chessy give Monica a run for her

money—just their characters, of course, but Monica knew
this writer, and she knew damn well she wasn't just referring
to rivalry between Roxie and Claire.

Put the magazine down now, she commanded herself. But
she couldn't. Some masochistic inner demon drove her to
turn to the gossip column, which she knew was penned by the
same vituperative writer under the lame pseudonym of Suzy
Scuttlebutt. She skimmed again, her breathing catching as
she found her name in bold.

The writer speculated that the comment *W and F*'s executive producer made in the Chessy article might mean he
thought Monica was resting on her laurels, and that the Roxie
character was becoming "predictable." The column referred
to Monica as "semireclusive" and noted that she hadn't had a
man in her life for months. "What *is* going on with Monica
Geary?" was how the paragraph concluded.

"Cow!" Monica spat, hurling the magazine in the trash.
She was not reclusive. That was a lie. Then again, she couldn't
remember the last time she gave an interview or attended a
fan function. As for not having a man, it was no one's business! Not only that, but what the hell did it have to do with
anything?

She tore her dressing room apart, knowing that she still
had a pack of cigarettes hidden somewhere. She found two
behind a picture of herself with a movie star, who had once
done a cameo on the show as Roxie's former pimp. Now she
just had to find a light. She contemplated going to Gloria, but
she didn't want her friend to see her so rattled. Further root-
ing around rewarded her with a book of matches. She lit up.

Okay, think. She needed to up her profile beyond just acting. Things weren't supposed to turn out this way. She'd
trained at Julliard, for chrissakes. Had studied privately with
Monty Kingman, considered one of the greatest acting teachers of all time.

After Julliard she found herself waiting tables, the actor's
cliché. Crappy roach-infested apartment, meager wages, but
the nighttime job freed her to audition during the day. She auditioned her ass off—she and a gazillion other good-looking,
talented young women. When her agent told her about the

part of Roxie on *W and F*, she went for it, never in a million years thinking she'd get it. But she did. Told herself it would just be temporary, until a "real" acting gig came along. After all, hadn't Julianne Moore started on soaps? Hadn't Meg Ryan? Starting on soaps was almost a rite of passage. It was a stepping-stone to bigger, better, more respected forms of entertainment. She was supposed to have won a Tony by now. Or an Oscar.

But oh my, how time flies when you're making bundles of money. Every time her contract came up for renewal, she was in agony. Should she renew, cling to the job security? Or should she venture out into the bigger world and try to get the admiration for her talent that she craved? In the end, she always signed on the dotted line. The salary was just too good to pass up. And truth be told, she liked the attention. That was one of the primary reasons people became actors. They *needed* the attention. They wanted to be loved.

Monica wanted to be loved.

She picked up her phone, dialed the number of her personal publicist, Theresa Dante, and made an appointment to come in.

THREE

"How the hell are you?!"

"I'm good." Monica melted into Theresa Dante's hug, put at ease by her warm greeting. She knew of other personal publicists who excoriated their clients for remaining under the radar for a while, calling them endlessly to urge them to do more, more, more. Theresa wasn't like that, perhaps because she didn't need to be. FM PR, the firm Theresa had started with her best friend, Janna, boasted a huge client list.

"Sit, sit," Theresa urged. Monica settled on the large leather couch in Theresa's cluttered office, her eyes lighting on the picture on Theresa's desk of her husband, Michael, and their three kids. "I can't believe how big the kids have gotten!"

"Their mouths are bigger, believe me," Theresa replied wryly. "Did Terrence come out and offer you any coffee?"

"He's brewing a fresh pot. Said he'll be in, in a minute."

"Good boy. He got a promotion, as you can tell from our new receptionist. He's my PA now." She sat down on the couch beside Monica. "Give me all the dirt from *W and F*."

Monica chuckled, remembering that Theresa had gotten

her start as a publicist at the show. "Who do you want to know about?"

Theresa thought a moment. "Nicholas Kastley."

"You mean Nicholas Ghastly." Both women laughed. "Well, he's about a hundred and five now, and blind as a bat. He can't remember his lines, so he has them taped all over the place: on the backs of chairs, on banisters. He won't wear contacts for some insane reason."

"He's always been that way. One time he mistook me for a coat stand."

"Well, about two months ago, he tripped over a coffee table and broke his left leg. He wouldn't admit it was his fault. He claimed Gloria Hathaway was trying to kill him."

"Oh, God." Theresa's palm flew to her mouth, but Monica could see she wanted to laugh.

"There are rumors that when his contract is up, his character is going to be killed off. Buried alive, I think."

"Ooh, that's good," said Theresa with wide eyes. "I don't think they've ever done that."

"Knock, knock, who's there," a haughty voice called from the doorway. "Terrence. Terrence who? Terrence, Theresa's personal slave."

Theresa rolled her eyes, beckoning him inside. "Just give us the coffee and be gone with you."

"See how she treats me?" Terrence lamented, handing over two coffees. He clasped his hands reverentially as he stood before Monica. "I just have to tell you, I think the show has been great lately. *Great.* I TiVo it and watch it when I get home from work around nine o' clock at night—if I'm lucky." He gave Theresa a pointed look, which she ignored, then turned back to Monica with worshipful eyes. "I loved that scene with you and Gloria Hathaway where you tore off her wig to reveal Antonia was bald."

Monica bowed her head with pleasure. "Thank you."

Terrence sighed. "Well, I'm off to put my chains back on and resume breaking rocks." He regarded Theresa. "Anything else, boss lady?"

"Nope. Just close the door behind you."

Terrence obeyed and was gone. Theresa took a sip of coffee, put it down on the coffee table, and lightly slapped the top of her thighs, getting down to business. "So, what's going on?"

Monica fished the latest issue of *Soap World* out of her bag, handing it over to Theresa, whose eyebrows lifted when she saw the headline. "It gets worse. Read it."

Monica didn't want to watch Theresa as she read it, so she busied herself by studying the walls of Theresa's office. Athletes, politicians, restaurateurs, other actors—FM handled them all. She turned back to Theresa when she heard her close the magazine with a sigh.

"It's not that bad. Seriously. They did a piece just like this on you when you started, remember?"

"Yeah, but they didn't ask if I was the next so-and-so."

Theresa paused for another sip of coffee, studying her. "What upsets you most about this?"

"That she has no acting experience!" Monica hesitated. "And that it might not matter, that she still might . . . outshine me." She looked down into her coffee. "You must think I'm really shallow."

"No, I just think you're a very popular actress, and no actress wants to be upstaged or risk losing her adoring public to someone else. And don't forget: you *do* have an adoring public."

"I know." It should have cheered Monica, but it didn't.

"You have been MIA for a while," Theresa said carefully. "Is anything wrong?"

"Just tired."

Which was true, but it wasn't the whole story. The fact was that until now, she didn't feel like she had any juice left to give to the public, especially since—and here she felt like a horrible, bitchy snob—it wasn't the public she'd always dreamed of having. Yet the minute her status was threatened, what did she do? Scurry off to her publicist so they could figure out a way to keep her prominent among soap fans. What a hypocrite.

"Well, we need to get you untired and reinspired. Get you on board with some charity events, some film openings, have you seen dining in chichi restaurants. Doing some soap fan events would be good, too. But you already know all this, Monica."

Monica nodded, feeling mildly chastised, which she supposed she deserved.

"What we really need, though, is to have you seen out and about with someone incredibly suave and gorgeous." Theresa paused, biting down on the tip of her pen. "You ever hear of Eric Mitchell? He was just traded to the New York Blades. He was voted one of *People* magazine's 'Top Fifty Bachelors,' and next week he's going to be on the cover of *New York* magazine. I cannot tell you how hot this guy is right now, both in terms of popularity *and* looks."

Monica was horrified. "And I cannot tell you how obnoxious he is. He just did a cameo on the show. He was awful, Theresa. And he hit on me!"

"So you two already know each other—great!"

"Theresa, I am not going out with Eric Mitchell. Seriously."

"I'm not asking you to get romantic with him. Just make people think you're a couple. Be seen with him here and there for a while. People will eat it up: the actress and the pro athlete. The public will love it, and so will the execs at *W and F*, believe me. It'll make great copy. Plus you're both so gorgeous, everyone will love the eye candy."

Monica put her face in her hands. "Oh my God. I can't believe you're asking this of me."

"Do you want your name on people's lips again or not?" Theresa asked, sounding irked. Why did Theresa always have to be so blunt? It was that Italian American thing. No beating around the bush. Call it like you see it.

Monica lifted her head, feeling desperate. "Of course I want that. But isn't there something else we could do?"

"Hmm. You could leave the show and enter a convent. Maybe come out as a lesbian. Or better yet, a hasbian—you know, harboring a deep, dark lesbian past, but now you're straight as a ruler with an insatiable sexual appetite for men."

Monica scowled. "Very funny."

"Trust me on this Eric Mitchell thing, Monica. I know what I'm doing."

"What if he tries to hit on me again?" asked Monica.

"You can handle him."

Yeah, by shooting him with a tranquilizer gun. "How much time would I have to spend with him?"

"That would depend on how much press you two generate." Theresa's expression was encouraging. "Look, I've met Eric. I know he comes off as a bit of a jerk at first, but deep down, he's a nice guy."

Monica drew back, puzzled. "How do you know Eric?"

"My husband is the assistant coach for the Blades, remember?"

"Oh. Right." Monica had met Michael Dante a few times and liked him. He was smart and funny, the first man to destroy her assumption that all jocks were lacking when it came to gray matter.

Two famous people who are hot, the big city at night . . . how about you give me your number, and we set the world on fire . . . Shit, could she really pretend to be involved with someone who'd actually said that to her? The thought made her contemplate throwing herself under a cab. Then again, it would give her another opportunity to act, which she loved doing.

Theresa was looking at her expectantly. "Well?"

"Fine," Monica huffed. "But if he mauls me in the back of a limo, I'm holding you responsible."

"I seriously doubt that will happen." Theresa crossed her long legs, stretching her arms out along the back of the couch. "Now, we just have to figure out where the two of you should make your debut."

"Well, there's going to be a black tie dinner at the Temple of Dendur next Friday night to honor James Dempsey."

"Perfect. The place will be swarming with paparazzi. I'll get in touch with all my contacts and let them know you'll be showing up with a delicious little surprise on your arm."

Retired actor James Dempsey had been one of Hollywood's brightest stars until his fortune changed—kind of like Gloria, Monica thought. Determined to keep working, he eventually landed a job in television, spending six years on a popular detective show called *Chim Chim and Jones*, about a private investigator whose sidekick was a monkey. His final acting job was on *The Wild and the Free*, playing the grand patriarch of the Deveraux clan until illness forced him to retire. Monica adored him; he was a great actor and a wonderful person. She was glad his peers would be honoring him.

"Wear something stunning," Theresa instructed.

"As if I wouldn't."

Monica moved to collect her bag, then stopped. "Oh, hell. I have to call him, don't I? Eric?"

"Relax. I'll handle the whole thing."

FOUR

"You look gorgeous."

Monica smiled at Eric's compliment, impressed that he had slid out of the stretch limo to meet her beneath the awning of her building and walk her all of six feet to the back of the waiting car. His eyes did a tour of her body, but in this case, she couldn't really complain, since that was exactly what she was angling for, though not for his benefit, but for the press. The dress was midnight blue, with a plunging neckline and a slit up the side to show off the fabulous legs she maintained through endless Pilates sessions. She'd chosen the color because it brought out her sapphire blue eyes, "the most beautiful eyes since Elizabeth Taylor," *Soap World* had once said. She'd worn her hair up. It was loosely tousled, soft curls cascading around her face. When Gene the doorman whistled and told her she looked like "hot stuff," Monica knew she'd nailed it. She just hoped the paparazzi agreed.

She turned to Eric. "Ever been in a limo before?"

Eric looked offended. "Uh, *yeah*."

"Just checking. Ever seen the Temple of Dendur?"

"No."

"It's pretty amazing. It's an Egyptian temple that has its

own wing at the Met. One of the walls is sheer glass, and there's this reflecting pool . . . it's really impressive."

"You go to museums a lot?"

"Not really," Monica confessed, feeling a little embarrassed. Her mentor, Monty, always said you couldn't be a real artist unless you had appreciation for other branches of the arts. Monica always felt she didn't read enough, didn't go to enough concerts or dance recitals or art museums. Maybe that's why she wasn't a real actress yet. Maybe she wasn't well-rounded enough.

Since Eric had had no qualms blatantly giving her the once-over, she did the same to him and was impressed by what she saw. Obnoxious as he might be, the man looked positively Bond-like in a tux. "You look nice."

Eric grinned. "I agree."

Jerk. How had she let Theresa talk her into this? Two seconds in his presence, and already Monica was irritated. *Act,* she reminded herself. *Use your skills.*

"You a James Dempsey fan?"

"Oh, yeah," said Eric. "It's a bummer that he died."

Monica blinked. "What?"

"He's dead, right? I thought this dinner is to honor his memory."

"He's not dead! This dinner is to honor his contribution to the world of entertainment."

"Oh. Well, that's good." Eric paused. "Is Chim Chim going to be there?" he asked hopefully.

"Chim Chim?"

"You know, the monkey from *Chim Chim and Jones.*"

"I know who Chim Chim is. I don't know."

"I hope so. Maybe I can get an autograph. My brother and I used to love that show. Chim Chim was amazing."

"He's a *monkey*, Eric. I doubt he does autographs."

"You're wrong. I'm sure he's been taught to hold a pen and scribble. Hell, he fired a pistol on the show."

Monica wished she had a pistol. So she could point it at her own temple and pull the trigger.

"I remember when James was on *W and F*," Eric continued. "He was great."

"You actually watch *W and F*?" Monica was surprised.

"The whole team does. It passes the time when we're on the road, stuck in a hotel during the day while waiting to play at night. We watch it when we're working out, too."

"Oh." Monica was surprised as well as pleased. It was kind of cool that big, macho jocks watched soaps.

Eric slid closer to her. "About this date . . ."

"Actually, it's not really a date. You're my escort. I'm sure Theresa explained the whole thing to you."

"Theresa used the word *date*." He inched closer. "Look, you don't have to apologize for the way you treated me on the set. I knew you'd come round," he murmured. He was doing that hooded, bedroom eye thing again. She wondered if he'd learned it from watching Royce's bad acting on *W and F*.

He was almost next to her now. Monica tensed, discreetly opening the beaded clutch she'd brought with her; inside was a small can of mace. She'd use it if she had to, so help her God she would.

"You're my escort," Monica repeated.

"Call it whatever you want," Eric replied with a dismissive chuckle. "The fact remains, you asked Theresa to contact me, and here I am."

"Here you are," Monica repeated with false gaiety. She made a mental note to fire Theresa in the morning.

Please *don't let him mention Chim Chim,* thought Monica as she and Eric made their way to their table at the Met. She was glad to see Gloria was at her table, as well as Devlin O'Dare, who played the newly zombified bartender in Garrett City. Unfortunately, Royce was there, too.

"Well, well," Gloria murmured with a lewd smile, her heavily made-up eyes raking Eric's body, pausing extra long at his crotch. "Who have we got here, Monica my love?"

"Everyone, this is Eric Mitchell, my—"

"Date," Eric finished smoothly, taking Gloria's hand and raising it to his lips. "It's a great honor to meet you, ma'am."

Gloria looked pleased. "I love men with manners."

Eric was amiable as he regarded Royce. "Hey."

"Met Gar's own Laurence Olivier," said Royce dryly. "What an *unexpected pleasure*"—he smirked as he looked at Monica—"to see you again. I guess you two really hit it off last week."

"Yes," said Monica. She turned to Eric. "Let's sit, shall we?" Eric nodded, pulling out her chair for her.

What happened next shocked her. Eric's demeanor was smooth as glass as he chatted with others at the table. It was as if he'd left his jerk persona behind him in the limo, some-how turning into a thoughtful, charming companion. Who was this chameleon?

To be honest, Monica's urge to fire Theresa flew out the window the second she and Eric had stepped out of the limo and walked up the steps of the museum together. Cameras clicked wildly with the paparazzi yelling out her name, want-ing to know if she was dating Eric. It was frightening how natural he was in front of the cameras, pausing with her for photos, his hand holding hers, the two of them smiling. He even knew to beam at her with unabashed affection, but she couldn't think about that now. All she knew was they'd be in all the gossip columns tomorrow, along with their picture. Mission accomplished.

"Can I get you anything at the bar?" Eric asked solici-tously during a break in conversation. He was unfailingly po-lite, no sign of the smug egomaniac she'd walked in with.

"No, I'm fine, thanks." Small waves of guilt were begin-ning to lap at her conscience. It was obvious Eric was thrilled to be here, doing his best to be the perfect—well, escort. And what was she doing? Using him. The longer the evening wore on, the worse she felt. It wasn't right. She didn't care what Theresa's master plan was. When the night was over, she was going to tell him the truth and apologize.

"Darling, shall we hit the little girls' room?" Gloria said to her.

"Certainly." Monica rose. "Be back in a minute," she said with a light touch to Eric's shoulder. A nice theatrical touch.

Eric rose. "Perfect timing," he murmured in her ear. "I'll go pay my respects to Chim Chim."

Monica smiled tersely. "You do that."

* * *

Walking with Gloria to the ladies' room, Monica worried about her friend slipping on the tiled floors. She was wearing rhinestone-studded spike heels; if she fell and broke her hip, it would all be over. Monica laced her arm through Gloria's. "Having fun?"

"God, yes. That boy toy you brought with you is *delicious*. Very nice, too. I sincerely hope your plan is to bring him home with you tonight and ravish him until neither of you can walk by the morning."

"I barely know him."

"Well, get to know him." Gloria pushed open the ladies' room door and separated from Monica, teetering toward the bank of mirrors and pulling a lipstick out of her purse. "I'm surprised your good friend and mentor, *Monty*, isn't here," she said in a venomous voice, applying color to her mouth that looked like spilled blood. Gloria hated Monty; they had acted together for years, and she thought he was a pretentious ass. Monica always suspected they had some sort of sexual liaison that ended badly.

"I think he and James had some kind of falling-out years ago," said Monica.

"I'm not surprised," said Gloria. "Well, if you see him, tell him I hope he ends up with Alzheimer's and covered in shingles."

"Will do."

A new guilt swept over Monica. She hadn't visited Monty in a while. She made a mental note to pop in and see him on Sunday, the one day she let herself relax.

"Chesty starts next week," Gloria noted.

"I know," said Monica, slipping into one of the stalls to pee. She heard the bathroom door open. Seconds later, a woman's head appeared beneath the stall door. "What the hell—?!" Monica shrieked, covering herself up.

"Miss Geary, I'm your biggest fan," the woman said breathlessly, trying to crawl forward.

On the other side of the door, Monica heard Gloria inhale sharply. "Dear *God*!"

Monica stared down at the woman in horror. "Do you mind?!"

The woman seemed surprised by her request. "Oh, sorry." The woman slid back out on her belly.

Shaking, Monica yanked her panties and stockings back up and smoothed her dress back down. How the hell did this lunatic get into the Met?! How did she even know Monica was *here*? She knew she had some hard-core and flaky fans— like the one who sent her cookies that were supposed to look like her, or the one in the process of having plastic surgery to look like Monica—but this took the cake. There was no way Monica was coming out of the stall. No way.

"Can I have your autograph?" the woman asked.

"Not right now."

"I have a pen and a picture of you," the woman persisted.

Monica leaned her head against the stall door. *Jesus help me. Well, this is what you wanted, right?* she chided herself. *To be prominent in the public eye?* Not like this, though. Not while she was trying to *pee*.

"Fine," Monica said wearily. "Hand them to me under the stall."

"Okay," said the fan, sounding disappointed.

Monica bent down and snatched the Sharpie and picture of herself from the fan's pudgy hands. It was a glossy black-and-white photo, the standard studio PR pic.

"What's your name?" Monica asked.

"Judy."

Dear Judy, Good luck with your electroshock therapy treatments, Monica Geary.

That was what she wanted to write. What she did write was, *"To Judy, All Best, Monica Geary."* She passed it back out to Judy.

"Wow, thanks," said Judy.

"Young lady," Monica heard Gloria say sternly. "Do not ever, ever do this to anyone you're a fan of again. Do you hear me? It is rude, and it gives all fans a bad reputation. Now go, before I notify security of this breach." Monica could picture her pointing to the door dramatically.

Monica waited until she heard the bathroom door swing

shut, then ventured out of the stall. Gloria was wide-eyed, her
hand clutching her crepey throat. "Horrifying," Gloria whispered. "Are you all right?"

"A little shaken up, but fine." She looked at herself in the
mirror. The color had drained from her face, making her look
like the world's only blonde Kabuki actor. "I feel like leaving."

"So go," Gloria urged. "Things will be winding up soon,
anyway. Take your blond-haired, blue-eyed stud home and
let him *calm* you."

Monica flashed back to the dream she'd had about Eric.
Shut up and fuck me. Heat wound through her. She wished
she could be that woman, the uninhibited one in her dreams.
But she wasn't. Not only was she not big on one-night stands,
but she could also be a little uptight when it came to sex, perhaps even a wee bit puritanical. She attributed it to her WASP
upbringing. She'd never seen her parents so much as hold
hands, and when she was small and her mother decided to
have the big Sex Talk with her, her mother couldn't even use
the word *vagina.* She referred to it as "your flower," then
made a disgusted face before handing her a book about repro-
duction and fleeing. Later that day, Monica had confusedly
peered between her legs, expecting to see a daisy or a rose
growing there. The thought was extremely alarming. At any
rate, she'd been left with the vague impression there was
something dirty about sex, an impression she'd never really
managed to shake, which sometimes impaired her pleasure.
Except in her dreams.

Monica pinched some color back into her face and squared
her shoulders. She would say her good-byes, apologize to
Eric Mitchell, and call it a night. No more bathroom stalls for
her tonight. She'd pee when she got home.

How do you confess to someone that you've used them? Is it
right to do it in the back of a limo idling outside your apartment building? Do you call them the next day to avoid doing
it face-to-face and endure being called every nasty name under the sun, all of which you deserved? Neither option seemed

palatable to Monica, which left inviting Eric up to her apartment for a coffee, and facing the drubbing she had coming to her.

"Would you like to come in for a ni—coffee?" Shit, she'd almost said *nightcap*. Did people even *say* nightcap anymore? They did on *W and F*, which is why she almost slipped. Characters were always inviting each other in for nightcaps, where one of them would pour brandy from a cut crystal decanter sitting on a brass drink trolley. Monica had never met anyone in her life that had a drink trolley. She needed to talk to the exec producer about this. It was one of the anachronisms that helped make daytime a butt of jokes.

Eric's eyes flickered with intrigue as he accepted her offer. Maybe this was a mistake. She still had her mace with her in case Mr. Hyde reemerged.

"Did you have a good time?" she asked Eric in the elevator as it rose twenty-seven stories up into the sky.

"It was weird," said Eric, loosening his bow tie.

"Because Chim Chim couldn't sign his name the way you expected?"

Eric ignored the barb. "Because you're all so phony with each other."

Monica blinked. "Excuse me?"

"All that air kissing and 'Darling, you look stunning,' and 'Isn't so-and-so wonderful,' and 'Yes, we must to get together.' And then the minute someone turns their back, you're all whispering about how their ass looks enormous and did he have work done and whom did she blow to get that movie part. It's kind of sickening."

"As sickening as you crawling up the ass of everyone at the table, telling them how much you love their characters?" Monica snapped.

"I do!"

"You were being just as disingenuous as anyone else. I heard you tell Gloria she didn't look a day over fifty."

"I was trying to be nice! I was trying to be a good date!"

Monica gritted her teeth. "Escort."

"You said *date* when you introduced me," Eric maintained stubbornly.

The elevator doors slid open. "If I'd said *escort*, it would have sounded like I was paying you."

Eric touched her cheek. "I can think of ways for you to pay me."

Monica jerked away from him. "Jesus," she hissed, storming to her apartment and throwing open the door. Bad idea, having him up here. Bad, bad idea. Christ, she wished she *did* have a drink trolley. She'd drink the brandy straight out of the decanter.

Eric followed, closing the door behind him. "I was just trying to be a good date," he repeated. He regarded her coolly. "You're not the only one who can act, you know."

Monica whirled to face him. "Really? So which one is the real Eric Mitchell? The self-absorbed egomaniac who thinks women should fall at his feet, or the fluid, conversant charmer in the tuxedo who seemed oh so interested in everyone else?" His face fell, a trace of mortification in his eyes. A new wave of guilt washed over Monica. "I'm sorry," she said with a sigh, tossing her bag onto the couch. "I'm tired and a little cranky." Even so, the question she'd just posed was a valid one.

"Apology accepted," said Eric, looking impressed as he gazed around the apartment. "This place is huge."

"Ten years of *W and F* provides a very nice paycheck." Visitors tended to be most impressed with the size, but it was how it was decorated that always made Monica proudest: English cottage style, with lots of dried flowers, stripped pine, baskets, and brass. Her home was her oasis, and she wanted it plain and homey, her own little piece of the Cotswolds on the Upper East Side. "What kind of coffee would you like?"

"I'm fine, actually. No coffee for me."

"I don't want any, either, to tell the truth."

Eric's gaze was unnervingly direct. "So why am I here?"

Now that the moment of truth had arrived, Monica wished she'd opted for the coward's way out back in the limo. Telling the truth could easily undo the PR coup of the past evening. What was to stop him running to the paper and telling them that Monica Geary had used him? Nothing. But she was willing to take the risk. She didn't want to be the type of person who used someone else that way.

She sat down on the couch. "Why don't you sit—at that end," she added hastily, pointing to the opposite end of the sofa. Eric complied. "I'm not really sure how to say this."

Eric raised a hand. "Don't worry," he said kindly. "I know what you're going to say."

"You do?"

"Yeah." He radiated self-confidence.

Monica steeled herself. "What, then?"

"That you're totally into me."

"Actually, I'm not. I'm totally *not* into you. In fact, I think you're an egomaniacal jerk who may very well have a personality disorder. This whole evening was Theresa Dante's idea. I need to up my profile in the public eye, and she told me you'd be the perfect escort for me, since you're the hottest thing on skates or something. We even discussed my stringing you along to keep the public tantalized." Her cheeks were burning. "But it's a crappy thing to do, and I—I won't do it. So I'm telling you the truth. I'm sorry for using you, Eric."

She made herself continue to look at his expressionless face, waiting for the inevitable storm of curse words to come. "Wow," he said, sounding awed. "You're a total bitch."

Ashamed, Monica looked down at her hands. "I know."

"But this is a great idea."

Monica slowly raised her head. "What?"

"Here's the lowdown, okay? I'm new to the Blades. Yeah, I'm a great player—that's universally agreed upon—and yeah, I'm totally hot, but I kind of got off on the wrong foot with my teammates."

"Alienated them by being a jackass?" Monica murmured sweetly.

"Something like that," Eric muttered. "Anyway, I have to prove myself on the ice, obviously. But I also need to do something to prove I'm not a dick off the ice, that I'm kinda cool. The guys all love you, Monica."

Monica felt a warm glow inside.

"They were totally impressed I did a cameo on the show, and even though they all thought I was bullshitting them about being your date tonight, the proof will be in tomorrow's paper."

"What are you getting at?" Monica asked warily.

"We commence a mutually beneficial relationship."

"You're kidding, right?" This was the last thing Monica expected to hear.

"It'll help each of us get what we want, right? This could even help me out with Blades fans, who are kind of gunning for me, too, since the team traded one of their most beloved players for me."

Monica nodded her head, impressed. "You must be good at what you do."

"Babe, I'm good at a lot of things."

"Oh, God. Look." Monica pointed a warning finger at him. "If we're going to be spending time together, you cannot say icky things like that. Got it?"

Eric looked mildly wounded. "But what if it's true?"

"Then keep it to yourself. I don't care if you have the biggest package east of the Rockies; (A) I'm not interested, and (B) it makes me want to stick a fork in your eye. So save your breath."

Eric frowned. "Fine," he said, his expression reflective as he gave a stretch. "How do we do this?"

"By constantly being in the public eye, doing couple type things. Dinner, stuff like that." Monica gave a small frown. "I suppose I could go to a hockey game sometime, meet your teammates. And you could visit the set."

"Sounds great." Eric stood, stifling a yawn. "So, we've got a deal?"

"Deal," Monica said, rising.

"Can we at least seal it with a—"

"Handshake?" Monica cut in, glaring at him.

Eric rolled his eyes. "Fine." Eric extended his hand, and Monica took it. His hands were big and strong, the grip firm. She pulled away as soon as politely possible. "I'd love to stay and talk, but believe it or not, I've got practice tomorrow. My coach is a bit of a fanatic."

"Should we set up our next rendezvous?"

Eric shrugged. "Sure. What do you want to do?"

"There's this new restaurant called Dijon that just opened up on East Seventy-ninth. I'll make reservations for Thursday night and have Theresa alert the press. My car will pick you up."

"Your *car*?"

"Is there a problem with that?"

"No. I've just never had a girlfriend—"

"*Business partner*—"

"—who had her own car service before."

"I told you: daytime's been very good to me."

"Sounds like it's going to be very good to me, too." He paused. "Don't you think I should kiss you sometimes, just so it looks realistic?"

"If we must." An unwanted streak of heat shot through Monica as she remembered another detail of her dream: they'd had sex here on the couch. "You should go," she said, hustling quickly to open the door.

Eric sauntered after her. He appeared to have only one speed: saunter. "Well, thank you for a very nice evening, Miss Geary."

"You, too, Mr. Mitchell."

He smiled at her—a sincere smile, which was somewhat unnerving—and sauntered out into the hall. Monica quietly closed the door behind him. Their arrangement was nuts, she thought, but Eric was right: it could help the both of them immensely. Still, what did it say about two people willing to use one another for their own purposes? She worried about that, but then again, as long as there was no risk of anyone getting hurt . . .

She yawned, suddenly tired. She couldn't wait to see the papers tomorrow.

FIVE

Eric sat on the bench behind the rink's Plexiglas, watching as his brother and five of their teammates were put through a two-on-one headman drill. Maybe it was a testament to his desperation, but the minute he'd woken up that morning, he'd hustled to the deli around the corner to pick up the Sunday edition of the *Sentinel*. Coffee in one hand, he'd hurriedly flipped to the entertainment section of the paper as soon as he got home. There, among pictures of other luminaries, was a picture of Monica and him from the night before, posing on the steps on the way into the Metropolitan Museum. He stared, amazed and pleased at how goddamn *great* they looked together. Forget Brangelina: he and Monica resembled a jaw-dropping vision of blondness that had come down from the heavens to give mortals the pleasure of looking upon them. It was unbelievable.

He was on a bit of a roll, PR wise. Tomorrow, an interview he'd done with *New York* magazine would hit the stands. He'd made sure to talk about how thrilled he was to be traded to the Blades, since they were the best team in the NHL. He'd made a point of saying he hoped he could follow in Guy Le Temp's footsteps and continually improve as a defenseman. In short, he'd said all the right things.

As if attention from print media wasn't enough, his cameo on *W and F* would be airing this week, and he had every intention of watching it with his teammates. He knew he'd be able to deftly handle any ribbing that came his way, and in fact welcomed it. Eric liked a challenge, both on the ice and off.

The lines switched, and six more players hit the ice. Eric felt a bump to his right shoulder and turned to see Barry Fontaine sliding down on the bench to sit beside him, helmet in one hand as he raked the other through his tousled, sweaty hair.

"Mitchell."

"Fontaine."

"I saw that picture of you and Monica Geary in the paper this morning."

Eric pretended to be concentrating hard on the ice, watching the drill. "Yeah?"

"How come you didn't say anything about it to anyone?"

Eric turned to him. "Because none of you putzes believed me when I told you we hit it off on the *W and F* set. I thought, Why even bother?"

By now, he could tell everyone on the bench was tuning in to their exchange. All Barry had to say was "Monica Geary," and the team was all ears.

"Where were you guys going, anyway?" Barry continued nonchalantly.

"A dinner honoring James Dempsey."

"Oh, man," said Thad Meyers, seated two players away. "Was Chim Chim there?"

"Yup."

Ulf Torkelson, who up until now had been intermittently scowling at Eric as he sat on his left, turned to him, goggle-eyed. "You met Chim Chim?"

"Shook his hand and everything."

"Lucky bastard." He gave Eric a begrudging once-over. "I guess you can't be all bad if Monica Geary likes you *and* you met Chim Chim."

Score!

"So, what is she like?" Ulf murmured, back to looking at Eric dubiously.

"Who, Monica or Chim Chim?"

Barry looked stricken. "Chim Chim's not a girl, is he? I mean, Dempsey's character always called him 'My dear Mr. C,' remember?"

"So?" Ulf snorted. "A female chimp could play a male part."

"Chim Chim's a guy," Eric assured them. "He had a tux on."

"Cool," said Barry.

"As for Monica, she's great. Great sense of humor."

There was a glint of envy in Ulf's eye. "Are you guys seeing each other?"

Eric shrugged. "I guess so. We're having dinner on Thursday."

Admiration rippled up and down the bench. He was the man. He'd have to tell Monica that even though they'd only been out once, already his teammates were holding him in higher esteem. Their ploy was going to work like a charm, at least on his end.

"Yo, Mitcho."

Eric frowned upon hearing Lonnie Campbell call him by his nickname. His brother's nickname was Mitchy, so he'd been saddled with Mitcho, which he hated. It sounded like one of those cheap gizmos peddled on late-night TV that always sold for just $19.99. *Prevent stove splatters and stains with the amazing Mitcho! And if you order now, we'll throw in a free electric scalp massager!*

"Yeah, Lonnie?"

Lonnie swallowed nervously. "Do you think you could—if it's not too much trouble—get Monica's autograph for me?"

"I can do better than that: I can have her come down here one day to meet you guys."

"Oh, yeah!" Ulf high-fived Eric, with everyone on the bench following suit. It amazed Eric how you could never get tired of hearing the phrase "You rock" from your teammates.

Just wait until they saw what he could do on the ice. He'd be a bona fide Blade in no time.

"Stanley!"

By now, Eric should have been used to Jason's giant Newf drooling all over him the minute he walked through his brother's front door, but it still got to him. Why Jason didn't put one of those dog bibs on Stan was beyond him.

"Stan, lie down!"

At Jason's command, Stanley lumbered back to his dog bed, grumbling. The bed was large enough for two small children to sleep on comfortably. Delilah's three dogs had barely lifted their heads at Eric's entry, and for that he was glad. One dog greeting him he could handle; a four-dog welcoming committee was a bit much.

"Hey, Delilah." Eric ambled over to the couch, leaning over to kiss his sister-in-law on the cheek. For a long while, Eric wasn't Delilah's favorite person, having stolen her father's fiancée out from under his nose. But it all worked out for the best: Delilah's parents had reconciled, and the fiancée, mackerel-brained Brandi, was history. By the time Jason and Delilah tied the knot a few months back, Delilah had forgiven Eric and even seemed fond of him.

He momentarily diverted his attention to the TV. Delilah appeared to be watching some show on cougars; in fact, three of them were tearing apart an antelope with glee. Charming. Again Eric wondered where Jason's head was at; *Pardon the Interruption* was on ESPN right now. What was wrong with his brother? Jason claimed Eric spent too much time glued to the tube. Easy for him to say; he didn't live alone.

Delilah smiled at Eric. "Good to see you. Do you want to stay for dinner?"

"That would be great." Delilah was turning out to be a decent cook.

"Why don't you just move in?" Jason grumbled.

"Hey, that's not nice," Delilah chided. "Eric's not here that much."

Which was true; Eric was making a concerted effort to

give the newlyweds their space. But this visit had been Jason's idea, not his.

"*You're* the one who invited *me* over," Eric pointed out. He grinned impishly at his brother. "You're dying to hear all about Monica, aren't you?"

Delilah's ears pricked up. "Monica who?"

"Monica Geary," said Jason. "Apparently she's deranged and asked Eric to accompany to her some party last Friday night."

Delilah sighed. "My mom once told me she's gorgeous in person. They were at the same sample sale, and my mom almost took out one of her eyes with the hat she was wearing."

"What was it, three-cornered?" Jason asked. He regarded his brother dubiously. "So? Are you really seeing her again?"

"Yup."

"Wow." Jason slowly shook his head. "That's amazing. Though it is kind of cool we'll all get to meet her—assuming your relationship lasts beyond a week, which I doubt."

"Oh ye of little faith and immense jealousy."

"Yeah, right." Jason perched on the corner of the couch, brushing aside his wife's curly hair so he could press his lips tenderly to the nape of her neck. "I've got all the woman I need right here, Bro."

Eric's eyes darted away. He was glad his brother and Delilah were so affectionate, but sometimes it made him feel like a third wheel. Affectionate interlude over, Eric parked himself on the couch on the other side of Delilah, absently petting her white-haired, weird-eyed dog, the one who'd had multiple cataract surgery. "So," he said to Jason, "you summoned me because—?"

Jason looked perturbed. "I spoke with Mom and Dad a little while ago. They wanted to talk about the farm."

Eric and Jason had been raised on a small dairy farm in rural Flasher, North Dakota. It was a great place to grow up, but both of them knew from an early age that they wanted to play hockey, and they'd left the minute the minor leagues came calling.

Eric felt a nip of jealousy. "How come they always call you?"

"Maybe because I pick up the phone and check my messages more than once a month?"

"Anyway."

"They're thinking of selling," Jason said with a pained look on his face.

"What?"

The Mitchell dairy farm went back generations to their mother's great-grandfather. Both their parents were from farm stock and had often said they could never imagine doing anything else.

"It's killing them financially," Jason continued. "Dad said they can't compete with those bigger, corporate farms."

Eric blinked, trying to imagine no farm to come home to twice a year. He was overcome by memories: Jason and him playing pond hockey in the winter; the two of them racing their bikes down the winding country roads the minute the snow melted; their father teaching them how to milk cows; the first calving he'd ever witnessed; the bare, stark beauty of the landscape in winter; and the summer sky stretched tight as a blue canvas.

And yet, it was unfair of him to be sentimental and rhapsodize. He had no interest in returning to North Dakota and taking over once his hockey career was through. Their folks in trouble . . . it was inconceivable. And frightening.

"Maybe they could switch product," he suggested. "Sell off the cows, start farming corn. They've got enough land."

"That would cost a shitload of money, Eric, which they don't have. Plus you know Mom: 'We're a dairy farm, always have been.' "

Eric rubbed his right temple, he and his brother catching each other's eye. He could tell Jason was thinking the same things he was: Who were their parents without the farm? Who were they without the farm to come home to?

"I think what we should do," Jason said slowly, "is offer to give them some money to hire some more help so they can at least keep up. I just hope they'll take it."

"We'll just remind them of all they did for us," said Eric. "All those years of shelling out for hockey equipment and driving us to practice at five a.m."

Jason chuckled. "I can still hear Dad bitching about the truck refusing to turn over in the cold, cursing out the coaches for setting practice so early."

"We owe them," Eric said softly.

"Of course we do."

"Talk to Dad, don't talk to Mom. You know he'll be more open to it." Eric paused. "Maybe we could do a conference call and *both* of us could talk to him."

"That's a good idea."

Delilah looked back and forth between Eric and his brother with admiration. "You're good sons."

Both men ducked their heads, mildly embarrassed. Jason was a better son than Eric was, of that Eric was certain. He was definitely worse than Jason about calling, but part of that was because his mother was always hounding him about meeting a nice girl and settling down the way Jason had. Maybe the Monica hookup would appease her somewhat, since she was a longtime fan of *W and F.*

Delilah rose. "I'm going to go see what I can conjure up for dinner." She disappeared into the kitchen, leaving Jason and Eric with a silence as vast as the North Dakota plains.

"No farm . . ." said Jason, stopping with a swallow. Eric was relieved when he didn't finish the thought.

"Who's there? Who is it?"

"It's Monica, Monty," Monica called out to her mentor, Monty Kingman, who was in his bedroom. His question made her wonder who else might have a key to his apartment besides her. Then she remembered: Rosa, the cleaning lady Monica paid for who came once a week.

As always, the first thing she thought when she entered Monty's apartment was, *What a firetrap.* Piles of old newspapers and magazines that he refused to part with covered every surface. In addition, the place smelled musty, despite Rosa's best efforts to clean. The carpet had been shampooed numerous times, the curtains laundered. Monica suspected the stale smell had a lot to do with the fact that Monty had some innate aversion to opening the windows. Rosa would open them, and Monty would close them—their own little cold war.

"I'll be there in a minute," she called to him, heading into the kitchen to put away some groceries she'd bought. Despite being one of the most well-respected acting teachers in the business, he had no savings, and his pension from Actors' Equity was so small it was laughable. It was this situation that had driven him into teaching on his own so many years back, a situation Monica knew he resented but one that had benefited her greatly in terms of her training.

Making her way to his bedroom, she gazed at his walls, taking in all the framed photographs of Monty from when he was younger, acting on the stage. He'd acted opposite some of the greats: Brando, Newman, Robards . . . it was unbelievable.

She found him sitting in his orange plaid Barcalounger circa 1970, watching TV. The bed was unmade, and the air in the room was stagnant, tinged with the sourness of old age. Monica marched to the window and opened it. Monty's arm jerked up, and he shielded his eyes, recoiling like a vampire who hadn't made it back to his crypt in time.

"What on earth are you *doing*?"

"Getting some air in here."

He harrumphed at her, turning back to the TV to watch two red-faced talking heads yell at each other about gun control. Despite his disheveled nature, he could still cut a dashing figure, Monica thought, with his maroon smoking jacket tied tight around his stick-thin waist, and his long, bony feet shod in monogrammed black velvet slippers.

"What are you watching?" Monica asked.

"Some *crap*," Monty replied vehemently. "TV is nothing but crap. Have you noticed?"

Monica felt her cheeks flame, which always happened when he said this. She tried not to take it personally, but it was hard. She worked in TV; therefore, by extension, in her old teacher's eyes, *she* was crap.

"Why don't you watch the Shakespeare DVDs I brought you?"

His blue eyes, still the bright sapphire color of his youth, flashed. "I couldn't figure out how to work the goddamn DVD player!"

"I showed you, remember?"

"Well, I guess I'm just a fucking idiot, then," he snapped.

"I'll show you again before I leave," Monica said patiently. "Why don't you get dressed, and we'll take a walk?"

Monty waved a dismissive hand at her, which Monica knew meant, "Subject closed." She wondered when the last time he'd been out was. She suspected he was becoming slightly agoraphobic in his old age, though she'd never bring it up to him for fear of incurring his wrath, which could be formidable. She'd invited him to accompany her to the theater numerous times, but he always declined, his mind already made up before even seeing the play in question that it was "tripe pandering to the idiot masses." Maybe it was hard for him to see others treading the boards now that he couldn't.

"I watched you this week," he murmured.

Monica smiled to cover the churning already starting in her stomach. Monty tuned in to *W and F* religiously so he could critique Monica's performance. For ten years she'd listened to his notes and observations, but it always made her tense.

"Okay."

"First of all, you're gesticulating too much. You certainly didn't learn that in *my* class."

"The director told me to!"

"The director is a fucking moron," Monty declared. "If he wasn't, he wouldn't be directing in daytime."

Monica's cheeks burned brighter. *I'm a fucking moron, too,* she thought. *That's what he thinks. That's what he's thought for a decade.* "Go on," she urged quietly.

"I don't think you're inhabiting your character anymore. I don't think you're really trying to get at the emotion behind the text. Your performances are becoming less and less nuanced."

Monica blinked with alarm. What if Monty was right? What if that was why the executive producer talked about Chessy helping to bring the show in a new direction? What if she *sucked*?

"You need to really dig," Monty continued.

You try digging when you have to memorize an eighty-page script five nights a week, Monica longed to say, *or when you have one day to shoot a show.* She did the best she could. But clearly it wasn't good enough.

Monty sighed heavily. "I hate to see you wasting yourself this way, Monica. You have incredible talent. And yet there you are on that ridiculous *soap opera*—and acting badly as well, in my opinion. You have to decide which is more important," Monty sniffed. "Money or your art."

Monica swallowed. Was it really that black and white? Maybe it was. She looked at Monty, the beloved teacher who had helped her excel at Julliard, the man who had told her she could make a living doing what she loved, unlike her parents, whose stance had always been, "Acting is a nice hobby, but you'll never make a living from it." She'd proven them wrong—because of Monty and what he'd been able to pull out of her.

"When it's time to renew my contract, I'll think about it," she promised. "In the meantime, I need to make a living, Monty, so I'm working as hard as I can to maintain what I have. You can understand that, can't you?"

"Artist or hack, Monica. You decide."

SIX

"Stop winking. You look like you have something in your eye."

Eric looked momentarily crestfallen as he escorted Monica to their window table at Dijon, NYC's hottest new restaurant. Theresa had worked her magic again: there were paparazzi waiting outside, snapping pictures, demanding to know if she and Eric were a bona fide item. Monica smiled coyly but said nothing. Eric winked at them while giving the thumbs-up twice: once while they were going into the restaurant, and yet again through the window once they were seated. This was going to be harder than Monica thought.

"What's wrong with winking?" Eric asked. "It tells them, 'Yeah, something is definitely going on,' while at the same time maintaining the mystery."

"You're a master of the media now, huh?"

Monica opened the menu, stifling an exhausted yawn. She was in the majority of scenes filmed earlier in the day, and she was incredibly weary. She'd gone above and beyond to really dig into the character of Roxie the way Monty advised. If anyone noticed, they hadn't said anything.

"How was your week?" Eric asked.

"Long. Tiring. Yours?" Christ, they sounded like some old married couple finally sitting down to dinner on a Friday night, eager to forget the nine-to-five grind.

"Great. Those pictures of us really boosted my profile with my teammates. I think our arrangement is going to work out great."

"I think so, too." Monica had heard through the grapevine that one of the pictures of them at the museum was going to run in tomorrow's *Soap World*. People were taking an extra interest in her again. This was a good sign.

Monica glanced sideways out the window. The paparazzi were still there. Eric noticed, too.

"We should probably hold hands across the table," he suggested. "And you might want to look enchanted by everything I say."

"Good thing I'm an actress," said Monica. She stretched her hand to meet his in the middle of the table. It was large and warm, comforting somehow. They twined fingers.

"How's that?" Eric asked.

"You're cutting off my circulation."

"If I do it too loosely, it will look fake."

"For God's sake," Monica replied, exasperated, "do you really think they're looking that closely?"

"You never know."

"Fine," she huffed. She waited for her fingertips to turn blue, but they didn't. They ordered drinks, then dinner. Monica refrained from sucking down her Bellini in one go.

"Look like you're hanging on every word I say," said Eric.

"How about you look like you're hanging on every word *I* say?" Monica countered.

"I could do that."

She watched Eric rearrange his facial expression so his eyes were caressing hers, his mouth parted slightly in wonderment. Jesus, this guy was good. It was almost scary.

"You missed your calling; you should have been an actor."

"I told you: I am an actor. When I need to be. Why else do you think I'm such a babe magnet?"

"Tell me," Monica asked sweetly. "What's it like to be a legend in your own mind?"

Eric chuckled. "I told the guys you had a great sense of humor. It's good that we're getting to know each other a little, right? Adds to the realism."

Monica sipped her drink with her free hand. "Do you feel at all guilty about this little ruse?"

"No. Do you?"

Monica paused. "A little. At some point we'll have to figure out who breaks up with whom."

"I think I should break up with you."

"I disagree."

"What if they can read our lips and know we're not having an intimate conversation?" Eric said worriedly.

"You're an idiot," said Monica, smiling at him with false adoration. How the hell was she going to get through an entire meal alone with this man? The dinner for James Dempsey was one thing; there were lots of other people for them to talk to, and of course, Chim Chim. But this was different.

Eventually, the waiter brought their dinners. "Looks good," said Eric. He had let Monica order for him, confessing that his knowledge of French food extended to fries and yellow mustard. She appreciated his honesty. She hated when men tried to bluff their way through sophistication.

"You'll have to let go of my hand if we want to eat," Monica pointed out.

"Oh. Right."

He released her hand, and for a split second, she missed the contact. When was the last time she'd held hands with a man? Helping Monty get to the bathroom didn't count.

Acutely aware of their surroundings, Monica noticed a woman and a man tucked away at a table for two in the back of the small room, trying to be discreet as they took turns glancing at Eric and Monica. Fans, Monica thought happily. When the woman stood and began walking toward the table, Monica squared her shoulders, sitting up a little straighter and smiling a friendly smile. An autograph, posing for a picture . . . this would be perfect. And the woman wasn't crawling beneath a bathroom stall. This was her type of fan.

The woman stopped at the table, twisting her hands shyly.

"Excuse me—are you Eric Mitchell?"

Eric smiled at the woman warmly. "Yeah, I am."

"I'm a huge Blades fan, and I'm just so thrilled that you joined the team. Can you pose for a picture with me?"

"Sure."

The woman handed her digital camera to Monica. "Do you mind?"

"No, of course not." Monica was smiling so hard she thought her face might crack. *Eric?* The woman wanted a picture taken with Eric and not *her*?

Eric rose, putting his arm around the starstruck fan. "Whenever you're ready, honey," he said to Monica. He was grinning at her like the cat that ate the canary. Or the jock that had outshone the actress. Monica held back a glare.

"Say cheese," Monica instructed cheerily, snapping a bunch of pictures. She handed the camera back to the fan, who thanked Eric profusely, but not her. The fan was babbling excitedly to her companion as she returned to her own table.

"Pissed, huh?" Eric observed dryly as they sat back down.

Monica toyed casually with one of her earrings. "I beg your pardon?"

"I saw your face when that chick said she wanted to pose with me and not you. You were stunned."

"No, I wasn't."

"Yes, you *were*." Eric seemed to be enjoying catching her out. "What a little egomaniac you are, Ms. Geary."

"Look who's talking," Monica snorted. "You practically knocked the table over trying to get out of your chair to pose."

"I didn't want the woman's dinner to get cold."

Monica rolled her eyes. "Spare me."

"I promise that the next time that happens, I'll ask them to take your picture, too, okay?" Eric said with a mischievous look in his eye.

Monica ignored him.

Eating their dinners, they actually had a decent conversation, talking about their jobs. Monica was surprised at how easy it went, and then she remembered watching him turn on the charm at the museum bash the other night. She wondered: Was *this* the real Eric, or was jerk Eric the real Eric? Well, it didn't really matter, since they were just playacting the whole romance, anyway. Still, she couldn't resist asking a question or two.

"What kinds of women actually fall for your 'I'm a stud' act? I'm not criticizing you for doing it. I'm just curious."

"Women who think it's cool to be with a professional athlete. Women who want to be seen with me."

"Like me."

"This is a partnership," Eric reminded her.

"So these women are just trophies, in other words. Nothing real. Nothing *substantial*."

Eric's jaw set. "I don't like complications."

Fascinated, Monica put an elbow on the table, cradling her chin in the palm of her hand. "So what happens when you get bored with your eye candy? Do you dump them? Pull the old 'Love 'em and leave 'em'? Or is 'Leave 'em before they want a commitment' more accurate?"

"What do you care?" Eric retorted.

"I don't, really," Monica replied, feeling mildly rebuked. "Like I said, I was just curious."

"What about you?" Eric challenged. "You only go for deep, artistic types? You're so sophisticated you're un-pick-up-able?"

"I never said that, though I'm not big on relationships that are all about status—until now. Not that this is a relationship," she was quick to add.

"Just two people helping each other out. Though I wouldn't mind knowing, just because I'm 'just curious,' what kind of guys you usually date."

Monica sighed, swirling her dessert spoon through the melted peach sorbet in her bowl. She supposed she owed him an answer. "The wrong kind. I've dated a couple of my costars, which is colossally stupid. 'Showmances' rarely work out. At least not for me."

"They probably can't handle how popular you are."

Perceptive, Monica thought. "That can be part of it. The other part is I've picked jerks."

"My sympathies," said Eric, sounding sincere.

Monica shrugged dispassionately. "You live, you learn."

The waiter left the bill, and Eric snatched it up. "I've got it."

"We should split it."

Eric made a face. "Yeah, because nothing says 'We're a couple' like splitting the bill."

"Fine." Monica raised her palms in surrender. "You get this one, I'll get the next one."

"When *is* the next one?"

"I don't know. Let me talk to Theresa."

"Oh, hey, I know," said Eric, his face lighting up. "How 'bout you come down to Met Gar and meet the guys? You wanna talk about doing me a solid? Plus they'll be so thrilled to meet you, you'll get the ego fix of a lifetime."

Monica smiled. "Sure. Call me, and we'll figure it out."

"Great."

Bill paid, they left the restaurant. The paparazzi had long since dispersed, leaving the two of them standing alone on the sidewalk in the quiet Upper East Side neighborhood.

Eric looked uncomfortable, rocking on his heels with his hands in his back pockets. "You gonna call for your car?"

"Actually, I think I'm going to walk."

"Oh." He paused. "I'll walk you, if you want."

"That's okay. I like to walk alone sometimes. Helps me clear my head."

"Right." He stopped rocking. "Well, bye, then." It looked as though he was going to plant a friendly kiss on her cheek. Instead, he touched his lips softly to hers. "Just in case there's someone from the press staked out somewhere we can't see, watching us," he explained.

Monica nodded briskly, still feeling the heat from his mouth. "Yes. Of course."

She turned from him and started walking home. For a split second, she was tempted to look back over her shoulder to see if he was watching her, but she didn't. They were just "helping each other out," playing their respective parts. Nothing more.

Monica double-checked her appearance in the mirror in the ladies' room deep in the bowels of Met Gar before heading to the locker room to meet Eric's teammates. Maybe it was a sign of her not being as well-rounded as she should be, but she'd never set foot in a sports arena before, nor had she ever been to a professional sporting event. She supposed she'd have to attend a hockey game soon, just to keep the relationship thing looking realistic.

She'd been careful not to dress too provocatively, showing just enough cleavage to entice but not so much she'd be surrounded by drooling men who thought her body began below the neck. She was surprised to find herself battling a mild case of nerves. Meeting and mingling with fans from all walks of life was one thing; but this was the first time she was meeting exclusively with a group of men, and not just any group of men, either: these guys were all jocks. Classic alpha males. The testosterone level awaiting her had to be staggering.

She'd brought a stack of photographs to autograph and fully anticipated posing for a picture with each of them. She could lie to herself and say it was a burden, but the truth was, she liked posing for pictures. She hated that Eric could tell it irked her when the woman in Dijon wanted her photo taken with him and not her, but she supposed she shouldn't. Actors were supposed to be egotistical, after all. She just wished she were getting the ego boost from performing in a more respected branch of entertainment.

She pushed open the ladies' room door, heading down the hall toward the locker room. She could hear a hum of excited voices coming from inside, which was flattering. She knocked once; the humming abruptly stopped. "Is that you, baby?" Eric called out.

"It's me," Monica trilled, chafing at the sexy tone with which Eric said *baby*. But a ruse was a ruse, right? She opened the door, finding herself confronted with nineteen goggle-eyed hulks. "Hi, honey."

Now in character, she walked straight over to Eric, giving him a more-than-friendly kiss on the mouth, just so there was no doubt among his teammates that they were truly a couple. Eric embraced her hard, his hands going a little lower on her back than she would have liked. In fact, one inch lower, and he would have been cupping her ass. Such provocative realism, enough to make her want to pop him one. There was a definite feeling of testosterone swirling around the room, a uniquely condensed male energy that Monica had never experienced. "So, guys, here's my girl," Eric said proudly as they broke their embrace. "Try not to drool all over her, or you'll have me to answer to."

Monica chuckled, quickly observing the hockey players. Most of them were in jeans and T-shirts, Eric included. He had just come from the shower; his thick, blond hair was wet, his scent lemon fresh. Something rippled through Monica that she didn't care to address.

Holding her hand (at least this time he wasn't cutting off her circulation), Eric led her around the packed locker room, introducing her to each of his teammates. Their names and faces all blended into one, as did their eyes, which always flicked down to her chest before returning to her face to stare worshipfully at her. The only one who seemed not to be awestruck by her presence was Eric's dark-haired brother, Jason.

Jason held out a hand. "Nice to meet you."

"You, too." Monica could see a slight resemblance between him and Eric around the eyes, but that was it.

"I need you to explain something to me, Ms. Geary," said Jason.

"Please, call me Monica."

"Monica. I'm a little mystified as to why you'd want to go out with my brother here. He's got the emotional depth of a paramecium." The other players laughed.

"Perhaps there's a side of him you don't know," Monica murmured mischievously. Eric smirked at Jason, who made a disgusted face.

Eric and Monica dropped hands, and Monica sat down on

the nearest bench. "Eric said you guys have tons of questions," she said affably. "Fire away."

"Why didn't you get a priest in to perform an exorcism when Grayson was possessed by Satan's right-hand man, Rodrigo?" Thad Meyers asked.

"You mean, why didn't *Roxie* get a priest," Monica corrected gently. This happened all the time: Viewers confused her with her character. She got mail addressed to Roxie, and a woman had once tried to slap her on the street after Roxie had stolen another character's husband on the show.

Thad just blinked.

"Everything is up to the writers," Monica continued.

"I gotta say, that was really low of you, that time you buried your cousin Willow alive in that glass coffin," said Ulf, nostrils flaring with disapproval. "How could you *do* that?"

Monica's teeth gritted slightly. "*Roxie* did it. I'm not Roxie. She's just the character I play."

But Ulf wasn't done. "But don't you think it was a rotten thing for Roxie to do?"

"She went to jail for it," Monica pointed out.

"Yeah, but then you got off on a technicality, which was soooo wrong," Tully Webster chimed in, shaking his head.

Monica closed her eyes a moment. Clearly, the "I'm not my character" distinction was a lost cause among these guys.

More questions came fast and furious.

"Remember that time you and Grayson discovered Dr. Clifford's secret dungeon?"

"Remember when your ex-pimp, Benny, tracked you down?"

"Are you going to be turned into a zombie?"

"Are you really trying to get hold of a secret potion that might help Grayson walk?"

Monica answered each question as best she could, but after fifteen minutes of verbal bombardment, she held up her hand. "Guys, I really hate to do this, but I'm on a supertight schedule, and I want to make sure I have enough time to pose for pictures with you and sign autographs. So, one final question."

"What do you like about my brother?" Jason Mitchell asked.

Monica flashed a charming smile and looked at Eric, who shot her a quick, almost imperceptible look of mild alarm. She reached out and took his hand, hoping he could read the message in her eyes: *Relax, buddy, I'm an actress. I can sing your praises in my sleep.*

"There are so many things about Eric, I'm not sure where to start," Monica murmured, staring into Eric's eyes as if she were Juliet and he her Romeo. "He's smart. He's funny. He's passionate about what he does."

Actually, she was beginning to discover that all those things were true. Mildly unnerved, she shifted her gaze to Jason, who looked unconvinced. Monica would have to ask Eric about him later.

She posed for photographs with each of the players, as well as a group photo with the whole team. The autograph signing went smoothly, though none of these guys wanted the standard, "To So-and-So, Love, Monica Geary," scribbled on the picture. No, she found herself writing things like, "To Thad, The Most Talented Player in the NHL"; or "To Tully, You're Truly Irresistible, Love, Monica Geary." To a man, they hung her picture up in their locker. It was very, very weird.

She said her good-byes, and Eric escorted her out into the hall.

"That was great," he raved.

Monica took a small bow. "Thank you. Though it was a little scary, them addressing me as my character."

"They were just a little nervous, that's all. And not all of them did it."

"True." Monica put a hand on his arm. "Look, that picture that was taken of me with the team? Could you get it to Theresa? I'm sure some publication would love to print it."

Eric looked baffled. "How will that help *you*?"

"You can never have enough publicity," said Monica. "Even bad publicity is better than none at all, and so far, that's not something we've had to worry about."

Eric shrugged. "Okay. I'll run it up to our in-house PR guy, Lou, too. Maybe we can put it in the program for the next game."

"That would be great."

After comfortably playacting with one another for over an hour, awkwardness suddenly descended. "So . . . what's next?" Eric asked.

"Why don't you visit the set next Monday, if you can? There's going to be some journalist from *Soap World* prowling around. Seeing us all lovey-dovey will definitely get me some ink."

"Why do you need ink?" Eric asked. "I mean, you're *Monica freakin' Geary.*"

Monica fought a blush. "And I've got a freakin' ingénue trying to unseat me."

"No one can unseat you," Eric declared. "Deep down, you have to know that."

Monica glanced away, uncomfortable with the naked praise. *He's saying that because he's a fan,* she thought. But other thoughts were trying to kick their way front and center: why should she care if Chesty began gaining in popularity, if Monica really thought that acting in daytime somehow didn't count?

She checked her watch. "Gotta run. I'll firm up the details about Monday and call you."

"Sounds good."

More awkwardness; was he deciding whether to give her a small kiss the way he did when they'd parted ways outside the restaurant? There was no one in the hall to perform for.

She made the decision for him. "See you Monday," she said, starting down the hall.

"Thanks again," he said softly, his voice trailing after her.

Just as she did the night after their dinner, she resisted turning around.

*   *   *

High fives and whistles awaited Eric when he returned to the locker room.

"You are totally my hero," said Tully Webster with a hearty slap on the back.

"And one fuckin' lucky bastard to boot," said Ulf.

"I know," Eric agreed, looking at the pictures of Monica tacked to each guy's locker. Man, she *was* gorgeous. Somehow, in the midst of their playacting, he sometimes forgot that. It was hard to believe she didn't have a *real* boyfriend in her life, or that someone as smart as her habitually hooked up with jerks, or so she claimed. For a split second when she'd come into the locker room and kissed him, he'd forgotten this whole relationship thing was a bunch of bull, because the kiss was so realistic. Well, she was good at what she did, right? He wondered if that was how she kissed Royce in all those love scenes between Roxie and Grayson. Had to be. It was part of their job. But did she enjoy it? The thought pricked him.

"Yo, dickhead."

Eric turned to find his brother standing behind him. "Yes, shit for brains?"

"I cannot believe Monica Geary has fallen so hard for you. The way she was looking at you . . ." Jason frowned. "I don't know if I can watch *W and F* anymore. Seriously."

"Why the hell not?"

"Because all I'll be able to think is, 'That poor, deluded woman has totally fallen for Eric's line of bull.' "

"No line of bull, my man. The sparks are there. You saw it yourself."

"Yeah, well, let's just see how long it takes them to fizzle out. With your track record—"

"This is different," Eric snapped. Jesus, Jason was a pain in the ass. Jealous, no doubt, now that he'd settled down to a life of Delilah, dogs, and the in-laws from hell.

"We'll see," said Jason. He and Eric picked up their gym bags, and they began walking out of the locker room together. "Nervous about tomorrow night?"

"Not at all."

Tomorrow was the season opener on home ice, Eric's first

as a Blade. He'd been going above and beyond in practice, winning the occasional curt nod of approval from Ty Gallagher, which was about as much validation as he could expect at this point. But tomorrow night would be different. Tomorrow night they'd all see he wasn't just a hero off the ice but on it as well.

SEVEN

Blow. Suck. Disappointment. Unfocused. Those were just a few of the words Eric was able to come up with to describe his virgin performance as a New York Blade. He wished he could put it down to bad luck, but the bottom line was his reaction time had been poor, his concentration worse. He'd choked when he should have been blowing everyone away.

Maybe it was the booing when he first stepped out onto the ice. He knew Guy Le Temp's skates were big ones to fill, and that he'd played for a hated rival, but Jesus Christ, it wasn't like he was some newbie fresh up from the minors. Too bad he played like one. By the time the game was over and the Blades had lost to Tampa Bay 4–1, he was surprised his teammates weren't booing him, too.

"Mitchell."

The stern timbre of Ty Gallagher's voice boomed through the depressed haze in the locker room, rendering it silent. Gallagher had already done a postmortem with the team right after the game, and hadn't, much to Eric's relief, singled him out. So much for that.

Eric stopped toweling his hair. "Coach?"

"My office in five."

"Gotcha."

He turned back to his locker, looking at the small gold cross hanging there that he wore during games for luck, just like his brother did. Maybe he should start wearing it all the time—not that it had done him any good on the ice.

He could feel some of his teammates' eyes on his back, could imagine their thoughts: *Can't believe we got rid of Guy for you. Not a good start, bucko.*

David Hewson walked up to him, and Eric tensed. "So you sucked," Hewsie said. "It's just the first game, and you were nervous. You'll get your legs."

"He fuckin' better," Ulf growled. "Maybe you should concentrate less on banging Monica, Mitcho, and more on your new *job.*"

"Stop calling me Mitcho, okay?" Eric snapped. "I fucking hate it."

Ulf sniggered. "Hear that, boys? Mitcho hates being called Mitcho."

"Why do you hate it, Mitcho?" Thad Meyers asked.

"Yeah, Mitcho?" Barry Fontaine chimed in. "What's wrong with Mitcho?"

Eric rolled his eyes. Assholes. He should have kept his mouth shut. For the rest of his time on the Blades, he'd have to endure being called Mitcho every three seconds.

He dressed, trying to concentrate on getting his head on straight before going to see Ty. He felt the same way he did when he was a kid being sent to the principal's office, a weird combo of vulnerability and defensiveness. Ignoring the jeers of "Good luck, Mitcho," he squared his shoulders and prepared to meet the one-man firing squad.

"What the fuck just happened out there?"

Eric blinked, blindsided by Ty's hitting him between the eyes before he'd even had a chance to close the door behind him. He wished there was a hint of concern in Ty's voice, but there wasn't. It was pure incredulity laced with anger.

Eric turned his palms up apologetically. "I don't know."

"You were tentative with the puck. You didn't even try to

skate into the zone. We traded Guy for you because we needed an *offensive* defenseman. That's what I need from you. That's what I've been telling you I need you to be at practice. That's what I've seen you *do* at practice. If all I wanted was somebody to dump it into the corners, I would have stuck with Guy." He shook his head. "You know the papers are going to tear you a new asshole tomorrow, right?"

Eric rubbed his forehead. "Yeah, I know." Truthfully, he hadn't even thought about that yet. His mind was still back at picturing himself on the ice, sucking.

Ty leaned against the front of his desk, eyes narrowed, arms folded across his chest. "I hear you're dating some actress?"

"Yeah."

Here it comes, thought Eric. The "live, eat, and breathe hockey" speech everyone in the league knew about. The "relationships come second" talk. Judging from what his brother had told him, he was surprised it had taken Ty this long.

"Anyone I know?"

"Monica Geary from *The Wild and the Free*."

"*Really.*" Ty looked impressed. "Haven't watched that show in ages. I think the last time I tuned in, Grayson Lamont's face had been burned off in a warehouse fire."

Eric brought him up-to-date. "Grayson's face was perfectly reconstructed by the top plastic surgeon in Garrett City, Dr. Jessica Schmidt, and he married her, but it didn't last."

"Huh," Ty grunted before his trademark glare returned. "Actresses are high maintenance, correct? Lots of parties. Public appearances."

"I guess," Eric mumbled. "We haven't been going out for that long."

"Keep a lid on the social side of things," Ty warned.

"I will."

"I mean it."

"*I will.*"

Ty pushed off his desk, walking toward Eric. "You need to live hockey. You have to eat it and breathe it. It has to be the only thing you think about. The only thing you *dream* about."

"I will, Coach," Eric promised.

The speech. Finally. In a weird way, it made Eric feel like he was really part of the team. Now he just needed to prove it—not only to everyone else, but to himself as well.

"You're late."

Monica practically pounced on Eric as he walked through the door of her dressing room, his name written neatly on the name tag the security guard had given him declaring him a "Guest." For the past fifteen minutes, she'd been stalked by Carolyn Shields, the *Soap World* writer whom Monica despised. Carolyn, on the set for the day to write what seemed to Monica to be her fiftieth "A Day in the Life of *W and F*" article, had oh so coyly been asking about Eric. Monica had oh so coyly responded that Eric was in fact going to be visiting her on the set today, and if Carolyn wanted, she could talk to them together and get a *Soap World* exclusive. All they were waiting for was Eric's arrival.

Eric smiled at her as she tugged him inside by the arm and closed the door. "Am I imagining things, or are you actually glad to see me?"

"Damn right I'm glad. That journalist I told you about is prowling around the set, just dying to talk to us. Let's go get it over with."

"Right." Eric looked amused. "Give me a moment to put on my adoring face." He turned away from her, putting his hands over his face and mumbling some kind of incantation. Then he whipped back to her, his "I worship you" expression firmly in place.

"Very funny," said Monica, though she was amused. "What's next? Changing into your Superman tights in a phone booth?"

"Do they still have phone booths in New York?"

"Good question. Now put your arm around my waist."

"Your wish is my command."

Eric put his arm around her waist, and Monica put her arm around his. She could feel the hardness of his flesh through the lightweight material of his tennis shirt and resisted the urge to run her hand up and down his side. "Let me do the talking," she said. "I've dealt with this woman before."

"Jesus, you're bossy." He paused. "Your waist is so tiny," he marveled.

"I don't eat," Monica confessed.

He seemed for the first time to notice that she was in a white lab coat. "What's up with the coat?"

Monica sighed. "Roxie is posing as a doctor. She's going to slip into the hospital and try to kill Grayson's father."

"Excellent! He deserves it, the lying bastard. The way he's had no sympathy since Grayson was paralyzed—"

"Eric." Monica felt a wave of pressure threatening to push her eyes from their sockets. "It's time to put Fan Boy away, okay? I need you to be Boyfriend Man."

"No prob." He opened Monica's dressing room door. "Shall we?"

"Eric Mitchell. *Enchante*."

Eric reached out to shake Carolyn Shields's plump hand, keeping his other hand firmly around Monica's tiny waist. He wasn't sure what he expected the journalist to look like, but this wasn't it: the woman's thinning hair was dyed raven black, her eyebrows painted on to look like teacup handles. She looked kinda, well, insane.

Monica was smiling at the woman as if they were old friends, though Eric was astute enough to pick up the subtle tension between them. The woman must have dissed Monica in print. The thought ticked him off.

"So here we are," Monica said gaily to Carolyn. "What would you like to know?"

"Well, obviously, everyone knows you two met when Eric here was doing his cameo—which by the way, was fantastic."

"Yeah? You think so?" The compliment pleased Eric, especially since his teammates had laughed so hard watching him he thought half of them might wet themselves. He'd gotten all the ribbing he'd expected from them and more. But it was worth it; the envy had outweighed the derision.

"Oh yes, you were wonderful," Carolyn was gushing, but she wasn't even looking at him as she spoke; instead, she was staring hard at Monica. "You're quite a *good actor*."

Eric felt Monica's arm tighten around his waist. For a moment, he feared Monica might dig her nails into *him*, since she couldn't rake them across the writer's puffy cheeks, even though she deserved it.

"Isn't he?" Monica agreed. "We were all pretty amazed."

"So, *lovebirds*, who approached whom first?"

"I approached her," Eric said, even though Monica had opened her mouth to speak. He wasn't a complete dolt; he could handle questions like these. "I've been a fan for a long time. I had to tell her."

"It was very sweet," Monica continued, glancing up at him with a happy smile. How did she get her eyes to dance that way? Eric wondered. It was starting to unnerve him a bit, how real this thing could appear sometimes.

"He was very shy at first, which was surprising, given his rep."

"Yes, the consummate ladies' man, I hear," said Carolyn, licking her lips hungrily as she looked him over before scribbling on her reporter's notepad. Eric felt a shudder pass through him. He didn't mind when hot babes dug him. But when forty-something women with crayola eyebrows gave him the once-over, it weirded him out.

Carolyn glanced back up at him. "Obviously, Monica is gorgeous. But what, beyond her physical attributes, attracted you to her?"

"She's smart and funny," said Eric, pausing to tenderly kiss Monica's cheek. "And she's very cultured. She's teaching me a lot."

Eric felt a nail dig into his side. Time to shut up.

"What about?" Carolyn purred.

"Theater," Monica interjected. "Art. Though mainly we just enjoy each other's company, you know? Talking. Laughing. We're still in the getting-to-know-each-other phase."

"Mmm." Scribble, scribble. Carolyn cocked a fake eyebrow. "Is Monica the woman who might tame you, Eric?"

"Could be," said Eric with a wink. Tame him? What did she think he was? A circus lion?

"Do you need any more?" Monica asked Carolyn sweetly. "I have to be on the set soon."

"One more," Carolyn said tartly. She turned to Eric. "You said you're a longtime fan of the show?"

"Yup."

"What do you think of the new character, Paige?"

"I think she can't act her way out of a paper bag," Eric said without hesitation. He glanced at Monica; she looked uncomfortable. "Everyone on the Blades agrees," he added, hoping it would back up his observation. "We all watch the show."

"Interesting." Carolyn looked at Monica. "That should do it—for now. Will you be available if I need to ask any further questions?"

"Of course," Monica said graciously. "Just call my personal publicist, Theresa Dante. I prefer working through her than the publicist for the show."

Carolyn nodded. "Would you two mind posing for a picture?"

"Our pleasure," said Monica.

"Roddy! Over here!" Carolyn boomed.

A nervous, clean-cut-looking young guy hustled to Carolyn's side. Monica obviously knew him; her face lit up when she saw him.

"Hi, Roddy," she said. "How are you?"

"Great," Roddy replied.

Monica turned to Eric. "Roddy's been with *Soap World* three years now. He takes great pictures."

"That's good to know." Eric held out his hand. "Eric Mitchell."

"Nice to meet you. You're a lucky man."

"Don't I know it."

At Roddy's command, Eric posed with Monica. He was starting to like posing with her. It was fun.

"When is this going to run?" Monica asked Carolyn.

"Next week, hopefully. We might want a longer feature at

some point in the future—*if* you two manage to go the distance."

Eric and Monica chuckled in unison, as if Carolyn's inference that their relationship might be a short-term thing was absurd. It did make Eric think back to their earlier conversation about who should eventually dump whom. He was of the mind now that it should be mutual. That way they'd both save face.

"Thanks for your time," Carolyn sniffed.

"Anytime," said Monica.

Eric and she watched her make her way up to the control booth, mild-mannered Roddy in tow.

"What a bitch," Eric murmured under his breath. He wasn't surprised when Monica looked pleased that he said that.

Back in her dressing room with Eric after the shooting of her scenes were postponed by the delay of Wallace Mendelson, the actor who played Grayson's father, Monica parsed the interview in her mind. The way Carolyn had commented on what a *"good actor"* Eric was—obviously she thought their whole relationship was bull. Perhaps she even suspected Monica of trying to counteract Carolyn's obvious championing of Chesty. Monica decided she'd wait and see how Carolyn's piece about her and Eric turned out. If it was snotty and full of insinuation that they weren't the real thing, more drastic action might need to be taken.

"How did I do?" Eric asked, settling down on the couch.

"Okay," Monica said flatly.

"Just okay?"

"What was that 'she's teaching me a lot' comment? It made me sound like Henry Higgins."

"Who?"

"Henry Higgins? *Pygmalion*?"

Eric shrugged. "Don't know it."

"You don't know *Pygmalion*?"

Eric looked annoyed. "Should I?"

Should he? Probably not. He was a jock, not a culture vulture. Though if Chim Chim had starred as Eliza Doolittle, it might be different. Even so, Monica again found herself admiring his lack of pretense. A lot of guys might have said, "Oh, yeah, right. *Pygmalion*, great play, Henry Higgins, ha-ha-ha." Not Eric. He seemed perfectly comfortable with who he was.

"I thought I did pretty well," Eric continued.

"Not to nitpick, but I also could have done without the comment you made about my costar's acting, too. Carolyn probably thinks it's a line I fed you."

"She can think what she wants," said Eric. "That new girl blows."

"I agree." Monica sighed. "Sorry if I seem pissy. I just find Carolyn really, really annoying."

"She doesn't seem to like you very much."

"I know, and I don't know why! I've never been anything but gracious to her!"

"Jealousy," Eric declared.

"That's very sweet of you."

A knock sounded at the door. Gloria, no doubt, come to feast her eyes on Eric. She'd been badgering Monica about him since the dinner at the Temple of Dendur. Had they made the "beast with two backs" yet? Was he wining her, dining her, letting her run her hands up and down his rippling six-pack abs? Monica told her it was a faux relationship, figuring that if anyone would understand, it was Gloria, who'd supposedly once staged her own kidnapping back in her glory days. Gloria didn't seem to care. As long as Monica was getting some "satisfaction" from the Adonis on skates, that was all that mattered.

"Come in," Monica called.

The door swung open. "Hiiiii."

Chesty, not Gloria. "Can I come in?" Chessy asked demurely.

Monica wondered what would happen if she said "No."

"Of course," said Monica.

Chessy floated inside like a fairy princess entering an enchanted garden. "Oh," she said breathlessly.

Oh yourself, you brain-dead twit, thought Monica. "Chessy, this is my boyfriend, Eric."

"That's why I'm he-ere," Chessy sang. "I wanted to meet my favorite hockey player *ever*."

Monica glanced around, looking for a garbage pail she could throw up into. Eric started to rise from the couch, but Chessy waved him back down. "Oh, don't get up," Chessy said. "There's no need."

Eric sat back down as Chessy came slinking over to him. From Cinderella to vamp in three seconds flat. Maybe she could act after all.

"I'm Chessy," she said breathily, leaning so far over him that her boobs were practically touching Eric's face.

"Uh . . ." Eric appeared too stunned to speak. When Chessy stood back up, Monica caught the gleam of lust in Eric's eyes. She was certain that if he parted his lips, he might drool on himself. Pissed, she turned to Chesty.

"Shouldn't you be on the set?" Monica asked sharply.

"In two," said Chessy. "But I wanted to make sure I met Eric in case he was leaving soon." She glanced back and forth between Monica and Eric. "We should all go out sometime. It would be fun."

Oh, yeah, thought Monica. *As enjoyable as an enema.* "Would you mind leaving Eric and me alone now?" she murmured, perching on the arm of the couch so she could run her fingers through Eric's hair. "We have some things we need to talk about, if you know what I mean."

Chessy flashed a terse smile. "Of course." Her eyes moved to Eric. "It was so great to meet you," she said in a low, kittenish voice. "I'm sure we'll cross paths again sometime."

"Sure," said Eric, sounding slightly dazed.

"Au revoir," said Chessy, blowing a kiss.

Monica forced a smile and waited for the door to close.

"Ow! What the hell are you pulling my hair for?!"

Eric looked upset as Monica released the hank of his hair she'd twisted around her knuckles. The second Monica estimated Chesty was out of hearing range, she'd given Eric's locks a good yank, since her hand was in his hair anyway.

"How stupid are you?" Monica hissed.

"What?" Eric asked confusedly.

"We're supposed to be a *couple*, remember? But there you were, ogling the silicone twins."

"I was not ogling. I was appreciating."

"You're my boyfriend! You shouldn't be appreciating anything but me!"

"But I'm not really your boyfriend!" Eric protested.

"But you're supposed to act like you are!"

"Well, even guys who are part of a couple sometimes *look*," Eric insisted.

"Not when they're with me," Monica said with a glare. She made a beeline for the bathrobe she kept hanging on the back of the door, digging out the one pack of cigarettes she kept stashed in one of the pockets. She knew it was bad, but she'd started smoking again—not a lot, just one or two a day to get her through. Eric looked horrified as she lit up.

"Don't say it, because I don't want to hear it," she warned him.

Eric was silent.

"If people are going to believe we're together, you can't stare at other women's boobs!"

"She shoved them in my face!"

"No kidding." Monica snorted. "I half expected her to offer to nurse you."

"That is totally gross." Eric coughed. "I can't breathe."

"Oh, for God's sake," said Monica, snuffing out her cigarette. "Better?"

"Much." Eric paused. He smiled slyly. "It really bothered you, didn't it?"

"What really bothered me?"

"My finding Chessy attractive."

"Don't be an *ass*."

"It's okay, you can admit it. In fact, it would be highly unusual if you hadn't developed a little crush on me by now." He leaned toward her. "Don't worry. I won't tell anyone."

Monica had never slugged anyone in her life, which is why, when she took aim at Eric, she wound up landing a blow to the side of his head and not his face, the way she intended. Eric recoiled, staring at her like she was nuts.

"*Jesus Christ!* What is wrong with you?! Do you beat up all your boyfriends this way?"

"Only the smug egomaniacs." Monica couldn't believe how irate she was. Beneath the lab coat, her chest was heaving. "Let's get something straight: I am not bothered in the least that you find that top-heavy little spider attractive. In fact, I find it a little sad. But it does bother me when you say or do something that plants even the smallest seed of doubt in someone's mind that what we have isn't real. So do me a favor: the next time Chesty or some other mewling little imbecile throws herself at you when you're with me, keep your eyes in your head, your tongue from hanging out of your mouth, and"—her eyes flicked to his crotch—"Little Eric in place. Got it?"

"Chesty?" Eric hooted. "You call her Chesty?"

"Shit," Monica muttered.

"I have to tell the guys that."

"You do, and you die."

"I'll pretend I made it up myself."

Remorse swept over her as Eric rubbed the side of his head. Maybe she was crazy. She put an apologetic hand on his shoulder. "I'm sorry I took a swing at you."

"It's okay. I kind of liked it." His smile was tentative. Was he flirting? She contemplated fishing the barely smoked cigarette out of the ashtray and lighting it up. Her mind was turning into one big maze of confusion.

Monica stood. "C'mon. I should probably get down to the set."

"Can I just stand on the sidelines and watch?"

"As long as you don't get in the way of the technicians, that should be okay. And if Carolyn corners you in between scenes with any questions about us, just tell her you're not comfortable talking about it any further, okay?"

"Gotcha." He rubbed the side of his head. "Not bad for a girl."

Monica smiled.

EIGHT

*ROXIE (ENTERING TUCKER LAMONT'S HOSPITAL
ROOM): Hello, Tucker. Enjoying your hospital stay?*

*TUCKER (HORRIFIED): Roxie! How did you get in
here? There are supposed to be guards outside the
room!*

*ROXIE: You'd be amazed at what a little cold, hard cash
can buy. (SHE APPROACHES THE BED AS TUCKER
FUMBLES FOR WHAT LOOKS LIKE A REMOTE
CONTROL.) Don't waste your time trying to ring for
the nurse. That connection was cut hours ago.*

*TUCKER (SHRINKING BACK AGAINST THE PIL-
LOWS): What do you want, Roxie?*

*ROXIE: For Grayson to walk again. But that's never go-
ing to happen as long as—"*

Wallace Mendelson, who'd been playing Tucker Lamont for
three decades, opened his eyes wide in surprise. A millisec-
ond later, he closed them as his head lolled to his left side.

"Cut!"

Jimmy the director came flying out of the control booth.
"Jesus H, Wallace! You do that *after* Monica gives you the

shot! You've still got five more lines! What the hell is wrong with you?" Wallace didn't move. Jimmy thrust his head forward. "Wallace?"

Alarmed, Monica gently patted Wallace's cheeks. No response. She jostled his arm. No response. She glanced up at her director uneasily. "Um . . ."

Jimmy clutched the sides of his head, squeezing his forehead so hard it began wrinkling like a shar-pei's. "Oh, no. Oh, Wallace. You bastard. Do not do this to me, man!" He looked around wildly. "Does anyone here know CPR?"

"I do," Eric volunteered, hustling toward the bed. "Call the paramedics. I'll start working on him."

"Call 911!" Jimmy yelled to no one in particular.

Monica stood frozen as Eric tore open the old actor's hospital gown, pried open his mouth, and began administering CPR.

"He's dead," Jimmy moaned to himself. "I know it. In the middle of a scene. I can't believe this. He's always been difficult to work with. Always. I can't—"

"Now isn't the time, Jimmy!" Monica yelled. "Go take some aspirin!"

A tense hush fell over the studio as Eric switched back and forth between puffing breath into Wallace's mouth and giving his chest thirty short pumps at a time with the heel of his hand. Watching him, Monica felt an odd surge of pride that she knew she wasn't entitled to. He wasn't her boyfriend, after all. But there was something about the fact that Eric didn't even hesitate to leap into action for someone he didn't even know that made her proud to know him.

Eric glanced up at Monica briefly, shaking his head no almost imperceptibly. Wallace was dead. Monica's eyes began welling up. Eric kept working on him until the paramedics arrived. Wallace was pronounced dead on the scene. He'd had a massive coronary.

Neither cast nor crew seemed to know what to do once Wallace's body was wheeled away. Some sobbed outright; others huddled in groups, talking in low voices laced with disbelief. Some actors trudged like sleepwalkers back to their dressing rooms.

Looking exhausted, Eric came to Monica's side. One by one, the cast and crew remaining on the studio floor came over to thank him, including the executive producer, who declared the show "dark" for the rest of the day. The only one still present who didn't come to thank Eric was Jimmy, who was holed up in the control booth, sobbing.

"That was really something," Monica murmured, touching Eric's cheek.

He glanced back at the empty hospital bed. "Poor bastard. At least he died doing what he loved."

"True. When did you learn CPR?"

"Years ago." Eric shrugged dismissively. "In the back of my mind, I've always toyed with the idea of being an EMT when my hockey career is over."

"That could be interesting."

"I guess. Hopefully, it's a long way off." Eric looked uncomfortable as he checked his watch. "Look, I'm going to take off. You going to be okay?"

Monica nodded. "I'll be fine. I'm going to stick around and help Jimmy pull it together."

"Okay." Eric stuck his hands in the front pockets of his jeans, hunching his shoulders. "Well, if you feel like you need to talk or anything, you know where to reach me."

"Thanks," said Monica, genuinely moved. "I'll be in touch about—you know. Something over the weekend, probably."

"Yeah." There were still lots of cast and crew milling around. "I guess I better make our good-bye look realistic," Eric murmured.

Taking his hands from his pockets, he gently cupped the back of Monica's neck with one hand, pulling her to him. Monica's heartbeat, which had just returned to normal after the adrenaline rush prompted by Wallace's sudden death, surged again as Eric pressed his lips to hers. If he was acting now, he was doing a damn good job of it. There was real feeling there as his mouth generated heat against hers, until finally he gently parted her lips with his tongue. Was anyone watching? Monica didn't care. In this moment, the rest of the world had burned away, and it was just her and this heroic man who'd tried to save another's life, a man who didn't pretend to be an intellectual when he wasn't, a man who used his strong, muscled body to make his living. Monica gave herself over to the heated blue spark of their kiss, the thrill of it something she hadn't experienced in a long, long time. When Eric slowly took his mouth from hers, Monica's dramatic instincts immediately kicked in; she did not want him to see her disappointment, and so she hid it.

"What do you think?" Eric asked, gently breaking their embrace.

Monica nodded approvingly. "Very convincing."

"Think your coworkers believe we're the real deal?"

"How could they not?" Monica was glad she was still wearing the lab coat. It covered her still-rioting heart, which felt as though it might thump its way right out of her chest. She glanced up at the control booth. "I really should go see how Jimmy's doing."

"Right." Eric's hands went back into his front pockets. "Well . . . see you."

"See you."

He gave her a small peck on the mouth and was off. Monica watched him go—her pretend boyfriend who, for a few seconds, had felt like a real one. Rattled, Monica went up to see her friend.

Jimmy sat with his elbows resting on the control panel, his face in his hands. He didn't move when Monica quietly came through the door.

"Jimmy," Monica said gently as she sat down next to him. "Talk to me."

Jimmy slowly lifted his head, his brown eyes reduced to swollen red slits. "I've worked with Wallace for thirty years, Monica. Can you believe that? *Thirty years.*"

"I know." Monica gave his shoulder a consoling squeeze. "I'm sorry I snapped at you down on the floor. It's just that you weren't helping things."

"I know." Jimmy wiped at his eyes with the back of his hand. "But I can't believe he fuckin' died in the middle of a scene, Monica. I mean, really."

Monica winced. "I'm sure the writers can work around it."

"I'm sure they can't. This is a major story line we're talking about here."

Monica paused. *She* might not know what lay far up the road for her character, but Jimmy did. Would it be crass to ask him in a moment of grief how much he knew about Roxie's future? Oh, God, the temptation. But she couldn't.

"We're back on our regular shooting schedule tomorrow," Jimmy lamented. "What are we going to do? Put a dummy in the hospital bed?"

"No." An idea whispered itself in Monica's ear. "I know someone we can get on really short notice to do the scene tomorrow," she said carefully.

"Who?"

"Monty Kingman."

"What?" Jimmy's expression went from despair to disbelieving. "That old theater queen? Are you nuts?"

"Monty is not a queen," Monica countered angrily. "He's a metrosexual. One of the first." Her expression turned pleading. "You know he's got the chops, Jimmy. And he needs the money."

"How do you know he needs the money?"

"He's a friend of mine," Monica said softly. "He was my acting teacher. He taught me everything I know."

Jimmy narrowed his eyes. "And you know for a fact he can be here first thing tomorrow for us to reshoot this scene? Know his lines?"

"He can learn them in two minutes. Believe me."

Jimmy sighed as he hoisted himself out of his chair. "Let me talk to Michael. You get your metrosexual friend prepped and bring him in here at six a.m. sharp tomorrow."

"Thanks so much, Jimmy."

"Speaking of thanks, thank your boyfriend for doing the kiss of life on Wallace. That was . . ." Jimmy shook his head, choking up again. "Just thank him."

"I will."

Monica gave Jimmy a big bear hug, then headed to her dressing room to collect her things before she left for the day.

She knew Monty might balk at first about appearing on a *soap* (she could hear his disgusted voice in her head), but in the end, he would thank her. Maybe he'd start getting small parts here and there. At the very least, maybe it would change his mind about the medium, make him see that what she did was legitimate, not garbage. She was saddened by Wallace's sudden demise, but hopefully, some good might come out of it that could help her mentor.

"You tried to resuscitate Tucker Lamont? *You?*"

Eric stared at his brother, annoyed with his incredulity. Jason knew Eric knew CPR. What was so shocking about him using it on someone who needed it?

They were hanging out at Jason's, sharing a couple of Heinekens and intermittently watching *American Idol*. Delilah had gone to visit her parents out on Long Island. Jason had begged off; he could only take his in-laws in short doses, since their primary mode of communication was yelling. Having met Delilah's parents on countless occasions, Eric didn't blame his brother for not going.

Jason took a swig of beer. "Well, the character was going to die anyway, right?"

"Yeah. But still . . ."

"How did Monica take it?"

"She was pretty shaken up."

Jason smirked. "Then what are you doing here?"

Good question. Eric had felt a small twinge of guilt leaving Monica at the studio. She claimed she was okay, but that might have been her putting on a brave face. The right thing to do would have been to see her home. The way a real boyfriend would, which was what he was supposed to be.

"She and a few of her costars wanted to go out on their own," Eric lied quickly.

Jason looked at him dubiously but had no further comment, so Eric assumed he believed his explanation. Jason leaned over to pet the head of his Newfie, Stanley, who always lay faithfully at his feet. "What did Gallagher say to you last night after the game?"

Eric shifted his gaze to the TV. "You know what he said. Play offensive. Do what we hired you to do. And then he gave me his famous 'live, eat, and breath hockey' speech."

"Why didn't you?"

"Why didn't I what?"

"Play aggressively."

Eric turned back to him. "I fucked up," he snarled. "Obviously."

"I thought you never fucked up," Jason taunted.

"You're enjoying this, aren't you?"

"Hell, yeah," Jason chortled. "Same way you enjoy the rare times I mess up." Jason stopped stroking Stanley's massive black head. "I spoke with Dad yesterday."

Eric stiffened resentfully. Goddamn, why did their parents always call Jason? It hadn't always been that way. Maybe because Jason was married now, so they saw him as the responsible one? Or perhaps they didn't want to shell out for two long-distance phone calls now that money was tight? Eric knew he hadn't always been consistent when it came to contacting his folks in the past, but he'd really been making an effort lately. It would be nice if once in a while, they called *him* first. He was the older sibling, after all, even if it was by only three minutes.

Eric took a sip of beer. "What did Dad have to say?"

"He wanted to know if we could come out for a visit soon. Mom's really depressed. She's been baking her head off."

"Uh-oh."

Whenever their mother was stressed, she turned into a bake-o-maniac. Pies, cakes, cookies . . . it was awesome, at least if you were the recipient.

Jason looked troubled. "I think they just need to see us in person and talk. He kept mentioning 'the loan' we're giving them."

Eric frowned. "I thought we made it clear that it's not a loan."

"You know Dad and his pride." Jason looked solemn. "Anyway, we do have a break next weekend, so I think we should go."

"Absolutely. Is Delilah coming?"

"Of course. The dogs, too."

Eric nodded. Maybe it was silly, but he loved seeing his sister-in-law on his parents' farm. She'd grown up in the burbs, and she was such an animal lover you'd think she was born to milk cows and muck out barns. The last time she and Jace were there, they brought all four of their dogs with them. The canines were in heaven with all that land to run around on. Eric was actually envious of his brother's contentment and of the life he'd carved out for himself.

His mind jumped to Monica and to the kiss he'd planted on her at the studio. He started out doing it just for show. Really. But then there was some connection, and— Oh, man, he didn't want to think about it. He took a slug of beer. He was pretty sure, now that Monica was slowly beginning to see that he wasn't a total jackass, that he could probably get her into bed for a one-nighter if the circumstances were right. But part of him didn't want to, which freaked him out. He really needed to get a grip.

Maybe it was the twin thing, but Jason seemed to be clued in to the fact he was thinking about Monica.

"The guys were really impressed with Monica," said Jason, sounding almost disappointed.

"Of course they were. She's great."

Jason frowned. "Which is why I'm still trying to figure out why she's with you."

"Yo, what is this, abuse Eric night?"

"C'mon, Eric. You have to admit she's not your usual MO. It just seems weird to see you with someone who can actually string a sentence together."

"Very funny. There's chemistry between us, Bro. You saw it with your own eyes." Faux chemistry, maybe, but chemistry nonetheless.

"Why don't you bring Monica to Mom and Dad's next weekend?"

"What?"

Jason's taunting tone returned. "Don't you want Mom and Dad to meet your girlfriend?"

"It's not a serious relationship yet, Jace," Eric countered.

"You know Mom. I bring Monica home, and the wedding banns are in the *Bismarck Tribune* the following week."

"She's gotten better about that stuff."

Eric grinned. "You mean she's stopped knitting booties for you and Delilah?"

Jason sighed. "She knits sweaters for the dogs now. How bizarre is that?"

"Good old Mom."

Jason took another drink of beer. "So can I tell Mom and Dad we'll be there? Maybe we'll catch a flight Friday night?"

"Definitely."

They went back to watching TV. Monica at the farm—talk about hell. They'd be thrown together for an entire weekend, having to pretend to be a couple for his *parents*. Jason would be on them constantly, watching, listening, looking for any little discrepancy that might reveal that Monica wasn't as into Eric as she appeared to be. Knowing Jason, he'd probably try to talk Monica out of dating Eric, the SOB. He and Monica at the farm. Never in a million years, Bro. Never in a million years.

NINE

"Monica, darling, light of my life. Could you come up here a moment?"

Monica responded to Jimmy's request with a queasy smile. Squaring her shoulders, she made her way up to the control booth to face Jimmy and Michael, the executive producer. They were about to tear her a new one for suggesting Monty to replace Wallace; she knew it. Right now, the shooting schedule was at least an hour behind, and it was all Monty's fault.

As Monica had expected, Monty had flared his nostrils at her and hurled choice words of disdain when she suggested he fill in for Wallace. But the mention of money as well as the possibility that some work might come of it turned him around, as did half a bottle of brandy. He learned his few lines in no time flat. It was executing them in front of the camera that was turning out to be the problem.

Monica entered the booth, striking preemptively. "I know what you're going to say."

"No, you don't," said Michael with a glare. He looked down at the set, where Monty was now sitting up in the hospital bed, smoking a cigar in between takes.

"He's awful," said Jimmy. "What's with the booming voice?"

"He's used to acting in the theater," Monica tried to explain. "He's *projecting*."

"He thinks he's doing King fuckin' Lear," said Michael.

"He's a classically trained actor."

"I don't give a rat's ass if he's a trained gymnast," said Jimmy. "I need him to stop pretending he's Peter O'Toole and just looked terrified and die. Do you think you can get him to do that? Because he sure as hell isn't listening to me."

"I think so," Monica said nervously.

"Go do it, then," said Michael.

"Now," Jimmy added. Monica turned to go.

"You owe us big-time for this," Jimmy called after her as she was leaving.

"I was just trying to help," Monica replied tearfully. *Help you, help my friend, and maybe even help myself.* Their criticism of Monty shook her. Yes, he was a little over the top, but he wasn't *that* bad. The embarrassing part, for her, was his unwillingness to take direction. As if he knew better, even though he'd never worked in daytime before. What had she been *thinking*? This was one of the stupidest ideas she'd ever had. As it was, everyone was still upset and stressed over Wallace's death, and now she'd made things worse by bringing Monty in, even if it was just for the day. She intended to apologize profusely to Jimmy and Michael at the end of the day. For now, she had to deal with Monty.

"They must be *insane*," was Monty's melodramatic response when Monica told him he need not project quite so much.

"TV is different than the stage, Monty," Monica explained as nicely as she could. "Your voice and your gestures don't have to be quite as big."

"That's rubbish."

"Just do what the director asks, okay?" Monica pleaded.

Monty leveled her with a frosty look. "They've brainwashed you. I taught you to question. To explore. The text beneath the text, remember, Monica?"

"There is no text beneath the text in this scene. You just need to die."

"But what's my motivation?"

"Oh, God." Monica could not believe she was having this conversation. "Your motivation is to advance the plot, okay?"

Monty looked disgusted. "Cheap melodrama. I cannot believe I agreed to this."

"It's work, Monty," Monica shot back angrily. She found herself trembling. Rarely did she challenge her old teacher this way. It felt scary. "Do you know how many unemployed actors would kill to lie in this bed and die? You should be grateful."

Monty got back under the covers with a sneer. "For debasing myself? Never. I'd rather starve than compromise my integrity as an artist."

Like me? Monica wondered. Was that what he was leaving unspoken? A lump formed in her throat. Monty's words sent her into a tailspin. She wasn't an artist. She was a hack. She had no integrity. If she did, she would have held out for meaningful roles, no matter how scarce. She would not have taken this job ten years ago.

Get out of your own head, she told herself. *Focus on the task at hand.*

"Just do the scene," Monica coaxed. "As a favor to me. Die quietly, and I'll never ask you to do anything again, all right?"

"As you wish."

Monica looked up at the booth. "He's ready to go."

"You and Eric are getting great ink."

Monica was reassured by Theresa's smile as she pushed a copy of that week's *Celebrity* magazine across the desk, pointing out the "New Romance" pages. There were two pictures of Monica and Eric: one of them on the steps of the museum, the other of them outside of Dijon. The caption read, "Considered one of Manhattan's hottest bachelors, NHL star Eric Mitchell has been seen out and about in New York with

W and F's favorite leading lady, Monica Geary. Will he be a bachelor for long?"

Monica smiled, pleased, pushing the magazine back. "That's great." She had to admit, she and Eric looked so good together it was scary. She was pretty sure she'd never "gone out" with anyone so attractive.

"Lou Capesi called me," Theresa continued. "He's going to be able to get the picture of you with the Blades into the Blades program for home games for the rest of the season. It would be wonderful if you could go with Eric to some charity functions."

"That seems doable," Monica said unenthusiastically.

Theresa raised a quizzical eyebrow but continued, "I love that you and Eric are generating copy. But I'm not sure how much of an impact that's going to have on your standing on the show. We need to do some things that reach your fans specifically. I hate to ride you on this, but when was the last time you met with the New York chapter of your fan club?"

Monica looked down at her hands. "Last year," she admitted.

"Not good."

"I know."

"You need to get in touch with the fan club president and arrange to do a lunch with them. You need to do some signings with your costars. You haven't done any of those in a while, either. I checked."

Monica turned pink. "I don't know why I let it slide."

"Content to rest on your laurels, maybe?" Theresa suggested.

Monica fought the urge to slink out of the office in shame. She'd been leading lady on *W and F* for close to a decade now. She'd paid her dues and had gotten to the point where she assumed things would keep rolling along. But now, sitting here today, hearing Theresa bluntly call her out, her presumption embarrassed her. It was the fans who had helped make her the star she was today, and she'd taken them for granted.

"I hate admitting it, but you're right," said Monica. "I *have* been coasting."

"Easily remedied," Theresa assured her. "Do the fan club thing, do more signings, and let the soap press know you're available to talk about anything and everything. I'll also call in-house PR at the show and speak with them." Theresa hesitated. "I have noticed that new actress is getting a lot of coverage in the daytime press."

"I've been trying not to think about it."

"Wrong move. Read every word that's written about her. Then we can strategize about how to position you in comparison."

Monica bit at the tip of her thumb. "Is it wrong for me to want to make sure she doesn't eclipse me?"

Theresa looked at her as though she were crazy. "This is your livelihood we're talking here, Monica. Being the hot new thing sometimes trumps talent. You have to start working it, girl."

Monica wondered what Monty would say about all this. They hadn't spoken since he finished his deathbed scene. Monica was still too upset to call or check in on him. One minute she'd think, *You ungrateful old bastard.* The next, her insecurity would creep to the fore. What if he was right? What if she was completely without integrity? Especially now, when it felt like her primary concern in life was making sure Chesty didn't become more of a fan favorite than she was. At least she had the comfort of knowing that deep down, lots of actors were insecure.

"I'll begin working it," Monica promised Theresa.

Theresa looked pleased. "Good. One more thing: You should probably go to a hockey game. Be supportive of your man."

Monica frowned. "Right. Eric mentioned that, actually."

"How's it going with Eric?" Theresa murmured, ignoring her ringing phone.

Monica sounded noncommittal. "All right."

"Is he as horrible as you thought he'd be?"

"No," Monica muttered reluctantly.

Theresa looked at her with interest. "You holding out on me?"

"What?" Monica felt confused. "What would I be holding out on?"

"That maybe the you two are enjoying each other's company for real?"

"He's as good an actor as I am, Theresa. Period. The fact that I can tolerate him—in short bursts—doesn't mean we're on the road to real romance."

Theresa shrugged her shoulders. "You're seeing him this weekend, I hope? Out and about in public?"

"Of course."

"Any place where I should steer the press?"

"I'll let you know."

Eric had invited her to his place to talk after she was done with Theresa. She had been racking her brain, trying to think of things they could do this weekend. She didn't want to go to dinner again. Maybe a play? A trip to a museum? She nixed that idea fast; paparazzi wouldn't come to a museum. Maybe they'd just take a walk in Central Park. She'd talk to Eric and see what Mr. "I live for the cameras when I'm off the ice" had to say.

A thought suddenly gripped her. "How much longer do you think the paparazzi will even continue to care?" she asked Theresa.

"As long as you're out there working it," Theresa replied. "And if Eric's getting a lot of press as a Blade, winning over the New York fans, that will help a lot, too."

Monica rose. "Whatever you say."

"Trust me," said Theresa.

"I do," Monica said simply.

She had to.

"So this is it," said Eric. "Chateau Mitchell. At least one of them. My brother lives up the street. So his place is Chateau Mitchell, too."

Eric seemed slightly nervous as he ushered Monica into his apartment. She wasn't sure what she'd been expecting. A pair of bronzed skates on a coffee table? Back issues of *Sports*

Illustrated stacked in a corner? Mirrored walls so Eric could adore himself? Her assumptions made her realize what a snob she could be. Just because he was a jock didn't mean his place would be decorated badly.

In truth, his apartment had a touch of the interior designer about it. Sisal rugs, modern art on the walls, nice leather furniture. Monica turned to him. "Who was your designer?"

Eric seemed surprised by the question. "What? Me."

"Oh, c'mon. No straight man could pull a place like this together."

"On behalf of all straight men everywhere, I'm insulted." He gestured toward the couch, and she sat down.

"Seriously," Monica said, running her hand over the buttery leather arm of the couch. "Who did your place?"

Eric sighed. "Some woman named Thea McNamara. She almost bankrupted me. But I didn't have the time or inclination to do it myself."

Monica nodded approvingly. "She did a good job."

Eric sat down beside her. "How are you?" he asked quietly, rubbing her shoulder. "Coping okay?"

It took Monica a moment to realize he was referring to her costar's death. She was suffering brain freeze, the direct result of his hand being in contact with her body.

"I'm fine," she said crisply, removing his hand. "There's no one here watching us," she pointed out to him when he looked surprised. "You don't have to put on a show."

Eric reared back in surprise. "I was just trying to be *nice*."

"And I appreciate that," Monica replied, maintaining her brisk tone. She'd decided it would be all acting from now on. No more being impressed by his knowing CPR and the concern he just showed for her. No more losing herself in kisses designed to deceive those around them. "Let's talk business."

"Fine." His voice was now as brisk as hers.

"I saw Theresa Dante before I came here." Monica frowned. "Why *did* I come here? Why did you want to meet here?"

Eric rolled his eyes. "You sound like Roxie."

"What the hell does that mean?"

"Suspicious and melodramatic."

Ouch. Who was being slapped down now? Monica felt a

sense of creeping apprehension. What if Eric was sick of their charade? If he ended it now, she'd wind up looking like one of the blonde scalps on his belt.

"I didn't mean to sound that way," she said hastily. "It just seemed unusual."

"We *are* supposed to be going out. What's so unusual about you coming over to my place? I've seen your place. I just thought a little reciprocation was in order. That's all. No big evil agenda." Eric folded his arms across his chest, the classic defensive posture. "You were saying about Theresa?"

"She said we were doing well. I need to do some more soap things to keep my profile high with my fans. As for us, she suggested I go to one of your games. She said as long as you're getting a lot of press as a Blade, that'll help us, too." Eric grimaced with pain. "What's wrong?"

"Oh, yeah, I'm getting press all right," he muttered. "I'm sucking out on the ice. Completely sucking. I don't know what the hell is going on. I've played two games so far and have played like shit in both of them. This is not the way to kick off being the new guy in town, okay? Especially not in this town."

Monica hesitated a moment, then put her hand on his shoulder. "It'll get better. From what I've heard and read, you're really talented."

"Yesterday doesn't matter," Eric countered harshly, as if her compliment didn't matter. *He's hard on himself,* Monica thought. The way she was. Monica removed her hand. "I'll come to your next game," she suggested, hoping to cheer him up. "Maybe I'll be your good luck charm."

"Yeah, maybe," Eric said listlessly. "Shit, I haven't offered you anything to drink."

"I'm fine. Really."

Eric shrugged. "Whatever you say."

"So, this weekend," Monica said brightly, trying to pull him out of the nosedive she could see him going into. "I was thinking we could—"

"I'm not going to be around this weekend. I'll be in North Dakota."

"Game?"

"Visiting my parents. On their farm."

"I'll come with you," Monica offered immediately, maybe too immediately. Eric was staring at her as if she'd just revealed she kicked little old ladies for fun. "Think about it," she continued as the idea began taking firm root inside her. "Theresa tells the press, and they start to speculate that things are getting serious. Isn't there a mall in Bismarck or something? We could do an appearance."

Eric looked perturbed. "I don't think this is a good idea."

"Why not?"

"Because we'd have to act all weekend, day and night. In front of my family."

"So?"

"I don't know if I can do it," said Eric. "Also, my mom will go totally mental if I bring you home. Not only is she a huge fan, but I've never—" He abruptly stopped.

"Never what?"

"Brought anyone home to meet my folks."

Monica stared at him incredulously. "Ever? In your life?"

"Does high school count?"

"No."

"Then no, I never have."

"Why?"

"Because my mother would go mental, like I said."

And because you've never really had a serious relationship in your life, Monica thought to herself, though she had no proof of that.

"Have *you* ever brought anyone home?" Eric challenged.

"Twice. Once in college. I was going out with a guy who was a mime." She glared. "Laugh, and I'll punch your lights out."

"Won't. I promise." He looked on the verge of howling.

"Anyway," Monica continued, "you can imagine how that went over with my blue-blood clan. My brother asked him to mime being penniless and standing in the unemployment line." Eric started to laugh, but Monica shot him a sharp sideways glance, and he halted mid-guffaw. "The second guy was an actor."

"Lance Ormond," Eric supplied.

"How did you know that?" Monica asked uneasily.

"I'm a fan, remember? I know lots of things."

"Riiight." Monica didn't want to think about it. "One of my disastrous showmances. Anyway, I brought him home to a big family party. Two hours later, I found him necking with my cousin in the pantry. That was the end of Lance."

Eric whistled. "That must have been tough."

"It is what it is," Monica declared stoically. The memory still smarted, which pissed her off. It was years ago. Maybe there were some humiliations you never got over, like when a boyfriend not fit to lick your boots cheats on you, confirming every feeling of insecurity you've ever had about yourself.

Eric's expression turned suave. "What do you think your folks would think of me?"

"I think they'd be thrilled I brought home someone with testosterone."

"God knows I've got enough of that," Eric murmured in a low, sultry voice.

"News flash: Jerk Eric is making an appearance. Not liking it."

"Wow. You're really critical today." He absently scratched his forearm. "Forget coming with me to the farm. My parents would drive us insane, and there's no way I could be 'pretend boyfriend Eric' for forty-eight hours, especially with my asshole brother watching our every move. He totally suspects this whole thing is bullshit. At the very least, he finds it very hard to believe that *you* could ever be into *me*."

"I've been nominated for three Daytime Drama Awards. I can make him believe it."

"Yeah, well, I don't have any acting awards, so I don't know if I can keep it up for that long."

Suddenly realizing what he'd said, their eyes met. And they both laughed.

"That wasn't intentional," Eric explained.

"I know," Monica admitted, smiling.

Monica was surprised: She was eager to go to North Dakota with him. It would be an adventure. She was always game for new experiences, and spending time at a farm was something she'd never done. It might even help with her acting somewhere along the line; it would give her memories and feelings to draw on.

"We can pull this off, Eric."

"I worry it's a crummy thing to do to my folks."

He has a conscience, thought Monica, pleasantly surprised. *Doesn't matter, doesn't matter, doesn't matter . . .*

"You don't have to tell them what's up. You can just tell them we split up later on."

Eric contemplated this. "That's true." He sighed. "Okay. I guess you can come. But I don't think a signing at the mall is a good idea. Let's just keep it a family deal, all right?"

"Fine. What should I bring to wear?" Monica asked brightly.

"You got any overalls? Maybe you and I could pose for a picture outside my folks' house with me holding a pitchfork."

"Excuse me, it's a legitimate question," Monica huffed.

"Bring jeans. Sweaters. Some shoes or boots you don't mind getting mud on. Oh, and bring your appetite. My mom is going to try to stuff you with food, and she'll be insulted if you don't eat. So none of this poking-at-your-salad actress stuff."

Monica hid her distress. *Food?* "I'm not going to find anything on my plate that was in your parents' barn mooing the week before, am I?"

"Relax. It's a dairy farm." Eric grinned. "I can show you how to milk a cow if you'd like."

"I don't think so," Monica said primly. She rose. "I'll call Theresa and let her know we're going to North Dakota. Maybe she can alert the local papers there, and someone can take our picture at the airport."

"Sounds good." Eric stood slowly, stretching his arms high above his head. His tennis shirt lifted slightly, revealing a straight, dark line of hair running down from his belly button, disappearing into his jeans. Monica looked away, chastising herself for the small dart of heat that shot through her body. *Jesus, you'd think you'd never seen a man's torso before. This is your business partner,* she reminded herself sternly.

*Relationship of convenience. All professional. No lust for the
biggest womanizer on earth allowed.*

"Call me when you have the flight plans worked out," she
said, heading toward the door. She paused. "And thanks for
asking how I was doing after my costar's death."

Eric raised his clasped hands high, miming being a cham-
pion.

"You're a jerk, you know that?" Monica hissed.

Eric just laughed.

TEN

"OhmyGodohmyGodohmyGod."

Eric pressed his lips together hard in an effort to cover his mortification over his mother's first words to Monica. His mom was hopping from foot to foot, while his father stared at them bemusedly from behind his mother. Eric was glad Jason wasn't here to witness it. He and Delilah had loosed their dogs the minute they arrived and were walking around the yard with them.

"Mom, calm down, okay?" Eric asked patiently.

"I'm trying," his mother insisted, fluttering a hand in front of her chest. "It's just—I've been a fan for so long."

"Mom."

"It's okay," Monica assured Eric, extending a soft, slim-fingered hand to Eric's mother. "It's nice to meet you, Mrs. Mitchell."

"Oh, it's so nice to meet you, too," Eric's mother returned breathlessly. "And you can call me Jane. And this is Dick behind me." Eric's father nodded in greeting. "Oh, I haven't even said hello to you yet!" she said to Eric, throwing her arms around him and smothering him with kisses.

"Mom!" Eric was glad to see his mother, too, but Jesus.

This was totally over the top. His mother had practically fainted on the telephone when he'd told her who he was bringing with him.

His mother broke their embrace. "Can I kiss you, too?" she asked Monica shyly, opening her arms. "Just a little one?"

"Of course," said Monica.

Eric rubbed his forehead, wishing he had a tranquilizer gun. If this was the way it was going to be for the whole weekend, he'd never make it. Hopefully, his mother would calm down soon and start acting *normal*. He hadn't seen her this crazed since Tom Jones played Bismarck when he and Jason were in eleventh grade.

Eric's eyes caught his father's while his mother gathered Monica in a rib-crushing embrace. They stared at each other, each knowing what was going through the other's mind about the farm, each knowing that this wasn't the place to discuss it. They'd talk about it later with Jason.

His mother released Monica, who still seemed able to breathe, much to Eric's surprise. "Oh my," Eric's mother said in a chiding voice to Monica. "Honey, you are just skin and bones. We've got to fatten you up."

Monica laughed pleasantly, a great acting job if Eric ever saw one. He'd love to know what was going through Monica's mind right now. Probably something along the lines of: *Who is this insane farmer's wife?* Well, she'd been warned.

"Let's go upstairs," Eric's mother said giddily. "I've got your room all made up for you kids. Dick, grab their bags."

"I can do it, Dad." Eric picked up his and Monica's bags, following his mother, father, and Monica up the stairs. They had no sooner started their ascent than Monica whipped her head around to look at him. *"Our room?"* she hissed, eyes popping with distress.

"I told you before we left New York," Eric murmured under his breath. "There are twin beds."

Upstairs now, he peeked into his mother's old sewing room, where there was now a double bed and a dresser. Jason and Delilah's room. As he told Monica, this meant they would be in his and Jason's old bedroom in the single beds. His mother would give her speech about how what they do back in New York was their business, but until they were married, they wouldn't be sharing a bed under *her* roof.

"Here we are," he heard his mother trill. Eric hauled his and Monica's bags into his old bedroom, freezing as he walked over the threshold. Gone were the old single beds with the scratched pine headboards; in their place was a double bed.

"Now I know you two aren't married," his mother said, twisting her hands nervously, "but your father and I discussed it, and we decided it was time we joined the twenty-first century. So here's your room. It's the one closest to the bathroom," she added significantly. The better for Monica to throw up her meals in, Eric thought. He couldn't look at Monica.

"You two get settled, and then come down to the kitchen, and we'll have some coffee and cherry pie," Eric mother's instructed, beaming at him. "I made it just for you, sweetie." She winked confidentially at Monica. "It's been his favorite ever since he was a little boy." Monica nodded, a queasy smile on her face.

"Thanks, Mom," Eric said hollowly. He held his breath as his parents departed. Then he turned to face the music.

"Tell me you didn't know about this," Monica said, glaring at him.

"I didn't! Last time I was here, there were twin beds."

"I don't believe this." Monica moved to the window at the front of the room, pulling back the white eyelet curtains to look down at the yard below. Eric could hear Jason and Delilah's dogs barking happily as they played.

"I'm sorry about my mother frothing all over you."

"It's okay. It was kind of cute, actually." Monica turned back to him. "You're sleeping on the floor."

"The hell I am! I'm a professional athlete, Monica! I can't afford to mess with my back!"

Monica put a hand on her hip, indignant. "Oh, so you expect me to sleep on the floor?! How gentlemanly!"

Eric sat down on the edge of the bed, wearily running his

hands over his face. They'd been here five minutes, and already it was a disaster. No way was he going to be able to keep up this charade for a whole weekend. No way.

He uncovered his face. "Neither of us has to sleep on the floor," he reasoned. "We can erect a barrier. Put a line of pillows between us."

Monica stared at the bed. "I suppose," she muttered. She narrowed her eyes. "If you breach the barrier and touch me, you're dead."

Eric snorted. "Same to you!"

"Oh, right," Monica said scornfully. "As if *that* would ever happen."

Eric chuckled, joining her at the window. "Judging by your reaction to that kiss I gave you at the studio, I think it could."

He watched Monica's cheeks turn pink before her whole face flared into a deep red.

"I was *acting*," she barked at him.

Eric smirked. "Is that how you 'act' when your costar Royce kisses you?"

"What do you care?" Monica shot back.

"I don't." Eric glanced down into the yard. Delilah and Jason were ushering the dog pack into the house. He and Monica would have to wrap up this little debate quickly, unless his mother lured Jace and Delilah into the kitchen right away. Eric looked at Monica smugly. "I was merely pointing out that if *that* was acting, then I'd love to see your reaction when you're really feeling something for a guy."

"Well, you'll never know, will you?"

Eric's hand shot out, impulsively grabbing Monica's wrist. The molecules in the room were changing shape, moving faster and faster, threatening to break down into a million tiny sparks as heat rushed to the place where their skin touched. Eric stared into Monica's eyes, waiting for her to jerk her hand away. But she didn't. Instead, her gaze was locked on his, watching and waiting. "You felt something. Admit it."

Monica put her face right up to his. *"No."*

Eric tightened his grip around her wrist as his pulse began scrambling. *"Admit it."*

"You admit it first," she jeered. "Admit you're the one who deepened the kiss, and it wasn't because you wanted it to look real. You *wanted* to kiss me."

Eric laughed. "Of course I did," he replied, as if it were obvious. "I came on to you the first time I met you, remember? Why would you think I still wouldn't find you hot, annoying as you are?"

Monica jerked her hand from his grasp. "So the kiss was purely physical. It meant nothing to you beyond that."

"Uh, no."

"Then why are you so hot for me to admit that I felt something?" Monica challenged.

Eric yawned with boredom. "I want to make sure I hadn't lost my touch."

He had to extricate himself here, and fast. This debate was headed into emotional territory.

Monica's blue eyes turned steely gray, flecked with challenge. "You're lying."

"So are you."

The thump of dog paws clambering up the stairs put a quick end to the discussion, at least for now, since Eric knew Jason and Delilah would be following their hounds up within seconds.

Monica moved past him, deliberately slamming her shoulder into his in a not-too-friendly gesture. "Touch me in that bed tonight, and you're dead," she repeated, going out into the hall.

"Back at ya," he called to her departing back. Two could play the ego game.

"How's it going, Dad?"

Eric's question was met with a grim smile as he, Jason, and their father strolled around the barn. Sights and smells from childhood came rushing back to Eric the way they always did when he was home. The scent of feed and of animals. The cows in their stalls, lying down in their straw. The hum of the ventilators ensuring a never-ending stream of clean air. Eric wondered if Jason was feeling the same tug in the gut he was. He glanced sideways at his brother. The answer was yes. Jason's expression was wistful.

"The ladies," as his mother insisted on calling herself, Monica, and Delilah, were still assembled around the dining room table, lingering over coffee and a selection of coffee cake, cherry pie, and peanut butter cookies. Dinner had gone well. Eric had left most of the talking to Monica, since she was the better actor. She fielded all the questions about their burgeoning relationship with aplomb, especially those being lobbed at them like grenades by Jason. He and Monica looked at each other with appropriate affection, though behind her loving glances, he knew she was still smarting over his calling her out on their kiss. Well, let her smart if she wanted to. He knew when a woman liked being kissed by him, and whether she admitted it or not, Monica Geary liked it.

His father paused before one of the new Holsteins. "This is Tallulah," he said.

Jason raised an eyebrow. *"Tallulah?"*

Their father chuckled. "That was the name your mother always wanted to name a girl if we had one."

"Good thing you just had us, then," said Eric.

"You didn't answer Eric's question, Dad," Jason said gently.

Their father's eyes were glued on Tallulah, unable to look at them. He'd never been good with expressing emotion. "I don't know when I'll be able to pay you boys back," he said quietly. He paused. "I don't know *if* I'll be able to pay you back."

"It wasn't a loan, Dad," said Eric. "We told you that."

Their father finally looked at them. "That was a helluva lot of money you boys gave us."

Eric and Jason glanced at each other. "We make a helluva lot of money, Dad," said Jason.

"Did you use it to hire some more help?" Eric asked.

Their father nodded his head. "Two more workers. Maybe you boys could come home and replace them," he said in a joking voice.

Eric and Jason both laughed. "You'd underpay us," said Eric.

"We'd give you free room and board," said their father. "And unlimited pie."

Jason chuckled. "Then it's definitely worth considering."

"Is the extra help—well, helping?" Eric asked.

"Yes. Obviously, it's lifting some of the burden off your mother and me. We still have Tommy from Carson coming down three days a week."

"Well, that's good," said Eric. Tommy had been helping his parents for as long as Eric could remember; plump, bald, and wizened, he was even more taciturn than their father.

"I still don't know how long we're going to be able to keep things going here, boys," their father continued in a choked voice. Eric filled with panic that he saw reflected in Jason's face. Neither of them had ever seen their father close to tears. Ever. He was the rock of the family, the practical, stoic one. *The father.*

Eric put a hand on his father's shoulder. "Dad . . ."

"You know what the situation is," his father said angrily. "Goddamn agribusiness, always trying to streamline to increase profits. It's driving down prices, forcing family-run operations like ours out of business. You have any idea how many family farms around here have gone into foreclosure?" He shook his head in despair.

"What if we gave you enough to compete?" Eric suggested. "Increase the herd, get a milking parlor?" He couldn't believe the sense of quiet desperation beginning to take hold of him. The thought of his parents losing or having to sell the farm distressed him more than he ever thought possible.

"We've got the money to do what Eric suggests, Dad," Jason reiterated quietly.

Their father returned to his usual stoicism. "I'll think about it." He was a man of incredible pride. Eric suspected it was entirely possible that the idea of being rescued by his sons made him feel like a failure.

"We're here for you Dad," Eric murmured. "In whatever way you need us to be."

His father patted his shoulder. "You're good boys. Now, let's get back to the house before all that pie is gone."

* * *

"Not enough pillows."

Monica looked at the two flimsy, feather-filled pillows dividing the double bed in Eric's old bedroom into equal halves. She'd barely been able to concentrate when she, Eric's sister-in-law, Delilah, and Eric's mom had been chatting over after-dinner pie and coffee. All she kept thinking about was how she was going to be in the same bed as Eric later in the evening. Also, she couldn't stop eyeing the cherry pie. It was so good she wanted to eat the whole thing, career be damned.

Eric sighed, adding his only pillow to the lineup. "Better?"

"Are you sure it won't affect your precious athlete's back?" she asked sarcastically.

"Oh, darling," Eric murmured with the affected expression he'd perfected. "I knew you cared."

Monica gritted her teeth. "Jerk."

She glanced around the room, rubbing her arms briskly, growing tenser by the moment. Beneath her thin, blue silk bathrobe she was wearing a matching blue silk baby doll with a sexy side opening and a matching G-string. She'd never been one of those women who could sleep in one of their boyfriend's rumpled old T-shirts. She'd always liked silky things, pretty things, even when sleeping alone, which is what she'd assumed she'd be doing tonight.

"Turn around," she commanded Eric.

"What?"

"I want to slip into bed without you seeing what I'm wearing."

Eric rolled his eyes. "I've seen women's bodies before, you know."

"Well, you're not seeing this one."

"Whatever."

Eric turned around as Monica shed her robe and quickly slipped into bed. The sheets were deliciously cold as she pulled them up to her neck.

"You can turn around now."

Eric turned, a hint of amazement on his face. "You look like some kind of terrified virgin bride on her wedding night. By the way," he said, stretching casually, "I sleep in the nude."

Monica bolted upright in bed, the sheets falling to her waist. "Not tonight you're not."

She saw Eric's eyes roam over her bare shoulders, then dip lower to her cleavage. She pulled the sheets back up again. "I mean it," she warned.

Eric grinned at her. "What are you so afraid of, Miss Geary?"

"It's just weird," she insisted.

What if the pillows shift and you roll over and we make contact and you have a hard-on and it's burning against my leg and I'm hot and bothered and—? she thought feverishly. Could he tell that's what she was thinking? Why was she thinking that, goddammit? She would not fall for this man. She'd fallen for too many jerks before, always thinking, *I'll be the one to change him.* But men didn't change. They might try to change their outward behavior, but their fundamental nature remained intact, and Eric's fundamental nature was that of a jerk. She would have to be vigilant against her own emotions. Against her own starved libido.

"I'm going to close my eyes while you get into bed in *your underwear*," Monica told him.

"Suit yourself," said Eric.

Monica screwed her eyes closed tight, at least to the point where she heard his jeans fall to the floor. Then she cracked one eye open, just a teensy-weensy bit, immediately wishing she hadn't. Gray Calvin Klein boxer briefs. Tightly hugging his muscled thighs. A magnificently sculpted body. *God knows everything you're thinking, and he's going to punish you, Monica Elise Geary,* she scolded herself, closing her eyes.

Eric slipped into bed, flashing her a seductive smile. Then he turned out the light.

ELEVEN

Monica was familiar with torment. In her early twenties she'd experienced the torment of auditioning and then wait-ing to hear if she got the part. She'd felt the torment of Monty telling her she was wasting her gifts. Then there was the on-going torment of knowing you could act but having to per-form with others who couldn't, worrying if it would drag your performance down.

Now she knew a new torment: lying less than two feet away from a gorgeous man.

Should she be insulted that Eric fell off to sleep so fast? Shouldn't he be at least a *little* tortured, especially after claiming that he still found her hot? A cool breeze was kick-ing through the half-open windows. It should have calmed her fiery desire. But it didn't help at all.

Monica lifted her head, peering at Eric over the pillow barrier. He was on his back, legs splayed beneath the sheet and a thin layer of blanket loosely covering his hips, his arms behind his head. Even in the darkness, there was enough light coming from outside the window for Monica to see his chest very clearly. There was some hair curling around his nipples, but not much. The physique . . . so perfect. Delicious. Another surge of heat crackled up her skin. What if she were to reach out and lightly, just lightly, press a palm to his chest? Would her burning skin wake him? Was it a bad thing to do?

She swallowed, reaching slowly across the divide separating them, but halfway there, she stopped herself. What if she were the one sleeping, and he did that to her? She imagined it. She was a light sleeper. She'd wake up and feel violated. Or would she?

Frustrated, Monica sank back down on her side of the bed. Perhaps because she wanted it to be so, she swore his body was radiating heat, too. Subconsciously, maybe, but heat nonetheless. She closed her eyes, trying to ignore the deep, regular rhythm of his breath. She wished he were a snorer. Or one of those guys who farted their heads off in bed. Anything that would disgust her and cool this embarrassing desire.

She closed her eyes, trying to drive thoughts of him from her mind, her pulse pounding like a hammer. What would it be like to feel his weight on top of her while his mouth devoured hers? What pleasure would her body experience feeling his fullness against her, knowing he wanted to put himself inside her? She felt her nipples go hard and reached her hands to her breasts, softly rubbing them with the pads of her fingers. Electricity flew through her body.

She took a deep breath, pulling her hands away, not wanting to incite herself further. But the images kept coming. She saw Eric stunning her with that sexy, crooked grin of his before his mouth began streaking down her body, an intoxicating prelude to his tongue greedily lapping between her thighs until she was unable to control her quaking body. She imagined him thrusting hard inside her, her cries of pleasure matching his own strangulated groans as they climaxed together. She saw herself curled in his arms in the afterglow, both of them sweaty but not caring, his still-fevered mouth tenderly pressing itself to her brow before he nuzzled her neck and told her how much he—

Her hands curled into fists. Enough. That was enough. What she was doing was insanity. It was desperate and masochistic. She knew that if she ever seduced Eric, he would jump at the chance to sleep with her. But Monica could never screw just for the sake of screwing. The act would have significance for her but not for him. She could never risk that, even though he was the reason she was now lying here, roused and tense at the same time. Feeling like her own worst enemy, she turned on her side away from him, waiting for the tension to leave her body so she could sleep.

Every morning for as long as Eric could remember, he woke at 4:30 a.m., the exact time he and Jason always had to be up to make the 5:30 a.m. hockey practice before school. Usually when he woke, he'd take a few seconds to get his bearings, then fall quickly back to sleep. But not this morning. This morning there was the soft rise and fall of breath coming from the other side of the bed: Monica, defending her virtue by erecting a goose-down pillow barrier between them. As if that could stop him if he really wanted to initiate something.

He propped himself up on his left elbow and looked at her. She was on her back, her lips parted slightly, her blonde hair tousled, her deliciously long neck cocked to one side. The stupidest cliché imaginable came to mind: Sleeping Beauty. But it was true. She was sleeping, *and* she was beautiful.

Watching her, he felt himself begin to harden. God, how many times over the years as a fan had he fantasized about making love to her in a hundred different ways? And now, here she was lying beside him, sleeping, at his *parents'* house, no less. He had kissed her deeply once already, and he wanted to kiss her now. Kiss her and hold her and eventually feel her bucking in his arms while she screamed his name. Simple, straightforward sex. Except it wasn't.

He lay back down, waiting for the intense feeling churning within him to abate. The more time he spent with Monica, the more clouded his mind became. They were supposed to be pretending to be a couple; but more and more—at least in his opinion—the lines were blurring, acting bleeding into real life. Monica could protest her gorgeous head off, but she was physically attracted to him, and he knew it. He wondered: Couldn't they just run with that, the way he did with every woman he'd ever dated? *I pleasure you, you pleasure me, no promises, and when it gets boring, we split and each look for another someone else to give us that heady rush that comes with initial seduction.*

Maybe he was in over his head with this pretending thing. He'd assumed Monica was as shallow as he was; she wasn't. And somehow that was changing his feelings. He worried about that; it could wreck his rep in the long run. He was the inveterate bachelor, for chrissakes. He wanted to maintain that image.

God, what bullshit. Right now, he didn't know what he wanted, apart from ravishing Monica Geary.

He heard a door open in the hallway, light footsteps walking to the bathroom. Delilah. His brother seemed blissfully happy with her, and she with him. But relationships seemed incredibly complicated to Eric. The compromises. Having sex with only one person for the rest of your life. Having to remember birthdays and anniversaries. Being dragged to spend time with her relatives. Endless negotiation on everything from what to have for dinner to when to have kids.

Then again, there did seem to be perks, too. Someone to come home to. Someone to laugh with. Someone to listen to you bitch and be there when you had a shitty day. Someone who loved you despite your flaws, maybe even because of them.

Mind somersaulting, he turned on his side to face the window. He wanted his old life back, the simple one where he was a player on and off the ice. They needed to talk about when to end this thing.

Eric was pleased when Monica agreed to take a walk with him after dinner, even though she'd already had a tour of the farm that morning with Delilah. He was feeling restless ever since not being able to get back to sleep that morning. It had been an odd day: him and Jason helping with chores, interspersed with long bouts of the two of them discussing the farm situation with each other, as well as with their folks. Surprisingly, their mother was just as tight-lipped as their father on the issue of Eric and Jason continuing to help out financially. He and Jason decided to leave it alone for now. They knew their parents; they shut down if you nagged them. Better to just let it go for now, gingerly picking up the thread of conversation when he and his brother were back in New York.

Monica had told him about her stroll with Delilah that morning; how thrilled Delilah and Jason were that Eric seemed so happy. The fantasy versus reality debate kept nudging itself back into his thoughts. Was he happy hanging out with Monica? Or was he just good at *pretending* to be happy hanging out with Monica? He was overthinking this whole stupid charade. It was time to turn off his brain and enjoy the endless black ocean of the sky above them, the twinkling silver stars luminous as pearls. He'd never lost his sense of wonder when it came to the sky out here on the farm. He hoped he never did.

Monica was looking skyward, too. "This is unreal. It just seems to go on and on forever."

"I know. Jason and I used to sleep outside sometimes in the summer. It was awesome."

"I'll bet." There was a long pause. "How come you didn't tell me your parents were in danger of losing the farm?"

His mother must have filled her in. Eric tensed, unsure how to answer. "I guess I thought it wasn't something you needed to know, since this isn't real."

Monica nodded. "I like your parents a lot. Your sister-in-law, too."

Eric chuckled. "Not Jace, though, huh?"

"No, I like him, too, now that he's given up the third degree. You two love each other," Monica observed.

"Yeah, yeah, yeah," Eric muttered, embarrassed. "Whatever."

Monica turned to look at him. "Are you upset they might lose the farm?"

"They're not going to lose it," Eric shot back fiercely. "Jason and I are going to help keep them afloat, even expand, if that's what they need to do. It's been in the family for three generations."

Talking about it was beginning to upset him, perhaps because that's all he'd talked about all day. Right now, he just wanted to walk around and enjoy it as much as he could.

"I'm sorry," Monica murmured, slipping a warm hand into his. "I didn't mean to upset you."

"It's okay."

Her hand in his—was it a gesture of sympathy or comfort? They continued ambling through the grass. Would it insult her if he gently broke the contact between them? The thing was, he didn't want to. And he didn't think she wanted him to, either.

He could feel sexual tension pressing down on them, solid and real as a weight. Eager to override it, he began talking. "Winters here can be really brutal. Jace and I used to freeze our asses off waiting for the bus in the morning. Summer is great, though. Sometimes thunderstorms kick up in a flash. The sky is amazing then, too, a really eerie gunmetal gray that's sometimes streaked with red, if you can believe that. It was a really great place to be a kid, but once you were a teenager, it sucked. At least Jace and I had hockey. We were pretty bad students; we knew sports would be our way out. Neither one of us wanted to stay on the farm." He realized he was babbling, most likely boring the hell out of her by talking about himself. "Did you always know you wanted to be an actress?"

"Yup. I played Cinderella in my first grade play, and it was all downhill from there."

Anther thing they shared: knowing their calling at an early age. Eric stole a sideways glance at her. She seemed calm, despite the tension still hanging over them like a cloud. This was the way real couples talked, he realized. This was how they got to know each other. The realization had his mind twisting in agony.

He cleared his throat. "So, when we get back to New York? How are we supposed to proceed?"

"Just carry on," Monica said briskly. "Theresa said I should go to one of your games. Maybe accompany you to a charity event. Do you do any of those?"

"Yeah, I've been doing stuff with the Ronald McDonald

House in north Jersey ever since I moved to the city. It's a
place where families can stay free when their kids are under-
going cancer treatment."

"I know what it is," said Monica, sounding impressed.
"That's wonderful."

"What can I say?" Eric replied jauntily. "I'm a great guy."
He needed to drag Eric the egomaniac out of storage, and
fast. The night sky, her beauty, opening up to her . . . all were
conspiring to make him want to gather her up in his arms and
kiss her.

"Can we stop walking a minute?" Monica asked. "I just
want to look up at the sky for a while."

"Sure."

Eric dropped her hand, ostensibly to button up his well-
worn denim jacket. But when he was done, he didn't know
what to do with his hands. He wanted to put an arm around
her waist but opted to put it around her shoulder instead, the
way a friend might.

Monica seemed comfortable in the crook of his arm. They
stood there, silent, both stargazing. The dark tension was in-
creasing, distracting them. Making him *want*. Usually his
damn brother was the one with impulse control issues. But
this time, it was him.

"Monica," he said softly.

She turned to look at him. Eric tilted her chin up gently,
her face luminous in the glow of the crescent moon, which
had slowly arced over the plains while they walked. She was
so heart-stoppingly beautiful, he feared he'd lose his nerve.
But the ache inside him, confusing as it was, needed to be
sated. Eric slowly lowered his mouth to hers, teasing as his
lips played over hers.

Monica jerked her head away. "Tell me," she said sharply.
"Is this another one of your kisses designed to make sure you
haven't lost your touch?"

"No." His mind was aswirl with confusion.

"What, then?"

"I just want to kiss you," he admitted, feeling sheepish.
"I've dreamed of it since before we met, and as you can see, I
dream of it now. If you don't want me to, I understand."

His heart was hammering as he waited for her to answer. "You can kiss me," Monica said with a hint of warning in her voice, "but don't think it really means anything. I just feel badly for you because of the situation with your family."

A mercy kiss. She was lying. She knew it. And he knew it, too. But it was a lie that worked for both of them. He lowered his mouth to hers again, the feel of her lips against his a particularly addictive form of torment. There was something in her response—the urgency, perhaps the neediness—that sent pins and needles shooting through his body. He matched her hunger, intent on pleasing not only himself but also her. All those years dreaming of kissing Monica Geary . . . But those dreams were of Monica Geary the fantasy. This was Monica Geary the woman, lovely and soft in his arms. *Real.*

It was more than his desire could take. He'd made love to lots of girls under these stars; he knew how drugging it could be. The longer he and Monica remained pressed together like this, exploring, probing, becoming familiar, the more he'd want and the more he'd try to take. Garnering every ounce of his self-control, he tore his mouth from hers.

They both blinked as they looked at one another, seeming to need to recover. Sexual tension still hovered, but now it was tempered with awkwardness.

"We should probably get back to the house," Monica suggested quietly. "And just for the record," she added, flipping her hair over her shoulder, "that wasn't half bad."

"I agree: you weren't half as inexperienced as I thought you'd be," he replied, suppressing a smile as they turned back in the direction of the house. Maybe he'd wait on talking to her about ending things.

TWELVE

A wave of delight swept through Monica as the crowd of more than three hundred women erupted into applause as she entered the ballroom at the Grand Hyatt New York. She was there for a special meeting of the tristate chapter of the Monica Geary Fan Club. They still loved her. They still wanted her. Take that, Chesty!

Monica was escorted to the dais in the front of the room by Debbie Glazer, the woman who had founded the fan club ten years before within months of Monica joining *W and F*. Debbie, a slightly overweight stay-at-home mom of three from Long Island was, without a doubt, Monica's most ardent fan. Sometimes it scared Monica how much Debbie knew about her, but Monica knew this came with putting yourself in the public eye. She hated celebrities who whined about having no privacy. They chose to put themselves out there; they wanted to be famous. Monica believed celebrities owed something to these people, since they did help put you where you were. However, there *were* limits—like fans crawling under the bathroom stall when you were trying to pee.

"Debbie, I can't thank you enough for putting this together on such short notice," Monica said gratefully.

Debbie's face lit up. "My pleasure. It's so great to see you again, Monica! You might end up being here all afternoon; there are so many questions people want to ask!"

"That's great."

Looking out over the crowd, Monica saw many familiar faces from the past. Maybe it came from years of memorizing lines, but she remembered many of their names and made a point of greeting them personally. It was such a simple thing, and yet they looked so happy. It helped assuage her guilt for being out of touch with her audience for so long.

Of course, there was some soap press there, too: Carolyn Shields from *Soap World* (who, surprisingly, had written positively about her and Eric in her "A Day on the Set of *W and F*" piece), and another woman named Delores Clarkson from *Soap World*'s rival, *Daytime Today*, who was a longtime Monica fan.

Sitting up on the dais, Monica took the mike. "Ask away!" she urged her fans with a smile.

Hands shot up in the air like weeds. Monica selected a petite, nervous-looking woman down front who'd been jiggling her left leg madly ever since Monica's entrance. Being an actress had made Monica a keen observer of people. She knew it would drive this woman nuts if she had to wait too long to have her question answered.

The woman stood, accepting the mike Debbie would be passing around the room. "Yes, um, Rox—I mean Monica—" the woman momentarily cast down her eyes, mortified by her mistake—"um, are Grayson and Roxie going to get married?"

Monica smiled slyly. "Good question. I'm not at liberty to answer that, but I can tell you, there will be a wedding on the show in the not-too-distant future."

"Ooooh," the fans said collectively.

Unfortunately, Chessy's character, Paige, was slated to seduce Royce's character, Grayson, after a drunken one-night tryst, resulting in a pregnancy. Wanting to "do the right thing," Grayson was going to dump Roxie and marry Paige, breaking Roxie's heart. This would spur Monica's character on to wanting revenge on Chesty's character, which would be a joy to play.

"Thank you," the woman said meekly, handing the mike back to Debbie so she could pass it on to the next fan.

Monica answered as many questions about the show and her character as she could. But she knew that eventually, the topic of Eric would come up.

"Monica," boomed a woman with all the stentorian warmth of a high court judge. "How serious is your relationship with Eric Mitchell?"

The room sucked in its breath, every eager eye glued to Monica. She smiled warmly. "We're taking it one day at a time."

Shoulders slumped. These people wanted dirt. They were her fans. They wanted to be on the inside track.

"Of course, who knows where it might go?" Monica added coyly. The room erupted in cheers and whistles. Monica knew she was deliberately tantalizing them, but that was the point, wasn't it? At the back of the room, Carolyn Shields and Delores Clarkson were scribbling furiously on their reporter's pads. Monica could already recite the headlines: "Wedding Bells for *W and F*'s Monica?" She wondered if her answer would get back to Eric. Probably. Hadn't he said he and his teammates read soap mags in addition to being addicted to the show? She'd cross that bridge when and if she came to it.

Though only a week had passed, the whole weekend in North Dakota was beginning to feel like a figment of Monica's imagination. After their passionate kiss beneath the stars, they resumed playing their parts as if it had never happened. All Monica could think was: we're both cowards. But now, her impromptu addendum to her fan's question—"Who knows where it might go?"—made her wonder. Where *did* she want it to go? She was willing to admit to herself that she was physically attracted to him. But emotionally? Could it go to that level? And if it did?

She put these thoughts aside, concentrating on pleasing her fans. Which was easy—until the door at the back of the ballroom opened and Chesty stepped inside.

"Hi, everyone!" she chirped loudly, waving as if she were the queen of England greeting her beloved subjects. "Since I'm one of Monica's biggest fans myself," she declared as she made her way to the dais, "this was one event I couldn't miss!"

Monica dug her nails into her thighs to keep herself from jumping up and coldcocking her. *Oh you bitch. Oh you bitchedy witchedy little bitch on wheels.*

Monica's fans looked unsure of how to react. Some looked delighted: two soap stars for the price of one! Others looked confused: Was this a planned surprise? But most of them looked resentful. This was *their* event for Monica, *their* private audience with their idol. Monica wanted to circle the room and give every one of them a big kiss.

Meanwhile, Chessy had effortlessly commandeered the mike from a shell-shocked Debbie and joined Monica on the dais. She laid a hand over her heart—assuming she had one—in what was no doubt supposed to be a gesture of sincerity. "I just had to be here. I've been a fan of Monica's since I was a little girl"—she smiled at Monica with wide, adoring eyes—"and I just had to come and pay tribute. Isn't she the best?" The room erupted into applause. "I cannot tell you what it's like working with her. She's been acting *for so long*, enabling a fresh-faced newcomer like me to learn so much. Did any of you ever have an old, wise teacher in school whose every word you savored, hungry for that knowledge? That's how I feel about Monica. She's my mentor, my own version of a wise teacher. If any of you have anything you want to ask me about Monica and what it's like working with her, learning from her, please feel free."

The room was silent as Monica's fans stared at Chessy coldly. These people were not stupid. They knew Chessy had come to steal Monica's moment, and Chessy was such a crappy actress that even someone on the level of, oh, say, Chim Chim could see through her words. The longer the silence dragged on, the harder it became for Monica to suppress a triumphant smile, especially when Chessy began to squirm.

"Nice try," Monica whispered to her. "Very professional.

There are two journalists in the room. Can't wait to see what they write about this."

Monica deftly plucked the mike from Chessy's fingers. "Sorry about the interruption, folks. Now where were we?"

I will not suck tonight, Eric vowed to himself as he dressed for the game against Toronto. He kissed the cross from his mother five times before putting it around his neck. Usually he only did this for away games, but tonight he needed all the divine intervention he could get. He put on his left sock first, then his right. Shoulder pads, then kneepads. This had been his ritual since he was fifteen. Sometimes the mojo worked, and sometimes it didn't. It had better work tonight, or his confidence in himself, and perhaps his team's confidence in him, would be seriously damaged, especially since he'd once again *totally sucked* in a game two nights before. Starting out the season in a slump? Not good.

Theresa had called him yesterday, urging him to get Monica to come to a game, especially since the Blades' program was now running the picture of her with the team. Theresa advised Monica to sit on the arena's first level, rather than sit in a skybox, so that she didn't look aloof and could interact with Blades fans as well as whatever soap fans might be there. Thankfully, Monica had no problem with that, though she did ask him to reserve two seats for her, which was reasonable. Unless she was a rabid hockey fan, who would want to go to a game alone? He did wonder, though, who she was going to bring with her.

His brother sidled up to him. "Almost showtime."

"Yeah."

"I saw you kissing your cross," Jason whispered. "You scared of fucking up again or what?"

"Fuck off," Eric snarled. He'd already had to endure dirty looks from his teammates, cracks about how if his on-ice performance mirrored his performance in bed, Monica Geary would be dumping him any second. You'd think his own brother would cut him a little slack, but no. When it came to hockey, Jason could be as much of a jerk-off as anyone else.

"If you've got anything else unhelpful to say," Eric muttered through gritted teeth, "say it now."

Jason put a hand on his shoulder and looked at him with a sincere expression on his face. "Good luck tonight."

"Thanks." Okay, so maybe his brother wasn't such a jerk. Saying another quick prayer, Eric followed his teammates out of the locker room.

"What on earth are they *doing* down there?"

Monica turned her attention from the Blades home ice to answer Gloria's question—or, more accurately, not to answer it, since she had no idea. Why she'd decided to bring Gloria with her to the hockey game, she didn't know. In typical Gloria style, she was wearing a leopard print catsuit and matching turban. The latter had to be removed the second they sat down and the fan behind Gloria growled, "Hey, Aladdin, I can't see a fuckin' thing here."

"Charming," Gloria sniffed, but she'd taken the turban off and was now holding it in her lap. "Why are we here again?"

"Because I want to see my boyfriend play," Monica replied. *Because we need to keep the PR machine rolling along.* "Besides, if you didn't want to come, you could have said no."

"Wouldn't miss it for the world," Gloria insisted. "I believe in trying everything at least once, if you can."

They were almost at the end of the first period, and Monica had already seen the camera pointed at her a few times, and waved. In fact, one of the newscasters wanted to talk to her between periods. Perhaps stupidly, she'd agreed to it. She hoped they didn't ask her any hockey questions, or if they did, she hoped she could bluff her way through them. She was pretty certain, though, that the questions would center on her and Eric.

"So, as I was asking . . ." Gloria began.

"I have no idea what they're doing," Monica confessed quietly. She felt like a simpleton watching the action down on the ice.

She kept her eyes glued to Eric. At one point, there was

something called a "power play," and Eric seemed to have the puck on his stick a lot, which the crowd liked. When someone on the power play scored, the crowd went crazy, their roar of delight almost deafening. It reminded her of movies she'd seen set in ancient Rome, where the toga and sandal crowd roared every time a Christian was thrown to the lions. But Monica understood their joy. She remembered the first time she'd ever gone to a play on Broadway, how she wanted to stand up and cheer, it was so amazing. These sports fans were no different than any other sort of dedicated fan. They delighted in their idols' victories, felt disappointed in their defeats. It was a wonderful thing to behold.

Hearing their cheers, Gloria peered at Monica and in a dry voice said, "I suppose I should toss my turban up in the air." Monica really wished she'd brought Jimmy instead. Jimmy knew about sports; he could explain to her what was going on. Plus, it probably would have helped cheer him. Wallace Mendelson's death was still affecting him.

"Which one is your boyfriend?" Gloria asked again, her gaze scouring the ice. "I can't keep track. There are so many of them down there, buzzing around like little bees."

Monica pointed. "Right there, skating back to the bench, number sixty-five."

Monica watched as Eric sat down on the end of the players' bench, grabbing a water bottle and squirting the contents into his mouth. His eyes were glued to the ice, but then, for a split second, they lifted, catching hers. He gave a quick smile. Monica smiled back. Pride ballooned inside her, the same way it did after Eric had tried to revive Wallace on the set. Again she thought, *I don't have any right to feel this. He's not really my boyfriend.*

"I heard about that little harlot showing up at your fan lunch," Gloria remarked casually. "How you didn't punch her in that retroussé little nose of hers is beyond me."

"I wanted to, believe me. But I'll let my character do it for me in a couple of months."

"I know I've told you this before, but *watch her*. She's got it in for you."

"I know that, Gloria."

"I've been in this business longer than you. You can't trust anyone. Someone will claim to be your friend one minute, then stab you in the back the next to further their own career." Monica held her tongue, even though she thought Gloria was beginning to sound a little paranoid.

"Don't forget: that blonde little fluff ball can open her legs to someone who makes the decisions about whose contract gets renewed and whose doesn't," Gloria continued. She held a declamatory finger up in the air. "Never underestimate the power of the muff."

Monica cringed. The woman on the other side of Gloria leaned over to stare at them, appalled. "Alzheimer's," Monica whispered to the woman with an apologetic smile. "She doesn't know what she's saying sometimes."

Gloria's mouth fell open, but Monica silenced her with her best glare.

"Honestly," Gloria huffed. She riffled through her purse for a cigarette.

"You can't smoke here," said Monica.

"My God!" Gloria sputtered in exasperation. "What is this? The Soviet Union under Stalin?"

Monica laughed. Gloria's penchant for melodrama sometimes reminded her of Monty's. Her anger at the old man had abated, replaced by a niggling sense of responsibility. She should go over and see him soon.

The buzzer sounded, signaling the end of the first period. Monica briefly caught Eric glance her way again before he followed his teammates into a tunnel. She wondered if he was glad she was here. Probably, if only to impress his teammates. The newscaster who wanted to speak with her was already rushing toward her. "You keep your lips zipped," Monica instructed Gloria. "Understand?" She had an image of Gloria putting her turban back on, telling the newscaster what a hunk she thought Eric was and how if she were thirty years younger . . .

"Aren't we bossy tonight," Gloria drawled. "Must be from all the time you're spending with that lovely, testosterone-filled athlete. You're getting very assertive. But very well, I'll hold my tongue."

"Thank you."

Two women in Blades jerseys approached Monica shyly, asking for her autograph. Monica happily complied. By the time the journalist reached her, her mood was downright cheery. This ruse was working like a charm.

THIRTEEN

"What did you think of the game?"

Eric could barely contain his excitement as he and Monica headed uptown toward their respective apartments in her hired car. To say he'd slaughtered out on the ice tonight was an understatement. He'd scored on the power play two minutes into the second period, and he'd orchestrated the team's other three power plays as if he had the puck on a string. They'd scored three out of four chances on the power play, in addition to their two even-strength goals. He'd excelled in his own end as well, skating the puck and making crisp breakout passes.

"I thought it was interesting," Monica said carefully.

"I caught some of the interview you did between periods. You did well."

"Thank God they didn't ask me anything in depth."

He remembered the first time they'd shared this car, when he escorted her to the tribute dinner for Chim Chim's old partner. That night, Monica had sat as far away from him as she could, her body pressed up against the window. Tonight, they were sitting close enough that their shoulders were touching. It hadn't been planned, it just was, and it felt natural—not to mention completely terrifying.

Eric resisted the urge to brush away the blonde bangs that had fallen over her forehead, settling instead for a friendly squeeze to her knee. "Look, I need to ask you a favor."

He could feel her tense slightly against him. "What's that?"

"I need you to come to the next home game."

"What for?" Monica asked suspiciously.

"It's an experiment."

She brushed her own fallen bangs from her eyes, the better to eye him. "What kind of experiment?"

Eric hesitated. "I need to see if your being there brought me good luck."

"You're kidding, right?"

"No, I'm not." He looked at her earnestly. "How can I explain this without sounding nuts?" he mused aloud. "Hockey players have rituals, little things they do to protect themselves. For example: One guy on my team has to puke before a game or it's bad luck for him. Another guy has to kiss a picture of Giselle Bunchen. My brother brought his dog to Met Gar when the Blades were in the running for the Cup two years ago, and it brought them luck. They won."

"Because of a *dog*?"

"It helped," Eric insisted.

"What about you?" Monica asked. "Do you have any personal rituals?"

"I have to, uh, put my socks on in a certain order. My pads, too. And I have this cross my mom gave me that I have to kiss."

He waited for her to start mocking him, but she didn't. "Actors have certain superstitions, too," she shared with him. "Like, you never say 'Good luck' to someone before they perform; you always say 'Break a leg.' And you never say the title *Macbeth* aloud; you call it 'The Scottish Play' or it's bad luck."

Her admission made Eric feel much better. "What about rituals? Do you have any?"

Monica thought. "I always read the *Daily News* while I'm in makeup and hair. Does that count?"

"I'd say so."

"You think you did well on the ice tonight because I was there?"

Eric thought he detected a note of pleasure in her voice.

"That's what I need to find out."

"You did do well, right?" Monica asked uncertainly.

Disappointment tackled him. "Yeah. I mean, you couldn't tell?"

"I told you, Eric: I know as much about hockey as you know about acting."

"I could explain it to you sometime, if you want."

"That would be nice," Monica murmured noncommittally. Eric wasn't sure he agreed. He could imagine her eyes rolling up in her head from boredom, begging him to shut up.

"So, what if I come to another game, and you do great? Does that mean you'll want me to come to every home game?"

"If you can," Eric admitted. A thought occurred to him: if Monica was his good luck charm, it meant they'd have to keep their ruse going through the whole season. That was a long time, much longer than he imagined this thing going.

"I can't," Monica said without hesitation. "It's after eleven right now. Do you know what time I have to be at work tomorrow? Five thirty in the morning. I can't come to games two or three nights a week! I have lines to learn! I need to get some sleep!"

"Okay, one game a week," Eric begged. "Just one. And it's not like we're home every week! We go on the road."

Monica sighed. "Let me think about this. It's asking a lot. Seriously."

"Do you want this thing to look real or not?"

"Oh, please. This has nothing to do with faux us and everything to do with real you."

"I'll pay you."

Monica's hands flew to cover her ears. "Stop! You're getting pitiful! I can't stand it!"

Eric pulled one hand away with a force akin to that of

when he'd grabbed her in his old bedroom. They both felt it: the shock of hard contact, the sparks. "You don't understand, Monica. This is my first year as a Blade. They traded a beloved player for me, which means I was supposed to come out of the starting gate dazzling the shit out of everyone. But the exact opposite happened: I've sucked from the minute I hit the ice—until tonight. Tonight was the first time I could feel all my teammates and the coaches thinking, 'Yeah, this guy was worth the trade.' It was the first time since the season started that *I* felt worth the trade." He hesitated. "Maybe your being there inspired me—just a little," he added quickly. "But I really need you to help me out here. Please. One more game." He slowly let go of her hand, the heat fading from where they'd been touching.

"Fine," Monica said quietly. "One more game. But I need to leave as soon as the game is over so I get home at a decent hour. No waiting for you to shower and then hanging with the guys awhile or anything like that."

"I promise you can rush right out of there as soon as the final buzzer sounds." He took her hand. "I really appreciate you helping me out like this," he murmured, lifting it to his mouth and kissing it tenderly. He saw the swoon in Monica's eyes, quickly followed by a look of minor desolation. She was falling for him; it was obvious. He lowered her hand, regretting this kiss, because it made him look like he was playing her, the way he'd done with so many women before her in order to get what he wanted. He wanted to tell her that his gratitude was real, that he wasn't just turning on the charm, but the words stuck in his throat. *I don't know how to do this,* he thought miserably. *I don't know how to be the one made vulnerable by the truth.*

"That's what friends do for each other: they help out," said Monica, looking out the window. "Which is why you're coming to a party with me Saturday night."

"What kind of party?" Eric loved parties, because—well, strike that. He usually loved them because they were filled with hot babes and he had his pick.

"An actor party," said Monica, still looking out the window. "One of my old classmates from Julliard is holding a little reunion. I haven't seen her in a while, so I thought it might be fun to go."

"We'd be going as a couple, right?"

Monica turned back to him. "Of course we are. Why wouldn't we?" There was a note of panic in her voice.

"The reason I asked," Eric replied calmly, "is that when you invited me a few seconds back, you said, 'Friends help each other out.' So I just wanted to be sure of my role before going in. Whether I'm going as a friend or—a lover."

"I need us to keep pretending," said Monica, skirting the word *lover* entirely. "Most of my friends are married now, or at least have partners. The last time I went to a party solo, I could see the 'Poor Monica, still alone' in their eyes."

"Don't worry," said Eric. "We'll blow them away when they see how in love we are."

Monica slowly broke into a confident smile. "We will, won't we?"

FOURTEEN

Eric had been to a lot of upscale parties since he'd moved east, and this ranked with the best of them. It was held in a loft that seemed the size of the ground floor of Macy's. The loft, owned by Monica's old buddy from Juilliard, Desiree, and her husband, Raymond, was fashionably spare, with lots of original art hanging on the walls and a minimum of furniture, which explained why most of the guests stood rather than sat, talking in small groups. Three waiters circled the room with trays of hors d'oeuvres and champagne. In one corner, a short woman in a glittering green dress tickled the keys of a white baby grand piano.

Eric did a quick scan of the crowd, his old habit of assessing women hardwired into him. It was a mixed bag: some were drop-dead gorgeous; some he could never imagine trying to pick up in a million years. None held a candle to Monica.

The partygoers were a mixed bag, too. There were lots of people whose simple but tasteful attire subtly signified wealth, and others who looked a little down-at-the-heel. Eric assumed they might be struggling actors, but this was New

York, so you never knew. They could deliberately be cultivating that New York boho thing.

A waiter approached him and Monica, and they each took a glass of champagne.

"Which one is your friend?" Eric asked.

Monica indicated an Amazonian redhead about thirty feet away dressed entirely in white, the biceps of her tan arms so cut they indicated hours spent at the gym. Her lips seemed to be moving—kind of—and her eyebrows were frozen in place. Botox. She had to be, what, thirty? Eric supposed he could understand it, being good-looking himself. But she still seemed a little young to be injecting her face with botulism, or whatever the hell it was.

He pressed a hand to the small of Monica's back. "Do you want to go over and say hi?"

Monica hesitated, looking uneasy. "She looks a little busy right now. Let's wait a few minutes." Eric got the sense that Monica was somewhat wary of Desiree. He was glad to see her uneasiness fade when a scruffy-looking guy with John Lennon specs and a day's worth of stubble on his face waved to her, motioning for her to come join him on one of the few couches in the room. Monica grinned. "There's someone I'd like to talk to."

His hand still on her back, Eric helped maneuver her through the crowd toward him.

"Monica!" The scruffy guy bounded off the couch, drawing Monica into a tight embrace. "It's so great to see you!"

"You, too, John." Monica turned to Eric. "Eric, I want you to meet my old friend, John. John, this is my boyfriend, Eric."

John shook Eric's hand warmly. "Nice to meet you."

"You, too."

"John blew everyone away when we were at Julliard. We all envied him."

John frowned. "Yeah, that's why I'm still waiting tables."

Monica reached for his hand, squeezing it. "It'll happen. It will. You just have to have faith."

"Yeah, well . . ." John didn't look too sure about that.

"Are you still auditioning? Doing showcases?"

"All the time." John seemed self-conscious as he gazed down at his feet. "You know what it's like. For some people, it happens, and for some it doesn't. After ten years, I'm starting to think it's time to throw in the towel." He smiled at her sadly. "At least it happened for you. God knows you deserved it."

John and Monica weren't chatting very long before John turned to Eric and said, "I'm so sorry; I'm being totally rude. Tell me about you."

"I play defense for the New York Blades."

"No way," said John, impressed. He nudged Monica in the ribs playfully. "About time you hooked up with someone manly. Monica here was renowned for hooking up with these skinny, pasty losers—"

"He knows all about that, John, thank you very much."

John chuckled. "Sorry. Anyway," he said to Eric, "a pro athlete? That's totally cool."

"Hey, if you ever want me to hook you up with tickets, just tell Monica."

"Thanks, man," John said, wide-eyed with unabashed gratitude. He gave Monica's shoulder a little shake in an unmistakable sign of approval.

Monica gave an uncomfortable little cough. She turned her faux adoring gaze on Eric. Which, he thought, might not be so faux anymore. But now wasn't the time to think about that.

John gestured toward Desiree. "I think she wants to talk to you."

Monica hugged her friend. "It was great seeing you, John. I've told you a million times; *call me.*"

"I know, I know," John muttered sheepishly. "I just worry about bothering you, big-time busy actress and all that."

"Don't be ridiculous," Monica chided. "I'm still just me."

"Thank God." John extended his hand to Eric again. "It was really great to meet you."

"You, too." Eric slipped his free hand into Monica's. "Nice guy," he murmured to her as they walked across the loft to talk to Monica's friend Desiree.

He could feel something surge through Monica as she held

his hand tightly: Happiness? Pleasure at making a connection with an old friend? Pleasure that they were holding hands? Whatever it was, he was glad she felt it.

"Monnie, Monica, Monniemoo!"

With over-the-top glee, Monica's old friend Desiree, threw her tanned arms open wide and embraced Monica, kissing both her cheeks.

"Good to see you, Desiree," said Monica.

"You, too, sweetie pie. I'm *soo* glad you could come."

Monica looked a little shell-shocked as Desiree released her from their embrace. Monica's eyes gripped Eric's apologetically.

Finished with her effusive greeting, Desiree pursed her lips as best she could, turning her attention on Eric. "You must be the boyfriend."

"I must be," Eric replied. Monica shot him a sharp look.

"Hockey player, right?"

"Yup. New York Blades."

"See," Desiree said to Monica, "I keep up with all the *star* gossip." The sarcastic way she said *star* irked Eric immediately. She flashed Eric a patronizing smile—at least he thought it was a smile; it was hard to tell with her frozen face. "You have to forgive me, but I've never understood the appeal of sports. It's so—violent. And it just seems so silly."

"Yeah, I know," Eric replied. "It's not an important profession like acting."

Desiree inhaled sharply, looking mildly stunned before launching into a tinkling little laugh as she waved a palm in the air. "I suppose that's one way of looking at it."

Monica drew closer to Eric and gripped him tightly at his waist but not before digging her nails into his side. Eric ignored it as he put a protective arm around her shoulder. If Monica thought he was going to let this pretentious phony insult her, then she hadn't learned a thing about him.

"So, Mon," said Desiree, absently twisting the giant diamond stud in her left ear, "you're still on the soap?"

Eric felt Monica stiffen. "Yes."

"Interesting."

"Are you doing any acting?" Monica asked.

"Actually, I am. I just got a part in an off-off-Broadway play by a hot new Irish playwright. I'm playing a leprechaun sorceress."

Eric suppressed a snort.

"That's great," said Monica.

"It is," Desiree agreed. "I'm so glad I can use my training and talent in a way that's true."

"True?" Eric repeated.

"Eric," Monica hissed under her breath.

"Yeah," said Desiree. "You know, not go—commercial," she explained, her expression disparaging.

"Can I ask you a question?" said Eric. Monica gave his side another dig.

"Sure," said Desiree.

"What does your husband do?"

"He manages a private hedge fund."

"So you don't really have to worry about making a living as an actress. I mean, you can afford to play a leprechaun because, hell, you've got a rich husband."

"What's your point?" Desiree snapped.

"My point is that you're really just *playing* at being an actress, whereas Monica makes her *living* using her talent."

"Eric," Monica hissed.

"It's okay," said Desiree coolly. "Your boyfriend obviously doesn't know anything about artistic integrity."

"She's right," Monica murmured miserably under her breath to Eric.

"No, she isn't," said Eric. *Why the hell was she agreeing with this snobby bitch?*

"Can I ask you another question?" Eric said to Desiree.

Desiree's mouth cracked into a polite smile. "Of course."

"How many times have you been nominated for a Daytime Drama Award?"

"I don't see how—"

"Just answer the question," Eric demanded. "How many?"

"None," Desiree sniffed.

"Well, Monica has been nominated three times."

"Mmmm."   •

Eric could feel Monica trembling, struggling to control it. He hoped it was because she was as angry as he was. He paused, waiting for Monica to counter her old friend's elitism, but she didn't.

"Look," said Desiree, "I know daytime has provided you with a good income, Monica, but you're wasting your talent. You should be on the stage. Or doing brilliant little indie films. Not *compromising* yourself like this."

"I know," Monica said bleakly.

"Can you excuse us a moment?" said Eric as he plucked Monica's champagne glass from her hand, depositing it with his own on the tray of a passing waiter. Firmly gripping Monica's hand, he began pulling her toward the loft entrance.

"What are you doing?" Monica sputtered.

"I'm taking you outside so I can talk to you." He practically punched the button of the elevator.

"I can't believe what you said to Desiree," Monica spat the minute they stepped inside, and the doors slid shut.

"I can't believe what you *didn't* say."

Eric's incredulity continued to build as the elevator descended. Monica had pointedly pulled her hand from his. *Fine,* Eric thought. *If she wants to be pissed, let her.* But he was going to say what needed to be said. They seethed in mutual silence as they made their way outside, halting on the sidewalk in front of Desiree's apartment building. For a minute Eric thought Monica was going to walk away from him. But she stood there facing him, her trembling evident now, her eyes fiery with anger.

"What the hell was so pressing that you had to drag me out of my friend's party as if I were some child who was misbehaving?"

"I wasn't going to stand there and let that bitch insult you anymore. I'm sorry."

Monica blinked. "What did you just call her?"

"Bitch. You heard me. Your friend John? He was great. But Desiree? Total snob bitch. She can afford to talk about remaining 'true to art' or whatever the fuck it was she said, because she doesn't have to worry about money."

"But—"

"Let me finish," Eric said with a glare. "Why the hell did you let that bitch make a value judgment about what you do?" Eric took her by the shoulders, wishing he could shake some sense into her and make her see herself as others saw her: as a success, someone to admire. "You have fans, Monica. You've won awards, which means you have the respect of your peers. So what if you're not starring in *Hamlet*? What's wrong with acting on a show that gives people pleasure and an escape five days a week? Why is that less valid than playing a fucking leprechaun in a theater that probably seats twelve people?"

"You don't understand," Monica gulped tearfully. "I was trained—"

"To act. You were trained to act. And that's what you do."

"No one respects daytime!"

"That's not true. I bet half the people who think it's crap have never tuned in to a soap in their lives."

"You don't understand," Monica repeated stubbornly.

Eric folded his arms across his chest. "Then explain it to me."

Monica huffed with frustration. "Imagine you trained your whole life to be in the NHL, but when push came to shove, you couldn't get there, and you had to settle for playing in the minors. How would you feel?"

"Grateful that I was at least making my living doing something I love. Maybe it wouldn't be exactly what I dreamed, but it would be a pretty good gig—one I'd sure as hell appreciate for as long as it lasts."

Monica began shaking her head, but Eric took her chin in his hand, tilting her face up so she couldn't avoid his eyes. "Listen to me. Your friend, John? Don't you think he'd kill to have a regular acting gig the way you do?" Monica said nothing. "Oh, wait, I get it: waiting tables is noble. It means John is a 'real artist' while you're a hack." Monica looked down at her feet, so she missed Eric shaking his head. "I don't get this.

If you're such a hack, if working in daytime is such an embarrassing compromise for you, then why are so intent on holding on to your popularity and position?"

"Because it's all I have!" Monica cried.

"That's not true," Eric countered fiercely. "You have me!"

The minute the words slipped from his mouth, Eric felt thunder in his head; he'd never said anything like that to any woman in his life. Meanwhile, Monica was looking at him warily.

"What does that *mean*, Eric?"

Eric struggled to put it into words. "It means I'm here. It means I'm your friend. It means . . . I don't know."

"That's great. Very helpful."

Eric looked away, feeling like an asshole. He could feel what she wanted from him and what she needed him to say. But he couldn't get the words out, afraid it would come out all wrong. Who was he kidding? He was afraid, period.

He glanced back to Monica. She looked upset. He was beginning to get the distinct feeling that she wished he wasn't there.

"You realize she's jealous of you, right?" he said. "Your leprechaun friend?"

"I can't talk about this anymore," Monica said wearily.

Eric dropped it. "I'll call us a cab."

"No. I'm going back to the party."

"For more self-abuse? Be my guest. I'm sorry; I can't stand around and watch that."

"Fine. Call yourself a cab, then." Monica started back into the building, then turned to look back at him. "When's your next home game?"

"Friday."

"Get me the same seats, and I'll be there."

Eric felt his heart leap. "You'd do that, even though you're pissed at me?"

She wouldn't look at him. "It means a lot to me that you tried to defend me to Desiree, even though your behavior was out of line and you mortified me. But," she added, "if you win the game, do not think I'm going to every home game you play." She began walking away from him. "Call me," she called over her shoulder as she ducked back inside.

"I will."

Alone on the street now, Eric hailed a cab, sliding into the backseat. He didn't know what to think. Or to feel. But he did feel something; something *new*, and it frightened him.

"Yo, Mitcho. I'm hearing wedding bells."

Eric looked up from lacing up his skates to see Ulf Torkel-son approaching him with a huge grin, waving a copy of *Soap World* magazine.

"Huh?"

Ulf waved the magazine in front of his face. "Your lovely lady seems to be planting seeds."

Eric snatched the magazine from him, his eyes immediately drawn to the picture of Monica sitting up on a dais. He skimmed the text. "Fan club luncheon . . . blah, blah, blah . . ." And then he found what Ulf was referring to. "When asked about her red-hot romance with hockey star Eric Mitchell, Monica told the crowd they were 'taking it one day at a time,' before adding coyly, 'but who knows where it might go?' "

Eric handed the magazine back to Ulf with a shrug.

"C'mon, buddy, admit it," Ulf goaded with a slap on the back. "She's got you roped and tied."

"Eric Mitchell, the ultimate bachelor, totally whipped," Tully Webster chimed in. "Who'd have ever thought?"

"Man, to wake up beside that body every morning for the rest of my life," Barry Fontaine said enviously. "You're one lucky bastard, Mitcho."

She's more than just a pair of tits and a pretty face, Eric wanted to retort, surprising himself, since that was precisely how he'd always thought of her until recently. "I have no idea what the hell she's talking about," Eric maintained gruffly.

"Yeah, right," said Ulf with a snort.

"I'm serious."

"Then I guess you better talk to her, because it sure as hell sounds to me as if she's hinting at matrimony."

Eric stood, avoiding his brother's eyes. He knew Jason was listening closely to everything being said, which meant Eric would soon find himself on the hot seat. *What the hell are you doing, Monica?* He thought. It was beginning to feel like this thing was spiraling out of control, and if there was one thing Eric cherished, it was control.

She was at Met Gar tonight. He'd gotten her the tickets she wanted, same seats, except this time, she didn't have Gloria with her, but Jimmy the director. Eric assumed Jimmy was a fan, so he'd probably be able to explain to Monica what was happening on the ice, if she even cared. Even though she'd requested ice-level seats, he wondered if he shouldn't have told her to go up in the skybox with Delilah instead. She and Monica liked each other, and now that Delilah was a fan, she'd be able to explain the game to Monica, probably in simpler terms than Jimmy would. Well, if she ever attended another game, that's where he'd suggest she sit. It would be more comfortable, and she'd still get attention. The announcers frequently noted who filled the boxes; she could easily wave to any cameras trained on her from there.

They'd talked once on the phone since the party, but their conversation was brief. That whole party experience had shocked him. The Monica she presented to the world was confident and no-nonsense; she could certainly dish it out to him when she felt it was called for. But the Monica he'd witnessed talking to Desiree was another person entirely, uncertain and willing to be bullied. Things were getting complicated. He didn't do complicated.

"This is a surprise."

Despite having told Eric she'd be leaving the minute the game ended, Monica had changed her mind. It was Friday night; she didn't have to work tomorrow. And Jimmy had explained to her that Eric had played well. Besides, she was thrilled by the reception she'd gotten from the crowd. During a break in the second period, they showed her on the scoreboard screen, and she waved. Then, in a television time-out in the third period, the crowd started chanting. It started as a low, rhythmic hum she couldn't make out. Then it got clearer and louder as more and more fans picked up the chant: Mo-ni-ca, Mo-ni-ca, Mo-ni-ca! And when they showed her face on the scoreboard again, and the crowd cheered, she laughed and waved. She was in heaven.

She wished she hadn't gone back to the party the other night. Desiree sent icy vibes her way the rest of the evening, and as other classmates spoke of their plays and auditions, she'd gotten more and more depressed. Eric's excoriation had stuck with her. Why did she let Desiree put her down?

She was glad Eric looked pleased when he found her waiting in the Green Room. "I thought you said you'd be making a run for it the minute the final buzzer sounded."

"It's Friday. I don't have to work tomorrow."

He had just emerged from the shower. He was freshly shaved, his blond, wet hair combed back. Faded jeans hugged his body, topped by a simple white button-down oxford shirt. He looked sexy as hell, but then again, when didn't he? Perhaps they'd share a kiss. Maybe it was time to admit to him she wanted the relationship to become real.

She noticed a lot of the other players eyeing Eric with envy, which was good, she supposed. Some of their wives asked for her autograph, which she gladly gave. Eric looked on proudly as she scribbled and chatted with them. But was it real Eric or fake Eric?

She shook the thoughts clear of her head. "It's a beautiful night," she said to him. "What if we cab part of the way uptown and then walk the rest?"

Eric swung his gym bag up onto his shoulder and shrugged affably. "Sounds good to me."

They'd chatted easily as they walked along, Monica demonstrating to him all she'd learned about hockey. Which of course brought them immediately to the good luck charm issue.

"You might not want to hear this," he began gingerly, "but your being there tonight—"

"Brought you good luck," Monica finished for him with a

heavy sigh. "Here's the deal: I can go to home games on Friday and Saturday nights, unless something else comes up." She didn't want him thinking she had no life outside work apart from masquerading with him and visiting Monty, even though that was the case these days. "Otherwise, no."

Eric's jaw set. "But what if—"

"Deal with it, big boy."

Eric laughed. "I guess I have no choice." He glanced at her curiously. "Where was *that* Monica the other night? The one who just put me in my place? Why didn't that Monica deal with Desiree?"

It was a good question. "I don't know," she admitted shyly.

"Worth thinking about."

"I know."

They rounded the corner of Monica's street, and she abruptly halted. There, standing right outside her building, was Rennie, a man she'd had to take out a restraining order against three months ago, a crazy, menacing fan who'd sent her threatening letters and once told her to her face that if she didn't accept the fact they were meant to be together in this life, he'd see to it they were together in the next life, and soon. A streak of rage flew through her before her heart began pounding with fear; why the hell hadn't Gene the doorman called the cops?

"What is it?" Eric asked. He'd picked up immediately on her distress.

"See that guy up there? The one who keeps pacing back and forth?"

Eric's eyes zeroed in on the guy. "Yeah."

"He's a psycho fan of mine. I have a restraining order against him. He's threatened me."

Eric's expression darkened. "Let's just try to walk past him into the building and ignore him. I'm sure he's not going to try anything while I'm with you."

Monica gripped Eric's hand tightly as they began walking toward her building. With each step Monica could feel her panicked heart jolting higher and higher, until finally it was in her mouth. Thank God Eric was there. If she'd had to try to breeze past Rennie alone, the terror would have been almost unbearable.

They were at the building now.

"Monica," Rennie said softly. "I got the wedding rings. Do you want to see them?"

"Keep walking," Eric commanded.

"Monica, don't ignore me," Rennie crooned in a menacing voice, following them closely. "You know what might happen—"

"Listen up, asshole." Eric's bag fell off his shoulder as he turned and grabbed Rennie by the lapels, shoving him up against the apartment building wall. "Get inside," he barked at Monica. "I'll be in, in a minute."

Frozen with panic, Monica found herself unable to move. What if this lunatic had a knife or gun and hurt Eric?

Eric was pinning Rennie so hard he was yelping in pain. Monica looked down. Rennie's feet were off the ground.

"Listen, asshole: If you ever—*ever*—go near Monica again—whether she's here, or at the studio, or just out in the city—I will murder you, but only after putting you through so much pain you'll be begging me to kill you anyway. Do you understand?"

Rennie nodded but said nothing.

"Do you fucking understand?" Eric yelled in his face, pulling him away from the wall, then smashing him into it again.

"I hear you," Rennie spluttered. "Now let go of me."

Eric turned to Monica. "Get inside."

Monica reflexively reacted to the command but turned back as soon as she got inside the glass doors. She saw Eric head butt Rennie, drop him to the ground, and then stand over him, yelling. Rennie rose up, bleeding from the nose, and ran down the street. Eric pulled out a handkerchief, wiped his forehead and hands, and then calmly picked up his bag and walked into the lobby.

"Thank you," Monica said, unexpected tears of relief suddenly springing to her eyes. "I don't know if I could have coped if I had to deal with him on my own."

"It was no problem."

"That's twice you've defended me," she sniffled.

"That's just the kind of guy I am."

"Don't do that, Eric," she said quietly. "Don't deflect."

Eric didn't respond and instead looked down at the ground for a moment. He raised his head, looking around the quiet street. "You need to report this to the cops."

"I know. I'll do it tomorrow morning. I promise."

"I guess I should be going home."

"Don't," Monica begged. "I—I'm still a little shaken up. Would you mind coming upstairs for a while and just staying with me until I feel better?"

"Sure."

Holding on to Eric's arm for security, they went up to her apartment.

Monica checked the locks on her door—twice—and went around pulling down all the shades in her apartment. Even the blinking light on her answering machine made her feel vulnerable. Suppose Rennie had somehow managed to get her phone number? Still shaken, she braved playing her messages back. One was from Gloria, asking if she wanted to go to the movies. The other was from Monty, wondering when he'd see her. He sounded sheepish and subdued; perhaps he realized what an ass he'd been to her at *W and F* that day and was ready to apologize.

Eric had shed his coat and his gym bag and was sitting on her couch. "You okay?" he asked worriedly.

"I'm getting better." She licked her lips, nervously glancing back in the direction of the kitchen. "Do you want anything to drink?"

"No."

"Me, either." She moved toward the couch, wondering, *How close do I sit to him, now that it's just us, alone, being real?* She decided to sit right beside him. Eric didn't move away. "Thank you again," she repeated as he put a hand on her arm to still her.

"You don't need to keep thanking me. Any guy would have done the same."

"I don't know about that."

Tentative, Monica laid her head on his shoulder. She felt Eric stiffen, but then he seemed to relax, putting his arm around her.

"We need to talk," he said, sounding serious.

Monica took a deep breath. "Okay."

"Did you tell the soap press we were on the verge of being engaged?"

"No," Monica said evenly. "I teased them a little bit, hinting at a possible long-term future. That's all."

The answer seemed to satisfy Eric, at least for now.

"Now I need to ask you a question," said Monica as her mouth suddenly went dry.

"Okay." Eric turned to look at her. She wished he didn't. It would be so much easier to ask if his eyes weren't that deep, piercing blue that made her wilt—those eyes that could devastate her if she didn't get the answer she wanted to hear.

"The other night, when you said, 'You have me'?" she asked tentatively. "What did you mean? And don't say you meant we were friends. Because you and I both know that on a certain level, that's bullshit."

Hunger stole into Eric's eyes, taking her breath away. "It meant I want you," he admitted, his voice turning into a tortured rasp. "Right here. Right now."

Monica's mind flashed back to the sexual dream she'd had about him months back, the one where she begged him to fuck her on the couch. *That's what I want now,* she thought, as heat burned its way through her body. She knew that Eric's primary language when it came to women was sex, so that was the language she'd speak to him in, even if she couldn't manage to get out the words she longed to say. She'd never been able to talk dirty.

"I want you, too," she whispered back. "Right here. Right now."

Eric groaned, pulling her onto his lap so she was straddling him, kissing her hard. The power of his mouth clamping down on hers, the heady sensation of her thighs tightly pressed to the outside of his, made her head swim. She'd tasted him before, but not like this, not with the naked lust they were both feeling so blatantly exposed. It was a kiss she didn't want to end, one she'd waited months for without even knowing it. Eric's groans were soft, almost secret. She felt his hardness rising against her, saw his eyes watching her to see if she noticed. To make absolutely sure what she wanted.

It surprised her, then, when she was the one who finally tore her mouth from his. Monica wanted to hold his face in her hands, feel his bones and skin beneath her fingers the way an artist feels and then molds clay. Her fingertips went to his face, first caressing softly, then a little firmer, memorizing the shape and feel of it. She looked down at Eric; his eyes were hooded and dark, watchful. Wanting. Bold, she was the one who lowered her mouth to his this time. The hunger she felt there seared her mouth as she nipped at his lips, pushing her tongue inside. For the first time ever, Monica felt powerful, like she was the one in control.

Pushing up against her with a small groan, Eric took a fistful of her hair and gently pulled her head back as he barely kissed her throat, his short breaths tickling her skin. Monica opened her mouth to moan, but she couldn't. For now, she'd been robbed of speech and sound. When his mouth began gently biting, a want so deep wound through Monica that she feared she might lose control before they even really started.

Gasping with pleasure, Monica forced her head forward to look at him. Eric's eyes were fastened on her face, a storm blowing up in those sapphire blues of his. "Tell me what you want," he commanded low, his breath as fast and shallow as her own.

Monica swallowed, forcing the power of speech to return to her. "You."

Eric grabbed her wrist as he'd done before, and again, she felt her skin burn. "No," he said gruffly. "Be specific. So I can make it good for you."

Monica blinked her eyes, as much in shock as with quickening excitement. No lover had ever offered this to her before. For a split second she felt shy. But the feeling sizzled away as a burgeoning wantonness began snaking its way through her.

"I want you to tear off my blouse."

Eric slowly released her wrist, his hands gliding up her arms to grasp her shoulders hard, maybe even leaving little bruises, his mark. Monica held her breath and closed her eyes. The anticipation of it, the intensity of the need beginning to build inside her, was creeping its way toward unbearable. Eric's strong, sure grip on her shoulders seemed to be going on forever. But then suddenly, he grabbed the lapels of her blouse and ripped, the sound of the tear like the rending of the heavens, and Monica knew in that moment what it was to teeter on the edge of danger, understood the thrilling subcurrent of violence that could walk hand in hand with lust.

Her breath was coming in short, staccato bursts as she waited impatiently for his hands to start roaming over her flesh and his mouth to fasten itself to her breast. But Eric did nothing; instead, he sat back, watching her, his smile a tease.

"Now what?" he whispered.

Monica's breath hitched. She kept her eyes locked on his, her body taut with want. "I-I want you take my blouse off, and my bra, and . . . kiss my breasts."

Languid enough to cause her delicious agony, Eric slid her blouse off her shoulders, sparks raining down on Monica's skin as the silky garment fell from her arms. Eric's hands circled her small waist, pressing hard, his fingertips running up and down her back before he began caressing her sides. It was a sweet eternity before he finally reached around to unclasp her bra and free her. Monica felt a jolt between her legs as blood began beating its way through her body. Eric paused again, drinking her in.

"Do you know how long I've dreamed about this?" he asked, his tortured gaze devouring her body. Monica shivered, the feeling reminding her of having a fever followed by a breeze gliding over her body. Hot and cool at the same time.

"Please," she heard herself begging.

Eric inhaled sharply, peeling off her bra and tossing it aside as he'd done with her blouse. She could feel him pulsing and twitching beneath her, his erection straining against his jeans. *Slow,* Monica told herself, restraining herself from rocking and pressing her body tightly against his. *Let it build slow; enjoy being wanted this way.*

She sat tall, reading him, momentarily surprised when he tenderly reached out a hand to tuck a loose strand of her hair behind the delicate shell of her ear before his hands came to her breasts. Rubbing. Touching. Brushing the pads of his thumbs over her hardened nipples as Monica whimpered with pleasure. When Eric's hands stopped moving, she almost stopped breathing. Then her breath did come to an unexpected halt as his head came forward, and he began suckling her, hard. Monica arched back, unable to stop herself from pushing herself deeper into his mouth as she lost the battle against rocking against him, her hands on his shoulders for support. Eric's groans were beginning to sound desperate, enflaming her even more. He seemed so greedy for her, so hungry, as his teeth nipped at her, and his tongue flicked.

He jerked his head and looked at her, his breath ragged. "More?"

Monica shook her head no. Any more stimulation of her breasts, and she would climax now, and she didn't want that. She wanted to feel his mouth elsewhere—on her collarbone, openmouthed on her ribs. She told him so—directly, easily, with no hesitation. And then, again, she waited.

She thought he would plant kisses up and down her torso. Lick at her sides like a cat. But instead he bit her torso—not hard, but tantalizing enough to induce delirium. Small gasps tumbled from deep inside her, coming faster and faster as he tilted her back, unbuttoning the top button of her jeans and pulling down the fly so he could nip lower on her belly. Monica writhed beneath his touch, her hands leaving his shoulders to grip his hips, hard. When he reached a hand down the front of her panties to part her and explore with his fingers, Monica heard a roaring rush in her head, so loud it drowned out the sounds of her own pleasured screams as she climaxed, digging her nails into the sides of his legs, bucking with pleasure.

She came to slowly, looking at him dazedly. "You" was all she could say, dragging his mouth to hers..

Wide-eyed, moaning into her mouth, Eric lifted her up

high so there was no contact between them save his hands on her waist, allowing Monica to hurriedly shimmy out of her pants and panties and kick them free. Monica eagerly settled back down on him, her fingers flying as she opened his shirt. She ran her hands over his heated skin in amazement, licked at his nipples that tasted faintly of sweat. She moved to press her chest against his, reveling in the contrast of hard and soft, but Eric gently held her off for a moment so he could free himself of his shirt. Neither of them seemed able to tear their eyes from the other now. *No secrets,* Monica thought. *No hiding.* The denim of his jeans beneath her naked thighs felt rough; she wanted him free of them, to feel him fully naked beneath her. Desperation making her almost clumsy, she began fumbling with the zipper of his jeans.

"Hold on," Eric said hoarsely, reaching into his back pocket and pulling out a condom.

"Please tell me you haven't been carrying that around since high school," Monica said.

They laughed together, the comfortable laughter of friends who have now become lovers. Monica crawled off him a moment so Eric could free himself of the remainder of his clothing. He was naked now, completely unselfconscious. Monica reached out to caress his erection, and Eric's head fell back with a groan.

"Don't," he begged. "I'm about to explode as it is."

A ripple of delight ran through Monica. She was thrilled she could prompt such a reaction. She watched hungrily as he put on protection and then pulled her back atop him, holding her hips high.

"We're gonna do this slow," he murmured sexily.

Monica held her breath as he lowered her onto him—but not all the way. She looked at him in surprise.

"Slow," he commanded.

Monica nodded, closing her eyes, letting him control the rhythm. It was making her crazy—riding him, but not fully, not deeply. But gradually, as her skin grew slicker with sweat, as she wrapped herself around him and squeezed harder and harder, that began to change. Up she rose, and then Eric pulled her back down, hard, driving into her fully.

Monica gasped, lightning crashing in her head as she, of her own volition, began pumping wildly atop him, setting the pace. Eric threw his head back again, the corded muscles of his throat betraying the self-control she knew he was exercising. Every time she rose up and slammed herself back down on him to take him inside, she felt a bit more of her consciousness being punched away. She wanted burning oblivion. She rode him harder and harder until finally, her body rose up one final time in furor and a second climax ripped through her seconds before Eric's own. Eric shuddered beneath her, his release feeding hers as they shared a relaxation of muscle and mind. Panting, Monica rested her fevered forehead against his, waiting for her breath to return to normal. She might not have said the words she'd longed to say, but her dream had come true.

FIFTEEN

They'd moved to the bed. She'd asked him to spend the night, and he'd agreed, and now they were lying there, entwined, silent but close. Monica was afraid to talk and break the spell. Eventually, though, his silence began to alarm her.

"You okay?" she asked, smoothing back some hair from his face.

Eric nodded. "Yeah, I'm just, you know . . ."

No, she didn't know. "What?" she made herself ask gently.

Eric was quiet a long time. "I'm kind of confused."

"Why?"

"Because I—my history with women . . ." He shook his head. "I'm not explaining this very well."

"Want me to explain it for you?" Monica offered.

Eric looked guarded. "Sure."

"You've never had sex that meant anything to you before. And what we just shared meant something. You fantasized about me for years, but the woman you fantasized about was just that: a fantasy. Now you know me and want me—the real me—and it scares you." She searched his face. "Am I right?"

Eric rolled on his back with a sigh, looking up at the ceiling. "Yes. But it's more than that. It's the expectations that go with what just happened."

Monica rested her chin on his shoulder. "What do you mean?"

Eric turned his head to look at her. "You want to define this as a 'relationship' now, right?" There was distress in his eyes.

"I guess," Monica said cautiously, afraid of saying the wrong thing.

Eric scrubbed his hands over his face. "I do care about you—the real you," he admitted. "But I don't know if I can be what you want me to be. I don't know how to *do* that."

"What is 'that'? Be a real boyfriend? Have you ever tried?"

"No, because it's never interested me." He rolled toward her, running a finger up and down her shoulder. "Can we just keep this simple for now?"

"What does *simple* mean? Just have sex and tell ourselves we're just getting off on each other?"

Eric drew back, stung. "No, of course not. Just take it one day at a time, without any expectations or preconceived notions of where we want it to go."

"Because you're afraid of where it will go," Monica said tersely. "Because you want an easy out in case you want to dump me."

"No." Eric gripped her shoulders tightly. "Tell me: Do *you* know where you want it to go?"

Monica hesitated. Did she know? She wasn't imagining herself walking down the aisle with him or moving in with him. She was simply imagining them having what they had now, maintaining the new emotional connection that existed between them, with wonderful sex thrown into the mix as well.

"No," she said quietly.

"Well, there you go, then."

"It's not that simple, Eric," she insisted.

Eric's jaw set. "It has to be. Simple is what I do, Monica. Simple and uncomplicated."

"Forever?"

"I don't know," he said with a deep exhalation of frustration. "See, this is what I'm talking about. I'm feeling pinned down here, and I don't like it."

Monica blinked. "Okay, let me make sure I'm getting this straight: we're going to have a real relationship, but we're not going to call it that, because you can't handle that definition."

"I guess," Eric murmured, looking uncomfortable.

"So you think having a real relationship, not calling it that to ourselves, but acting to the outside world like we're having a real relationship, is simple and uncomplicated?" Monica asked.

"I don't know," Eric snapped.

"And what happens if it gets more and more intense?"

"I can't think about that right now. That's where the 'take it day by day' comes in."

Monica thought. "Okay," she eventually capitulated. "If that's what you need to do, then okay."

Even as her mouth was forming the words, she wondered if she was now compromising herself personally, just as she did professionally. Why should he get to set the terms? Wasn't she entitled to at least *some* expectations? She could tell this was the real Eric: he wasn't just handing her a line of bull; laissez-faire *was* all he could handle right now. He'd admitted he cared. For someone who'd spent his entire life doing nothing more than bagging babes until they bored him and he moved on, this was progress. Monica sensed that if she pushed him, he'd bolt, and she didn't want that. *Patience,* she told herself and settled back peacefully in his arms.

"I don't appreciate this torture."

Monica ignored Monty's comment as she walked with him slowly around the Pond in Central Park. As usual, she'd found him holed up in his apartment, growling at the TV in his musty bedroom. Barking like a drill sergeant, she instructed him to get dressed because she was taking him out.

Monty issued his standard protest, but it stemmed more from tradition than any genuine resistance. She could tell he was glad to see her.

It was a lovely Sunday, the sun dappling the swaying leaves on the trees as well as glinting magically off the water. The episode of *W and F* featuring Monty had aired recently.

"Did you watch yourself on my show this week?"

Monty gave a pained shake of the head. "Awful. A rote, wooden performance, just as they demanded of me. I hope to God no one I know watched it."

"I bet you liked the nice, fat check you got for one minute's work, though."

Monty just grunted.

She'd come to the conclusion that Eric was right: it was time to show some backbone. She decided to broach the topic of Monty's disdain for what she did.

"I know you probably don't mean to," she said, "but it hurts me when you put down daytime. It's how I make my living."

Monty said nothing.

"You say it's compromising my talent, yet when I came to you to fill in—"

"That was for one day," Monty interrupted sharply. "There's a difference between compromising for one day and compromising for a decade."

"I'm not sure I agree," Monica said bravely. She took a deep breath. "And I also think you owe me an apology for your behavior on the set that day."

Monty seemed to get very still despite their strolling the lake. This was probably the first time in all these years that she'd ever challenged him. Maybe *challenge* was too strong a word; perhaps *disagreed* was better. The first time she'd ever disagreed with him. How sad was that?

"I saved this for you," was Monty's response. He reached into the pocket of his coat, pulling out the print edition of *Back Stage*. "I think you should audition. You'd be perfect for it. You could keep your day job and display your true talent at night."

Monica took the paper and unfolded it. Circled was a casting call for a new play opening on Broadway written by one of England's top playwrights. The producers were looking for "tall, blonde women between the ages of thirty and thirty-five, capable of doing an impeccable, upper-class British accent. Agented submissions only, please." Monica could do a British accent in her sleep. In fact, she was adept at a multitude of accents: Irish, Scottish, Cockney, Australian, French, American South, New England Yankee . . . mimicry was a gift she'd had since she was a small child.

Monica swallowed. "Thank you for thinking of me."

"Auditions are on Friday."

"Yes, I see that."

"Promise me you'll go."

She wanted to but found she couldn't. Her life wasn't that simple anymore. Her job was demanding, and now that she was in a whatever-you-wanted-to-call-it with Eric, she had even less time to play with. Excuses, excuses. What if she auditioned and didn't make the cut? She appreciated Monty's belief in her, but after ten years of not having to audition, she feared she'd be rusty. Still, this could be her chance to prove the depth of her talent. She thanked Monty again, folded the paper, and continued at a snail's pace with him around the Pond. Later, she thought she heard him say, "And I'm sorry," under his breath as she was leaving his apartment, but she couldn't be sure.

"Balls to the lot of them."

The vehemence in Gloria's voice did nothing to assuage Monica's pain as she lay with her head in the older woman's lap, winding down from a crying jag. Despite her trepidation, she'd decided to audition for the play. She'd aced the upper-crust British accent the producers desired. When she was called back to read two days later, she half allowed herself the thought that she might get the part.

The ensuing two days, spent waiting for her agent, Renee, to call with news, were torturous. The minute the phone rang and she heard the deliberately measured tone of Renee's voice, she knew she'd been rejected. "They thought you were great, Monica," Renee assured her, before adding after a slight hesitation, "but they didn't want to cast a soap actress. They were afraid the production wouldn't be taken seriously."

Monica's first reaction was fury. Why couldn't she be seen simply as an actress, not a "soap actress"? If she had the chops, what did it matter? Jesus Christ, it wasn't like she'd been earning a living doing porno films for the past ten years!

Her anger was short-lived. She segued quickly into despair and self-doubt, followed by utter devastation. She sucked. She shouldn't have tried to stretch herself. She would always and forever be Monica Geary from *W and F*. The soap opera actress. She knew there were worse brushes to be tarred with. But it still hurt.

Her first impulse was to call Eric. But as she dialed his number, she realized she needed to talk to someone who could understand her anguish. And so she sought out Gloria.

"You have to understand," Gloria said, stroking Monica's hair as they sat together on the couch in Gloria's flower-filled living room. "Not only is the industry competitive, but they like to put actors in nice, tidy boxes where they're easily definable. So this one is labeled a character actress, and that one is branded the kooky best friend, and this one over here is Mr. Action-Adventure. Try to do something different, and the powers that be—idiots that they are—become spooked. 'What if I can't sell this person in this new role?' is all they can think. They're terrified of risk."

"But if you've got the talent—"

"It doesn't matter."

"But other actors have made the jump from soaps to movies. Or the stage."

"My angel," said Gloria, cupping Monica's cheek, "for every Meg Ryan, there are one hundred other actors who leave daytime and find themselves starving or offered the most insulting roles imaginable. Why do you think so many return?"

Monica swallowed, closing her eyes. "I know. I just thought—"

"You'd finally be taken seriously?"

"Yes," Monica whispered.

"Sit up."

Monica did as Gloria said, rubbing her eyes, which now felt raw.

"You are taken seriously," said Gloria sternly. "Your peers take you seriously. Your fans take you seriously. Don't you realize that until you stop letting *others* define success, you're never going to be happy?"

Monica glanced away, not knowing what to say. She knew Gloria was right.

"I know that the way you're feeling right now, you probably won't give a tinker's damn about this," Gloria continued, "but I wanted to show you something, just in case you hadn't seen it."

Gloria picked up the latest issue of *Soap World* and handed it to Monica. There were two pages of polls, ranking favorite characters for each of the shows. Monica was ranked the number one character on *W and F*, followed by Gloria, and then Royce. Chesty was sixth.

Monica looked up at Gloria. "Okay, that does help," she admitted with the hint of a smile.

"Especially since Titty LaRue didn't even make the top three."

Monica laughed.

"Feel better?"

"A bit."

"Still going hot and heavy with that ice boy of yours?"

Monica blushed. "Yes." Hot and heavy was the perfect way to describe it. Her patience ploy seemed to be working; it sometimes felt like she and Eric couldn't get enough of each other, both in and out of bed. She was now a fixture at, at least one Blades' home game a week, her name chanted with such affection by the fans that she always left the arena touched. She still got the sense that Eric was holding her at arm's length emotionally, but he'd come a long way. Even so, there was no way she was going to risk telling him she loved him. He was going to have to say it first.

"Why aren't you with him tonight?" Gloria asked.

"His team is away, playing on the West Coast."

"Then let's you and I go out and wreak havoc," Gloria said with a wicked glint in her eye.

"What do you have in mind?"

"Anything that doesn't involve my potentially breaking my hip."

Monica chuckled. "C'mon. I'm sure we can figure something out."

"Talk to Mom and Dad lately?"

The cautious tone in his brother's voice got Eric's full attention as they sat at the Blades' favorite bar, the Chapter House, nursing beers. Up until now, Eric had only been half listening anyway, his mind preoccupied with Monica. The press was still eating up their relationship, which was great. He was playing well, in part, he was sure, because she was his good luck charm. But their day-by-day thing had turned into a month-by-month thing, complete with "real" couple activities, like hanging around the apartment (usually hers) in their sweats watching TV and eating pizza, or else hanging out with Jason and Delilah at *their* apartment, doing much the same thing. He knew she was falling in love with him, and it was freaking him out. So were some other things that he didn't care to explore too closely. Too bad he couldn't talk to anyone about it.

Eric took a bite of a stale pretzel, chasing it with a sip of beer. "Dad left me a message, but I haven't had a chance to call him back yet."

"Well, I talked to him last night." Jason looked grim. "He and Mom turned down our offer for more money."

Eric blinked. "Are you kidding me?"

"They said it was stupid, pouring that kind of money into a failing venture. They said we needed to keep our money for 'our future.'"

"Did you remind them of how much money we make?"

Jason frowned. "Of course I did. But you know Mom and Dad."

"What happened to the farm being in the family for three generations and all that?" Eric heard the rising panic in his voice. He couldn't believe what an emotional subject this was for him.

"I think they're just tired," Jason continued with a sigh. "Dad mentioned selling and he and Mom buying an RV and driving around the country in it."

Eric could picture it. He'd never seen two people who got along as well as his parents, even after all these years. Sometimes the affection between them even made him uncomfortable. He and Jason recently had a really uncomfortable conversation about whether their folks still "did it," a discussion they both swore never to repeat.

"An RV," Eric mused. "They'd like that."

"Anyway"—Jason took a long pull on his beer—"Delilah and I came up with an idea."

"Yeah?"

"We're going to buy the farm from Mom and Dad."

"What?"

"Hear me out," Jason said quickly, as if he were fearful Eric's gut reaction would be negative. "You know Delilah loves it out there. It could be our summer home—of course, you and Monica would be welcome to use the house whenever you wanted, too. We'd pay Mom and Dad way above the market value of the house, the cattle, and the equipment. They'd be in a really great financial position—*and* the land would remain in the family. What do you think?"

Eric mulled it over. "I think it's a great idea."

"Are you upset?" Jason asked, looking at him with concern.

"No, of course not." Eric paused. "Well, maybe a little. I'd like to feel like I was doing something more to help out. I grew up there, too, you know," Eric reminded him testily as he reached for another stale pretzel.

"I didn't mean to insult you," Jason apologized.

Eric clapped him on the back. "You didn't. Honestly. You just took me by surprise."

"I know."

"What if Mom and Dad won't go for it?"

"I think they will," said Jason, finishing the last pretzel in the bowl and holding it up for the bartender to refill. "Especially if Delilah suggests it to them. They think Delilah walks on water. Monica, too," he added significantly.

Eric ignored the comment, draining his beer.

"You two seem to be getting very serious," Jason continued. Eric just nodded.

"I have to say, I never thought I'd see you in a serious relationship, you know?"

Eric forced a smile.

"You guys up for a movie Thursday night?"

"Can't. I have to go to that charity ball for Ronald McDonald House, remember?"

"Is the Mrs. coming?" Jason teased.

Eric leveled him with an irked look. "Don't push it, okay?"

"Jesus, Eric, lighten up." Jason threw a crumpled wad of bills on the bar. "So you're definitely okay with the house purchase?"

"Let's go in halves. That way I'll feel like I'm doing something."

"No problem," said Jason.

"You know, there aren't many people I know who want a summer place in North Dakota."

"It's the right thing to do."

"Totally," said Eric. "I just hope Mom and Dad agree."

Eric was one of the few Blades who actually enjoyed attending charity dinners. He knew he looked great in a tux, and he was always up for superficial glad-handing and schmoozing. But tonight he was in no mood to don his humanitarian persona. The Blades' road trip had been a disaster, the team losing three out of four games. He'd played like crap.

He knew he'd been unusually quiet on the ride with Monica to the Four Seasons, where the dinner was being held. When she told him about not getting the part in the play because of her work in daytime, he'd expressed genuine outrage on her behalf, but he couldn't maintain it for long. Within seconds he sank back into his own misery, worried about being subpar on the ice, worried about his parents' plight. "I'm sorry," he told her, meaning it. "I'm just in a bad mood tonight. I'm sure I'll snap out of it once we get inside."

Unfortunately, he didn't. They usually split up to mingle at these functions. But not tonight; tonight Monica was glued to his side, beaming at him with love that was all too real. Of course he was proud to be seen with her, but tonight's Velcro act was making him feel smothered. He was actually relieved when she excused herself to go to the bathroom.

"Can I say something?" said Ulfie, the minute Monica left the Blades table.

"Shoot," said Eric.

"You're totally pussy whipped. It's like she's got you on a choke collar or something. Everywhere you go, she goes. You don't hang out with us that much anymore, dude. You're still an asshole, but you were a shitload more fun when you were a horn dog, my man." Ulf shook his head sadly.

This wasn't what Eric wanted to hear right now. He turned to Thad, who'd been listening while trying to build a series of pyramids out of all the drink straws littering the table. "What do you think? You agree with Ulfie?"

Thad nodded. "Yeah, it's like you're boring now that you're not Mr. Tomcat."

Eric began to panic. "You clowns don't get it, do you? It's not a serious relationship. It's just a status thing for me, same as every other hot chick I've ever bagged."

"Yeah, but you were always done with those other chicks pretty quick. This thing has been going on for months," noted Thad, giving up on his architectural efforts.

"Of course it has," said Eric, "because she's the hottest thing on two legs. What kind of an idiot would pass up that kind of opportunity? Admit it, she's the best piece of eye candy I've ever nailed, right?"

"You got that right," said Ulf.

"I don't *care* about her," Eric scoffed. "All that's mattered to me is that I've been banging Monica Geary. If I can keep getting laid by the most gorgeous woman in daytime, why not just let it roll on?"

Thad coughed uncomfortably, his eyes cutting quickly to the left. Eric turned. The hottest thing on two legs was standing not two feet away.

SIXTEEN

"Get the hell away from me."

Monica wanted to run. Sprint away from the asshole who'd just told his friends she was nothing more than a status symbol for him. Tear into the night and hop into the nearest cab, telling the driver to get her home as fast as he could so she could relieve her heaving stomach and puke her guts up. But she couldn't run; her heels were too high; she'd break her neck. So instead, she was storming away from Eric the best she could, but it wasn't fast enough; Eric caught her arm before she'd even reached the hotel's front doors.

"Monica, listen to me."

She jerked her arm from his light grasp. "I just did, you asshole."

She wouldn't look at him, because she knew what she'd see in those blue eyes: the false bullshit sincerity he'd been laying on her for months. She could hear his voice in her head: *Of course I care about you—the real you.* Fuck him. She'd talked herself into believing he cared about her, Monica Geary the woman, when all he cared about was Monica Geary the image. She wished she could spit in his face. Truly. She would never forgive Theresa for suggesting this little ruse, never. And she would never forgive herself for thinking she could be the one to change him. Surprise, surprise: superficial Eric was the *real* Eric; caring Eric was the part he played. Some student of human behavior she was.

"All I ask is a minute," Eric begged.

"Why? So you can hand me some line of bullshit and tell me that what you told your friends wasn't true?" She felt herself becoming tearful and suppressed it. She was an actress, goddammit. She would cover her pain with anger and indignation.

"I exaggerated to my friends. I had to save face with them."

"And what a job you did of it," Monica sneered. "Throwing me under the bus, making me look like some kind of desperate loser."

"I apologize for that," Eric said sincerely.

Monica snorted. "You think I care?"

"I know you do." He looked like he felt sorry for her. She wondered what would happen if she kicked him in the balls, watching him crumple in pain and humiliation right there in the lobby. God knows he deserved it.

"You are such a jerk, you know that?" She was talking louder than she intended. Heads were beginning to turn. She concentrated on lowering her voice; the last thing she needed was a story in the press about her having a hissy fit.

"This is over," Monica declared. "You've saved face. Now get the hell *away* from me."

"I never meant to hurt you," Eric insisted softly. Monica suppressed a flinch of pain as she watched the expression on his face change from sincere to defensive. "We entered this purely as a business agreement, remember? I shouldn't have let it go any further."

"Oh, right, I forgot," Monica replied sarcastically. "When you told me you cared about me, the real me, that was just an act, right? Even though there was no public there to witness it. Gotcha."

"We'd agreed at the beginning it would end at some point," Eric continued.

"And now it has," Monica shot back airily. "So why don't

you go back inside to your stupid jock friends and tell them another lie: that you just dumped me, when in reality, I just dumped you."

Eric paused. "I think we should tell Theresa to tell the press it was mutual."

"Fuck you, Eric."

His mouth fell open in indignation. "You think I'm gonna let you say you dumped me? No way."

Monica shrugged like she didn't care. "Lie. I mean, you do it so well. Tell the press you dumped me. And I'll counter and say I dumped you. And the press will just lap it up, won't they? Lots of headlines, the kind we both love, saying the split is acrimonious. Who really dumped whom? they'll speculate. Was one of them having an affair? Can we get one of them to talk? Eric the puck-passing stud, on the loose again. Who'll be his next conquest?"

"Monica—"

"Good-bye, Eric. When your hockey career ends, you should seriously consider becoming an actor. Your powers of pretending are amazing."

She pushed through the glass doors of the lobby. Cabs were lined up at the curb outside the hotel. Monica hopped into the nearest one, pulling the door closed with a slam as she gave the cabbie her address. She'd never wept in the back of a cab, and she wasn't about to start now. She distracted herself by talking to the driver, who told her all about his father's failing mango farm in Bangalore and how he was saving up money to bring his whole family to the States. He'd had to leave his wife behind, and he missed her terribly. Monica wished the cabbie's tale put her own problems—so inane in comparison—in perspective, but it didn't. By the time she got home, she had a headache from clenching her jaw to hold back her tears. The headache was a blessing; she took two Valium, put on her favorite silk pajamas, and collapsed into bed, grateful for the rapidity with which her mind plummeted into darkness.

*   *   *

"Eric! What happened?"

Delilah was staring at him in utter and complete shock as she handed over a slice of pepperoni pizza. For two days, news of his split from Monica was all over the media, though it was deliberately vague, as Theresa had advised. She'd issued a statement saying the split was mutual, and that he and Monica wished each other all the best. Eric had been "no commenting" his head off. Monica was doing the same. It was all very polite and civilized.

His brother was staring at him across the kitchen table like he'd never seen anyone so pathetic, which Eric didn't appreciate. "What's your problem?" Eric asked sharply.

"You know what my problem is. You blew it, didn't you? All this 'The split was mutual' crap all over the press? It's bull, isn't it? You cut her loose, didn't you?"

Eric bit into his pizza, taking his time answering. He could still see himself standing in the lobby at the Four Seasons, shocked by how quickly Monica had pulled the plug and walked away. Well, what the hell else was she supposed to do? He'd expected to feel relief as she drove away in the cab, but he didn't. Instead, he felt hollow. It was just the shock of how they parted, he told himself. He squelched the feeling and went back to his teammates, raising a champagne toast to the return of Eric Mitchell, horn dog supreme.

"Well?" Jason pushed.

"Jason," Delilah chastised quietly. "Give him a chance."

"I dumped her," said Eric matter-of-factly.

"But why?" Delilah asked, frowning at her husband as he slipped a piece of pizza under the table to his Newf, Stanley. "You guys seemed so perfect together. And you seemed so happy."

"That's why he dumped her," Jason jeered. "Because things were getting too *real*."

Eric lowered his slice from his mouth. "What is with all this hostility?"

"Monica was great," said Jason.

"Yeah, I know, but—"

"Let me finish," said Jason with a glare.

Eric frowned. "Fine."

"And one of the reasons she was great was because she humanized you. She brought out your good side—the side very few people know exists, the one that isn't a womanizing dick."

Delilah looked uncomfortable. "That's a bit harsh, honey."

"You know it's true," Jason said. He looked at Eric contemptuously. "I guess you're going to go back to your studly ways, huh?"

Eric shrugged.

"You are one sad bastard."

"I want you to listen carefully to what I'm about to say, and if you ever breathe a word of this to anyone, I *will* kill you," Eric said in a controlled voice, tired of being abused. "My and Monica's relationship? The whole thing was an act."

"What the hell are you talking about?" Jason scoffed.

"The whole team was upset about losing Guy. No one was thrilled about my taking his place, as you may recall. I put my foot in my mouth by acting like a smug asshole on day one. I was sucking at practice. Meanwhile, the soap press was buzzing about that new actress on *W and F* unseating Monica."

"That blonde chick that sucks?"

"Yeah. Monica was panicking, so she went to Theresa Dante. After Monica told her we'd met on the set, Theresa suggested she raise her public profile by dating me. Remember all those articles at the beginning of the season about me being the hot new bachelor in town? And of course, the *People* magazine list—"

"Cut to the chase," Jason grumbled.

"So Theresa approached me, pointing out how mutually beneficial this would be to both of us. I knew the guys all loved Monica, and it would impress them if I were dating her, so I agreed. And that's all it's been: a fake relationship to keep both of us in the public eye."

"No way."

"Yes way."

Jason was shaking his head vehemently. "*No way.* What about at Mom and Dad's, with you guys in the same bed?"

"We made a barrier of pillows between us."

"Really?" Delilah asked, looking crestfallen.

Jason still wasn't buying it. "You're full of it. There's no way someone in a fake relationship could look at you the way she looked at you. The way she touched you."

"She's an *actress*, you idiot, remember? Sadly for her, though, she did come to develop feelings for me."

Jason looked scornful. "Oh, and I suppose you didn't develop any for her?"

"Nope," Eric garbled through a mouthful of pizza. "Total acting job on my part."

"God, you are so full of shit. You can't act."

"Yes, he can," Delilah pointed out quietly. "Remember when he posed as you and charmed my mother? He did a great job."

"Well, there's no way he could keep up an acting job like this for months," Jason insisted.

"Obviously, I'm more talented than you know," Eric replied cockily.

"Okay, so tell me this," said Jason, reaching down to give another piece of pizza to Stanley, but Delilah snatched it from his fingers before it reached the dog's jaws. "If this act was working out so well for you two, why end it?"

"I told you: she was beginning to get emotionally attached to me. You *know* me, Jace: I don't like to be tied down."

"Did you *ever* sleep with her?"

Eric grinned. "Hell, yeah."

"Doesn't make sense," Jason said more insistently than before. "Why would you be having sex if the whole romance wasn't real?"

"Ever hear the expression 'Friend with benefits'?"

Jason crossed his arms across his chest. "Bullshit, Eric. I'm your fucking twin. I know you like I know myself. It might have started as an act, but you cared for her."

"I agree," Delilah piped up. "You have feelings for her, and it's just like Jason said: you were getting nervous because it was getting 'real.'"

"Getting real for *her*," Eric maintained angrily. "I didn't want her to fall more deeply in love with me. I like her. I didn't want to hurt her."

"You're lying." Delilah picked a slice of pepperoni off her pizza and popped it in her mouth. "You two spent a lot of time here with us. You were not acting."

"Yes, I was," Eric maintained through gritted teeth.

"I'm never going to believe that," Delilah said stubbornly.

"That's your choice. But it's the truth."

"I'm with Delilah," said Jason. "You might be able to bullshit everyone else in the world, but you can't bullshit me."

Eric chuckled. "You know what I don't get about this, Jace? You were the one who, in the beginning, said you couldn't believe someone like Monica Geary would fall for a jackass like me. Now I'm here telling you the whole thing was bullshit, and you refuse to believe it. What's the deal?"

"She brought out the best in you, Eric." Jason turned serious. "I love you, Bro, and it bothers me you haven't found someone. It just seems sad."

"Maybe I think *your* fuckin' life is sad," Eric shot back. He quickly turned to Delilah. "I don't mean that. I'm just . . . I don't know." He stared at his brother. "Different people want different things."

"Whatever." Jason reached for another piece of pizza. "So, you going out tomorrow night with Ulf and Thad to pick up some bimbos?"

"Maybe."

"Same old Eric," Jason sneered.

"Leave him alone, Jason," said Delilah. She looked sad as she finished off her slice. "You know what's best for you," she said to Eric. "We love you. And we're here for you. But I'm really going to miss Monica."

SEVENTEEN

GRAYSON *(HOLDING ROXIE IN HIS ARMS): My own, sweet Roxie . . . I-I don't know how to tell you this.*
ROXIE: *What is it, my love?*
GRAYSON: *I-I've been unfaithful. I was drunk, I didn't know what I was doing—*
PAIGE *(BURSTING OUT FROM BEHIND THE LONG VELVET CURTAIN IN GRAYSON'S LIBRARY): Don't lie to her, Grayson! You knew exactly what you were doing!*
GRAYSON: *Paige! What are you doing here?*
PAIGE *(CLOSING IN ON GRAYSON AND ROXIE): I wanted Roxie to hear the truth, not the candy-coated version I knew you'd feed her (SMILES AT ROXIE TRIUMPHANTLY). Grayson and I are getting married, Roxie! I'm carrying his baby! And there's not a damn thing you can do about it!*
ROXIE *(GASPING AS SHE CLUTCHES THE BACK OF THE COUCH FOR SUPPORT): No . . . it can't be true . . . Oh, Grayson (FAINTS BEHIND THE COUCH).*

"Cut!"

Monica got up from behind the couch with a sigh, her eyes glancing up at the control booth to catch Jimmy's. He was frowning. He was always frowning these days. After all these months, Chesty still had the acting ability of a rock. Monica had heard through the grapevine that she was getting private coaching, but it didn't seem to be helping. Oh, well. If the popularity polls in *Soap World* were any indication, it wasn't Monica's problem.

"OMG, Monica. I can't believe you and Eric Mitchell are splitsville!"

When Sartre wrote, "Hell is other people," he wasn't kidding, Monica thought to herself as Chesty cornered her on the set. News of her and Eric's "amicable split" was being reported everywhere, with speculation running high as to why this "golden couple had called it quits," as the *Sentinel* so unimaginatively put it. Because of Eric's high profile as an athlete, they were even generating some chat on ESPN. The guys on *PTI* were debating whether Eric had been unable to change his womanizing ways. Months ago Monica would have been thrilled at the response. Now she just wanted the buzz to die down so she could get on with her life.

She'd allowed herself a one-day pity party of weeping, moping in her pajamas, and eating junk food. The next morning she resolved not to waste any more time and emotion on an asshole like Eric Mitchell. Instead of putting her heartbreak into exile, she'd channel it into work. It would come in handy now, especially since Roxie had just gotten the earth-shattering news that Paige was pregnant with Grayson's baby.

Chesty seemed to be holding her breath, anticipating, perhaps even longing for, some kind of emotional outburst from Monica. *You can hold your breath till your face turns blue,* thought Monica. *The day I let you see I'm upset is the day Burt Reynolds stops getting plastic surgery.*

"The split? No big deal," Monica said with a big yawn. "It happens."

"Yeah, but you guys seemed so—so in love," Chesty continued, as if she were really, truly stunned by Monica and

Eric's split. Unfortunately, her breathless shock was about as real as her breasts.

"It happens," Monica repeated. If Chesty didn't catch on at this point that Monica wasn't going to discuss it with her, then she really was a dimwit.

"Was it because of the age difference?"

Scratch *dimwit*; fill in the word *bitch* instead. Monica rolled her eyes. "I guess this is the part where I'm supposed to reply, 'What age difference?' and you make a surprised face and say cattily, 'I thought you were older than him,' right?"

Chesty looked caught. "I was just making a joke," she insisted.

"Ha-ha," Monica deadpanned.

"So, um," Chesty began twirling a piece of hair around her finger coyly, "this is kind of awkward, but since you seem so, well, over Eric, would it bother you if I got in touch with him?"

Monica felt steam beginning to build in her veins. By the time it reached her head, it would come hissing out her ears. She knew *hate* was a strong word, but she really, truly hated Chesty.

Monica gave a devil-may-care shrug. "No skin off my nose."

"You sure?"

"Absolutely."

"Cool," said Chesty, bouncing on her heels.

She walked away, wiggling her tight little tush. Chesty and Eric . . . Monica could see it. Chesty was just his type. If she threw herself at him, Eric would go for it, of that Monica was certain. Monica felt herself beginning to slide down the surface of her pride. If Eric hooked up with Chesty right away, then people would think Monica had been as disposable as every other airhead he'd bedded. It would put her on the same level as Chesty. Sure, their "relationship" lasted longer than any in Eric's previous history, but who cared? Once he hooked up with someone else, no one would remember about him and Monica; no one would care. Oh, she might get a passing mention in the beginning ("Eric Mitchell, whose relationship with soap star Monica Geary recently ended, has been seen out and about with a bubbly blonde"), but then she'd be wiped from the slate.

The current forecast: rain in her heart, humiliation on its way. She'd pour all of it into Roxie, every last ounce. Chesty usurping her on *W and F* was no longer a concern. Monica was about to show them what acting was all about.

"There's some actress in the Green Room who wants to see you," Lou Capesi growled as Eric and his brother trudged out of the Blades locker room following a miserable loss to New Jersey. Eric was a step slow all night. Twice he was beat wide and had to pull down Jersey skaters both times. Jersey scored on both power plays. To add insult to injury, Eric misplayed a couple of scoring chances on Blades power plays. The only saving grace was the rest of the team played almost as poorly. He refused to chalk it up to the absence of Monica at the game, even though that was what he feared. A couple of the Blades half jokingly asked him to get back together with Monica so she would return to Met Gar and bring back the magic.

Jason peered at him curiously. "What actresses do you know besides Monica?"

"None, unless Brandi decided to pay a visit." Brandi, his ex with the mackerel-sized brain, considered herself an actress, though for the life of him, Eric didn't know why; the only acting she ever did was a few years back on a tacky mattress commercial, where she rolled around on a king-sized bed, dressed as an angel, cooing, "Oooh, this mattress is heavenly." He really hoped it wasn't Brandi.

He and Jason paused outside the Green Room. "Want me to wait?" Jason asked.

"No. I need you to come with me. That way if it's Brandi, we can make our excuses and get the hell out of here fast."

"Hey, maybe Brandi's got a little bundle of joy to present you with," Jason teased.

Eric scowled at him. "Don't even joke about things like that, okay?"

He followed Jason into the Green Room, which was abuzz

with friends, family, and Met Gar "guests," as they were known, those in the public eye who had gotten clearance to meet one or more of the players. The mood was slightly subdued because of the Blades loss, but people seemed to be enjoying themselves, helping themselves to the food and drinks, some waiting for the local sports news to come on the huge, high-def TV at the end of the room.

Eric's eyes scoured the crowd, eventually lighting on a small, lithe blonde waving to him.

Jason jerked his head in her direction. "Isn't that what's her name—Paige from Monica's show? Maybe she's bringing you a message from Monica," said Jason hopefully.

"Her name's Chessy. And she and Monica hate each other," Eric informed him. "Come with me."

Jason shrugged. "If you insist."

Eric made his way across the room, his brother in tow. "Chessy," he said, sounding as surprised as he felt. Her tight, white angora sweater was so low-cut, Eric half expected to see her navel. Form-fitting jeans hugged her hips and thighs so tightly they looked painted on. She hesitated a moment, then hugged him as if they were old friends. Eric stiffened. When Chest—Chessy—pulled away, she was looking at him with concern.

"I've been worried about you."

"Uh . . ." said Eric, unsure how to react. Deflection time. "Chessy, this is my brother, Jason."

"Great to meet you," Chessy bubbled, her eyes momentarily brushing Jason's wedding ring before refocusing on Eric's face.

"You, too," said Jason, glancing at his brother perplexedly.

"So," said Chessy, inhaling so deeply her breasts rose a good three inches. "Like I said, I've been worried about you."

"Because—?"

"Well, you know, the split with Monica."

"What about it?"

"You must be devastated."

"I'm doing okay," Eric said cautiously. This whole thing

was too weird. Why should Chessy care? A second later, his
question was answered.

"I thought it might cheer you up if you and I went out for a
drink."

Jason coughed into his hand, looking away. Eric knew just
what he was thinking.

"Not tonight," Eric said politely. "I'm kind of tired."

"You sure?" Chessy cajoled. "I'm a good listener."

"I appreciate the offer, Chessy. But I really need to get
some rest tonight."

He watched as the sweetness turned to coldness on
Chessy's face. "Your loss."

I don't think so, thought Eric. "You need me to call you a
cab or anything?"

"I'm a big girl," she snapped. "I can take care of myself."
She looked at Jason. "Nice to meet you," she said again.

"You, too," said Jason.

She tossed Eric one final nasty look, then sauntered away.

Jason's expression was serious as he regarded Eric. "We
need to talk. Let's go grab a brew."

Eric wanted to say no. His body ached, and after tonight's
pummeling, he really wasn't in the mood to chat. All he
wanted was to go home and go to bed. But he knew his
brother; he'd hound him until he said his piece. Jace was a
total pain in the ass that way.

"Fine," Eric acquiesced, motioning toward the door. "Lead
on."

They agreed on a bar called Fuzzy's three blocks from Met
Gar. Neither of them had ever been there before, which in-
trigued them; checking out new watering holes, the tackier
the better, was one of those twin traits they shared. And
Fuzzy's was tacky, all right: not only was the decor somewhat
schizophrenic (there was a nautical/Hawaiian theme, with
etchings of old whaling ships on the walls juxtaposed with
strategically placed tiki torches, all of which were lit), but it
also sold tourist merchandise: I Love NY T-shirts, Statue of

Liberty snow globes, Empire State Building pencil sharpeners, the whole shebang. Following Jason to a small, round table, Eric noticed the only other patrons in the place were old men with rheumy eyes who'd probably been coming here for years, pickling their livers. It was a great place; he and Jace would be back, teammates in tow.

"I wonder who Fuzzy is," said Eric, resting an elbow on the table. It was sticky. He pulled his arm away. Maybe they wouldn't be coming back.

"He's probably dead."

Eric looked around, noticing the anchor behind the bar and the shelfful of hula girl bobble-head dolls right above it. "Well, whoever he is—or was—I think he might have suffered a head injury."

"Maybe he was a sailor," Jason speculated.

"Or a schizophrenic."

"Or both."

They laughed, clinking their glasses together. "So what's on your mind, Baby Bro?" Eric began. "How much I sucked on the ice? Selling the farm?"

"Monica."

Monica. Jesus Christ, when is Jason going to let this go? "What about her?" Eric asked, frowning.

"You *do* care about her."

"We're back to this?" Eric tilted his head back, pouring beer down his throat.

"Do you realize what happened tonight?"

Eric swallowed quickly, looking at his brother. "No."

"A gorgeous babe came on to you, and you said no."

Eric could feel his hackles rise. "So?"

"The old Eric never would have said no to an opportunity like that in a million years. Never."

"I only did it out of consideration for Monica. I didn't want to hurt her by going out with her costar so soon after the split."

Jason snorted. "Since when did you ever care about hurting people? Brandi was Delilah's father's *fiancée*, for chrissakes."

"Yeah, but he didn't know I was fooling around with her," Eric pointed out. His heartbeat was beginning to pick up pace. "Monica would know if I started seeing Chessy."

He glanced over at the old men at the bar, wondering if they had brothers who liked to call them out. Their lives were probably simple: collect their pension or Social Security check, slip out of the house a few nights a week to escape the wife. Or maybe they weren't married. Maybe they were retired merchant seamen, and all they had left was Fuzzy's. Maybe—

Jason shook his shoulder. *"Eric."*

"What?"

"Why can't you just admit that you love Monica? Why is it so horrible? You and I both know your 'I don't want to humiliate her' excuse is total bullshit. You turned that bimbo down because you have no interest in chasing tail anymore, and the reason you have no interest is Monica."

Eric closed his eyes a moment. He was feeling intense pressure. His head was pounding so hard he thought the top of his skull might blow off. He knew the only way to get rid of it would be to say the truth out loud—admit it not only to himself but to Jace, too.

"Okay, yeah, you're right," Eric confessed heatedly. "I do love her."

Jason flashed the briefest of smirks but then turned concerned. "Then why—"

"Because I can't handle it, okay? It scares me."

"It scares everyone, you dickwad. Don't you remember what I was like when I was falling for Delilah? I was a mess."

"Yeah, but you didn't have a reputation to uphold with your teammates. I was at the Ronald McDonald House charity dinner the other night with Ulf and Thad, right? And both of them said I was pussy whipped and boring since I'd hooked up with Monica."

"Who the fuck cares what they think?"

"I do. I need the guys on the team to accept me, to trust me, to back me up on the ice."

"No offense, but you sound like you're fifteen years old. Listen to me." He drew his chair closer to Eric's. "In the beginning, it did help grease the wheels with the other guys that you were seeing Monica. But since then, it's your playing that's made you an accepted member of the team, not Monica. Don't you remember Gary Albertson?"

"The Ice Queen," Eric said, citing Albertson's nickname in the league.

"Yeah, the Ice Queen. Only after he scored four in the conference finals in '98, and six more in the Cup finals in 2001, did everyone on his team start calling him the Ice King. The guys can be rude and crude, but if you come through when it counts, they don't give a damn about anything else."

"Maybe," Eric muttered.

"You're a total fucking idiot to have let her go, Eric."

Eric looked down at the sticky table miserably. "I know."

There, he'd said it out loud to the person who knew him best, and the world hadn't burst into flames. Instead, a kind of relief started winding through him. He missed her, the horrible emptiness of waking up every morning and not seeing her face smiling at him from the other side of the bed. He missed her voice, her laugh, everything about her. The way she gave as good as she got, at least with him. Her talent. Her gentleness. Her kindness to that batty old costar of hers, Gloria. Coming to his home games. He'd had it all, and he'd let it go. And why? Because he was a fucking jerk, that's why.

"I'm a fucking jerk," he said to Jason.

Jason sighed. "I know. But you've always been a fucking jerk."

Eric put his head in his hands. "Shit," he whispered.

"Eric—"

"Just shut it a minute, okay? I need to think."

"Think away. I'll go get us a couple more brews."

I'm a fucking jerk, Eric thought to himself again. *Now, how do jerks redeem themselves?* He'd never felt the need to redeem himself before. *How about this: The jerk goes to the woman he's hurt, and he tells her that he loves her. Next, he says that he knows he's been a jerk, but that he'll do anything, including crawl over broken glass, if she'll just give him a chance to prove he's worthy of her love and is, in fact, no longer a jerk.*

Jason returned, handing him his beer. "How's the thinking going?"

"Tell me if I've got this right." Eric related his plan to his brother.

Jason nodded sagely. "That about sums it up."

"What if I beg her for another chance, and she tells me to take a hike?" Eric lamented.

"Why would she?"

"Because I'm a fucking jerk!" Eric reiterated with annoyance.

"You said she cared about you. That means she knew you were a fucking jerk but didn't care. I'm sure she'll tear into you at first—and you have to take it; don't even try to protest if you know what's good for you—but then once she gets it out of her system, she'll give you a tepid, 'Let's see how it goes,' which really means 'Yes, I'll take you back, but I'm the one in control now, got it, buster?' and everything will be fine."

"You know what's scary?"

"What?"

"This sounds like something I would have said to you a while back."

Jason paused. "True." He shrugged. "Well, we're twin jerks." He clapped Eric on the back. "You can do this, Bro. She's the one."

EIGHTEEN

"Hello, everyone. As you know, my name is Christian Larkin, and I'm the new executive producer of *W and F*. You can all just call me Christ for short. Just kidding."

Monica and Gloria exchanged wary glances. The entire cast and crew were gathered on the set. Rumors had been swirling for months that Michael, *W and F*'s long-suffering producer, had decided to leave, the pressure of the job combined with his wife leaving him being too much to handle.

Larkin's reputation preceded him. He was a renowned egomaniac who had executive produced three other soaps over the course of a fifteen-year career. One of the shows had tanked under his leadership; the other two had flourished. Monica heard he'd been lured away from *W and F*'s rival, *Shadows and Horizons*, with a big, fat pay increase and the promise of complete control over everything from salaries to set design.

"Now." Larkin clapped his hands together, the eager elementary school teacher addressing his new class. "This is going to be an exciting time for all of us. I've decided to bring in a new writing team to freshen things up, that's the first thing. The second is, I want you all to begin thinking of *us* as a team, one that wants to win. And for that to happen, we need to really know one another, trust one another. For that reason, the entire cast and crew will be going on a weekend cruise up the Hudson River. The goal is for us to relax and let our hair down, form even stronger bonds that will translate into superior work on every level."

Jimmy, perhaps infected by the schoolteacher vibe, raised his hand. "What if you can't go?"

"You *will* go. Everyone will go. It's mandatory."

Resentment rippled across the room. Monica knew most present had families, as well as one or two coworkers they couldn't stand the thought of spending time with in a space where it could be hard to escape. In her case, it was Chesty and Royce. She pictured Royce with a captain's hat on, asking her to be his "first mate." *God help me,* thought Monica. *This is going to be hell on the high seas.*

"I've brought a list of trust exercises we might spend some time doing," Christian continued authoritatively. "My assistant will be handing them out tomorrow. I'm looking forward to getting to know all of you, and to all of us working to make the show the best it can be when we return."

The cast and crew broke up slowly. Everyone looked slightly shell-shocked—even Royce, who was always up for a good time, especially if he wasn't paying for it.

"This is the most asinine thing I've ever heard of," Gloria railed. "The show *is* the best it can be! We win the Daytime Drama for Best Show year after year!"

"I know," said Monica.

"Is the man an idiot?" Gloria continued, practically foaming at the mouth. "What kind of fool books a cruise in February, for Jupiter's sake? I'm not going," Gloria harrumphed.

"You have to go," said Monica. "You can't make me face this all alone."

Gloria sighed, but the look of defiance remained. "All right, my dear, I'll do it for you. But that man is going to regret the day he ever forced me into this. Not only am I going to speak French to everyone but you, but I plan on being drunk as a skunk the whole time."

"I'm sure you won't be alone." Monica gave Gloria a hug. "I have to go get ready for my next scene."

A broken heart, a bone-stupid costar gunning for her, an enforced cruise . . . *Yeah, life's just great these days,* thought Monica as she headed over to makeup. Gloria always said bad things happened in threes. Perhaps this was her time for a run of bad luck. It couldn't last forever, right?

"You have got to be kidding me."

After a semitorturous day at work that had dragged on until 9:30 p.m., Monica, exhausted, starving, and punchy, slipped out of the back of her town car to find Eric milling anxiously on the sidewalk outside her apartment building. The sight sparked her sluggish senses immediately, putting her on high alert. Whatever he'd come for, she sure as hell didn't want to hear about it.

Spotting her, Eric rushed toward her. "Monica, I need to talk to you." He sounded desperate.

"Why? Leave some CDs or clothes in my apartment? Just wait here; I'll open the window and throw them down to you."

"Two minutes," Eric continued in an uncharacteristically pleading voice. "That's all I ask."

Monica pulled up her coat sleeve and looked at her watch. "And . . . go."

"C'mon, Monica." He shoved his hands deep in the pockets of his jeans. "Have some heart. I've been standing here for three hours."

"That's not my problem."

"I really need to talk to you."

"And I really don't want to talk to *you*." Monica glanced inside at the lobby. Gene, the doorman, was watching them closely. Monica waved a hand at him to indicate that all was well, and Gene nodded his understanding, and went back to watching the multiple closed-circuit TV screens fixed on the lobby, the elevators, and the stairwells.

"Two minutes," Eric repeated.

"Fine," Monica said in exasperation.

Not bothering to wait for him, she pushed open the door to the lobby. She couldn't shake the feeling that she was asking for trouble letting him in, somewhat akin to inviting the devil into her home. They rode the elevator in silence.

"Well?" Monica asked as they entered her apartment. "What do you want?"

"Can I at least take my coat off?"

"What's the point?" Monica asked, shedding her own jacket and putting it away in the closet. "You're only going to be here two minutes."

Stomach grumbling, she strode over to her couch and sat down, frantically trying to erase the memories of the last time they'd been here together: wonderful sex, ordering in Japanese food, watching *The Godfather* marathon on TV. It had felt so natural, so right. *Jackass,* she thought angrily, though she wasn't sure if she was addressing herself or him. Eric moved to join her on the couch, but Monica held up a hand to stay him.

"You're standing."

"I'll do you one better: I'll kneel."

Monica blinked confusedly as Eric knelt down on her Persian carpet and held his arms out to her. "Monica, I love you."

Monica stared down at him, then burst out laughing.

"I'm not joking," Eric continued, undeterred. "Last night, a bimbo came on to me—"

"Chesty?"

Eric looked surprised. "Yeah."

Monica rolled her eyes. "Figures." The little whore never ceased to amaze.

"Anyway, she came on to me, and I turned her down. You know why? Because I figured something out about myself: I don't want to chase tail anymore. And the reason is because I'm in love with you. I've been a jerk, Monica. I know that. But if you'll just give me a chance, I think I can prove to you that my love for you is real, not an act."

"Yeah, right," said Monica, frowning. She snatched her remote from the nearest end table and clicked on the TV.

"You and I both know what this is really about," she said, not looking at him.

"What?" Eric sounded puzzled.

"I saw on ESPN that the Blades lost to Jersey the other night. That guy with the mullet haircut said the team's on a losing streak, and you're in a slump. You just want me back because you think I'm a good luck charm," Monica accused.

Eric lowered his arms so they hung listlessly at his sides. "You really think I'm that shallow?"

"*Yes.*"

"Well, you're totally wrong on this one." Eric began inching forward on his knees like some sad penitent, but Monica glared at him, and he halted.

"Can I ask you a question?" said Eric.

"No."

He asked anyway. "Since when do you watch Barry Melrose on ESPN? You're following the team because you still care."

"Don't flatter yourself. They had *SportsCenter* on at the place Gloria and I went to dinner last night."

Eric's face fell. "Oh."

She was lying, of course. Though she hated herself for doing it, she had been tuning in to see how the Blades were doing and was happy when she saw they lost. Maybe she *was* his good luck charm.

"I love you, Monica," Eric repeated, holding out his arms to her once again.

"Stop saying that," Monica snapped, rubbing her temples. "And lower your arms and get up off the rug. You look like a fool."

"I don't care," Eric maintained fiercely. "If I have to make a fool of myself to win you back, I will. I'll do whatever it takes."

Monica narrowed her eyes suspiciously. He seemed serious. Still, no self-respecting woman would take back a man who'd done what he'd done to her, no matter what feelings she still had for him.

"Listen to me. And get up."

Eric reluctantly rose, grimacing. "My knees are sore."

Good, thought Monica.

"Here's the thing," said Monica with studied nonchalance as she glanced back and forth between Eric and the TV. "I don't trust you. How do I know you don't have some ulterior motive for hooking up with me again? Actually, that doesn't matter. You can't win me back, okay? Because I don't want you."

"I don't believe you."

"What you believe or feel is completely irrelevant to me."

"You're acting."

Monica jerked her head to look at him, teeth gritted. "I am *not* acting, you out-of-control egomaniac. It was fun while it lasted, whatever you want to define 'it' as. But now it's over. Time to move on. You cannot win me over."

"That's where you're wrong." Eric no longer looked or sounded imploring. Now he looked determined. "Maybe you haven't figured this out about me yet, but I'm one tenacious bastard. I get knocked down, and I get right back up again. I've won a Stanley Cup, Monica. If I have what it takes to win the Cup, then I have what it takes to woo you, and I have what it takes to win you. So get ready."

Monica stood, stretching her arms high above her head while letting out a long, tired yawn. "Knock yourself out," she said. She pointed to the front door. "You know your way out. Good night."

NINETEEN

"I would rather have my legs plucked hair by hair than ever go through anything like that again," Gloria told Monica. "*Quel* nightmare!"

They were stretched out on their respective beds in the small cabin they were sharing on the cruise boat, *The Washington Irving*. It was a "sanctioned" naptime, meaning Christian had graciously allowed the cast and crew—or "hostages" as they were calling themselves—an hour's respite from his lectures and exercises supposed to foster intimacy. Following a dinner of soggy vegetables and some unidentifiable meat the night before, Christian had made everyone sit in a circle in the dining room to "rap." He asked them to share their happiest and most traumatic experience to date. What this had to do with anything mystified Monica. Still, there was no escaping.

Many of her cohorts cited the birth of their kids as their happiest experience; others talked about the joy of getting their first part. Royce said his happiest experience was working with Monica, the biggest load of hooey Monica had ever heard in her life. Gloria said her happiest experience was having sex with Orson Welles during a break at the 1959 Academy Awards, even though his vigorous thrusting had broken the couch they were lying on. The closer it got to Monica's turn, the more she panicked. Her happiest experience to date had also been her most traumatic: Eric. There was no way she was going to reveal that, so she lied: she said her happiest experience was getting the role on *W and F*; her most traumatic experience was getting mugged when she was in college. Predictably, Chesty's happiest experience was the same as Monica's, though their traumas did differ; Chesty's biggest trauma to date was not making the cheerleading squad in high school.

"I can't believe Royce said working with me made him happiest," Monica told Gloria. She got up on her knees to look out the porthole, but since it was the size of a dessert plate, she couldn't really see anything. "He's so full of it."

"Don't trust him," Gloria warned. "He wants something. I bet he's scared of getting fired, and he's sucking up to you so that when the axe falls, you'll intercede on his behalf with the Antichrist."

"You've been telling me for as long as I can remember not to trust anyone in this business," Monica pointed out, coming to sit on the edge of the bed. "Who screwed you, Gloria?"

"You don't want to know. You'll be like Saul on the road to Damascus: you'll fall to the ground, the scales will fall from your eyes, you'll be terrified."

The scales were already falling. It wasn't terror Monica was feeling; it was the slow dawning of comprehension. "It was Monty, wasn't it?"

"Yes," Gloria admitted with a reluctant sigh. "I've always held my tongue because I know you adore that puckered old snake, and I didn't want to poison you against him. But the man cares only about himself. Believe me."

"I suppose I knew, the way you always talked about him, but I guess I didn't really want to know." Monica lightly kicked her feet against the bottom of the bed. "What happened?"

Gloria looked wistful. "We worked together quite a bit in the early days, Monica. I don't know if you knew that."

"Yes, you told me that." Monica could picture it: two acting powerhouses feeding off each other's energy. It must have been magnificent.

"We were the best of friends. We respected each other and helped each other get parts.

"Even though Monty preferred treading the boards to anything else, when an opportunity fell into his lap to direct a film version of *Othello*, he jumped at it. Who wouldn't? He phoned right away and said he wanted me to play Desdemona. I'd played the role onstage in London two years before and had gotten rave reviews. I was thrilled.

Gloria's eyes looked glassy. "We'd just started filming when one of the executive producers came to Monty and told him he wanted his floozy in the part rather than me. This girl could not act, Monica. She could barely put together a sentence. And so, Monty fired me."

"Oh, Gloria." Monica came to sit beside her.

Gloria's voice turned vehement. "The entire cast urged him to show some backbone and stand up to the producer, but he wouldn't. He kept saying he had no choice. But he *did* have a choice: he chose to protect himself rather than stand up for me.

"A few weeks later another producer visited the set and saw what an atrocity this girl was. He told Monty he was an idiot, that all he needed to have done was come to him and tell him what was going on, and he would have read the other producer the riot act. In the end the movie never got finished, and I never trusted Monty again." Gloria pointed a warning finger at Monica. "Always watch your back. People in this business, even those who claim to be your closest friends, will kick you in the teeth if it means saving their own skin or furthering their career."

"Not everyone," Monica murmured, leaning over to kiss the side of Gloria's powdery cheek. "You wouldn't."

Gloria chuckled sadly. "I'm too old to do you much harm." Gloria patted Monica's hand. "I'm sorry I told you that about Monty. I know you love him."

"It's okay," said Monica, though the story did make her feel ashamed of Monty. She took a deep breath. "Gloria, have you ever thought of forgiving Monty? It was a long time ago."

"I don't forgive, and I don't forget," Gloria declared, nostrils flaring. Monica didn't push it. When Gloria flared her nostrils, it was best to back off.

Gloria rose creakily from the bed. "I need to walk off some of my irritation at the sheer stupidity of this weekend. Care to join me?"

"I think I'll pass," said Monica. "I just want to close my eyes for a few minutes to fortify myself for whatever horrors are to come."

"You know," said Gloria, posing at the door, "you haven't said a word about your split from Eric."

"There's nothing to say," said Monica, lying down on her own bed and putting a cool pillow over her forehead. "He turned out to be a jerk like every other man I've ever dated."

"That's too bad," Gloria murmured sympathetically. "He really seemed to adore you." When Monica didn't respond, Gloria let it drop. "Pleasant dreams. If I'm not back when the fun and games resume, assume I've hurled myself overboard. I've always thought burial at sea was romantic."

Monica laughed and closed her eyes.

Two minutes later, there was a gentle rapping at the cabin door, prompting Monica to pull her pillow down over her face. Maybe whoever it was would go away if they thought no one was in there. Rap, rap, rap; no such luck. It was time to screen; if it was Royce or Chesty, she had a migraine. If it was Jimmy, she'd let him in.

"Who is it?" she called out groggily, a nice touch. Maybe whoever it was would feel guilty for waking her, and they'd leave quickly.

"It's Christian Larkin, Monica. I was hoping I might speak with you."

Shit, Monica mouthed to herself, sitting up. What could Christian possibly want with her? Could he tell she was lying in the "rap" circle? No, no way. She was Monica Geary; her acting had been impeccable.

"Just a minute." She stood, smoothing her hair, not wanting to look like a complete wreck. She opened the cabin door, trying to look welcoming. "Come in." *You pain in the neck,* she finished in her head.

Christian smiled broadly, closing the cabin door behind him. "My God," he said, looking around. "They've stuck you in a room the size of broom closet. As soon as I leave here, I'll fix that."

"There's no need." The truth was, apart from the dollhouse-sized window, the cozy cabin was okay. As long as she had a place to lay her head and a decent roommate, she was fine.

Monica noticed that the cabin had become somewhat chilly. Of course, Christian was clueless; he was wearing a bulky cable-knit sweater that nearly came down to his knees. *Short men shouldn't wear oversized sweaters,* thought Monica. It made him look even more diminutive than he was. In fact, he appeared about three feet tall, and with his wiry orange hair, he could have passed for a homunculus of Carrot Top.

"So," said Monica, rubbing her arms for warmth, "what can I do for you?"

"What can you do for me indeed," Christian murmured thoughtfully. "That is the question." He pointed to Gloria's bed. "May I sit?"

"Of course."

Damn damn double damn. Monica had blown her chance for escape. She should have told him she wasn't feeling well and asked if they could talk another time, rather than asking him what she could do for him. He might have gotten annoyed, but she'd have at least delayed the conversation.

He patted the bed beside him. "Sit, sit."

"This is fine." Monica sat down on her bed opposite him.

"Well." Christian clasped his hands and put them between his knees, leaning forward. "Let me start by telling you that I am absolutely, without a doubt, your biggest fan."

"Thank you." Monica felt a small flutter of panic tickle her insides.

"And you're incredibly beautiful." He came and sat beside

her, despite the warning vibes Monica hoped she was emitting, his eyes raking her body. "I think we'll make quite a team, both on and off the set." He leisurely lifted a strand of her hair. "I'm thinking of asking the new head writer to beef up Roxie's story line even more." He lifted his eyes to hers, kissing her hair.

Monica jerked away from him. "You're disgusting." Bounding off the bed, she flung open the cabin door. "Get the hell out. Now."

Christian laughed softly. "I wouldn't say no so fast, Monica. I'm sure you've heard about my 'prowess,' as they say."

Yeah, I've heard you come in three seconds flat, Monica wanted to say, even though she'd heard no such thing. Over the years, she'd had lots of men in the industry come on to her, but this was the first one who'd ever tried to talk her into sex as a means of furthering her career. She was shaking inside, she was so angry. She bit down on her tongue to keep herself from snarling every invective she could think of at him.

"Get out," Monica repeated.

Christian rose from the bed. "I really wish you'd think about this, Monica," he said.

He paused at the door, leaning in to touch her cheek, but Monica recoiled. "So beautiful," he murmured with a sad sigh as Monica jerked her head away. She slammed and locked the door behind him, her stomach heaving. Maybe Gloria was wrong; maybe bad things happened in fours, not threes. She checked her watch. Half an hour until naptime was done, and she had to face that pig again. At least she would be in a group. His face had gotten so close to hers . . . she shuddered. A rogue thought entered her mind: if Eric knew, he'd kick his ass. She laughed; it came out more like a bark, actually. That would be a bright move: have your boyfriend—ex-boyfriend—threaten your boss. Still, imagining it was pleasurable.

She was saved from sinking further into thoughts of her onetime hero by the sudden reappearance of Gloria, rubbing her gloved hands together, her aquiline nose red as a cherry.

"Jove's tits! Do you have any idea how cold it is out there?!"

"Christian was just in here. He implied that if I sleep with him, he'd beef up Roxie's part."

"Typical," said Gloria, peeling off her floor-length fur coat. "I hope you told him to shove it up his nose."

"Of course I did."

"Good girl. Don't worry about him; he's nothing but a boil on the backside of humanity. He won't last a year." Gloria pulled a flask from the pocket of her coat. "Now. Let's get nice and warm before we go back to having to do those idiotic group exercises." She paused. "I wonder if anyone brought any pot."

"Gloria!"

"Fine, fine, we'll make do with Jameson." She unscrewed the flask, took a sip, and handed it to Monica. "To acting with honor and dignity."

"I second that," said Monica, the whiskey burning a trail down her throat before turning into a warm glow in her belly. She might not have Eric, but she did have Gloria and Monty. For now, it would have to do.

"You really sucked out there, Mitcho."

Eric fought the urge to turn around and snap, "No shit," to Ulfie as the Blades left the ice following another defeat, this time to Washington. Ulf was right; he had sucked—again. The Met Gar crowd agreed. After they failed to capitalize on their fifth power play, some of the fans had started chanting "Mitcho sucks!" His confidence had taken a major hit, especially when Ty didn't put him on the ice for the power play in the third period.

"You gotta hook up with Monica again," said Tully Webster as they trudged to the locker room. "Since you two split up and she's not coming to games anymore—"

"—you're sucking," Ulfie finished for him.

Eric frowned incredulously. "I love you guys, okay? But how many times are you gonna tell me I suck? I know I suck.

Do you think repeating it over and over again is going to make me *not* suck?"

"Ooh, someone is on the rag," said Thad.

"You're a fucking idiot, you know that?"

Thad stopped. "You wanna take this outside, Mitcho?"

"Where?" Eric jeered. "Back on the ice?"

"Whoa, whoa, whoa." Team peacemaker David "Hewsie" Hewson stepped between them. "Let it go, guys. We're all just pissed off."

Thad hung his head apologetically. "Hewsie's right." He extended his hand to Eric. "Sorry, Mitcho."

"It's fine," said Eric, returning the shake. They continued into the locker room.

"Can I just say one thing?" Thad said cautiously after a small spell of silence.

Jesus Christ, will you let it go? Eric thought. "Sure," he made himself say.

"Since you dumped Monica, you haven't gone back to being the old horn dog we knew. No offense, but you're still being kind of boring, the way you were when you were with her."

"He's right," Ulfie chimed in. "All hockey and no pussy makes Mitcho a dull boy."

"I'm trying to show her a little respect, okay? She's devastated. If I start bagging babes right away, she might go off the deep end. You want her to have a nervous breakdown and leave the show?"

Ulf looked stricken. "Shit. Didn't think of that." He patted Eric's shoulder. "You should totally wait until she's over you before you go back to studding. *W and F* without Monica would be unwatchable, dude."

"Totally unwatchable," Thad chimed in seriously.

"There you go," said Eric. "I'm doing you all a service."

"Maybe you should get back with her," Thad offered tentatively.

"Which is it?" Eric snapped. "Return to horn doggery or make up with her?"

Thad looked down. "If you keep playing like shit, maybe get back with her. Even if it means you keep being boring."

Eric looked around the locker room. "You pussies feel the same way?"

No one would look at him.

"Great," Eric said, frowning.

"Let's stop talking about relationships and drown our sorrows at the Chapter House tonight, boys!" Ulf called out to the rest of the team. A raucous cheer went up. Eric caught his brother's eye. "Fuzzy's?" he mouthed. Jason nodded his head yes.

"Guys, Jace and I found a new place we have to check out. You up for it?"

Another cheer went up. Eric was glad. At this point, he was glad for anything that would take his mind off his shitty playing and off Monica.

"I'm so sorry." Monty held out a bony, sympathetic hand to Monica from his perch on his sagging couch.

It took Monica a minute to figure out what he was referring to. Then she remembered: the play that had passed her over because she worked in daytime. No way was she going to tell him the reason for the rejection. She squeezed his hand, sighing.

"You know how it goes."

"But didn't it feel wonderful auditioning again?" Monty asked before lapsing into a coughing fit, covering his mouth with a monogrammed handkerchief.

"I suppose," Monica murmured. She glanced around his living room, the dust seeming to have taken up permanent residence. "Did Rosa quit?"

"She was released," Monty corrected her haughtily.

"Jesus Christ, Monty! Do you know how long it took me to find her? Whatever you did, you're going to call her up and apologize and beg her to come back."

Monty pointed his nose up in the air. "I will not."

"You will. What did she do that was so awful?"

Monty didn't look at her as he folded his handkerchief back up into a small square. "She called me an old man," he said softly.

You are old, Monica thought. But she felt badly for him and for how wounded he seemed. Some people dealt with aging better than others. Monty had only last year stopped dying his hair when one of his old students told him he looked like Bela Lugosi. He hadn't had any plastic surgery, though occasionally, when he looked sallow, Monica had known him to pinch some color into his cheeks or use a dab of her lipstick instead.

"I'm sure she didn't mean it as an insult," Monica pointed out kindly.

"No one ever does." Monty looked up at her. "Growing old isn't for sissies, Monica, I can tell you that. And it's certainly not for actors. I should have lived fast, died young, and left a pretty corpse. Jimmy Dean and Monty Clift had the right idea."

"You're aging with dignity, Monty. That's more than some people can say."

"Fuck dignity, my dear."

"I thought dignity was very important to you," said Monica, surprised. "I thought it was one of the reasons you refused to do TV. Especially daytime TV."

"Yes, well." Clearly Monty wasn't in the mood to listen. "Where have you been? I phoned you a few times over the weekend, and there was no answer."

"On a weekend cruise. With my cast mates and our new executive producer, who's a nightmare."

"How so?"

"He made us do these trust exercises, talk about ourselves . . ." Monica shuddered. "And he came on to me. He insinuated that if I slept with him, he'd beef up my part. As if I need his help!"

"God, what a cliché," Monty sniffed. He leveled Monica with a stern gaze. "I hope you said no."

Monica's mouth fell open. "Of course I did!"

"Because integrity's very important in this business, Monica. Very, very important. You must never submit to blackmail. Or threats."

"The way you did?" Monica shot back. She couldn't help

it. She hadn't been unable to stop thinking about it ever since Gloria told her.

Monty's fingers curled tightly around the folded handkerchief in his hand. "I beg your pardon?"

"Gloria told me about what happened when you were directing *Othello*," Monica said quietly.

Monty raised an eyebrow. "Oh yes? And what exactly did the old boot tell you?"

"How you succumbed to pressure from the producer and fired her from the part."

"Yes." Monty licked his lips nervously and looked away. His voice was barely audible as he said, "It was quite unfortunate, and possibly one of the biggest mistakes I've ever made."

Monica rocked back slightly, shocked by his admission. She wasn't sure she'd ever heard her mentor admit to making a mistake about anything. His talent matched his ego; that had always been the case.

Monty seemed lost in thought, so lost Monica hesitated to break his spell. Eventually, Monty broke it himself, smoothing his handkerchief and shoving it back into the front pocket of his smoking jacket. "Well," he said with tense finality.

Monica searched his eyes. "Did you ever tell her you thought it was one of the biggest mistakes you ever made?"

Monty hesitated. "No."

"Why not?"

"I was ashamed."

"So you just let the friendship *die*?"

"She wouldn't have forgiven me anyway," Monty insisted. "Gloria is one of the most unyielding, unforgiving creatures to ever draw breath."

"Have you missed her?"

Monty's eyes turned cold. "I think we've discussed this subject long enough, don't you?"

No, thought Monica. She was bursting with questions she knew she could never ask. Had they been more than friends— lovers, maybe, or on their way to being in love when the *Othello* debacle tore them apart? Had he ever picked up the phone to call her only to get cold feet at the last minute? Each must have thought of the other over the years. In fact, she knew they did. Many was the time Gloria asked about him (calling him His Royal Ass or something worse) and vice versa. Monica resolved that next time she spoke to Gloria, she'd try to get more info out of her.

Monica forced herself to stay another hour, chatting with Monty, paying some of his bills. She was eager to go, which made her feel guilty, but she had things to do. It was only on the cab ride home that she realized why she so desperately wanted to depart: his loneliness reminded her of her own.

TWENTY

"I feel like I'm in some bizarre parallel universe."

Eric shook his head in disbelief. Sitting in a dark-paneled, trendy café in the Village with Jason, he'd just finished explaining how Monica had rejected him, despite his declaration of undying love. Two years ago, Jason had been the lovelorn sap seeking advice from Eric, the self-proclaimed expert on women.

"Did you tell her you know you'd been a fucking jerk?" Jason asked, blowing into his mug of hot chocolate.

"Of course I told her. She seemed unfazed."

"She's playing it cool," Jason said knowingly.

Eric just grunted.

"How did you leave things?"

"I told her that I've won a Stanley Cup, and that if I can do that, I can win her back, too."

Jason looked impressed. "Good one."

Eric puffed up. "Thank you. I thought that was pretty clever."

Jason leaned across the table toward him. "As you once told me, you gotta go for the big gesture. 'Chicks love the big gesture.' Do you remember saying that to me?"

Eric groaned. "Yes, unfortunately." He took a sip of his espresso. "Well, how much bigger a gesture can I make than saying I love her, admitting I'm a jerk, and begging her for a second chance?" he lamented.

"You have to woo her."

Eric squinted in alarm. He pictured himself standing beneath Monica's window, strumming a mandolin. Of course, that would be useless, since she lived on the twenty-seventh floor.

"Give me an example of wooing," he said to his brother. He knew he sounded pathetic, but he didn't care.

"Well, you could send her a big box of candy."

Eric snorted. "Yeah, right. She's an actress, Jace. She'd either throw it out or throw it up. She lives on coffee, cigarettes, and breath mints."

"I've seen her eat," Jason countered.

"Monica's not the candy type, believe me."

Jason drummed his fingers thoughtfully on the table. "Flowers. Send her flowers every day for a week."

"Not bad," Eric said listlessly. "It's a possibility."

"Jesus Christ, Eric, you're not an idiot—well, not most of the time, anyway. You can figure out something that will really wow her."

"Maybe you're right," Eric said, grateful for his brother's cheerleading as he stole a sip from Jason's hot chocolate.

Jason looked annoyed. "I hate when you do that. I've always hated when you do that."

Eric chuckled evilly. "I know."

Jason settled back into an expression of semiaffection. "I hope you get her back; I really do."

Eric frowned glumly into his espresso. "Me, too."

"You may be carrying Grayson's child, you little slut, but *I* have his heart." Monica sighed as she walked down the hall to her apartment after a long day's work. She'd already started learning her lines for the next day so she could make it an early night, but saying them aloud to herself, she wasn't sure she liked the cadence.

"You may be carrying Grayson's child, you little slut, but I have his *heart*."

No, the other sounded better, she thought to herself as she turned the key in the lock and opened the door. Somthing crinkled beneath her feet, and she looked down: there was a large pink envelope with her name on it. Puzzled, she bent to pick it up, at the same time becoming alarmed. What if Rennie, her stalker, had somehow managed to gain access to her building? Spooked, she hung up her coat, then pulled out the mace she kept in her bag and slowly crept from room to room, making sure she was alone. She was, thank God. Relieved, she made herself a cup of tea, curling up on the couch with the mystery envelope.

Inside was a pink piece of paper upon which was written a poem entitled, "Come Back to Me." By Eric. She knew it was Eric because she recognized the small, crabbed handwriting. "Oh, God," she thought, steeling herself. Then she began to read.

We met one day on a TV show
And you were the gal I wanted to know.
With your long blonde hair and your eyes of blue,
Babe, I had an instant thing for you.

In the beginning, our love was fake
Then we each took a bite of Sara Lee's love cake.
I loved you, and you loved me
More than a Band-Aid loves a skinned knee.

But then, one day, it fell apart.
I was a moron who trampled your heart.
You treat me now like the invisible man.
I cry all the time, even in the can.

Please, oh please, come back to me.
I love you so, and you will see
Just what a good guy I can be.
Please, dear Monica, come back to me.

Eric (Mitchell)

Monica put the poem down beside her and covered her mouth with her hands, speechless. This was, quite possibly, the worst poem she had ever read in her life. She glanced back down at the poem and began laughing, then abruptly halted. It was mean to laugh. It was. It had probably taken him hours to write it. She could imagine him agonizing over it at his kitchen table, crossing out lines, tearing at his blond hair. It had probably taken a lot out of him emotionally as well to make himself that vulnerable to her.

She picked the up poem again, thinking she should throw it out. That seemed kind of cruel, though it wasn't like Eric would ever know. She read it through a few more times, then decided to save it—*not* because she cared, but because no one had ever written a love letter to her before. Valentine cards exchanged in first grade didn't count.

She carefully folded the poem back into its envelope. She had to admit, she was touched by his effort, despite its ineptness.

But not enough to take him back.

TWENTY-ONE

ROXIE: You may be carrying Grayson's child, you little slut, but I have his heart.
PAIGE: By the time this baby is born, Grayson will love me, Roxie. You'll be nothing but a sad memory.
ROXIE: Then perhaps you can explain to me why Grayson made mad, passionate love to me last night beneath the weeping willow at the Deveraux mansion, Paige.

"Stop. Stop. Stop. Stop. *Stop.*"

All movement on the set halted as Christian made a beeline for Monica with a rolled-up copy of that day's script in his hand, his mouth pursed in displeasure.

"You," he said to Monica as if she were a peon. "You're completely phoning it in today."

"I most certainly am not," Monica scoffed.

"I'm the executive producer, and I say you are."

Monica flinched inwardly, mortified by an upbraiding by this moron. She never phoned it in, even when she was running a 101 fever with the flu or about to faint from bad period cramps. *Never.* How dare he—?

She tensed as Christian turned to Chessy with a big smile on his face. "You, on the other hand, are doing great, Chessy. Just great." He winked at Chessy, and she winked back at him, adding what she must have thought was an undetectable lascivious lick of her upper lip. Monica felt her guts turn and prepared for another take.

"You turned the midget down for sex, didn't you?"

Monica leaned against the console in the control booth, counting out how many aspirin Jimmy was about to down with his coffee. Six, by the look of it. She wondered how much of his stomach was left.

She'd deliberately sought him out because she needed his opinion on whether he thought she'd "phoned it in." She knew she could count on him to tell her the truth.

Monica stared at him. "How did you know that?"

"Uh, maybe because the guy has a rep for banging leading ladies?"

What? Monica had never heard this before! How was such a thing possible? Everyone knew everyone in this biz.

"I didn't know that," said Monica.

"Well, it's true. You turned him down, and now he's gonna make you pay, the petty bastard."

"He can try," said Monica. "But I'm not going to lie down and just take it."

"Maybe you should have," Jimmy wisecracked. He held up a hand. "Sorry. That was crude of me." He offered her half of his pastrami sandwich.

Monica shook her head no.

"Obviously he's banging Chesteroo."

Monica's eyes lit up. "You caught that, too?"

"Everyone did."

Monica began picking at the cuticle of her left thumb. "You think he's going to beef up her role?"

"It's possible," said Jimmy. "Depends how much control he can exert over the new writing staff."

"Know anything about them?"

Jimmy sighed. "I know the two new head writers are new to daytime."

"What?" Monica squawked. Usually, daytime writers were playing a constant game of musical chairs. A writer would get fired from one show and would immediately pop up on another, while a writer at yet another show would replace that very same writer from their previous job. Writers rarely left the genre, choosing instead to drop dead at their keyboards at a ripe old age. The money was simply too good to pass up.

Jimmy patted her shoulder. "I wouldn't worry if I were you. According to ratings, you're still the main draw for this show. Just keep doing what you're doing. Eventually, unless he's a complete asshole, Christian will back down. And no, you were not phoning it in, and everyone else knew it."

Monica blew a big sigh of relief. "Good."

"One word of advice, though: when he criticizes you, just take it."

"But—"

"Listen to me on this, Monica. Just nod your head yes to whatever he says and then do your job. You challenge him, he's going to keep busting your ass."

"All right," Monica reluctantly agreed. But that didn't mean she'd be happy about it, especially since Chesty would love every minute of Monica being called on the carpet. Still, she was a professional. She'd do what she had to do.

Question: *What's the difference between a stalker and me?* Eric pondered as he waited for Monica to get home from work. *Answer: the doorman doesn't let a stalker sit inside in the lobby.* Gene, the weeknight doorman at Monica's building, knew Eric on sight. Gene also knew that they'd broken up, which is why, two days earlier, he'd been sympathetic when Eric asked for his help in slipping his poem under Monica's door. Gene, too, was suffering from a broken heart and longed to get his woman back. He told Eric he admired his determination, and that it inspired him.

Eric had been going nuts, not hearing from Monica after he'd sent her his love poem. It was a great poem, in his opinion. Much better than that stuff in greeting cards. If what he'd written didn't prove he could do some top-notch wooing, he didn't know what would. He'd been up a whole night working on it.

A troubling thought crossed his mind: maybe it had been slipped under the wrong door, and that was why she didn't respond. "Are you sure you slipped it under Monica's door?" he asked Gene.

Gene scowled at him. "I'm not an idiot, you know. She got it."

"Okay, okay, just checking."

Eric settled back in his chair, absently tapping a thumb against his thigh. The Blades were leaving tomorrow for a four-day road trip down to Florida. Eric was hopeful that getting away from Met Gar might actually revive his play; Christ knows it couldn't get any worse. Ty wouldn't even deign to yell at him. Instead, all he got was glares. Michael Dante yelled, though. Right up in his face. In front of everyone. Normally it would have pissed Eric off, being treated like that, but in this case, he deserved it, which only made it worse. Met Gar brass were keeping a close eye on him, too, regretting their investment, probably. If he didn't turn things around, he was sure they'd try to get rid of him. He couldn't bear to think about it.

"Hey, Gene."

At the sound of Monica's voice, Eric looked up. She looked tired but gorgeous as usual. She didn't see him until he stood. Once again, his fantasies were dashed. He'd been imagining that when she saw him, she'd walk to him silently and slip her arms around him, no words needed. Instead she looked annoyed.

"Why did you let him in?" she asked Gene sharply.

Gene suddenly became tongue-tied. "I—I—uh—"

"Are you the one he persuaded to put that letter under my door?"

Gene nodded dumbly. *Please don't hurt me,* his eyes begged.

Monica clucked her tongue. "You could get in big trouble for that, you know."

Gene's gaze turned imploring.

"Don't worry," said Monica with a frown. "I won't say anything to management. But if it happens again . . ."

"Oh, it won't, Miss Geary, I swear."

"All right, then."

She turned and walked toward Eric like she was in no hurry to get there. There was no warmth in her eyes at all. Only irritation. She's acting, thought Eric. Doesn't want to show how happy she is to see me. Wants me to grovel. I can deal with that.

"Hey," said Eric.

"Hey."

"I was wondering: Did you get my poem?"

"Yes."

Yes. So she knew how much he loved her. He'd put it down on paper, proof that meant more than saying it, a record that could be kept forever.

"And—?"

"And I got it."

Eric took a deep breath. "Did you read it?"

"Of course."

Monica kept glancing distractedly toward the elevators, as if they were a limited mode of transportation whose onetime arrival she might miss. *She's totally playing it cool,* he assured himself. *Don't give up.*

"Well, what did you think?" he pressed. His eyes momentarily flicked to Gene, who scowled at him then looked away.

Monica pursed her lips thoughtfully. "I think . . . you put a lot of effort into it."

"A lot of effort." Eric felt a small scratch of temper beginning beneath his skin. "How about 'I poured my guts into it for you'? Did you even *hear* what I was saying?"

"Eric, I really need to get upstairs. I'm in a lot of scenes tomorrow, so I have a lot of lines to learn."

Eric chuckled. "I know what you're doing here, Monica. It's very obvious to me."

"What's that?"

"You're kicking me in the teeth, the way I kicked you. Okay, that's fair. I'll play along for as long as you want. We both know how to 'play.'"

Monica sighed, looking at him with pity. "You're really not getting this, are you? I appreciate the effort you took to write your poem, but it doesn't make any difference. Real or fake, we're done. Okay?"

Eric shook his head obstinately. "Nope. Not buying it."

"Here, maybe if I put it in the form of a poem, you'll understand. 'Roses are red / Violets are blue / There's no one on earth / I hate more than you.' Get it now?"

Eric shook his head again. "Nice try, but you forget: I know you, Monica. I know you still want me, but you just want me to twist in the wind. Totally understandable. But I already told you: if I can win the Cup, I can win you back, and I'm not giving up until I do."

Monica shrugged. "Fine. Waste your time. That's your choice."

"You better be ready, Monica. My next woo is going to blow you away."

"Woo is a verb, Eric. Not a noun."

"Doesn't matter. Just wait and see. By the time I'm done, you're going to be sad about all the time we wasted being apart."

"Go away."

Eric started to saunter away. "I will—for now."

God, she was stubborn, he thought as he left. Feisty—at least with him, which was so damn sexy. What would she do if he turned around, grabbed her, and crushed her into his arms, kissing her just the way he knew she loved to be kissed? Probably slug him. *No*, he told himself. *Keep it slow, keep it steady.* Tenacity was what would win her back. Tenacity and his undying love. Feeling not the slightest bit discouraged, he began walking home.

"I can't believe she didn't go for the love letter."

"I know."

Eric tried not to sound too down as he hit the Mute button

on the TV in his hotel room. The team was in Miami; having just finished their morning practice, they had nothing to do all day but hang around and watch TV. Naturally, they were tuned in to *W and F*, a tradition on the road. But Eric found he was having a hard time watching Monica. Every time she appeared on the screen, he felt like a sharp stick was poking at his insides. All the self-confidence he'd felt as he'd strolled out of her building two nights before was gone, replaced by depression. What if she really didn't want him? What if, no matter how hard he tried, he couldn't win her?

Ulfie and Thad were watching with Eric and Jason. Both of them were now convinced Eric had to get back with Monica to revive not just his own level of play, but the entire team's luck. The whole team was talking about him and Monica.

"You sent her a love letter?" said Ulf, chugging some bottled water.

"Yeah. And it didn't work."

"I sent a girl a love letter once," Ulf revealed.

"And—?"

"She chased me with a bat."

"What the hell did you say to her?" Jason asked.

"I think the letter itself was nice. But I addressed it to the wrong woman."

"Bright," said Eric.

"Okay, we have to move to plan B," said Jason. Eric could tell his brother was enjoying trying to solve the Monica problem. Eric would never tell the douche bag this, but he was feeling really close to Jace lately. Maybe he'd kick his ass later, just to show his affection.

"Perfume," said Jason. "The more expensive the better."

"You can't buy a woman perfume," said Eric. "What if you pick out something she hates?"

Jason tugged at his lower lip. "True."

"Boys, boys, turn up the sound on the TV!" Ulfie said excitedly. "I think Grayson is going to tell Roxie that he's gotta be faithful to Paige now that they're married."

Jason grabbed the remote and turned the sound back on. They all watched, transfixed, as the scene unfolded. Eric made himself watch, because he didn't want to miss it. Monica was amazing, as always. Her begging, her sobbing—by the time she was done, all of them were misty-eyed.

"They are so meant for each other," said Thad with a sorrowful shake of the head.

"I'm sure they'll get back together eventually," Ulf assured him.

"After Roxie does time for killing the old man," Jason put in.

"Guys, could we get back to me?" Eric asked. He knew he sounded kind of petulant, but he really needed help here.

"Sorry, Bro," said Jason. He lay down on the bed, crossing his feet at the ankles, hands laced behind his head. "Candy is out, you said. Flowers are too cliché. No perfume."

"What about a singing clown?" Thad suggested.

Eric stared at him. *"What?"*

"I've seen them advertised on TV. You hire them, and they go to the person's house and sing a happy love song to them."

"I'm fuckin' scared of clowns, man," said Ulf with a shudder. "Seriously."

"I am not going to try to win Monica back with a *singing clown.*" Eric stole a look at Jason, who rolled his eyes.

"Hey, I was just trying to help," Thad muttered.

"What won Delilah over?" Eric asked Jason.

"The first time? Took her to the dog show. The second time? Spent the night the Blades won the Cup with her."

"Pussy," Ulf snorted. "We all sat there waiting for you and Stanley at Snatcher's, and you never showed."

"Yet somehow you survived."

Ulf gave Jason a dirty look.

Eric rubbed his forehead forlornly. "I am so bad at this. I can't believe it. I can't believe I'm bad at something."

"Oh, spare me," Jason snorted.

Ulf snapped his fingers. "I've got it."

"Yeah?" Eric asked eagerly.

"A snake."

"Oh, Jesus Christ," said Jason.

"No, listen to me," Ulf pleaded. "Snakes are sexy, right?"

"Only to other snakes!" said Eric.

"Listen. A snake can twine itself around her, reminding her of your tight hugs. And it will make her miss the monster snake in your trousers, eh, Bro?" he finished lewdly.

Eric wished he had a spike to drive through his own head in frustration. Much as he loved these guys, it was time he admitted the painful truth: they were idiots. Well-meaning but dumb as rocks nonetheless. Snakes, clowns—who did they think he was wooing? Jace's suggestions, while sane, were totally lame, too.

Eric lay back, exhausted. "I don't think a snake will work, but thanks for the suggestion, anyway."

He closed his eyes. He was just falling asleep when an idea came to him, a fantastic idea that would leave Monica no choice but to take him back. He couldn't wait to get back to New York and totally blow her mind.

TWENTY-TWO

A week later, Monica was in her dressing room trying not to spit tacks as she read an interview in *Soap World* where Christian was singing Chesty's praises, when Gloria popped her head in. "Darling? There's a situation outside the studio that pertains to you. I think you might want to nip it in the bud before the law becomes involved."

Rennie. Monica felt a tightening in her chest. She'd taken out a restraining order. Eric had intimidated him. And now he was back with a deranged vengeance. She was beginning to fear for her life.

Doing her best to cover her fear, she followed Gloria outside. The usual cluster of faithful fans was there, the same faces she'd been seeing for years, rain or shine. She smiled at them warmly until she caught sight of "the situation": Eric was walking back and forth on the sidewalk, wearing a sandwich board which read, "I love you, Monica. Please take me back."

What was the expression her British friends used for being rendered speechless? Gobsmacked, that was it. Monica stared at Eric, completely gobsmacked. He winked at her and kept pacing back and forth.

Monica, determined not to lose her cool in front of the fans, walked over to him.

"Are you out of your mind?" she hissed under her breath.

"Yes. With love for you," said Eric, strolling past her, walking another twenty feet, then turning around again. When he reached her again, she quietly grabbed his sleeve.

"Please stop this. You're making an idiot of yourself."

"Maybe that's what I need to do."

"You're going to get arrested."

"No, I'm not. I'm not soliciting."

Monica glanced behind her; the fans were watching, goggle-eyed. *This is not happening,* she told herself. She felt herself strengthen as Gloria approached. Gloria would tell Eric in no uncertain terms to take a hike, and it would be over. Thank God.

"Young man."

Gloria's voice was characteristically imperious. *Here it comes,* thought Monica.

"The fact that you are willing to put yourself out here like this and risk being called a fool is a testament to the love you have for Monica. I admire you tremendously."

Monica turned to Gloria with a gasp. "Are you insane? Why are you *encouraging* him?"

"For one thing, it's clear he loves you and rues whatever he did that hurt you. For another, he's very creative! No candy or flowers for you, ay?" She nodded approvingly. "The boy's got guts. And heart. Reminds me of Orson."

"Thank you," said Eric, lifting his eyebrows at Monica as if to say, "What do you think of *that*?"

Monica pointed to the studio door. "Go," she said to Gloria. "You're not helping the situation."

"Banishment." Gloria sighed. "You're very cruel."

"Go," Monica repeated with a glare.

"Good luck," Gloria said to Eric, pausing to sign autographs for fans before she slipped back inside the studio.

"You realize this isn't going to do anything," Monica said to Eric, who had resumed pacing. *"Stop pacing."*

"Tell me you're not flattered," Eric challenged, halting beside her as she asked.

Monica looked at the ground. The truth was, she was flattered. It seemed that real Eric was wooing her; fake Eric would never do anything so dweeby. His efforts seemed heartfelt. Even so, she couldn't forget how quickly fake Eric had reared his ugly head the minute he was experiencing peer pressure with his teammates. How did she know that wouldn't happen again? How could she be sure he wouldn't be two-faced: real Eric when he was with her, and fake Eric when he was with them, claiming the relationship was nothing more than a status thing?

She was about to challenge him with that when a news van from Channel 22 rounded the corner.

Monica felt her guts sink. "You called the media, didn't you?"

"I want all of New York to know how I feel."

Monica shook her head. "You're unbelievable. You know that?"

"Yup. That's why you love me."

Monica turned away from him with a frustrated growl. It was only a matter of time before Theresa called her and asked her to make a statement she could send out to the media. Theresa probably thought Eric debasing himself this way was great.

The news van pulled up.

"Leave me alone, okay?" Monica said to Eric as she hurried inside.

"Not on your life. Make sure you watch the news from now on," he called after her. "And the home games. I have a few more tricks up my sleeve."

With that, Eric resumed his happy pacing in front of the studio.

"Do you believe this?"

Monica's question was addressed to Gloria, who was spending the night at Monica's after a leak in her upstairs neighbor's apartment had caused the ceiling above Gloria's bed to cave in. They were watching the late news when Monica heard her name mentioned while channel surfing, and she stopped. "Blades fans made no secret of their feelings about Eric Mitchell's recent breakup with soap actress Monica Geary at tonight's game against Philly," said the greasy-haired, mulleted hockey correspondent from ESPN. The news then cut to footage of that night's game at Met Gar, where fans were chanting, "Mon-ica! Mon-ica! Take Eric back!" over and over. Monica's mouth fell open.

Gloria was grinning. "This is fantastic!"

"You're as deluded as he is."

Monica turned off the TV. She couldn't believe Eric was doing this. What was next? Presenting her with a petition from the fans?

Gloria sighed, stretching out her long, bony legs from beneath her red silk robe and flexing her veiny feet. "You must have a heart of stone. I don't see how you can fail to be charmed."

"I don't have a heart of stone," Monica said quietly. The truth was, she *was* charmed. She was also frightened of being burned again. The fans knew she was the team's good luck charm; that was probably the reason they wanted her back. Hell, that was probably the real reason *he* wanted her back. Jerk.

"Monica, darling, I'm talking to you."

"I know, Glo. I'm sorry. The Eric thing . . . it's complicated."

"Explain."

"My whole relationship with him was fake at the beginning. We both wanted to up our profile."

Gloria seemed unfazed. "Big deal. Why do you think I went out with Jack Palance in the mid-sixties? We both needed a career boost. People do that all the time."

"Yes, but then it turned real, at least for me. He said it was real for him, too." Monica tucked her legs in tighter. "But he was lying." She told Gloria what she'd overheard Eric telling his friends at the charity ball. Gloria clucked her tongue.

"So he was trying to save face with his goon friends. Clearly, it was real for him. Why else would be walking up and down in front on the studio baring his soul to the world?"

Monica rubbed the crick beginning in her neck. "I know, I

know." She looked into her friend's eyes. "Would you take him back?"

"Yes. To love is to risk the pain of loss. But it's a risk that's worth taking. God knows I've taken it more times than I care to recount."

"Then why don't you risk becoming friends with Monty again?"

Gloria laughed softly.

"I saw him last week," Monica continued. "He told me one of the greatest regrets in his life was not standing up for you."

Gloria looked to the blank TV screen. "We haven't spoken in years, Monica. I suspect we'd have very little to say to each other."

"I think you're wrong. I think you'd have a lot to say to each other. You always ask about him, and he always asks about you. How can you encourage me to forgive when you won't?"

Gloria was silent.

"Life is too short," Monica continued.

"One could say the same to you, though in my case, it's too true. I'll probably be dead in ten years."

"Don't say that!"

"Well, it's true," Gloria said without the slightest hint of upset. "And that would be fine. I've led a wonderful life. And when you've reached the end, I want you to be able to say the same thing."

Monica slowly unfurled her legs as she stared down into her lap. "I have so far. But I don't think I'm ready to forgive Eric, not yet."

"That's your choice, my dear. But I'd think about it long and hard if I were you. I let too many good men slip through my fingers over the years, and now look at me: alone in my dotage. I don't want that to happen to you. Now put the damn TV back on so I can channel surf for my old beaus."

TWENTY-THREE

"Well?" Delilah asked quietly. "Have you thought about the offer?"

Eric was sitting with Jason, Delilah, and his parents in his folks' dining room.

Jason had suggested it might be better if Delilah opened up the discussion with their parents, and Eric agreed. Their folks adored her; plus, it might soften what would no doubt be an emotional discussion. Dinner was over, and they'd all run out of small talk. Delilah had used the gap to break the ice.

Dick and Jane exchanged telling glances, their faces etched with discomfort, their eyes asking each other, *Which of us will speak? Which of us will tell them?* In the end, it was Jane who answered, which didn't surprise Eric in the least. His mom's family had built this farm; Jane's attachment to it was greater than anyone's.

"We're going to sell to you boys. That way, the house and the land will at least stay in the family, even though it will no longer be a working farm."

Eric tried to read his father's face: stoic as ever.

"You're sure about this?" Jason double-checked.

"Very sure," Jane said calmly. Then she burst into tears.

Eric, sitting next to her, dragged his chair so it was right beside hers and put his arms around her. "It's okay, Mom. We know how tough this must be for you. But like you said, at least it will stay in the family."

"Yes," Jane said softly, sounding like she was trying to convince herself more than anyone else. "Yes, that's the most important thing."

Eric looked across the table at his father. "You okay?"

Dick nodded, his face still impassive.

Calmer now, Jane broke her embrace from Eric. "Dick, tell them the rest."

"We'll auction off the livestock," Dick explained. "But we won't let you pay more than market price for the house."

"Wait a minute," Jason protested. "Auctioning off the livestock is fine. But the real estate market is in the toilet. We'll decide what to pay for the house and the land, not you."

"We don't need charity," Dick snapped.

"It's not charity," Eric replied firmly but with obvious affection, trying to soothe everyone's rapidly fraying nerves. "It's gratitude for giving us a great life here growing up. You've worked yourselves to the bone all your lives. Now it's your turn to relax and have some fun. Buy that RV you've always dreamed of and travel around the country."

"Eric's right, Dad," Delilah added.

Jane looked hopefully at Dick. "The boys *are* right."

Dick drained his coffee cup, slamming it back down on the saucer. "I don't want to live in a damn trailer on wheels."

"We're not going to live in it, Dick," their mother said with mild exasperation. "We're going to travel in it. We can buy a smaller house close to here so we can see the boys in the summer."

"That sounds wonderful," said Delilah.

"We've already been over this," Jane reminded her husband. "Why are you getting so ornery all of a sudden?"

"Who the hell wants to retire?" asked Dick. "Not me."

"Tell me what the hell else we can do, mister," Jane challenged. "We can't afford to keep the farm."

"I know that," he said in a resigned tone. "But I can't stand the thought of being useless. Can you at least understand that, Jane?"

"You can find something else to do," Jane insisted.

"What? Work as a greeter in Wal-Mart?"

Eric and Jason glanced at each other covertly. Eric was pretty sure neither of them had ever heard their parents argue. Sure, they'd heard the occasional angry whispers down in the kitchen when they were kids and were supposed to be asleep, but that was it. It felt weird and uncomfortable.

"I can't believe you're bringing this up now," Jane said, glaring at her husband. "I thought we were in agreement about selling to the boys."

Dick pushed back from the table and walked out of the kitchen into the yard.

"I think he needs more time to process this," Jason offered tentatively.

"No, he doesn't," said Jane. "He's just a stubborn old fool who refuses to see reality."

"It's a pride issue, Mom," said Eric. "He feels like he's failed somehow."

"Look, there's no rush on this," said Jason. "We can do it whenever you guys are ready."

"We're ready," Jane insisted. "I just need to give your father a swift kick in the pants."

Eric and Jason both smiled nostalgically. "A swift kick in the pants" was one of her favorite expressions, especially when it came to their father. Eric had no doubt his mother would set his father straight. Sweet and loving as their mother was, she'd always been the stronger one, the one who ruled the roost.

"Excuse me," said Jane, following their father outside. Eric knew they'd have their chat in the barn so "the kids" couldn't hear.

Jason regarded Eric uneasily. "What do you think?"

"They'll go along with it," Eric assured him. "I think Dad's just freaking out a bit about making a major change. They've lived and worked here all their lives."

"You're right."

Eric began clearing the table, and Delilah moved to help him. "Anything new with Monica?" she asked.

"No."

He had no idea if Monica had seen the footage of the fans chanting her name. Maybe he should have Lou's office make a DVD and send it to her?

"I'd keep trying," said Delilah, ever the optimist.

"Yeah? And at what point do I stop because it's become pathetic?"

"You have to go with your gut on that one."

Eric was glad he was standing behind Delilah so she couldn't see him roll his eyes. He hated going with his gut. His gut was an empty, clueless black hole. All he knew was he loved Monica, and he wanted her back, but so far it wasn't working. Still, he'd keep trying. And it wasn't his gut telling him that, either.

It was his heart.

TWENTY-FOUR

Was it possible to love and hate at the same time? Monica wondered as she hung up the phone following a conversation with Theresa, who'd been fielding calls left and right from the media, wanting to know if Monica was willing to talk about Eric's tactics to win her back. Monica's unequivocal answer? No. She loved the continued media coverage, but she hated the way it was embarrassing her. Yes, Eric was creative, but encountering Blades fans in the streets that chanted, "Take! Eric! Back!" at her was beginning to pluck on her already frayed nerves.

Even so, Monica couldn't resist tuning in to the next Blades home game, if only to stop herself thinking about work. Chesty was now getting the lion's share of the dialogue in their scenes, while Monica's character was being slowly pushed out of the spotlight. These things tended to go in cycles, but Monica still found it so unnerving that Eric and the Blades were a welcome diversion.

The pregame warm-up was beginning. One by one, the players skated out onto the ice and began circling. Cheers went up when certain players emerged. Monica loved seeing the kids pressing right up against the Plexiglas, getting an up close view and hoping one of the players would flip a puck to them.

Eric skated out, and Monica could hear the early arrivals start chanting, "Monica! Monica! Take! Eric! Back!" She blushed, even though she was sitting all alone in her apartment. Eric waved, and a bigger cheer went up. The camera cut to the two hockey commentators from the Met Gar channel.

"The Blades are really going all out to help Eric win back Monica Geary," said the one who looked like a walrus. "Take a close look at the guys on the bench."

The camera cut to the home bench, panning its length. Every player on the team had an *M* sewn onto his jersey where the *C* or *A* for the captain or assistant captain usually went. Monica felt her heart lurch.

"Do you think it will work?" asked the balding commentator with the beaky nose.

"I hope so. The Blades need to turn their luck around."

"Maybe Eric's wearing his heart on his sleeve—or should I say, on his chest," chuckled the walrus guy, "will do the trick. It's sure brought the team together."

A flash of heat licked its way up Monica's body as the game began. God, he really did want her back; look at how foolish and desperate he was willing to appear. She focused on Eric when he hit the ice. Initially she'd been convinced he only wanted to reunite so he wasn't awful on the ice anymore. But more and more, it was obvious that wasn't the case—or was just a small part of it, anyway.

She hated to admit it, but she missed going to the games and getting cheered. And she missed watching him, even though she still didn't know what was going on half the time.

She looked up as Gloria came out of the spare bathroom to join her on the couch, her face slathered in cold cream. Monica loved her dearly, but she hoped Gloria's apartment was repaired soon. She was used to living on her own, to being quiet when she needed to be quiet. Gloria liked to talk all the time.

Gloria sighed as she sank down beside Monica. "For someone who claims not to give a tinker's damn about that little Hottentot, you certainly watch a lot of hockey."

"He asked me to watch tonight's game. There was something he wanted me to see."

"What's that?"

"See if you can figure it out."

Gloria squinted hard at the television. "Haven't a clue."

"Most of the Blades are wearing *M*s on their jerseys for Monica."

Gloria squinted again. "Oh, my. You're right." She put her hand over her heart. "That's so sweet that they're all helping him to get you back."

"It's only because he's been playing really badly since we split. They're all superstitious and think I'm some kind of living good luck charm."

"Dear God, you are so naïve when it comes to machismo," said Gloria with a cluck of the tongue. "That's what they tell themselves and each other: that it's because of their play. They can't admit they actually have feelings."

Monica made a sour face and went back to watching the game, pretending Gloria wasn't there. Perhaps, taking a cue from how hard Monica was concentrating, Gloria was largely silent, except when a break in the action came and some fans resumed the chant: "Monica! Monica! Take! Eric! Back!"

Gloria turned to her. "Monica! Monica! Take! Eric! Back!"

Monica squirmed and said nothing. The Blades didn't play poorly, earning a tie at the end of regulation. But then they gave up a goal in the five-minute overtime. Skating off the ice, the players looked as dejected as the fans. Monica switched off the TV, the fans' chant now embedded in her head, repeating itself over and over. It was ridiculous, but she was beginning to feel that she *was* responsible in part for the Blades' slump. *As if you're that powerful,* she chided herself. *You're just as egotistical as he is.*

She and Gloria rose simultaneously.

"Well, good night, my dear," said Gloria, covering her mouth as she yawned. "Enjoy sleeping all alone in that big bed of yours."

Monica glared at her, said good night, and went to her room, where she spent the night staring at the ceiling. The next morning, she was as fresh-faced and professional as ever on the set, even though she was only in two scenes and had two lines. She'd adopted her own chant these days: "These things go in cycles." Interesting that both she and Eric were having a downward swing these days. Christian might be trimming her role on the show, but her ratings were as high as ever. Chesty's ratings showed she was barely registering a blip with viewers. *That which does not kill me makes me stronger,* Monica told herself as she left the set hours earlier than she had in years, her own chant drowning out the realization that she had no idea whether she was coming or going these days.

"Dude, no offense, but I don't think the *M* on our jerseys did anything."

Eric ignored Thad's comment as he toweled off following a particularly brutal practice. His teammate was right, of course. They'd gotten a single point from the overtime loss but were still trailing Jersey by eight points in the standings. If they didn't turn it around soon, they could miss the playoffs entirely. The gesture hadn't helped personally, either. He still hadn't heard from Monica. She probably didn't even know about the chanting fans and the *M*s. He was fighting a losing battle, both on and off the ice.

Ulf swiped Eric's deodorant. "I told you: you should have sent her the snake."

"Or the singing clown," Thad put in.

Eric took back his deodorant, wondering if there was a doctor somewhere in New York who could reverse the lobotomies his teammates had obviously had.

"What are you going to do next?" Ulf asked.

"I don't know," Eric replied despondently. If he went after her one more time, he was pretty sure he'd be crossing the line from ardent pursuer to pathetic jerk. Maybe it was time to give it a rest. Then again, tenacity and relentless drive were how he'd achieved everything in his life, from getting out of Flasher to winning the Cup. He couldn't understand why it wasn't working with Monica.

Eric finished toweling off, grimacing as he dressed. He'd

been playing and practicing his butt off. As a result, he'd at least raised his play to mediocre. But he knew that wasn't good enough for Ty, his teammates, or himself.

As he headed over to Fuzzy's with a bunch of the guys, he resolved to drop his pursuit for a while and just focus on his game. What else could he do?

> PAIGE: *How dare you show up at my wedding to Grayson, Roxie? How dare you?*
> ROXIE: *I wanted everyone there to know what a sham it was. Plus, I had some news of my own to deliver to Grayson.*
> PAIGE: *What's that?*
> ROXIE: *You're not the only one carrying Grayson's child.*
> PAIGE: *You're lying!*
> ROXIE: *It's true, Paige. But mine is a child created from love, while yours is the result of a night of debauchery. Tell me, dear sister: How long do you think it will take him to divorce you and marry me?*

"Stop, stop, stop." Christian rubbed his beady eyes, crooking his finger to call Monica over to him. "How many times do I have to tell you," he said in a low voice, "to really put your guts into it?"

That's it, Monica thought. She wasn't going to let this little troll keep on humiliating her just because she'd refused to screw him.

"I am putting my guts into it," she snarled. "Which is why my ratings are through the roof. Too bad I can't say the same about the show. Notice how we've slipped to number two since you've taken the helm?"

"Temporarily," Christian sniffed. "Always happens when a show is transitioning."

"And what are we transitioning to?"

"Younger, hipper, more savvy." Christian narrowed his eyes. "What's with this antagonism, Monica?"

"Don't play stupid. I know I'm being punished. And if you

really gave a damn about this show, you'd put some energy into calling your talentless little girlfriend on the carpet, not me. Breasts and Kewpie doll eyes do not an actress make."

Christian's jaw clenched. "Watch it."

"You'd better watch Chessy before she—and you—destroy this show. Now piss off, I have some *acting* to do."

"Anything? Any packages or notes?" Monica asked Franco at the front desk of *W and F* as she left the building.

"Nope. Have a good night, Miss Geary."

"You, too."

"Anything?" she asked Gene the doorman when she arrived home. "Any packages or anything?"

"Nope."

"No one stopped by to see if I was home?"

"Nope."

"I guess Eric's decided to give up, then," Monica replied with a small, blasé laugh.

"Looks like."

Monica bade him good night and went up to her apartment. God, she was loathsome. For two weeks she hadn't gotten anything from Eric, nor had he ambushed her outside her building or the studio. Nothing. Neither he nor his teammates had the *M* sewn onto their jerseys anymore. At first she told herself she was relieved he was giving up. But as the days wore on, she found herself feeling neglected. And disappointed. If she missed his wooing, however over-the-top, by extension that must mean she missed him.

She turned on the TV as soon as she slipped into her sweats, knowing the Blades had a home game tonight. The fans didn't chant about her even once. Instead, they occasionally broke into a vulgar chant about someone named Potvin. They'd given up on her as soon as they sensed Eric had given up.

Monica drew her favorite quilt around her and curled up on the couch. Her home had never felt more of a haven to her. For the first time in her life, Monica dreaded going to work in the morning. Rumors were rife that the writers were going to have a plague from Mars kill off half the cast. Doing something that radical reeked of desperation. The show's slipping ratings were beginning to have an effect.

She closed her eyes, dozing. When she woke, the game was over, and the local news reported that the Blades had lost again. *He needs me,* she thought. *Do I need him, too?* She drew her comforter tighter around her, remembering the things he'd said to her the night of the charity banquet, how when she'd dumped him, his primary concern was that they tell the press it was mutual, so he wouldn't look like a loser. But then her mind jumped ahead to his appearing in her lobby, admitting his jerkiness, claiming he knew she was just giving him a taste of his own medicine, kicking him in the teeth the way he'd kicked her to teach him a lesson. Finally, she thought about Gloria telling her to risk a reconciliation, how it was so obvious Eric loved her by how willingly he'd made a fool of himself. She wondered if she would do the same if she were in his shoes.

Confused as ever, she turned off the TV. *Well, you got what you said you wanted,* she told herself. *He's finally given up.* Exhaustion overtook her, both emotional and physical. Alone of her own making, she slept on the couch.

TWENTY-FIVE

"What the hell—?"

The last thing Monica expected to see when she walked into Gloria's apartment was Eric. Gloria had called and invited her to lunch, after which they planned to hit Fifth Avenue and drop a bundle on whatever hit their fancy. Monica always enjoyed going over to Gloria's apartment, because it was so interesting and eclectic. Turn-of-the-century paintings mixed with Art Deco furniture combined with ornate Victorian pieces. Somehow, Gloria made it all work. The only thing Monica disliked was the ever-present aroma of tea rose. It made her think of funerals.

Eric looked up at her from where he sat on the couch, leafing through one of Gloria's leather-bound photo albums. There was a glint of mischief in Gloria's eye as she ushered Monica inside.

"I was just showing Eric some pictures from more glamorous times."

"You were quite the looker," Eric told her. Monica felt a shiver pass through her as her entire body gave a small leap at seeing him. This wasn't what she wanted to feel. She gave Gloria a dirty look.

"Was this your idea?"

"It was Eric's. He called me and wanted to know if I could help him see you."

"And of course, you just had to comply."

"Call me Cupid," Gloria replied with an angelic smile.

"I'd like to call you something else. You ambushed me." Gloria shrugged.

Monica's annoyed gaze shifted to Eric. "Very clever."

"I have my moments."

"What do you want?" Monica asked Eric icily.

"I need to talk to you." A look Monica wasn't sure she'd ever seen came to his face: desperation.

"Go ahead."

"Alone."

"I don't mind," Gloria the traitor quickly announced. "I'll just toddle off to the kitchen and mix myself a mai tai."

"Thanks a lot," Monica muttered under her breath to Gloria's back.

She could hear Eric draw a deep breath as she remained standing by the door. "Have you been watching any of our games?" he asked.

"No," she lied.

She felt stupid just standing there, so she moved farther into the living room, sitting opposite Eric in one of Gloria's vintage leather club chairs.

"Well, if you'd been watching," said Eric, looking somewhat dejected, "you'd have seen the crowd chanting for you to take me back. And all the guys on the team sewed *M*s on their jerseys that stood for Monica."

"I did read something about that in the paper."

"So will you . . ." Eric ran his hands over his face, whether in dejection or in an effort to wake himself up, Monica couldn't tell. He looked awful.

"Hypothetical question," he said. "If you were having trouble at work, and you knew there was someone who might be able to help you out, would you ask for their help?"

"Yes," Monica said cautiously.

"Okay, then. I'm asking for your help. I need you to come to the next Blades game." Monica opened her mouth to protest, but Eric swiftly held up a hand to silence her. "Hear me out. You were my good luck charm, Monica. I'm not kidding. If you come, maybe I can reverse the slump I'm in."

Monica stood up. "You selfish bastard!"

Eric looked alarmed. "What? What did I do?"

"I *knew* you were only trying to win me back because of your stupid superstitions! I *knew* it!"

"No, no, no," Eric insisted frantically. "That's not it at all."

"Bullshit."

Eric was edging his way off the couch. "Can't you just come to one game? Please? For old time's sake?"

"We don't have an old time's sake, remember?" Her voice was bitter. "Our whole relationship was fake for you."

"Not true. I'm begging you here, Monica. *One game.*"

"Fine," she harrumphed, thinking about all his inept wooing and the fondness it produced in her against her will. "You'll see me at the next game."

Eric's face lit up with gratitude as he rose from the couch. "I can't thank you enough for this."

"No, you can't. Now please leave."

"Fine. I mean totally. Right this minute," said Eric, bowing and scraping. "It worked," he called out to Gloria in the kitchen. "Thanks for helping me out."

Gloria tottered back into the living room, cocktail glass in hand. "Anytime." She looked back and forth between Eric and Monica triumphantly. "Should I lift my glass high to toast the newly reunited couple?"

"Bite your traitorous tongue," Monica snarled.

Eric gave Gloria a quick peck on the cheek. "The game is tomorrow night," he reminded Monica as he headed toward the door.

Monica looked at him coolly. "I told you: you'll see me there."

"*Adieu*, sweet prince," Gloria called after Eric. She turned to Monica. "How is it that you're not back together?"

"I'm helping him out professionally. That's all."

"Deep tissue massage?" Gloria teased.

"Not funny."

Gloria took a huge gulp of her mai tai. "Want one of these? Brando taught me how to make them perfectly when I visited him in Tahiti many years ago."

"No thank you."

"It might help loosen you up. You seem a bit fraught to me."

"Of course I'm fraught; you tricked me, Gloria," Monica repeated in a hurt voice. "That wasn't very nice."

"It was for a noble cause," Gloria insisted.

Yeah, so Eric could save his own ass, Monica thought.

"How would you feel if I tricked you into seeing Monty?"

Gloria clutched at her throat. "You wouldn't."

"Behave, and I won't."

Gloria relaxed, lowering her hand. "May I at least ask *how* you're helping him out professionally?"

"That's for me to know and for you to find out," Monica replied. "Now finish up your Brando mai tai so we can do some serious damage at Bergdorf's."

Eric couldn't remember the last time he was this excited to play as he cruised toward the Blades locker room, a spring in his step. He'd told his teammates at practice that morning that they'd see Monica at tonight's game, and to a man they were elated. Not surprisingly, he'd had a great practice. Whether Monica wanted to admit it or not, her defenses were slowly crumbling; it was only a matter of time before she took him back. *Damn, you're good,* he said to himself. *Perseverance: that's the key in sports, in life, and in romance.*

He opened the door of the locker room, jerking to a stop at the threshold. There, planted in front of his locker, was a life-sized cardboard cutout of Monica.

"Mitcho!" said Thad. "Check out what Lou just brought down."

Ulf grinned. "Awesome, is it not?"

Oh, it was awesome, all right. Cardboard Monica was wearing a low-cut, beaded red gown, her long blonde hair falling in soft waves down her shoulders. The expression on her face was sexy, but not overwhelmingly so; it was more kittenish than come-hither. Eric felt his face flame.

"Why's it in front of my locker?"

Thad shrugged. "Lou said that's where it's supposed to go."

"You mean, that's where Monica told him to put it," said Eric, feeling like an idiot.

Jason came up to him. "What's going on here, Bro?"

Eric frowned. "Monica's exact words to me yesterday were, 'You'll see me there.' Not 'I'm coming to the game.'" Eric was seething as he gestured at the cutout. "Well, there she is, guys. She's at Met Gar."

Low laughter rumbled through the room. "Oh, man, did she ever stick it to you," Barry Fontaine chortled.

"She got you, Mitcho," Ulf added. The Blades began clapping and whistling.

"You can all fuck off, thank you very much," Eric growled. He dropped his gym bag and started moving toward his locker. "Let's get it the hell out of here."

"Dude, no!" Thad stepped in front of him. "I think we should keep it."

"What the hell for?" Eric scowled.

"Maybe it'll bring good luck," said Ulf. "At any rate, she sure is fun to look at." He moved his hips suggestively as he slithered toward the cutout, putting his mouth on cardboard Monica's for a long, long time. "Mmm-mmm good."

Eric fought the urge to punch him in the face, even though he had no right to; she wasn't his girlfriend anymore. Besides, this was a cardboard cutout. "I don't want to see it," he declared emphatically, sizing up the locker room. "There's no room in here for it, anyway."

"We can put it out in the hall, right outside the locker room," Thad suggested. "A good luck charm for all of us. All those in favor say aye."

"Aye," said everyone but Eric and Jason. Eric shot his brother a grateful look for siding with him. Jason nodded curtly and began lacing up his skates.

"It's decided, then," said Barry. "Monica Geary will assume an honorary position—"

"You mean a missionary position?" Ulf interrupted with a smirk as the other Blades catcalled.

"—outside the locker room door." Barry picked up the cutout by its neck. "May I?" he said to Eric.

"Knock yourself out, asshole," Eric muttered. Any excitement he'd felt about playing had evaporated in a puff of mortification. It was time to get out of his head and start channeling all his frustration and disappointment over failing to win Monica back into playing his guts out. He avoided looking at cardboard Monica as he trooped out of the locker room with his teammates.

That night, the Blades won 4–2 against Philly. Eric was all over the ice, scoring once on a slapper from the point and assisting on two power play goals. His teammates were ecstatic. Ty slapped him on the back when the game ended, and Michael Dante gave him a hug when they got back to the locker room.

"Cardboard Monica brought your mojo back," Ulf proclaimed. "We definitely have to keep her around."

How could Eric argue? He reluctantly nodded his assent as he headed for the shower. But he couldn't help thinking his play would have been even better had flesh-and-blood Monica been there. Talk about sending him a clear message. He showered, but rather than joining his buddies for a postgame, celebratory drink at Fuzzy's, he headed straight home to lick his wounds. The day after tomorrow the Blades were leaving for a road trip, and he was glad, since everything he saw reminded him of Monica. He flicked on the TV, surfed, nodded off. Some bachelor life.

TWENTY-SIX

"I'm just going to say this straight out," Christian declared solemnly. "Next Friday is going to be your last day on *W and F.*"

Monica kept her expression neutral as she sat down on the giant couch in Christian's office, the one he probably screwed Chesty on daily. She thought she was going to be called on the carpet about her attitude and for challenging him in front of the cast and crew. She never thought she'd be fired. Monica blinked hard as a gash opened up in her chest out of which stunned incredulity poured.

She held her head high. "May I ask why?"

"We're taking the show in a younger, hipper direction. The character of Roxie simply doesn't fit into that."

"I see." Monica pressed her lips together hard, a dam against the torrent of expletives threatening to gush from her mouth. "And may I ask how Roxie is going to be written off?"

"She's going to be killed by a zombie on next Friday's show."

"I see," Monica repeated.

"I know this must come as a shock to you," said Christian,

who was a worse actor than Chesty. The sympathy on his face
was about as real as Chesty's boobs.

"It is."

"We will, of course, buy you out of your contract and pay
you accordingly."

*Don't expect me to say thank you, you spiteful little prick.
Legally that's what you're bound to do, unless you want me to
sue your pudgy little ass.*

"And of course we'll throw you a huge going-away party
after we finish shooting for the day."

"That's so sweet of you," Monica replied with just the
slightest tinge of sarcasm coloring her voice.

"Well, you are beloved by some of the cast and crew."

*Some. Screw you and the horse you rode into town on,
mister. You are so going to regret this.*

Christian stood. "That's it. Thank you for all the hard work
and dedication you've demonstrated over the years."

"It was my pleasure."

He came out from behind the desk to open the door for her.
"I know you'll flourish wherever it is you wind up."

"That goes without saying," Monica said with a false smile
as she breezed past him. Her pace quickened as she headed
for her dressing room. Chesty passed her in the hall, her pouty
pink mouth sporting a tiny smirk. She knew. The little bitch
already knew.

Monica fought the urge to follow her, burst into Christian's
office, and yell, "How dare you tell this stupid little tart before me?!" Oh, she could picture the genesis of her fate:
Chesty breathlessly urging the king of the Munchkins on as
she gave him head, encouraging him to tell the writers to
write Monica off the show; Chesty covering his lumpy little
face in kisses when he brought her the news that he'd fulfilled
her wish. It was disgusting. Disgusting, corrupt, and unfair.

Monica steamed toward her dressing room, struggling not
to slam the door. She closed it with quiet dignity before lock-
ing it. And then she sat down on the couch and cried her eyes
out.

* * *

"He's been gunning for you ever since you turned down his offer for nooky," Gloria said as she bit into a piece of rare rib eye steak, following it with a sip of her Johnny Walker. At Gloria's urging, Monica had joined her soon-to-be ex-costar for a meal at the Old Homestead Steakhouse, the oldest in New York. Gloria claimed that apart from mindless sex, nothing assuaged devastation better than a good hunk of meat washed down with strong booze. Monica wasn't sure she agreed, but she wasn't complaining. She was getting a nice buzz off her martini.

"But isn't it stupid to do something like this out of vengeance?" Monica asked plaintively. "Doesn't he care about how it affects the show?"

"It's not his brain that's doing his thinking. I'm going to enjoy watching him go down in flames."

"I guess." Monica took a sip of her drink, trying to ignore the thin swirl of watery blood on Gloria's plate from her near-raw dinner.

"Darling, do you know how many times I've been written off that show?"

Monica thought. "Three."

"That's right. Three. Once when I was dragged down to hell by Santo the Demon King to suffer the fires of eternity for stabbing Grayson; once when an iceberg cracked beneath me and I fell into the Arctic Ocean and drowned; and once when I fled town after starting the warehouse fire. It's not the most horrible thing in the world. You've been working like a dog for years. Now you can take a nice break; maybe pursue being a 'real' actress."

Monica peered across the table at Gloria in the dim light of the restaurant. "Are you being sarcastic?"

"Of course I am. I've never understood this fixation you've had about not being a 'legitimate' actress because you work in daytime. It's nonsense. No one can make you feel inferior without your own consent, you know." She gulped down the rest of her drink before waving her empty glass dramatically at their buff waiter to call him over. "Fill 'er up, laddie." After ogling the waiter as he walked away, Gloria turned back to Monica. "Why don't you think of this as an opportunity to try to spread your wings? You've been saying you wanted to do that for years."

"As you know, I tried to spread them a few months ago. Look where that got me."

Gloria slid a hand across the table, interlacing her fingers with Monica's. "How should I put this?" Gloria pursed her bright orange lips. "You're been in the business long enough to know it's filled with assholes who wouldn't know fine acting if it bit them in their asses. We have to take the good with the bad. So you had an encounter with the bad. Onward and upward, I say."

"I guess you're right." Monica cocked her head, looking at her friend admiringly. "How do you manage to keep so positive all the time, Gloria?"

"Booze and Prozac. You should try it sometime."

Monica laughed.

The waiter returned with Gloria's refill, and she blew him a kiss in thanks. "Here's another good thing that could come of this," Gloria said after taking a sip of her drink. "You will get a heap of PR. I wouldn't be surprised if the fans rise up when they realize you've been let go, and storm the studio with pitchforks and torches."

Monica brightened. "You really think so?"

"Don't be coy," Gloria chided. "You know how beloved you are."

Monica knew Gloria was right; Roxie's death would unleash a storm of protest from viewers. Requests would pour in from the media, all of them wanting to talk to Monica and get a quote from her about how she felt about being let go. Of course, she'd have to play nice and toe the party line, claiming it was time to take the show in a new direction, and she was ready for a break, eager to explore new things. But then the attention would fade, and she would just be Monica Geary, out-of-work actress, former queen of daytime. The thought of invisibility petrified her. It was shallow and egotistical, but she'd reconciled herself to that side of her personality a long time ago. Explore new things. Gloria was right. She should be excited about the possibilities her newfound freedom might offer, but right now, she just wasn't.

"Have you told the old snake yet?" Gloria inquired, motioning for their hunky waiter to bring her yet another scotch. Jesus, she'd sucked down that second one fast. Monica worried about what would happen when it was time to stand up.

"Do you mean Monty?"

"You know I do."

"No, but I plan to. I haven't been to see him in a while, and I really need to get over there. Want to come with me?"

"I'd rather snort Drano."

Monica cast her a worried look. "You've never done that, have you?"

"No, but Peter Sellers and I tried to smoke a banana peel once. Did nothing."

"Well, at any rate, I'll tell Monty you were asking about him."

Gloria stabbed a piece of bloody meat on her fork, waving it at Monica menacingly. "Don't you dare."

"You can't stop me," Monica replied, sounding like a child challenging a parent. Gloria's response was to pop the meat in her mouth with a glare.

Monica took another sip of her martini. There was someone besides Monty she longed to pour her heart out to, but she couldn't let herself. Wouldn't let herself. *Good-bye to all that,* she thought, trying to be positive. *New horizons. Freedom. Time to relax.* It sounded good—in theory.

"Dad called me with a closing date," Eric announced as he plopped down next to Jason on a bench in Central Park. They were both dripping with sweat after a run. Eric didn't want to sound superior, but he was thrilled his parent had finally called him with news rather than his brother.

Jason turned to him with interest, mopping his face with his T-shirt. "Yeah?"

"Friday, April first. He's auctioning off the livestock two weeks before that." Eric shook his head. "The stubborn old bastard is still insisting we're paying too much for the house."

"Did you tell him 'Tough shit'?"

"No. I conveniently played deaf the way he used to."

"Payback's a bitch," Jason joked. He squirted Gatorade into his mouth. "I know this sounds kind of dumb, but I'm actually excited about keeping the house in the family and all."

"Me, too," said Eric, though lately he'd been haunted by visions of himself as the lonely bachelor uncle to Jason and Delilah's future kids when they were all out there in the summer.

"Delilah is really excited," Jason continued. "She keeps talking about putting in a dog run and making Mom's garden bigger. I'm excited, too. Summer there is great, as you know. Too bad Monica won't be coming for a visit."

"Yeah," Eric added before falling silent.

In an effort to fill the vacuum that had just opened up, Jason said, "That cardboard cutout seems to be helping us turn the tide."

Eric just nodded.

"Miss her, don't you?"

"Yup."

"Any thoughts on a new strategy to get her back?"

"Nope," he said, watching a girl with long blonde hair as beautiful as Monica's jog past. Jesus Christ, even women's hair was making him wistful now. How effin' sad was that?

He tore his eyes from the girl to look at his brother. "I blew it, she doesn't want me, end of story. Time to move on."

"Sorry," Jason murmured with sincere sympathy. "If there's anything I can do, or if you just want to talk sometime . . ."

"Don't be a fag," snapped Eric, unsure how to handle this newfound kindness from the jerk who used to throw himself against the wall when their parents were out of the room, then howl with pain and claim Eric had hurt him.

Eric rose. "Twenty bucks says I can beat you home."

"You're on."

They took off, neck and neck as always. The Mitchell boys, Eric thought to himself gratefully. At least one thing in his life was still going right.

TWENTY-SEVEN

FATHER CHESSLER (LIFELESSLY): It's time for you to pay, Roxie. Pay for what you did to Tucker Lamont.

ROXIE (BACKING AWAY TOWARD THE DOOR): Oh, no. Not you, Father. Don't tell me the zombies have gotten you, too.

FATHER CHESLER: For so long, I lived in the light. But now I inhabit the shadow world between the light and the dark, between the living and the dead. Our ranks are growing. Soon we will take over. But you won't be here to see it, Roxie. You must pay for your heinous crime. You must die.

ROXIE (FRANTICALLY TRYING TO UNLOCK THE DOOR): Please, Father. I'll do anything you ask. Just let me live! Let me stay in the light. (SHE FALLS TO HER KNEES AS THE PRIEST PUTS HIS HANDS AROUND HER NECK AND BEGINS SQUEEZING.) "Noooo!!!"

(FADE TO BLACK.)

"Cut!"

Monica felt a lump quickly form in her throat. The entire cast was there for her final scene, whether they were shooting that day or not. Jimmy came down to the set, which had gone silent. He looked at Monica and began clapping as she rose from the floor. Everyone on the set joined in, the noise getting louder and louder. Christian and Chesty stood off to the side, grim-faced as Easter Island statues.

"Thank you," Monica managed. She would not give that midget bastard and his conniving whore the satisfaction of crying. No way.

Jimmy came up and put an arm around her. "That was one helluva Friday cliffhanger performance. The viewers are going to go crazy when they tune in and realize Roxie is really dead."

"I hope so," Monica said quietly.

Monica looked around for Gloria, who seemed nowhere to be found. A minute later she finally appeared, wheeling out a big sheet cake with icing that read Best of Luck to the Best There Is. This time Monica couldn't hide being choked up.

"I want to thank all of you," she said to the cast and crew, sniffling, "for giving me the ten greatest years of my life."

"Back at ya, babe," Royce called back in a surprisingly emotional voice.

"Don't be a stranger," Jimmy said to her. "Promise?"

"Of course not."

The show's top makeup artist, Josie, showed up with paper plates and forks, handing out pieces of cake to everyone as fast as Gloria could cut them. Everyone took a piece—everyone but Chesty, who was wiggling her way over to Monica.

"Christ," Monica murmured to Jimmy under her breath. "Here it comes."

"I'm really sorry to see you go, Monica."

"Thank you, Chessy."

What she really longed to say was, "You're not sorry at all, you lying little bitch." But Monica was going for dignity and class right up until the end.

The party was mercifully brief, as if everyone understood that the longer she lingered in the studio, the harder it would be for her. She said good-bye to them all individually, even Christian, who patted her on the back as of she were a baby in need of a burp. She'd already cleaned out her dressing room the day before, but her coat was there, and she had to go collect it.

She opened the door, remembering the first time she'd walked into the room, excitement zapping every nerve ending in her body as she realized she'd finally found steady acting work and would no longer have to wait tables or live in that crummy apartment of hers. She'd given a decade of her life to this job.

She grabbed her coat, slinging it over her shoulder Sinatra style, and walked out of the studio. The usual cluster of fans was there to greet her. As she always did, she stopped to talk to them. She felt guilty that she knew what was in store for her character when they didn't.

She waved good-bye, turned the corner, and stopped. What now? She looked up; the sun was shining, its rays reflecting off the smooth glass of surrounding skyscrapers. The lump in her throat was growing bigger. She was all alone now, aching for comfort. She fumbled for her cell, impulsively calling Eric's home number. Given the slump he'd been in, he'd understand her pain. She got his answering machine; the message said he was playing out of town and gave his cell phone number in case of emergency. Was this an emergency? Not yet, Monica thought, as she resumed walking. But it could be.

The next day, letting herself into Monty's apartment, Monica was pleased to see it was relatively clean. Monty had either hired Rosa back or found someone else. She went to the kitchen and put away the basics she always brought for him— bread, milk, fruit, soup, tuna—before padding to his bedroom, always aware he might be asleep. He was sitting up in his recliner in his smoking jacket and pajamas, puffing on a cigar.

Monica choked, waving away the awful smoke. "What the hell are you doing? The doctor told you not to smoke."

"The doctor can kiss my bony white ass," Monty replied, his deeply lined face relaxed with pleasure as he puffed away on the stogie still clenched between his teeth.

Monica plucked it from his mouth, eliciting a loud gasp from her mentor.

She snuffed out the stinky cigar in the crystal ashtray on Monty's dresser and threw open the window.

"Honestly, Monty. What gives?"

"What gives is that the Grim Reaper will no doubt be coming to collect me sooner rather than later, so I may as well do what I damn well please."

Monica rolled her eyes. "Jesus Christ, between you and Gloria, I've got more morbidity than I can take."

Interest flickered in Monty's bright blue eyes. "So the fat-assed wench is feeling the icy grip of imminent death as well, eh?"

"She's not fat-assed, as you well know. She's managed to maintain her figure."

"Girdles are a miraculous thing."

"She was asking about you, you know," said Monica, ignoring the jibe.

"Did she want to know if I was dead yet?"

"Enough with death!" Monica railed. "I swear, you're going to make me more depressed than I already am."

"And why is my star pupil depressed?" Monty murmured with concern.

Monica felt her lower lip quivering. "I was written off the show. My character was killed by a zombie priest."

"Mmm." Monty looked out the window into the middle distance, his expression unreadable. Monica thought maybe he'd rise creakily from his recliner to put a consoling arm around her shoulder or at least proffer words of wisdom, the way Gloria did. Instead, he turned to her after a considerable length of silence and said, "You'll still be able to help me out with the rent, won't you?"

Monica jerked back slightly, as if shoved by an unseen hand. No comfort. No advice. Just selfishness.

"I can't believe you just said that."

Monty quickly began to backpedal. "Well, of course I'm sorry you lost your job, though it could be a blessing in disguise, since the genre is so tawdry. But—"

"But all you care about is yourself." Monica gaped at him. "Is that all I am to you? A goddamn bank on two legs?"

Monty looked panicked. "Of course not, of course not. Monica, darling, I didn't mean to upset you. Please sit down."

"Forget it." Tears of humiliation were threatening to erupt. "All these years, I've worshipped you. Helped you get by. Treated your opinions about the acting profession as the word of God passed down from on high. And what for?" Monica clutched her head in disbelief. "You don't give a shit about me. All you give a shit about is that I help pay your rent." She poked his shoulder. "Well, you know what, Monty? You can find some other former student of yours to pay your bills and hang breathlessly on your pronouncements about art and talent and selling out. This jackass has seen the light. I should have listened to Gloria a long time ago."

"Monica!" Monty called after her as she stomped out of his bedroom. "Monica, darling, please wait!"

"Kiss *my* bony white ass, Monty!" she yelled back to him, slamming his front door. Slamming doors was very satisfying, she found. She loved when she got to do it on the show, and it was even better in real life. It was drama without words.

Out in the hallway she realized her chest was heaving. *Stupid, stupid, stupid.*

She leaned against the wall and closed her eyes. Panic-driven insecurity invaded her body, seeping through her skin, twining itself around her bones, burrowing itself into her heart. The only person she wanted to talk to right now was Eric. It was irrational, perhaps even cruel, to call him. She didn't care. She dialed his cell.

TWENTY-EIGHT

"What the hell are you doing?"

Eric turned to look at Jason, standing in the doorway of his hotel room. The Blades had played two of their four games scheduled for the West Coast, winning both. They were on a streak. All the players were convinced it was because of cardboard Monica, whom they'd managed to transport intact across the country. Her presence was beginning to disturb and depress Eric, even though he, too, was now convinced it really did exert some kind of mystical pull that was causing them to win.

Eric turned back to his suitcase. "I'm packing to go back to New York."

Jason came to stand beside him. "Eric, we have a game tonight."

"I know that. And I'm flying out right after it. Red-eye. Don't worry. I got the okay from Ty. I'll be back in time for Friday night's game."

Jason sat down on the bed, watching his brother carefully. "Did someone break into your apartment or something?"

"No." Eric zipped up his suitcase, pinning a note to it to remind himself to bring it to the arena tonight so he could leave from there after the game against Anaheim. He'd already booked a car to take him directly to the airport.

"Time to share with your brother," Jason cajoled.

"Monica."

She'd left a message on his cell phone so choked with tears he could barely make out what she was saying. When he'd called her back, she picked up the phone on the first ring and burst into tears, telling him the show had let her go. He calmed her as best he could, instinctively offering to fly back so they could talk about it face-to-face. Monica hesitated, then said, "Please, yes, come. I can't believe you'd do this for me," she managed to choke out over the phone.

"Yes, you can," Eric replied softly before telling her to sit tight, that he'd be there as soon as he could.

There was no question in his mind he was doing the right thing. She needed him; he'd be there; it was that simple. If it made him a chump, so be it. He'd deal with that later. For now, all he knew was that the woman he loved was in pain, and it was him she wanted to pour her guts out to. Nothing else mattered.

Jason looked leery at the mention of Monica's name. "What's up with her?"

Eric started to talk, then stopped, realizing Monica had sworn him to secrecy about Roxie being killed off.

"I promised her I'd keep it private," said Eric.

"You knock her up?"

Eric looked bored. "Do you know how many times you've said that to me throughout our lives? Get a new line. It's getting kind of stale."

"Ouch. Someone's testy." Jason eyed his brother's suitcase. "What time is your flight?"

"Midnight."

Eric swung the suitcase to the floor so he could lie down on his bed. "Would you mind leaving? I really need to take a nap before tonight's game. I'm totally keyed up."

"I'm going, I'm going." Jason made it to the door, then turned. "Whatever is up, I hope it turns out the way you want it to."

"Thanks," said Eric with genuine appreciation.

For an asshole, his brother wasn't a bad guy.

Opening her door to find a bleary-eyed Eric standing there, Monica fought the urge to throw herself into his arms and burst into tears. Ever since she'd phoned him, she'd alternated between stunned lethargy and intense agitation, one minute mindlessly channel surfing so she didn't have to think, the other pacing endlessly, trying not to look at the clock every ten minutes. She'd experienced the torture of waiting before, but not like this. Time seemed to be taunting her.

Eric came into the apartment and dropped his bag. "You look like you need a hug."

Monica squeezed her eyes shut tight, still trying to hold back tears. "I do."

"Then come here."

She let him wrap his arms around her tight, those strong arms that had held her through so many nights. She'd agonized after accepting his offer to fly back across the country as to whether it might be sending him the wrong signal. He would think it meant they were getting back together. But Eric was one of the few people who really knew *her*: how she thought, how she felt, how she needed. He'd seen the real Monica, and that's who she needed to be. She burst into tears.

The harder she cried, the tighter his embrace became. His chin was resting atop her head, one hand gently stroking her hair. *Let me hide here,* thought Monica. *Let us just stand here and sway and not speak any words.* But it didn't work that way.

Gently, almost gingerly, Eric broke their embrace. "Want to talk?"

"Yes." Monica swiped the back of her hand across her wet, swollen eyes. "I must look great."

Eric smiled. "I've seen you cry before. On TV, remember?"

"Oh," Monica sniffled, blushing. "Right." She wrung her hands nervously. "Can I get you anything?"

Eric glanced longingly at the kitchen. "Coffee. Strong."

"Of course. How was your flight?"

"I managed to sleep a bit."

"That's good." She motioned toward the couch. "Sit down. Please."

Feeling unsteady on her feet, she went to refresh the coffee she herself had been drinking all night in order to wait up for him. She wondered if she'd go back into the living room to find him dozing on the couch.

Fumbling for a mug, she swore she could still feel the protective warmth of his arms around her. She rubbed her right temple, closing her eyes. Her feelings were a jumble. He loved her. And yes, she did love him, the real him, the one who'd been so relentlessly pursuing her. But she couldn't go there right now. She could only handle one emotional crisis at a time.

She prepared his coffee the disgusting way he liked it (three sugars, a touch of milk) and brought it out to him.

He smiled wearily. "Thanks."

"You're welcome."

He took a sip of coffee. "Oh, man. I can't tell you how great that tastes." He noticed her empty hands. "None for you?"

"I've been guzzling it all night," she confessed. "Waiting for you."

His eyes searched her face. "So, you were fired?"

"Not fired. Let go. They wrote Roxie off the show." She pointed a finger at him. "Remember, you cannot tell *anyone*."

"I told you, you have my word. Jason asked what was wrong, and I told him I couldn't go into details. But you have to let me know what's going to happen," he insisted. "I mean, it's the least you can do for a fan who flew cross-country for you."

"She's killed by Father Chessler. He's a zombie now."

"Oh my God. The guys are going to go *mental*." Eric looked horrified. "How come Chessler didn't just turn Roxie into a zombie, too?"

"Because she has to pay for killing Tucker Lamont in the

hospital, remember? And because the executive producer is screwing Chesty, and she wanted me out of the way."

Eric looked surprised. "Really? Stuff like that can happen?"

"It happens all the time. But it's just . . ." Monica's eyes began watering again. "It's never happened to me. And to be let go so that talentless little ho can be in the spotlight—it hurts, Eric. It really hurts. And it makes me doubt myself. Maybe I've lost my touch. Maybe I suck at what I do."

"I hear you there," said Eric ruefully.

"That's one of the reasons you were the one I wanted to talk to. You're out there performing in front of the public, too. You know what it's like to doubt yourself. Which brings me to something I need to say."

"What's that?"

She looked at him, shamefaced. "I'm so sorry I sent that cardboard cutout. It was a mean thing to do."

"Actually, it's our new good luck charm. Before every game the guys—" he stopped.

Monica narrowed her eyes suspiciously. "Before games the guys what?"

Eric's eyes were glued to his coffee cup. "I can't tell you."

"You better," she threatened.

"You don't want to know. Seriously."

"Well, now you've *got* to tell me."

Eric still wouldn't look at her. "There's this ritual. Before every game, each of the guys puts his hands on your boobs as we walk out of the locker room."

Monica was too shocked to speak for a moment. "Let me get this straight," she said slowly. "You guys *feel up* the cardboard cutout of me?"

Eric jerked his head up. "I don't!"

Monica snorted in disbelief. "Oh, no, of course not! You're way above that!"

Monica knew she shouldn't ask the next question, but her curiosity was getting the better of her. "Do you have any pregame ritual that involves the cardboard me?" she asked nonchalantly.

"Maybe."

"Tell me."

"Nope."

She was dying to know but refused to beg. Maybe he kissed her cutout's lips. Or said something sweet. She liked the idea of that, then chastised herself for liking the idea of it.

"Anyway," Eric resumed. "You said *one* of the reasons you wanted to talk to me was because you knew I'd understand what it was like to doubt your abilities."

"Yes, but your career is going well now, and mine is over, so I guess it's a moot point."

"Your career isn't over. Something else will come along."

"You don't know that," Monica insisted gloomily.

"No, I don't. But you're not thinking clearly right now. Give yourself some time to work through this, and you'll see that *W and F* was stupid to let you go." He took another sip of coffee, his penetrating gaze pinning her to the couch. "What's the other reason I'm the one you wanted to spill your guts to?"

Monica felt her cheeks begin to burn. "Because you know the real me. I know that sounds stupid," she said hastily, afraid he might laugh or scoff. "But when we were together, there were things I told you that I never told anyone else. You understood me. The way I thought. All of it."

She held her breath, waiting for him to say something. He was quiet for a long time.

"You're really fucking my head up here, Monica. You realize that, don't you?"

"I don't mean to."

"I know you don't. But it's all so confusing. What was real and what wasn't. What's real now and what isn't."

"I know," Monica whispered. She went to cup his cheek and then stopped, knowing it would only add to the list of confusing signals she was sending him. Eric was right; she wasn't thinking straight, not on any front.

"I shouldn't have asked you to come," she said.

His expression was intense. "I'm glad you did." He pulled his eyes away from hers. "I've missed talking to you," he said quietly.

"Me, too."

"We did have some good times, right?"

The pain in his voice tugged at her heartstrings. "Of course we did. Do you think we could try to be friends for now? At least still talk occasionally?"

"Friends. That would be great," Eric answered unenthusiastically.

"Friends," Monica agreed, holding out a trembling hand for him to shake.

Eric clasped her hand tightly, the heat and familiarity almost too much for her to bear. She thought about the first time she met him, what an unbearable jerk he'd been. He'd been an unbearable jerk when she'd broken up with him, too. The two Eric's: jerk Eric and real Eric. This was real Eric, holding her hand. Handsome, blond-haired, blue-eyed Eric who'd hopped a cross-country flight to comfort her. The Eric she'd let go.

She knew she need only say she wanted him back, and they'd be in each other's arms. But ironically, she was now the one with suspect motives. She would hate to reconcile with him, only to realize a few months down the line that she was taking advantage of him because she needed the safety blanket of a relationship when it felt like the rest of her life was going to hell. It wouldn't be fair. And yet the woman deep inside her who yearned, and who knew what it was to be with this man, was somewhat disappointed that he hadn't, well, burst into the apartment and tried to seduce her. Didn't he find her attractive anymore? Was that possible? Oh, Jesus, what a mess she was. Confused didn't even begin to cover it; she had crossed over into the realm of well and truly fucked-up. There was no way she was going to inflict herself on him right now.

Their lingering handshake finally ended. "Are you going to be okay?" Eric asked, standing up. "I could sleep on the couch if you wanted. Purely G-rated."

"I'm okay now," Monica assured him, trying not to think of all the times they'd made love on the couch. "I don't know how to thank you."

Eric paused. "I do."

Monica felt her heart begin to race. He was going to ask

for no-strings-attached sex. The attraction between them was still so strong. It wouldn't be inflicting herself on him if the connection were purely carnal, right?

"Come to the Blades home game Tuesday night."

Monica thought about it. What the hell else did she have to do? It wasn't like she needed to learn her lines for the next day. And they were friends now, weren't they? "I'll come on one condition," she said.

"What's that?"

"Your teammates don't think they can cop a feel of my real boobs for luck."

Eric laughed. "They won't need to, with the real thing in the house. Your usual seat will be waiting for you, Miss Geary. No locker room detours. I promise."

"Okay, then."

Feeling almost shy, she walked him to the door. "Again, I can't thank—"

Eric put his index finger to her lips. "Ssh. No thanks needed." He tenderly pressed his lips to her forehead; it felt more like a benediction than anything romantic. "You know where to reach me if you need to, right?"

Monica nodded.

"So . . . see you." He hoisted his bag onto his shoulder, heading down the hall toward the elevator.

"See you, too," she called after him. "Tuesday night? After the game?"

Eric's shrug was noncommittal. "Sure. We'll grab a beer or something."

"Sounds good," Monica said, watching him walk away. He'd flown cross-country for her. And for what? A twenty-minute conversation with a selfish, needy bitch. She might have her head up her butt right now, but there was one thing she knew for certain: she didn't deserve him.

TWENTY-NINE

"Dude. Mitcho. You telling me the real thing is in the house?"

Thad did nothing to contain his excitement as Eric casually mentioned to his teammates there'd be no need to touch cardboard Monica's boobs for good luck: the lady herself was at the game. He hated that goddamn ritual. It made him uneasy; he could just imagine what his teammates fantasized about as they touched her. Plus it showed a total lack of sensitivity toward him. Hockey players and sensitivity: what an oxymoron. At least Jason had the decency not to feel his ex—his cardboard ex—up. The two of them were always the last to the leave the locker room these days. Jason's ritual was to touch cardboard Monica's hand as he walked by; Eric's was to look into her eyes and silently profess, "I will always love you." He'd blow his brains out if any of his teammates found out. Even Jace didn't know.

"Yup, she's really here," Eric said, affixing his shoulder pads.

"This is gonna bring us super good luck," said Ulf.

"That's the idea."

"I just called Capesi," Michael put in casually. "And Theresa."

I don't need the PR anymore, Eric almost said but held his tongue.

"She's been awesome on *W and F* lately," said Tully. The rest of the team murmured their assent. Eric was dying to tell them what was going to happen when they tuned in next Friday, but he knew Monica would never forgive him. He actually hated that he knew; it was going to detract from his own pleasure when watching it.

Ulf came over to him, grabbing him in a brotherly headlock. "So, you guys are obviously back together. You back to nailing her nightly, you lucky bastard?"

"Bite me."

Ulf released him. "My, my. Someone's panties are in a twist tonight."

"Just fuck off, Ulf, okay? Seriously."

Ulf shoved his shoulder, walking away with an insulted sniff. Eric wasn't pissed at his teammate; he was pissed at himself. He'd come damn close to reflexively answering Ulf's question the way the old Eric would have: *Oh, man, she is better in the sack than ever.* But he'd stopped himself; he had to give himself credit for that. Even so, it alarmed him that the old Eric still lurked just beneath the surface.

Dressed and ready to hit the ice, he hung back with his brother as, one by one, his teammates touched cardboard Monica's breasts. When it was Ulf's turn, he mimed an orgasmic moan, his index finger rhythmically flicking cardboard Monica's crotch.

"What a dick," Eric whispered to his brother.

"*Are* you guys back together?" Jason murmured.

"No. Not really," said Eric, sounding as miserable as he felt. "I don't think so. I mean, I know she cares about me. Who the hell knows?"

"See? You are a good luck charm."

Monica smiled, walking out of Met Gar with her "friend," Eric. The Blades had won 4–2 over the Tampa Bay Turks.

She was happy for Eric, as well as happy that the crowd went
nuts when her face was shown on the scoreboard, with the
Blades banging their sticks for her on the ice not once, but
twice. Despite this affectionate gesture, she and Eric had
agreed not to meet in the Green Room, because Monica had
no desire to see Eric's teammates. The thought of them touching her cardboard breasts still disturbed her.

Eric held the door open for her, and they walked smack into
a solid wall of photographers and reporters. While the photographers snapped away, the reporters yelled out questions.
Were they back together? Was it serious? Who called whom?

"No comment," Eric said with a smile as he ushered her
into the back of a waiting cab.

Nothing was secret in this town, Monica thought. It also
explained why Theresa had left an excited message on Monica's cell, asking her to stop by FM PR's office tomorrow
morning. *Why not? What else do I have to do?*

Monica glanced out the window of the cab as it sped uptown. "How do you want to handle things with the press?"

"How do *you* want to handle it?"

"I don't know," Monica admitted. "Let me think about it."

"Fine." Eric sounded tired. "Would it be too ballsy of me
to ask you to keep coming to games?"

"I don't mind, as long as I don't have anything else going
on."

"What else would you have going on?" Eric asked tersely.

Monica turned back to him, wounded. "I'm not a total
loser, you know. I might have been written off the show, but I
do have other things going on."

Eric held up his hands in surrender. "Okay. I meant no offense."

"No offense taken," said Monica, pushing her back against
the opposite door of the cab, mildly embarrassed about how
happy it made her feel that he might be jealous. "How are
your parents?" she asked suddenly. The claustrophobic New
York night was making her think of the wide-open spaces of
Eric's childhood home.

"They're doing okay. They're selling the farm to Jason,
Delilah, and me. We want to keep the house in the family."

Monica tried to picture Eric's father without his cows, his mother not talking to the "chickadees." "Are your folks sad?"

"Yeah." Eric looked depressed. "But my folks will finally be able to travel. My brother and I will just use it in the summer."

Monica felt sad she might never see Eric's folks again. "Tell them I wish them all the best."

"I will."

Eric gazed at her curiously as the cab jolted them over a pothole, making both of them wince.

"What's up with *your* parents? You never talk about them."

"There isn't anything to say, though I *am* going up there this weekend so they can insult me and tell me how I've wasted my life. They'll probably be happy I've been written off the show. That will give them an opening to tell me I should go to business school and get my MBA."

"Sounds like fun."

"Oh, it's a barrel of laughs."

"Is that why you never brought me there?"

"Yes," Monica said stiffly. "The only thing lower than acting on their totem pole would be a professional athlete. They'd assume you were an idiot."

"The way you did when you met me," Eric pointed out.

"You *were* an idiot when I met you." Monica became wistful. "Remember how you tried to pick me up the day you did your cameo on the show?"

Eric smiled. "That was my evil twin putting the moves on you, not me."

Monica lifted an eyebrow. "How's the evil twin doing?" she murmured.

Eric smiled wryly. "He's pretty much vanished since . . ." He trailed off.

. . . We broke up, Monica finished for him in her head. She was longing to reach out and take his hand, but again, she didn't want to send the wrong signal. She really needed to get her head screwed on straight before she approached the subject of reconciliation.

"I'm really beat," Eric said, yawning. "Would you mind if we canned going out for a beer?"

"I thought you were just being polite when you suggested t," Monica confessed.

"No, it was genuine. I told you: I miss talking to you."

"Me, too. Another time, then."

"Yup."

The cab pulled up in front of Eric's apartment first. He eaned forward, paying the driver the fare plus enough to :over the trip to Monica's and a tip.

"You didn't have to do that," she called after him as he slid ut of the cab.

"Wanted to," he said, heading into his building.

"Thanks," she said, but she wasn't sure he heard her.

She settled back against the patched and torn leather seat f the cab as it pulled away from the curb smoothly.

"Nice guy," the cabdriver noted in a thick West Indian ac-:ent.

"Very nice," Monica agreed, confusion enveloping her. No job, no boyfriend . . . one not her choice, the other very nuch her choice. She shook her head as if to jar her muddled nind back into a state of clarity. *Go home, go to bed, wake up omorrow, face the day, and take your time to figure it all out.* For now, that's all she could do.

"Have you seen these?"

There was no mistaking the jubilation in Theresa's voice is she directed Monica's attention to the pile of newspapers atop her desk, where she'd laid out issues of the *New York Post,* the *New York Sentinel,* the *Daily News*, and *Newsday*. All four featured photos of Eric and Monica leaving Met Gar after last night's game, the accompanying copy rife with speculation. Monica studied the pictures. It was weird to see herself and Eric together and think back to those months when their "relationship" was a calculated ruse.

"*Great* coverage." Theresa shut the papers, beaming at Monica, who had taken a seat across the desk. "I'm so glad you guys are back together."

"We're not."

Theresa's face fell. "What do you mean, you're not?"

"I went to a game last night. That's all."

Theresa sat down, beating out a slow rhythm on her desk with a pencil. "So what were you two doing together after the game?"

"Catching a cab back uptown together. We're friends."

"Friends. Interesting." Theresa paused, furrowing her brows. "Don't let anyone know that."

"*What?*"

"Keep the speculation going. It will keep people interested."

"Oh, I will, believe me. I need the attention more than ever."

Theresa's ears pricked up. "Why is that?"

Monica hesitated.

"Spill it," Theresa commanded. "I'm your publicist."

"You have to swear you won't tell anyone, especially Michael."

"I swear on the heads of my three beloved children. Now start talking."

"I've been let go from the show," said Monica, surprised to find herself tearing up. "Roxie is being killed by a zombie next Friday. My departure will be officially announced the following Monday."

Theresa's mouth fell open so wide you could have fit a baseball inside. "You're *kidding* me."

Monica gave her a withering look. "Do I look like I'm joking?"

"But you're the main reason people watch that show."

"You worked for the soaps. You know how it goes."

"They're jumping the shark," Theresa declared knowingly. "Ratings must be slipping."

"They are, but I don't think that's why I was let go," said Monica, trying not to sound as bitter as she was feeling. "The show's new little ingénue is sleeping with the show's new executive producer. She put the bug in his ear to get rid of me so she could be front and center, and voilà! It's bye-bye, Monica Geary."

"Who's the new executive producer?"

"Christian Larkin."

A gurgle of disgust came from the back of Theresa's throat. "He's a world-renowned asshole." She sat back, tenting her slim fingers thoughtfully. "You need to be in the public eye more than ever. I'd suggest you keep seeing Eric and accept any interview request about your departure."

"No problem." *What else do I have to do?* It was becoming the sad refrain of her life.

Theresa looked pleased. "Good girl. As for you and Eric, you know the drill: smile and 'no comment' your head off." Theresa paused. "Actually, you might want to hold hands every once in a while. Above all, keep going to the team's home games."

Monica narrowed her eyes. "Why?"

"Because everyone thinks you're their good luck charm. Go to the games, and we've got a chance for coverage from the sports reporters as well as the entertainment writers and gossip columnists."

"Did Michael tell you about the cutout?"

"Yes." Theresa chortled. "That was really brilliant, Monica, I have to say. I was so tempted to plant a piece about it, but I knew you'd kill me."

"*Kill* doesn't even begin to describe it." She wondered if Theresa knew about the boob-touching pregame ritual. Probably not, and Monica wasn't about to tell her, either. She didn't want to get Michael into trouble.

"So, you keep the public guessing," Theresa recapped, "and I will, too, giving the usual 'My clients have no comment at this time' line. I'll talk to Lou Capesi and Eric about this, too, so we're all on the same page."

"That would be great. Just make sure you tell Eric this new teasing of the media was your idea, okay? I don't want him thinking I came up with it."

Theresa looked baffled but shrugged. "Okay. Whatever you want. Anything else you want to talk about?"

"I don't know." Monica felt miserable all of a sudden. "I'll get another acting gig, right?" She hated the way she needed to get reassurance from everyone she talked to. What was next? Asking the doorman his opinion?

Theresa looked at her worriedly. "Is that a serious question?"

"Yes."

"Of course you will. Why don't you just enjoy your downtime, try to relax? And if you do anything interesting and press worthy, let me know, okay? So I can keep your name and face out there."

"You're a doll, Theresa."

"Hey, that's why I get paid the big bucks. Now get out of here. And don't forget: the Blades have a game on Friday night."

"I'll be there."

Not only for herself, but for Eric.

"Okay, let me make sure I can wrap my head around this."

Eric looked like he had a headache as he stared at Monica over a cup of coffee at Starbucks. He'd called and asked her to meet him after hearing from Theresa. Their simply sitting together was generating interest; Monica could see it: people glancing at them, people putting their heads together, whispering. She supposed she should have called Theresa, but it was too early in the morning.

"We want the public to think we're back together . . . maybe."

"Right," said Monica. She leaned toward him. "And lower your voice."

Eric rubbed sleep from his eyes. "And we're doing this because—?"

"I need the PR. Especially after all the hubbub dies down about you-know-what." It was T-minus one day until the show aired where Roxie was killed.

"Mmm." Eric took a long slug of coffee. "So, what are we, exactly?"

Monica blinked. "What do you mean?"

"*Are* we back together in some weird way?"

"I—we're friends," Monica said quickly, her heart beginning to pick up speed.

"So it's totally fake. Like last time. I mean, the first time."

"I guess." Confusion was beginning to nibble at her synapses again.

Eric ran his hand through his hair, a gesture Monica loved because he looked kind of sexy when he did it. "This would be real easy if I wasn't still in love with you." He blew out a deep breath. "Real, fake—I don't know if I can do this."

"Please." Monica slid her hand across the table and put it on top of his. "Please do it for me."

Eric's gaze sharpened. "I feel like I'm doing a lot for you lately."

Scalded, Monica slid her hand away from his. "You are," she admitted sheepishly.

"How about you do something for me, then?"

"Okay," Monica said cautiously.

"Tell me how you feel about me."

Monica's gaze dropped to the table. "It's complicated."

"Try," Eric demanded.

"I care about you," Monica said softly. "I just don't know how to define it right now."

Eric snorted. "Oh, that's rich."

"What? What's your problem?"

"When we were together and I said I didn't know how to define things, you tore me a new one, telling me I was scared to."

"You *were* scared," Monica countered vehemently. "Look, do you have any idea what a state I'm in right now about being written off the show? I can't think straight about anything, including you. Is that definitive enough for you?"

"No, actually. I want to know if any of your caring for me includes romantic feelings."

"Yes," Monica admitted reluctantly. "But I can't go down that road right now, Eric. I just can't. I need us to be just friends for now."

"Fine," Eric said, looking somewhat mollified. "As long as I know I still have a shot, I can deal with this latest charade."

Monica winced. "I wish you wouldn't use that word."

"What would you prefer we call it?"

"A mutually beneficial arrangement?" Monica offered

tentatively, remembering the phrase they used way back when this whole thing began.

Eric frowned. "Fine. Mutually beneficial arrangement, take two."

"This wasn't my idea, you know," Monica felt compelled to add. "It was Theresa's."

"So she said."

Monica heaved a sigh of relief. Theresa hadn't forgotten. She didn't look as desperate as she felt.

Eric drained his cup, and stood. "You'll be at the game tonight?"

"Can't. I'm having dinner with Gloria."

Eric looked mildly disconcerted. "I guess we'll have to make do with cardboard Monica."

Monica frowned. "I'm sure you'll survive." They began walking out of Starbucks together. "Do you feel better now that we've talked?"

"I guess. It's still an extremely fucked-up situation, if you ask me."

"Not as bad as a soap opera, though." They paused on the corner. "Will you be watching tomorrow?"

"We've got a team meeting tomorrow afternoon, so we'll be watching together in the Green Room. I kind of wish I didn't know." Eric checked his watch. "I've gotta fly. Call me to let me know when our next fake rendezvous will be, okay?" He leaned over and gave her a quick peck on the cheek.

Monica nodded, watching as he ducked into a cab. She waited until it was far enough down the avenue to touch the spot on her cheek where he'd briefly pressed his lips. He was right: the situation was absurdly complicated. But at least he still seemed willing to wait for her to sort her own feelings out. A lot of other guys wouldn't. But Eric Mitchell, it had finally dawned on her, wasn't like other guys.

THIRTY

Stunned silence reigned over the Blades as Friday's episode of *W and F* ended with a close-up of Roxie's lifeless
body on the floor. No one moved, even as the show's flowery
theme music began playing over the credits. Even though
Eric knew what was coming, he could barely breathe as Father Chessler squeezed the life out of Roxie, her eyes bulg-
ing, her body flailing, until she slumped lifelessly to the floor.
Looking like a zombie himself, Thad switched off the TV.

Tully broke the silence. "No way she's dead. No way.
We'll find out Monday she's just unconscious or something."

Eric heard sniffles in the back of the room and turned. Ulf
was wiping his nose with his knuckle. "Are you crying, you
pussy?"

Ulf's head shot up. "*No*. It's my allergies, you fuckwit."

Thad looked distraught as he began pacing the front of the
room. "I can't believe this. I can't believe they'd kill Roxie."

"It's cold, man," said Burke Dalton, shaking his head in
total disbelief. "Totally cold. I can't believe it."

"I know," Thad said miserably. "What's the point of watching now if Roxie isn't on?"

Eric made a mental note to tell Monica how upset all the

Blades were over Roxie's demise. He knew she'd love it; maybe it would help her get over her current insecurity.

Broken men, they began filing out of the Green Room. Jason held Eric's forearm to hold him back from the rest of the fray so they were walking some distance behind.

"You have to know whether Roxie is really dead or not," Jason wheedled in a low voice. "I swear I won't tell a soul. Not even Delilah. I'm your twin brother, dude. We're blood. You can't hold out on me."

Eric glanced around to make sure there was no one else behind them. "Roxie's dead," he whispered.

"God. Damn." Jason exclaimed loudly. A couple of Blades turned around. "Sorry guys, I'm just upset," Jason explained. Nodding, the players continued on their way.

Stealthily turning back to Eric, Jason whispered, "Is that why you flew back to New York? Was Monica freaking out?"

"Yeah."

Jason looked confused. "Are you guys back together?"

"We're friends," Eric maintained flatly.

"Haven't you ever seen *When Harry Met Sally*? There's no such thing as a man and woman just being friends, unless the guy is gay."

"Listen, I don't know what's going on between us right now," Eric muttered.

Eric knew he and Monica weren't strictly *friends*; they were in some weird limbo in between, one he hoped they'd get out of, though he had no idea if or when that might happen. Ambiguity wasn't something Eric could deal with for long. He always knew what he wanted and was used to getting it, when he wanted it. Patience wasn't his strong suit, despite declaring to Monica while wooing her that he would wait as long as it took to break through her defenses. He just hoped all his patience wasn't in vain.

"The ratings are in the toilet, and I'm thrilled."

Gloria looked positively gleeful as she stretched out languidly on Monica's couch, relating what was going on at *W and F*. Three months had passed since Christian had let Monica go, yet she was getting more fan mail than ever. So was the show, apparently, angry letters pouring in by the thousands, informing the network that a boycott was being organized. It made Monica feel cherished, valued.

Now that she'd lost her job, she realized what a gift the show had been. It had allowed her to do what she loved, and it entertained millions of people. There were struggling actors out there who would give anything to have the adulation, outlet for their creativity, and steady paycheck she'd taken for granted for ten years. She got sick to her stomach whenever she thought about how much time she'd wasted not appreciating what she had. She swore she'd never bad-mouth soaps again.

"Have you been watching at all?" Gloria asked, swirling her Rob Roy in its glass. Monica wasn't even sure what a Rob Roy was. Something her grandparents used to drink, she thought.

"I caught a few episodes," said Monica. "The one where Chesty's character kills off the zombie king, and the other where she gives birth to Royce's child." Monica suppressed a smirk.

"Go on, grin, you vain bitch," Gloria urged. "I know you want to. The crew were trying hard not to laugh during both scenes. She's a nightmare."

Monica grinned.

"We all miss you terribly," Gloria continued, looking miserable. "Royce doesn't make rude comments to anyone anymore. Jimmy doesn't even have the energy to yell; he's a shell of his former, manic self. It's just not the same."

"I miss you guys, too." She'd always hated it when actors told the soap press that the others on the show were "family," but now she knew it was true.

Gloria eyed her critically. "You've been awfully tight-lipped about Mr. Mitchell."

"I know."

"Any particular reason?"

Monica sighed. "It's complicated."

Gloria rolled her heavily lined eyes. "Honey, it's always complicated."

"We're doing the charade thing again, mainly to help me."

"But—?"

"But I want it to be real."

"So make it real."

"I'm afraid. I don't trust my own motives at this point. And I'm afraid he could turn around and hurt me again." Monica bit her lip. "I'm going to wait a little while longer. Until I'm completely sure."

"What are you waiting for? The Rapture?"

"The right time."

Gloria gave an exasperated sigh. "And how will you know when that is?"

"I don't know. I just will." Monica wondered if she sounded crazy—or worse, immature. But she couldn't help how she felt.

Gloria belted down half her drink and then got serious. "He's not going to wait forever. Men don't like to wait. I made that mistake with Anthony Quinn. When you're young, you assume you have all the time in the world. You don't. Do yourself a favor, and don't waste too much time thinking."

"I won't," Monica promised.

Gloria pursed her lips. "Speaking of not thinking, how's the doddering old bastard?"

"I don't know," said Monica. "I haven't spoken to Monty in months."

Gloria looked shocked. *"Really."*

"I don't want to talk about it."

Gloria just sniffed and concentrated on her drink.

The truth was, Monica missed Monty. She worried about him, too. She was glad she'd stood up to him, though she wished she'd been a little less emotional.

Gloria drained her drink, put it down on Monica's coffee table, and clapped her hands excitedly. "So, what fun are we getting up to today?"

"Movies."

"Porn?" Gloria asked hopefully.

"Oh, God, please. You must be kidding."

"You know, I starred in a blue film once. I—"

Monica covered her ears.

"Fine," Gloria huffed. "If you don't want me to share, I won't."

"Thank you."

"Just promise me we're not going to some artsy-fartsy film where two people sit in an empty restaurant for two hours, picking at shrimp and discussing the meaning of life. I want to see something where lots of things get blown up, and gorgeous young men hang out of car windows with bazookas chasing bad guys."

"I think that can be arranged."

Not what Monica had in mind, but she supposed it could be fun. Everything she did with Gloria was fun. Gloria was a good role model: no regrets, still open to new things. That's how Monica wanted to be in old age, with just one exception: she didn't want to squander her youth on love affairs. She wanted a relationship that was long, deep, and committed. And she knew who she wanted it with. She just needed to make the leap when the time was right.

"Here you go, boys."

Eric noticed the quiver in his father's hand as he handed over two set of keys to the family home, one to him and one to Jason. Outside in the driveway sat a gleaming white RV. The barn was silent and empty, the farm equipment gone. It had been surreal doing a walk-through of the house and seeing it devoid of furniture. Yet it wasn't empty; there were memories everywhere he turned, which was both comforting and disconcerting.

Eric gave his father a big hug. "You did the right thing, Dad. And we won't let you down."

His father pulled back, clasping him by the shoulders as he stared hard into his eyes. "Neither of you boys could ever let me down."

Eric and his brother looked down at the dirt at the same time. Off in the near distance, Eric could hear his mother and Delilah chattering away like two magpies. His father might still be stoic, but his mother was rarin' to go. They'd put their furniture in storage; the plan was to travel, then come back to

Flasher and buy a small house for the two of them near the farm.

"What's the first stop, Dad?" Jason asked.

"Your mother's goddamn sister Lucy in Kansas. Never liked me, and the feeling is mutual. At least we'll be able to sleep in the RV. The woman is the biggest slob I ever met."

"And then it's on to—?" Eric prompted.

"Texas," he said, looking happy for the first time in months. "I've always wanted to see the Alamo. And your mother wants to go to the beach."

"Sounds great," Eric and Jason said in unison. They turned and looked at each other. Whenever they were at the farm, their twin connection became especially strong.

Jane and Delilah wandered back to join their circle of three, the two of them looking happy. Jane squeezed Dick's arm. "You ready to roll, old man?"

"Who you calling old?" Dick shot back, his mouth curling into an affectionate smile. Eric felt relieved. If his dad could joke, he'd be okay.

His mother dug her sunglasses and a set of car keys out of her purse, swinging the keys on her index finger. "I'm driving."

His father turned to Eric and Jason. "See how she bosses me around?"

They all laughed, but it was a thin, forced sound, covering up for deep emotion.

Jane took Eric's face in her hands, kissing him hard on the cheek. "Be a good boy. We'll be in touch." She kissed Delilah in turn, then Jason. Dick hugged them all.

Eric watched as his mother hoisted herself up into the driver's seat of the RV.

"Jesus," said Jason worriedly. "How the hell is she going to back that thing out of the driveway? You know reverse has never been Mom's best gear."

Eric looked at his father's worried face through the windshield; he was obviously thinking the same thing as Jason. But his mother pulled it off.

"Good-bye, boys!" she called through the window, waving madly. "Good-bye, Delilah!"

"Good-bye!" Eric called along with Jason and Delilah as he watched his parents disappear in a cloud of dust.

"Ten bucks says they're only on the road ten minutes before Dad insists on driving," said Eric.

"That's a given," said Jason. He put an arm around Delilah's shoulder, squeezing tight. "Happy?"

She beamed up at him. "Very."

Eric felt a surge of envy watching them.

Delilah kissed Jason's cheek. "I'm going to go inside the house, think about decor."

"Go ahead."

Eric turned to his brother. "I'm glad we did this."

"Me, too." Jason kicked at a patch of dirt on the ground. "Think you'll be bringing Monica back here at some point?"

"Yup," said Eric.

He just wished he knew when.

THIRTY-ONE

"Miss Geary? There's some old guy down here named Monty who says he's a friend of yours. Should I send him up?"

Monica held down the intercom button in her apartment for a long moment, waiting for her incredulity to pass. In all the years Monica had known Monty, he'd only come to her apartment once: eight years ago when she threw him a birthday party. "Send him up."

"Will do."

Monty. Here. To see her. Apprehensive, she opened her apartment door to wait for him in the hallway. She was all too familiar with apprehension where Monty was concerned; it was the way she'd felt all those times he gave his weekly critique of her performance on *W and F*. This time it was different, though. Her anxiety was born of not having seen him in months, as well as her fear that he'd deteriorated. Masochistic, she knew that if he were in poor shape, she'd blame herself for pulling the plug on his financial and emotional support.

The elevator doors slid back, and out stepped Monty, his bearing as regal as ever, his trademark silk cravat around his neck. The man still had panache, even as he strolled toward

er at a snail's pace. He lifted his hand in an uncertain greet-
ng when he caught sight of Monica standing there. Monica
ifted a hand in return, catching a whiff of Monty's cologne
receding him. Another surprise: she'd never known Monty
o wear cologne in his life.

"Hello," she said coolly as he reached the door. "This is a
urprise."

Monty looked at her uncertainly. "An unwelcome one?"

"I don't know yet."

Monica ushered him inside, helping him off with his coat.
The temperature outside was edging up into the high seven-
ies, yet he was wearing a camel hair coat along with a V-neck
weater underneath.

Monty looked impressed as his gaze swept Monica's
apartment. "I'd forgotten how lovely your home is."

"Thank you."

She gestured for him to sit on the couch.

"Can I get you anything?" she offered as he slowly low-
red himself onto the plush cushions with a small grimace.

"No, no. I intend to be brief."

Monica felt the old familiar knot in her gut return. She
hated being wary of him, but that was his fault, not hers. De-
ermined not to show her uneasiness, she sat down opposite
him, her gaze as unnervingly direct as his had always been.

"What can I do for you?"

Monty cleared his throat. "I wish to apologize to you for
ll those years of belittling your career in daytime," he said,
his voice cracking slightly. "I've been thinking about it long
and hard, and I've come to the conclusion I'm a raging jackass. I hope you can forgive me."

Monica didn't know what to say. This was the first time
she'd ever seen him display humility. "Go on."

Monty took a deep, fortifying breath. "Dedication and talent is dedication and talent, no matter where it's practiced.
Don't ever put down what you do. And don't ever let others
put down what you do, either. You haven't squandered your
alent, Monica. If anyone's done that, it's me. When I think of
all the opportunities to act that I passed up over the years because I viewed anything commercial as 'selling out,' I want to

take my dear father's Luger out of the drawer and splatter my turtle-sized brain against the wall.

"I can't tell you how sorry I am." His deep blue eyes became teary. "I hope you can forgive me. I hope we can be friends again."

Monica's eyes welled up, too. "You can't imagine how much this means to me, Monty. Thank you." She came to sit beside him, squeezing his hand. "I know that was hard for you to do."

His smile was sentimental. "How well you know me." Monica was shocked at how cold his hand was. "Of course it was hard for me. But it needed to be said. I must confess, I was fearful you'd think I was just flattering you falsely so you would"—his eyes darted away in embarrassment—"assist me with some of the various aspects of living."

"You could never be that conniving."

"True, but I could be that selfish."

"*Are* you getting along okay?" Monica asked quietly.

"Perfectly fine. You'll be very pleased to know that I started auditioning again, and I've landed a small role in a sitcom pilot, *Her Majesty and Co.*, based upon the queen. I'm playing her butler."

"Monty! That's wonderful!"

"Yes, it is. But I never would have done it if weren't for you making me see the light. Take my advice: as long as you love what you're doing, keep doing it. That's it. End of speech."

Between Gloria and Monty, Monica was beginning to feel like she was continually being visited by the Ghosts of Acting Future, warning her about how her life might turn out if she made some of the same mistakes they did. Monty looked weary, as if his speech had worn him out. Still, a flicker of hope burned in his eyes.

"Are we friends again?" he asked tentatively.

"Of course. I've missed you terribly."

"I've missed you, too. I thought perhaps, to celebrate, I might take you out to lunch?"

"That would be lovely." My, this *was* a new Monty, offering to pay for something.

"Good." He rose slowly. "No chance of us running into the ogress, is there?"

"I don't know any ogresses," said Monica, flashing him a warning look.

Monty sighed, offering Monica his arm. "Onward and upward, my dear girl," he said, using the very same expression Gloria once had, which Monica found very telling. "Onward and upward."

THIRTY-TWO

"Oh, God, this is torture," Monica declared anxiously. "Pure torture."

Monica and Gloria were parked in front of Monica's TV set, waiting for the Daytime Drama Awards to be announced. It was a ritual they'd followed ever since they started working together: Gloria would come to Monica's at six a.m. bearing bagels and lox, and they'd turn on the RBC's early morning show, *Wake Up, USA*, to watch the nominations being announced live. This year, Elizabeth Taylor, a longtime soap fan, was making the announcements. When the show's hosts announced they were cutting over to Elizabeth live at her home, where she was gracious enough to be awake at three a.m. to do the honors, both Monica and Gloria leaned forward eagerly.

"She's been nipped and tucked a bit," Gloria snorted cattily.

"Ssh."

"She never knew about the solace Burton sought with me, the sweet, sweet nights—"

"Gloria, please shut up." Monica hated sounding irritated.

but she didn't want to miss a word, and six a.m. was just too early to start listening to tales of Gloria's sexcapades.

"Someone hasn't had their coffee yet," Gloria sniffed.

One by one, Elizabeth read out the nominees for a variety of categories.

Costume Design.

Direction.

Outstanding Writing. (For the first year ever, *W and F* wasn't nominated.)

Supporting Actor.

Supporting Actress. ("Sons of bitches," Gloria proclaimed when her name wasn't announced.)

Outstanding Lead Actor in a Daytime Drama. (Royce was nominated. "Oh, please," said Gloria. "A cardboard box has more ability than him. What are they *thinking*?")

And then, finally, Outstanding Lead Actress in a Daytime Drama.

"Here it comes." Monica bit down on her fist to stifle the scream she knew was coming if her name was announced—which it was. She screamed anyway.

"Thank you, God!" Monica began bouncing up and down on the couch.

"Ha, take that Christian Larkin, you little pissant! You, too, Chesty McTalentless!" Gloria cried. She threw her arms around Monica. "You deserve this, darling!"

"Wait, wait." Monica forced herself to calm down. The nominations for the final award had yet to be announced.

Monica held still, despite the excitement careening through her body.

"The nominees for Outstanding Daytime Drama series are," said Elizabeth Taylor in her tiny, breathless voice, "*Golden Days, Passionate Nights . . . The Heat and the Heart . . . Shadows and Horizons . . .* and *Reap the Wild Wind.*"

Monica and Gloria turned to each other, slack jawed.

"Disaster," Gloria snapped. "*W and F* has never not been nominated. Never!"

"I know." Monica was stunned. She was tempted to pick up the phone to call the show's former executive producer,

Michael, to comfort him and make sure he knew it was completely the fault of his successor, Christian, but not everyone got up to watch the announcements live.

Monica's phone immediately began ringing. The first of what would be many congratulatory calls throughout the day.

Gloria stifled a yawn. "Go answer your phone and accept your kudos. I'm going home and going back to bed. Kiss, kiss." She kissed the air and departed Monica's apartment with bagel in hand and a slightly despondent air.

By the time Monica hung up the phone hours later, her throat was sore from talking. She was about to crawl back into bed—she'd barely slept the night before, she was so keyed up about the nominations—when the biggest bouquet of red roses she'd ever seen in her life was delivered to her apartment. She fumbled eagerly to open the accompanying card. It read: "She shoots! She scores! Congrats on your nomination! Love, Eric."

Swooning inside, she put the flowers in a vase, carefully tucking the card back in its envelope. *The time's almost right*, she told herself.

She unplugged the phone and crawled between the sheets, feeling happier and more certain of herself than she had in months.

"I'm so glad you were able to come in on such short notice, Monica."

Monica smiled politely, trying not to gawk at the shelves full of Daytime Drama Awards lining William Drayton's palatial office. Drayton was the head of Daytime Programming, the man responsible for reviving *W and F* fifteen years ago by hiring the best writers, producers, and actors for a show that at that time had the lowest ratings in daytime.

At six foot three with the body of a linebacker, Drayton was physically intimidating. Always dressed impeccably in Italian silk suits, his legendary gaze was unnervingly direct, bordering on staring. Right now, he was staring at Monica, his expression serious. "I'm sure you can guess why you're here."

Monica did have an idea, but she wasn't sure she wanted to share it, just in case she was wrong.

"I've heard the show is in trouble," she replied guardedly.

Drayton gave a barking laugh. "That's one way of putting it. The show has been a disaster ever since Christian Larkin took the helm. This hasn't been formally announced yet, but Christian, Chessy, and the writers have all been fired. The old writing team is coming back. Michael hasn't agreed to come back yet as exec producer, but I'm working on it. I'd like you to come back, too, Monica."

His voice was somewhat formal; Monica sensed he didn't want to appear desperate. Well, she didn't care how *she* appeared. Her answer was a resounding yes. She was tempted to jump up and throw her arms around his neck and kiss him.

Drayton looked relieved. "I'm so glad."

"I love working on this show," Monica said softly.

Drayton smiled. "Good."

"I'm just curious: How will Paige be written off? And how will Roxie be written back on?"

"The zombies become enraged at Paige when they learn she's the one who actually killed the zombie king. They tear her limb from limb, then burn her body in a sacrificial rite that also releases them from their eternal hell.

"As for Roxie, she isn't really dead. Prior to Father Chessler attacking her, she discovered a secret antidote to make her appear dead if attacked. She's been hiding away in a mountain cabin, waiting for Paige's downfall and the zombies' demise. She'll return triumphantly to town, where she and Grayson will wed, then have their child."

"Sounds great."

This was Roxie's, what, third wedding? Monica loved it when Roxie got married, because it meant the show would go on location to shoot at some exotic locale. Last time it was Hawaii. Maybe this time they'd go to Paris. "When will you be announcing my return formally?" she asked, trying not to sound too eager.

"As soon as we announce the other changes to the show, which is Friday. Expect a press barrage."

Monica smiled to herself. As soon as she left the office, she'd call Theresa. Theresa lived for press barrages; so did Monica. She couldn't wait to tell Eric her good news. According to him, the Blades no longer tuned in to *W and F*. Her return would bring the team, and the multitudes of other fans that had been upset by her departure, back into the fold.

Drayton stood, his large hands spread on his glass-topped desk. "I guess we're all set, then. Expect your first batch of scripts the end of next week. In the meantime, I'll call your agent, and we can discuss the terms of your new contract."

Monica rose and went to the desk to shake Drayton's hand. "Thank you for your faith in me, Mr. Drayton—"

"William."

"William. I won't let you down."

"You never have. Welcome back to the *W and F* family, Monica."

"Stop jumping around. You're making me dizzy."

Sitting on Monica's couch, Eric watched in amusement as she pogoed around her living room, shouting out joyfully that *W and F* wanted her back. It was fantastic to see her happy; even more fantastic that he was the first one she'd called.

"Oh," Monica said, breathlessly, coming to a stop. "Can you believe it? I mean, can you believe it?"

Eric chuckled. "I think that's the thirtieth time you asked me that in five minutes."

"It's because I can't believe it," said Monica, launching into a series of small pirouettes. "I kind of knew what might happen when Drayton called me in. But I didn't want to get ahead of myself or come off as egotistical."

"You? Egotistical?" Eric teased.

"Very funny. So he told me Christian and Chesty were out, the writers were out, and the old writers were coming back in, and asked if would I come back to the show!" She started jumping up and down again, giving a small squeal. "This is so amazing!"

"No, it's not. It makes total sense. You're a great actress, and the show just isn't the same without you." He smiled at her cheekily. "I take it you've gotten over your 'Daytime is the lowest form of acting' fixation?"

Monica came back down to earth, plopping back down on the couch beside him, "Totally. Absolutely." She threw her hands above her head like an excited child. "I love daytime! I love my job! I love life! I love you!"

A shock wave hit the room. Eric could feel Monica tense as he slowly turned to look at her. "Do you realize what you just said?"

Monica dropped her gaze. "Yes."

"And you mean it?"

"Of course I do," Monica murmured.

"Are you sure?" Eric asked skeptically. "Because I'd hate to think it just slipped out because you're carried away."

Monica lifted her eyes to his. "It wasn't said in the heat of the moment." She was tentative as she took his hand, her twined fingers sliding up and down between his nervously. "I wouldn't say it if it wasn't true. I've felt this way for a while, but I was too afraid to say it."

"Why's that?"

Monica hesitated. "Well, I wasn't sure whether you really wanted me back, or just wanted me back as a good luck charm because you play well when I'm at games." Her fingers stopped moving. "But then I realized it had to be the real you wooing me, because the fake you would have been much smoother." She giggled. "Those things you did were so dorky, Eric. But I loved it."

"So now do you believe I love you, and that I'd never hurt you again?" he asked, overcome with remorse for all the pain he'd caused her.

Monica looked up at him, her body trembling slightly. "Of course I believe you love me," she said with a small quaver in her voice. "And of course I believe you won't hurt me again."

Relief dashed through Eric. "Good."

Monica turned apologetic. "I'm sorry it took me so long—"

"Enough talking."

He grabbed her and kissed her roughly, more turned on

than he ever thought he could be by the low guttural sound
that instantly rose in her throat, heralding desire.

"Bedroom?" Monica suggested huskily as she tore her
mouth from his. The wild desire in her eyes was matched
only by the hungry pout of her lips. He was tempted to take
her on the couch right now; to rip the clothes from her body to
reveal the perfect, soft skin beneath; to watch excitedly as she
rode him, her head thrown back, her long hair cascading
down her back. But he restrained himself. If she wanted to
make love in the bedroom, then he'd make love to her in the
bedroom. He wanted it to be all about her: *her* wants, *her*
needs, *her* happiness.

And so he picked her up and carried her to the room where
he intended to drive her crazy.

Jesus, thought Monica, *I can't take my eyes off him.* They
were as eager as teenagers, shedding their clothes the minute
Eric had kicked the bedroom door shut behind them. How
many times had she bitten down on those powerful shoulders,
making him cry out in hoarse but delighted pain? Run her
finger along the white scar across his knee from an old hockey
injury? Kissed her way down the taut abdomen and slim hips
to take him in her mouth? She felt her nipples rise just looking at him and thinking about it; saw him rise, too, nakedly,
unabashedly. Lust twisting through her, she tugged his hand
and led him to the bed. She lay down, Eric propped up on his
elbow beside her.

"Kiss me," she commanded, quietly reassured by the way
he was looking at her, as if she were a wonderment created
just for him.

Eric, sloe-eyed, leaned over and kissed her softly, his hand
brushing her cheek. "I love you so much."

"I love you, too."

Her words seemed to enflame him. Gentleness disappeared, replaced by the desperate ardor that had possessed
both of them once they hit the bedroom. His mouth claimed
her mouth, then her breasts, the kisses searing her skin, brand-
ing her as his and his alone. Monica returned his passion, run-

ing her hand along his solid hips and down his muscled
high, the skin hot beneath her fingers and hard, as an athlete's
body should be. The burning sensation licking its way through
er began transforming itself into complete fire as Eric began
stroking her inner thighs.

"Wider," he urged.

Shuddering, Monica opened her legs wider to accommo-
ate him. A gasp erupted from her lips as his fingers began
xploring her, teasing out all the wildness she usually kept so
well-hidden and under control. His fingers moved faster, but
Monica resisted the temptation to explode. She wanted him
to know the same delicious agony she was now in. Something
hey could share in together.

"Stop."

Eric stopped, panting lightly. A thin sheen of sweat coated
his body. Monica loved it; it was sexy, animal. She pushed
him gently so that he was on his back, then climbed on top of
him, her teeth biting down softly on his sculpted shoulders,
her hair brushing against his face. Eric groaned as his splayed
hands came up to run themselves up and down her back before cupping and kneading her bottom. Monica lifted her
head; she wanted to see the hunger in his eyes ignite as she
began a trail down his body, first with her fingertips, then with
her tongue. When she got below his hips, she grasped him,
hard. He was rigid, pulsing in her hand. Smiling at him wick-
edly, she lowered her head and began flicking her tongue
around the tip, moving her hand up and down him gently.

Eric groaned with pleasure. "You're torturing me."

"Good."

"Let's see who's better at it."

Pulling her back up his body, he flipped her so she was on
her back. He was poised above her, his face flushed and wanting. Monica could feel the heat rippling up and down his
body, the way it joined with her own, doubling the threat of
complete conflagration. Eric kissed her hard, then reached
over and opened the night table drawer, pulling out one of the
oil packets left there from when they'd been intimate months
before. He sheathed himself, then smiled down at her wick-
edly.

"Torture time for Miss Geary."

He parted her wide. Monica held her breath, waiting, waiting, excitement beginning to punch its way through her.

He entered her slowly, so slowly she thought she might go mad. The whole time, he was watching her, his gaze hooded and sure.

"Is this how you want it?" he asked, beginning to move inside her. Monica couldn't speak. Eric's hands reached to take her wrists, pinning them over her head. His grip was hard enough to leave bruises. It was what she wanted. She wanted him to love her so hard it hurt.

He began thrusting deeply, his thirst for her an assault on her senses. Monica's head thrashed wildly on the pillow, her juddering body arching up to meet his. Yet she could feel him holding something back from her as his grip on her wrists slowly slackened.

"What?" she asked, her own voice sounding strangulated to her ears. "What is it?"

"Ride me. Hard."

Monica let out a low moan as they flipped positions once again, and she mounted him, slowly taking him inside. His eyes were absolutely riveted to her, his gaze glazed. She began moving atop him, the rhythm slow and easy, her loving it as Eric threw his head back, the taut muscles of his neck rigid with self-control.

She was breathing hard now. Eric reared up, grabbing her face, kissing her with brute force, biting down hard on her bottom lip. Monica cried out in violent pleasure. He lay back down, watching her, his hands coming to stroke her hips before reaching around her to clasp her buttocks. Monica, full with the feel of him inside her, arched back, riding him as hard as she could, slamming her body down against his again and again, each jolt of flesh against flesh shattering her body into pieces. He bucked beneath her, clearly wanting release, but Monica refused to give it and kept riding him fiercely, this man whom she'd doubted for so long.

She wanted him to be the first to explode, but Eric tricked her as he began to tease and caress her most intimate place. Monica fell forward, a series of small sobs shaking her body as the room around her seemed to fall away and she lost control, her orgasm pounding through her as she screamed her pleasure. Barely able to breathe, she lifted her head just in time to see the pleasure on Eric's face as he grabbed her hips and pumped her wildly atop him until he exploded inside her, gasping and groaning.

The real Eric.

Her Eric.

THIRTY-THREE

GRAYSON: *My God, Roxie! You're alive!*
ROXIE: *Yes, my love. (RUNS INTO HIS WAITING ARMS, WHERE THEY KISS PASSIONATELY.) Nothing could ever separate us—not even a zombie priest!*
GRAYSON: *And now—now that evil has been vanquished and the zombies are no more, we'll never have to be parted again. My darling, will you marry me?*
ROXIE: *Oh, Grayson. Nothing could make me happier (PUTS HER HAND ON HER BELLY). You, me, and Grayson, Jr., all together as we should be. It's what I dreamed of all those lonely nights in the cabin.*
GRAYSON: *You'll never be lonely again, Roxie. Not as long as I draw breath.*

"Cut!"

Jimmy waddled down from the control booth, scowling. "Royce! That sucked! We'll have to do another take—as if I have goddamn time!" He turned to Monica, his scowl quickly transforming itself into a smile. "Great job."

Monica took a small bow. "Thank you."

"Everyone, take five."

Monica moved off set, where Gloria stood waiting, a proud smile on her face. "That was exquisite, darling. And that glow on your cheeks that you've been sporting all week—I assume it has nothing to do with being back in Roxie's fuck-me pumps and everything to do with Eric?"

"Yes," Monica said, on the verge of gushing like a lovesick adolescent. The two weeks that she and Eric had been back together were the way she'd always hoped her life would be: a man she loved, a job she adored—things were finally coming together.

Eric life's, however, had hit a major glitch: The Blades weren't playing well. The hot streak they'd attributed to cardboard Monica had run its course, and they were playing mediocre, inconsistent hockey, stuck at around the .500 mark. She tried to make him feel better about it, but soon learned there was no talking to a hockey player about his game unless you were a hockey player yourself. She was still front and center at every home game she could attend, but it seemed the magic had worn off.

Gloria continued to look elated. "I'm so happy for the two of you, darling." She shook her head, sighing contentedly. "What a change of atmosphere since you returned. Everyone is back to his or her old self. Jimmy's screaming. Royce is sucking. It's pure heaven." She leaned in close to Monica. "I've heard some rumors about the upcoming story line," she said under her breath.

Monica's ears pricked up. "From?"

Gloria shrugged. "Just around. Do you want to hear?"

"Of course."

"Apparently," Gloria said authoritatively, "Roxie's baby isn't Grayson's."

Monica drew back. "What?"

"It's going to turn out that Grayson has a twin brother he never knew about. He had Grayson kidnapped and put in prison in the Seychelles, and he's tricked everyone into thinking *he's* the real Grayson, including Monica, who slept with him."

"Wow." An evil twin story line. Monica had never done one of those. It was a daytime convention she wasn't fond of, but she supposed it could be fun.

"Then the brother gets killed fighting in Bovinistan—"

"That's not a real country!"

"Of course it isn't, darling. Anyway," Gloria continued breathlessly, "Roxie, thinking he's dead, finds love with the new hot attorney in town; except the real Grayson escapes from prison and returns, and Roxie must decide between the two men."

Monica's toes curled happily in her shoes. "Oooh, that sounds good."

"My role is being expanded, too. Antonia's old love, Thane Wintergreen, will be returning to town, and the two will re-kindle their love from years ago."

"That's great, Gloria. It sounds like bringing the old writing team back will really make a difference."

"Indeed. Have you decided what you're going to wear to the Daytime Drama Awards?"

"Not yet. You?"

"I'm going to wear a dress Diane von Fürstenberg designed for me back in the seventies. The neckline plunges so far you can see my toes," she said with a delighted laugh.

"Mmm." Monica suppressed a wince, not sure she wanted to picture it. Gloria . . . plunging neckline . . . her boobs so thin and droopy she could toss them over her shoulders like scarves if she wanted to . . . it could get ugly. Monica didn't want her friend to humiliate herself. Maybe she'd try to gently nudge her into choosing something else.

"I take it Eric will be escorting you?" Gloria asked suggestively.

Monica sighed. "God, you're the most lecherous woman in the Western Hemisphere. Of course Eric will be with me."

Discussing the Awards reminded Monica that she needed to speak to Eric about it. She was excited by the prospect of him being there if she won; just imagining the pride she'd see on his face made her dizzy with love for him.

"I'd better get back on set," said Monica.

"And I'm off to tighten my face." Gloria clucked her tongue. "Honestly, I don't understand women spending all that money on plastic surgery when Preparation H works just ıs well." She gave Monica a quick peck on the cheek. "Au evoir for now. And thank Thor you're back."

Which method of suicide do you think would be less pain-ul?" Tully asked his teammates glumly. "Blowing my brains ›ut, or mixing sleeping pills in my Wheaties?"

"Gun," Thad replied just as miserably. "Definitely gun."

Despondency dominated the Blades locker room as the ·eam slowly, sadly undressed following their loss to Jersey. ›espite winning a brutal game against Philly two nights be-·ore, they'd missed making the playoffs by a single point, vith Jersey beating them out tonight for the last spot.

"We could all kill ourselves together," Ulf suggested. 'Like a cult."

Eric frowned. "You're an idiot." Still, he couldn't help pic-·uring their motionless bodies in a heap on the ice. That'd ·ure get press coverage.

"I think we lost because Coach got rid of the Monica cut-›ut," said Burke, grimacing as he removed his shoulder pads, ·he result of suffering a serious hit in the second period. "I'm ·ot kidding."

"You lost because you weren't at your best. Period."

All eyes swiveled simultaneously to Ty Gallagher stand-·ng in the locker room doorway, his trademark scowl firmly ·ixed in place. The displeasure on his face sent a small bolt of ·umiliation through Eric. At least he knew he wasn't alone: ·is teammates looked just as degraded as he did.

"Listen up," said Ty, unsmiling, as he closed the locker ·oom door behind him.

Rank with sweat and in various stages of undress, the Blades did as their coach asked. He tortured them in his usual way, making prolonged eye contact with each and every one ›f them. He who flinched was a pussy. When it was Eric's ·urn, he held Ty's gaze despite the strong impulse to drop his ·yes to the floor.

"I'll make this brief," Ty began tersely. "We didn't make ·he playoffs because we didn't come together as quickly as we needed. A lack of chemistry on and off the ice led us to dig a hole too deep for ourselves to climb out of. We've gelled now, but unfortunately, it's too little, too late."

He sighed heavily. "We have the nucleus for a good run at the Cup next year. We've got the players we need. It's just a matter of you guys hitting the ice running the minute next season starts. You feel like shit right now, right?"

The team nodded.

"I've been there," Ty told them. "My advice is to savor your disappointment. Remember this feeling. Hold on to it. Keep it with you so that you'll do anything to make sure you're never in this position again."

He dismissed them with a curt nod of the head. Eric was turning to his locker when Ty gripped his forearm. "Come to my office when you get out of the shower."

Eric nodded. Singled out again. Shit. He hoped Ty didn't rip him too badly. He asked Jason to tell Monica to wait for him, since he'd be slightly delayed, and headed for the showers.

Ty didn't motion for Eric to sit, so Eric assumed his coach was going to be brief, which was fine with him. He squared his shoulders and waited for the verbal onslaught.

"You started the year off slow," said Ty.

Eric's shoulders slumped slightly. "Yeah, I know."

"But I've been happy with the caliber of your performances toward the end of this season. The trade for you didn't work out for us this year. But you showed glimmers of what we were looking for. Make sure you play that way all next season."

Eric tried to contain his elation. For Ty, that was a glowing endorsement. "I will." He couldn't wait to tell Monica, and Jace—especially Jace.

"Don't get fat in the off-season," said Ty. "I need you at your peak from the moment the puck drops on opening night."

"That won't be a problem, Coach."

He'd work out every day. Rent ice time with Jace so they could keep their skills sharp. He'd make sure he came into

training camp in game shape. The idea of rising to the challenge pumped him up.

Ty looked down at his notes, signaling the conversation
was over.

Eric turned to go.

"By the way," Ty called after him, "tell your girlfriend I'm
glad she's back on *W and F*. It sucked without her."

Eric turned back to him, grinning. "Will do. Have a good
summer, Coach."

"Really? He said that? That the show sucked without me?"

Monica couldn't hide her delight as Eric related to her the
details of his postgame conversation with Ty.

"Yup."

"I must be doing something right." She snuggled against
Eric in the back of the cab taking them back uptown to her
place. "I need to talk to you about something."

"Yeah?"

"The Daytime Drama Awards are in two weeks. I take it
you're going to be my dream date?" she said kittenishly, rubbing her nose against his.

"Uh . . . I meant to talk to you about that."

The undertone of apprehension Monica heard in his voice
made her sit up.

"Yes?" she said, trying to keep her voice from sounding
clipped.

Eric looked apologetic. "I'm not going to be able to go
with you to the Awards." He rubbed his neck; Monica imagined a knot of tension forming there, fast. She assumed this,
because a knot was also forming in her neck right now, too,
matched by one coalescing in her stomach.

This time she couldn't hide her upset. "Why can't you
come?"

"I probably should have talked to you about this a couple
of weeks ago, but I've been so preoccupied with the
hockey . . ."

Monica waited.

"I have a charity event I have to go to for the team."

Monica's heart sank. "Can't you get out of it?" she wheedled.

"No. I committed to it before we got back together."

Shit. She couldn't fault him for that.

"Please don't be pissed."

"I'm not. Just disappointed," she admitted sadly. "I would
love to have you with me if I win. I would have loved to have
you with me, anyway."

"Don't worry. I'll be watching you."

Monica brightened. "Really?"

"Yeah, really," Eric replied with a wounded look. "I'll
TiVo it. I wouldn't miss it for the world."

"I love you so much," said Monica, pressing her lips to his.
She wondered if kissing him would ever stop being an exhila-
rating experience; if, years from now, it would feel mundane.
She couldn't imagine that ever happening.

"I love you, too." Eric's arm snaked back around her
shoulder, drawing her to him. "This is the best," he murmured. "And you know what? It's only going to get better."

"I've a mind never to speak to you again."

Monica ignored Gloria's fuming as she sat down at one of
the *W and F* tables at the Daytime Drama Awards with Monty.
At first, she'd intended to come alone, since Eric couldn't be
with her. But then she thought: Why not bring Monty? It
would force him and Gloria to talk. Monica steered Monty to
sit down next to his old friend and supposed nemesis.

"Hello, Gloria," Monty said quietly.

Gloria turned her head dramatically so she was looking in
the other direction. "Don't talk to me, you desiccated old liz-
ard. You look a hundred years old."

"And you already look like you've been moldering in the
grave for years," Monty retorted.

Monica knew the remark was meant to get Gloria's goat,
and it did: Gloria jerked her head back to glare at him, though
Monica caught an almost imperceptible look of sentimental-
ity quickly pass over her friend's face before she forced her

features back into a sour mask. "You're a son of a bitch," Gloria said to Monty.

Monty sighed, debonairly straightening his bow tie. "Yes, I am. But I *have* missed you."

Gloria snorted.

"C'mon, Gloria," Monica intervened. "You're being silly. You know you've missed him, too. You always ask about him. It's time to forgive and forget."

Gloria's eyes flashed daggers, but Monica could see, in the nearly undetectable relaxation of Gloria's features, that she knew Monica was right. Gloria frowned, looked Monty up and down sniffily, and took a swig of champagne. "Beg me for forgiveness, old man. I'm all ears."

Monica, not wanting to eavesdrop, excused herself to go to the ladies' room. Men and women watched her as she sailed by, the women somewhat enviously, the men longingly. As she did every year, she'd taken great care to choose her dress: full length, black, strapless, the back plunging low. A string of pearls around her neck. Diamond teardrop earrings. Completely elegant. Completely classy.

She wished Eric were here to talk to, get nervous with, look at. She loved when he got dressed up; he looked stunning. His absence was a sad ache inside her, but she understood why he couldn't be there.

She didn't go as far as the ladies' room, standing instead in the back of the banquet room where she could watch Gloria and Monty from a distance. Focusing on them helped keep her mind off the butterflies bombarding her stomach every time she thought about the Award. It would be especially satisfying to go home with the statue this year, after Christian Larkin's short-lived reign of terror. She tried not to dwell on her three previous nominations. If she lost, she was in danger of becoming the next Susan Lucci.

She hadn't prepared any sort of speech, afraid that it would jinx her chances of winning. Still, if she *did* win, she had a pretty good idea whom she'd thank.

Gloria and Monty seemed deep in conversation, leaning into one another, their mouths going a mile a minute. It was possible they were arguing, but from what Monica could see, Gloria wasn't scowling, and Monty wasn't sneering. Gloria must have accepted his apology. Monica was glad she'd engineered this reunion. She was also glad Gloria hadn't worn her old von Fürstenberg dress. Unfortunately, she'd decided to wear a tiara.

Monica hung back a few minutes more, then returned to the table. Her friends' conversation was impassioned but appeared devoid of rancor, at least right now. Gloria glanced over at her as she took her seat next to Monty, and winked. Monica heaved a big sigh of relief and poured herself a glass of champagne. Hopefully, this was a harbinger of a wonderful night to come.

"Here it comes, darling."

Gloria leaned past Monty to squeeze Monica's hand. They were waiting for the presenter for Outstanding Lead Actress in a Daytime Drama to take the stage, where he or she would read out the nominations, tear open the envelope, and then—and then—Monica was too rattled to even complete the thought. On the outside she was cool as a cucumber, but inside, her guts were somersaulting.

So far, the big upset of the evening had been Royce winning the Award for Outstanding Lead Actor in a Daytime Drama. Monica had nearly choked on the shrimp she was eating, but she recovered quickly and congratulated her costar, who seemed so genuinely touched and humbled as he accepted his award that for a few seconds, she was able to forget she couldn't stand him.

"Ladies and gentlemen."

The ballroom murmur turned to silence in an instant. Monica was squeezing the stem of her champagne flute so hard she was afraid it might shatter in her hand.

"Here to present the Award for Outstanding Lead Actress in a Daytime Drama is longtime soap fan Eric Mitchell of the New York Blades."

Monica put down her champagne flute and tried not to faint.

THIRTY-FOUR

Eric. Onstage, in a tuxedo, beaming down at her. *I'll be watching you,* he'd said. He'd neglected to tell her it would be face-to-face.

Monica's heart was pounding so loud, she feared people would think there was drummer crouching beneath her table. She folded her hands in her lap like a polite little schoolgirl to keep herself from wringing them. How could a few seconds feel so damn interminable?

Eric cleared his throat—*He's nervous,* Monica thought, though how a man so suave and photogenic could be nervous about anything was beyond her—then focused his attention on the TelePrompTer. "The nominees for Outstanding Lead Actress in a Daytime Drama are: Monica Geary, *The Wild and the Free.*"

The audience applauded enthusiastically as a camera zoomed in on Monica's face, projecting her image on a huge screen behind Eric. She knew she shouldn't betray how she was feeling, but she couldn't help it; she gave a small, nervous smile.

"Tanya McKinnon, *Shadows and Horizons.*"

More applause. Monica noticed as Tanya's image flashed

on the screen that she gave the same nervous smile. Monica wondered if Tanya was on the verge of throwing up the way she was.

"Kim Calvados, *Golden Days, Passionate Nights*."

Applause, but no smile from Kim. She looked as grim as a woman crossing the prairie by covered wagon in the 1840s.

"And last but not least, Jessica Nevelson, *Reap the Wild Wind*."

Since Jessica was the final nominee, she prompted the final round of applause. The screen showed Jessica smiling confidently. *Ugh,* thought Monica. Tanya and Kim were worthy opponents. But Jessica ranked with Chesty in terms of talent. Monica hated being petty, but all she could think was, *If Jessica wins, I'll shove a dessert fork in my eye.*

The anticipation in the room had been building all night, a rumbling volcano eager to explode. Eric flashed one of his devastating smiles that made Monica weak at the knees as he began tearing open the envelope. "And the winner is . . . Kim Calvados, *Golden Days, Passionate Nights*."

Shit shit shit shit shit shit shit shit shit.

Okay, Kim could act. But still. *Shit shit shit shit.* Monica felt like someone had sharpened a flint and was scraping it up and down the inside of her throat. On the outside, though, she was completely professional. She'd been in this position four times now, so she knew that the polite thing to do was look happy for Kim. Afterward, she'd tell the press, "It was an honor just to be nominated." She wondered what would happen if just once, one of the losers told the truth and said, "I'm really upset! *I* deserved the Award!" Well, she'd never know.

Kim had already started crying before she reached the podium. Eric gave her a small peck on the cheek before handing her the Award, then moved off to the side so she could give her acceptance speech. Being a decent actor, he looked pleased for Kim. But Monica knew deep down, he was disappointed for her.

Thankfully, Kim's acceptance speech was short. Monica had been to enough Award shows to know that everyone in the audience hated when their cohorts went on and on, thanking everyone from their sainted granny in Missouri to their

et poodle, Daisy. Another round of applause accompanied
Kim's departure from the stage with the statuette that Monica
feared would never grace her own mantelpiece. Eric was supposed to exit the stage so the next presenter could come on
and give out the Award for Outstanding Daytime Drama. Instead, he moved back to the podium. The flint in Monica's
throat halted midscrape.

Eric's eyes sought hers, his expression unabashedly adoring. As far as Monica was concerned, there were only two
people in the room right now: herself and the man she loved.

"Anyone who competes for any prize is disappointed
when they don't win. I know: my team, the New York Blades,
didn't make it into the playoffs this year. But I think I have
something that might help Monica Geary over her loss tonight."

He reached into one of the front pockets of his tux and
held up a sparkling diamond ring. "I love you, Monica," he
said humbly. "Will you marry me?"

Monica felt her stomach plummet to her feet as he
mouthed, "I love you," to her. She took her eyes from his for
just a second as one of Gloria's pointy nails stabbed at her
bare shoulder.

"Go up there," Gloria hissed. "Go up there and accept!"

Monica turned back to Eric. It still felt as though all the
tables around her had vanished, and she and Eric were alone
in some enchanted place where time was suspended. She rose
slowly, floating toward the podium where the man she loved
stood waiting, the engagement ring in his hand refracting the
colors of the rainbow as the blazing lights above the stage hit
it.

Eric met her at the top of the steps.

"I can't believe you did this," Monica whispered in awe.

"C'mon. You know what a ham I am," he whispered back.
"You look incredibly beautiful tonight, by the way."

"And you're so handsome I could die." She gave him one
of her little pinches.

"How did you wangle becoming a presenter?"

Eric grinned. "Theresa arranged it for me. When I told the
producers of the show I intended to propose, they went nuts.

Real romance in a TV genre that specializes in it and all that."

"Smooth, Mitchell. Very smooth."

They were standing together in front of the miked podium now. Eric held out the ring to her. It was a gorgeous two-carat marquise-cut diamond, the band platinum. There was a slight tremble in his hand as he awaited her answer. Monica's breath hitched, moved. How could he ever doubt what it would be?

"Yes, I'll marry you," Monica said, voice cracking with emotion. She couldn't hold back her tears of joy any longer. She wept as Eric slipped the ring onto her finger, and the crowd broke into mad applause. Eric grabbed her tight, his face nuzzling her hair.

"You know who we are?" he whispered into her ear.

"Who?"

"Two famous people who are hot. How about you give me your number and we set the world on fire?" he murmured sexily, using the exact lines he'd tried to pick her up with the first time they met.

Monica laughed. "I'm so glad I went against every sane instinct I had and agreed to Theresa's crazy scheme."

"I'm glad you did, too." He held out his arm to her. "Shall we?"

"Where are we going?"

He kissed her softly. "Somewhere I can't wait to get to: the rest of our lives."

Enter the tantalizing world
of
paranormal romance

MaryJanice Davidson

Laurell K. Hamilton

Christine Feehan

Emma Holly

Angela Knight

Rebecca York

Eileen Wilks

Berkley authors
take you to a whole new realm

penguin.com

M4G0907

Discover Romance

berkleyjoveauthors.com

See what's coming up next from your favorite romance authors and explore all the latest Berkley, Jove, and Sensation selections.

Fall in love

- See what's new
- Find author appearances
- Win fantastic prizes
- Get reading recommendations
- Chat with authors and other fans
- Read interviews with authors you love

berkleyjoveauthors.com

M1G0907